D0271731

THE KNOW

Also by Martina Cole

Dangerous Lady
The Ladykiller
Goodnight Lady
The Jump
The Runaway
Two Women
Broken
Faceless
Maura's Game

THE KNOW

Martina Cole

headline

First published in 2003
by HEADLINE BOOK PUBLISHING

10 9 8 7 6 5 4 3 2

Cataloguing in Publication Data is
available from the British Library

ISBN 0 7472 6967 X (hardback)
ISBN 0 7472 6968 8 (trade paperback)

Typeset in Galliard by
Letterpart Limited, Reigate, Surrey

Printed and bound in Great Britain by
Mackays of Chatham plc, Chatham, Kent

HEADLINE BOOK PUBLISHING
A division of Hodder Headline
338 Euston Road
LONDON NW1 3BH

www.headline.co.uk
www.hodderheadline.com

For Jo and Lesley.
Onwards and upwards, girls.
Love and hugs.

For Avril and Timmy Petherick
(and Gra Geoff and Susan P).
With love to you always,
Minnie x

Also for Adele King.

It was such a privilege to have
you as my friend and as Freddie's
godmother. I will never forget the
kindness and the friendship I always had
from you and Darley.

Prologue

As Joanie Brewer opened her front door the first thing she saw was police uniforms. She tried, unsuccessfully, to close the door. Something she had done before on many occasions.

When a large foot was planted firmly on her front-door mat, she sighed.

'He ain't here, he just went out. But he was here all day with me, so whatever you want him for, he never done it.'

'Joanie . . .'

The plainclothes officer stared at her for a few seconds before dropping his eyes and staring down at her tiny feet encased in scruffy old mules: pink ostrich feathers and worn-down plastic heels. Her pretty face looked hard in the harsh electric light of her hallway. The faded blonde hair was scraped up on top of her head and her sharp features made her look almost feral. Devoid of her usual makeup Joanie looked older than her age; she looked what she was – used, worn out.

Only her blue eyes showed any real emotion. They were desolate. She knew now why they were here. And she didn't want to hear what they were going to tell her even as she knew she must.

'I'm sorry, Joanie love, can we come in?' said the plainclothes, DI Baxter.

As she opened the chipped and battered front door wide her whole demeanour changed.

'Better get it over with then, eh?'

None of the three men could look at her. A dark-haired policewoman with high breasts and a disdainful expression on her face took Joanie's arm gently, only to be shrugged off with such force she was nearly unbalanced.

The atmosphere was taut with tension. None of them wanted to be here and all knew equally they were not wanted.

In her front room Joanie felt a glimmer of satisfaction as she saw a look of collective shock register on their faces. The place was shabby but spotlessly clean. It was the forty-eight-inch TV set and the up-to-the-minute DVD system that had given them one up and she smiled to herself as she said, 'All bought and paid for. I have the receipts in the kitchen.'

No one said a word in reply.

The policewoman looked through a door and saw the kitchen; she walked towards it, saying: 'I'll make some tea, eh?'

No one answered. Joanie sat down and gestured for the others to do the same. 'You've found her, haven't you?'

DI Baxter nodded.

She was holding back tears now, and still none of the men could bear to look at her.

'She's dead then?'

The detective nodded again.

Joanie put her head into her hands and sobbed loudly, one harsh desolate sob before she forced herself to be calm. Wiping her eyes, she lifted her head and gazed around the room, battling her emotions as she had done all her life.

She was fucked if she was going to cry in front of this lot. Her eyes lighted on a photograph on the mantelpiece. Her Kira's last school photo, her blue eyes alive with merriment. She was a beautiful little girl, a dear child, and Joanie's last. Born out of wedlock like the others, and loved more than any of them.

Joanie could hear her heartbeat thundering in her ears and felt momentarily as if she was going to faint.

'I told you she wouldn't run away, but you never listened to a word I said, did you?' It was an accusation. 'My baby would never have left me. *Never.* But none of you would listen.'

The detective took a child's dress from a bag on his lap; it was small for an eleven year old's. Kira had taken after Joanie. Tiny. Petite. Once the dress had been white with tiny blue flowers on it. Now it was soiled. Joanie knew exactly what had happened to her child.

'We found this with the body. We need you to—'

She snatched it from him and held it to her face, but all she could smell was dirt – dirt and hatred. Not the flowery, sunshine smell of an eleven-year-old child on the brink of womanhood. A child with her whole life stretching ahead of her. In her mind's eye she saw Kira once more, laughing and joking. She had been a good child, easy to rear.

The tears came then, and with their arrival the WPC brought in the tea. Even in her distressed state Joanie was glad the girl had used the good mugs kept for visitors. It was important to her to have nice things around her.

Especially now.

They talked to her, she could see their mouths moving, but she could hear nothing. All she could hear inside her head was the sound of her child's voice, as she called for her mummy and her mummy never came.

She was rocking now, clutching the remnants of the dress and whispering over and over, 'My baby. My baby.'

One of the PCs said sadly, 'Shall I get the quack?'

The detective nodded and sipped his tea.

For all Joanie Brewer was, and she was legendary down at the station, at this moment she was just a woman who had had a child brutally murdered.

Bugger tea. He should have brought a bottle of hard, if not for himself then for the wreck of a woman before him.

She wasn't Joanie Brewer now, the prostitute, drunk, and all-round Mouth Almighty responsible for giving birth to a one-family crime wave. She was a bereaved mother grieving for a child who had been snatched from the street, used and abused and then disposed of like so much rubbish.

He finished his tea in silence.

Joanie was quiet now, staring into space, and he knew they would get nothing more from her today.

Eventually the doctor arrived.

Book One

'Ladies, just a little, more virginity, if you don't mind.'

– Sir Herbert Beerbohm Tree, 1853–1917

For without are dogs, and sorcerers, and whoremongers, and murderers, and idolaters, and whosoever loveth and maketh a lie.

– *Revelation*, 22:15

Chapter One

It was hot and, Joanie [illegible]
bedroom and rolled on more [illegible]
up nearly all the room [illegible]
overflowing dressing table [illegible]
Hedges Light. She also [illegible]
acid taste making her [illegible]

An overstuffed ward[illegible]
smell of Avon Musk hung [illegible]
feel like going to work [illegible]
outside the flats with all [illegible]
and gossip. It was lo[illegible]
stench of rotten rubbish [illegible]
being abroad. But then [illegible]
good imagination. Tene[illegible]

She smiled to herself [illegible]
sugar-pink lipstick. If sh[illegible]
tomorrow off and enjoy [illegible]

She was listening to Bob [illegible]
and singing along softly as [illegible]
makeup that was a prerequisite of her job. She made a point these
days of not looking too closely at herself, gone was the [illegible]
she'd taken a real pride in her appearance. [illegible]
with her, and the money that had [illegible]
only adequate. In fact, if she wasn't [illegible]
even consider getting [illegible]
for anything like that [illegible]
most respectable avenues [illegible]

She sighed heavily and [illegible]

Chapter One

It was hot and Joanie Brewer turned up the fan in the tiny bedroom and rolled on more deodorant. The double bed took up nearly all the room and she had to climb across it to get to the overflowing dressing table for a quick puff on her Benson & Hedges Light. She also took a large gulp of vodka and Coke, the acid taste making her belch loudly.

An overstuffed wardrobe spewed clothes everywhere, and the smell of Avon Musk hung heavy in the room. She really didn't feel like going to work tonight. What she wanted was to sit outside the flats with all the other women and drink and smoke and gossip. It was lovely in the summer here, apart from the stench of rotten rubbish and unwashed kids; it was almost like being abroad. But then again, she mused, she had always had a good imagination. Tenerife it ain't!

She smiled to herself and applied another layer of No. 7 sugar-pink lipstick. If she had a good earn tonight she would take tomorrow off and enjoy herself. She was due a break anyway.

She was listening to Bob Marley singing 'No Woman No. Cry', and singing along softly as she carried on applying the thick makeup that was a prerequisite of her job. She made a point these days of not looking too closely at herself; gone was the time when she'd taken a real pride in her appearance. The life had caught up with her, and the money that had once been plentiful was now only adequate. In fact, if she wasn't such a lazy bitch she might even consider getting a real job though it was a bit late in the day for anything like that; her criminal convictions would rule out most respectable avenues of work. It was a vicious circle really.

She sighed heavily and dragged once more on her cigarette. In her wildest dreams she had never thought this would be her life, but it was and her natural resilience made her accept that fact. In repose she looked haggard, the deep lines on her face more pronounced, but there were still traces of the pretty girl she had once been. Suddenly, looking at her reflection, she wanted to cry. Instead she finished her drink and forced a smile.

Now that was much more like it. If she wasn't careful she would scare the punters off! She could hear Kira laughing in the lounge and instinctively she smiled too even though she couldn't work out what was being said. Her youngest was a happy kid, always laughing and joking. Her son Jon Jon came into the room then with another large vodka and Coke.

'Get that down the old Gregory, Mum. Need a lift?'

Joanie shook her head.

'That's OK. I'm going in with Monika.'

He laughed. 'I meant, do you want a few Valium?'

Joanie grinned.

'I get worse, don't I? No, thanks, and I would appreciate it if you didn't go offering them about to all and sundry. You will get a capture, son, mark my words.'

Jon Jon didn't answer; he was too busy admiring himself in the dressing-table mirror.

She took a deep drink and spluttered.

'Bloody hell, Jon Jon, what's in this – rocket fuel?'

'Smirnoff Black Label. Carty gets it from the docks.'

Joanie sipped the drink and smiled.

'Just what I needed.' She was telling the truth though her son wasn't aware of that. He smiled back, and she looked at him and marvelled at this boy of hers. She knew how much he hated her work and yet he had brought her in a drink before she left the house since he was nine years old. Even though he had been ridiculed all through his schooldays because she was a brass, a tom, whatever epithet people wanted to call her, and hated what she did with a vengeance, he accepted the necessity for it and respected her as his mother.

'Be in now, won't you, for Kira? It's Jeanette's turn to go out, remember.'

He nodded.

'I don't need you to keep reiterating everything, Mum. I always do me bit, don't I?' He left the room with the affronted dignity of a seventeen year old who knew far better than his own mother.

For all the talk about him he was a good kid even if she was the only one who could see it. The police hated him; he was their first call for anything and everything that happened on the estate. Jon Jon was a little fucker when the fancy took him, but if they could see him reading! He read everything he could lay his hands on, and the words he knew! Joanie's pride in her errant son knew no bounds.

Her pride in all her children was unwavering despite the things that were said about the Brewers, herself included. She knew the talk and ignored it; they were just trying to survive like everyone else, and being the kind of person she was, Joanie let most of the gossip go over her head. It had never really bothered her – or at least that was what she pretended to people, making a joke of her job, being the first to mention it and consequently making herself a legend in her own lunchtime. She was also renowned around and about for being able to handle herself in a row, and that helped. She had chinned more than a few of her neighbours over the years and consequently people were wary of her and civil enough to her face. Why wouldn't they be? She was a soft touch for a few quid and always lent a friendly ear; she could also keep things to herself and knew most of the local gossip, the *truth* behind it as well. But she never let on; Joanie knew she could cause more than a few rows if she ever opened her trap.

She also ran every catalogue going and all the women bought from her, especially for Christmas and birthdays, so she also knew everyone's financial status. Which was exactly what most of the tear ups had been over: non-payment of debts. Joanie prided herself on never owing a penny to anyone, and she did not like people taking advantage of her good nature.

She also read Tarot cards for a small fee and that alone brought her status up in the community because everyone wanted to know *if*, or more importantly *when*, they would get away from this dump and what the state of their love life would be in the future. As most of the men hereabouts only lasted a few weeks her readings were in great demand. The thought made her smile. Women amazed her, ever the optimists. But then, as she knew herself, they had to be.

All in all she had her own little niche here and she enjoyed it, as much as she could enjoy anything. Life, Joanie believed, was what you made it, and she made it as good as she could given the circumstances. Happiness, she had always told the kids, was just a state of mind.

Slipping on a tight black mini-skirt and a black see-through blouse, she pushed her feet into impossibly high heels and strutted into the lounge, all tits, backcombed hair and perfume.

'Oh, Mum, you look beautiful!'

Kira's voice was tremulous with admiration. She loved makeup and perfume, and her mother's overabundance of both made her seem exotic and stunningly lovely to her youngest daughter.

'Thanks, darling. Now, you got your money, ain't you?'

Kira nodded, her bright blue eyes still drinking in her glamorous mother.

'You smell lovely and all.'

'She won't when she gets back. She'll smell like the men's lavs in Soho.'

This caustic comment was from Joanie's daughter Jeanette.

Joanie grinned.

'Been there a lot, have you, love? Only you seem to know the place well.'

Jon Jon and Kira laughed. Joanie laughed with them though inside the comment had hurt, but as usual she shrugged it off. She understood better than anyone did what her kids had to deal with on a daily basis because of her job, and made allowances accordingly. She lit a cigarette and tidied her hair absentmindedly as she smoked and watched out of the window for Monika's arrival.

The estate was a hive of activity as usual: kids running round, radios and stereos blaring, car engines revving – it looked like a bad day in Beirut.

But it was home to them and they liked it there, or as much as you could like it anyway.

She sighed.

'Late for her own funeral, Monika.'

Kira laughed.

'Her, Bethany and me are going to the pictures tomorrow.'

'That's nice, love.' Lighting another cigarette, she bellowed, 'Do us another drink, Jon Jon.'

He poured her another in the kitchen as he watched his microwave chips rotating. He was stoned and suddenly starving. He took another puff on his joint and walked back into the lounge with his mother's drink, the stench of skunk hanging round him.

'No wonder they call it skunk - it stinks.'

He smiled lazily.

Jeanette, who'd disappeared into her bedroom, came out and Joanie sighed.

'You ain't going out like that, are you?'

Jeanette had a full woman's body and a child's face. The combination was lethal. But both girls took after Joanie. Even Kira had a little pair of tits on her and she was only eleven. Tonight Jeanette was dressed like her idol Britney and she looked like sex on legs.

'You look gorgeous!'

Kira was once more in raptures.

'Is that your mate's new top?'

'No, it fucking ain't, it's mine.'

Kira's face fell.

'I was only asking.'

'Well, don't, all right?'

Jeanette had no time for her little sister and it showed; she just saw her as a nuisance.

'Don't talk to her like that, you rotten little mare. And anyway, she has a point. If it ain't your mate's, where the fuck did you get it?'

'She's been thieving again up the high street.' Jon Jon spoke quietly and the room went quiet. 'You've been out on the grab, ain't you?' he challenged.

Jeanette tossed her long curly brown hair over one shoulder.

'So what if I have? What's it got to do with you? You ain't me fucking dad.'

Jon Jon took a step towards her and Kira planted herself between her brother and sister.

'Don't start fighting, please!'

Joanie finished her drink and slammed the glass down on the scuffed wooden table.

'All right, that's enough. Why do I always have to walk out that door in a two and eight, eh? Once, just once, let me go to work in a bit of peace.'

Jon Jon poked his sister in the chest none too gently as he growled, 'Watch yourself, girl.'

She laughed.

'I ain't scared of you, mate!'

He stared into her eyes and Joanie watched as her daughter's bravado turned to real fear.

'Well, you should be, Jen. You should be very scared.'

Kira was visibly upset now. It seemed as if the whole room was charged with malice and all of them were affected by it.

The front door flew open then and Monika stumped in, overweight and sporting the most amazing Afro in recorded history.

'I been bibbing away down there,' she shouted. 'You ready, girl, or what?' She scratched one large boob as she adjusted the elasticated top she was wearing. 'Bloody thing, it's killing me.'

'Try buying one that fits next time,' Jeanette said sarcastically, without thinking.

Before Monika could answer Kira piped up with, 'I think it looks . . .'

Everyone, including Monika, said 'lovely' with her and once again they were all laughing.

Kissing the kids, Joanie went to work feeling more light-hearted.

Kira walked out of the flat and down the steep concrete staircase to the communal washing lines below. No one used them any more so it was a place for the kids to hang out. On the plus side you could hear the music from certain flats so at least you had a few sounds as you sat around jawing.

The overflowing bins were also housed down there so the smell, especially in summer, could get overwhelming. Last winter a newborn baby had been found in one of the large bins, barely alive. The kids had heard its mewling and retrieved it from the dustbin, called the police and were heroes for a few days. The mother of the unfortunate child had left the area after a near lynching from the neighbours and the child had been fostered out. It was still a major topic of conversation for them all, months after the event, and their parents didn't mind them hanging round here so much now.

Kira loved it here, it was her favourite place. Unlike most of the other girls she didn't live under a loose rein, was not able to sit out till all hours, so made a point of enjoying the time she did have with her mates. It was a bone of contention between her and her brother and mother that she was not allowed the same freedom as everyone else, but she was shrewd enough to know she was fighting a losing battle. Her mother had lost the war with Jeanette, she was not going to lose it with Kira. Consequently, she was watched far more closely and had come to accept and to understand why this was so. Basically she was a good kid anyway and did as she was asked. Tonight, as she settled herself on the low wall, she was happy enough.

'Little' Tommy Thompson watched the girls as they sat and chatted. His balcony overlooked the washing lines and he had a good view of them. He liked watching the kids, they made him laugh with their antics, especially Kira and her friends. He waved down, smiling, and the girls waved shyly back.

He had moved to this area a few months previously with his father. At thirty-eight, Tommy was cripplingly obese and unable to work because of that. And, as his father had always pointed out to anyone who would listen, he wasn't the brightest bulb on the Christmas tree either.

Tommy hated his father, and every fresh nasty comment sent him running to the fridge. 'Morbidly obese?' his dad would say. '*Anyone* would be morbid around him.' Tommy kept meaning to find out what this meant but he never had; he was always forgetting things. He hadn't liked to ask the doctor either because his dad was sitting there with him every time and Tommy had learned just to listen, to let his father talk. It was how it had always been even when his mum had been alive.

He moved his huge bulk in the chair. This heat was a killer for him and he knew he smelled. He could catch the sweet odour himself every time the wind blew through the flats. It was like a vacuum here because of the way the blocks were situated, and out on the balcony was the coolest place to be. Consequently Tommy spent a lot of time out there.

'All right, Fatty?'

The good-natured call made him smile. He waved back happily, glad to be noticed. He was practically beaming as he shouted down, 'Hot enough for you?'

The man carried on walking without answering and Tommy felt a moment's embarrassment. He settled himself once more and observed the girls below as they chatted and laughed. He could hear Beenie Man blaring out from Kira's flat so knew her brother Jon Jon was still around and that her mother had gone to work. They watched her like a hawk – and so they should after all.

The thought made him smile, but this was quickly wiped from his face as he heard the front door slam.

His father was home. Tommy waited patiently for the baiting to begin.

'Why do we come in so early?'

Monika's voice was slurred as she drank copiously from a bottle of cheap Bacardi.

'That'll get you in the end, girl. Quicker than anything, Bacardi is.'

'Oh, fuck off, Lena, and give me a break!'

Lena, a young Scottish girl, sighed and raised her eyebrows as she looked at Joanie who shook her head, telling her to mind her own business.

'I like that necklace, Lena. New, is it?' Monika commented.

The girl preened herself. She had just acquired a new pimp and so presents were still on the agenda; it was always the way with the younger ones.

'It was made for a much slimmer neck, of course.'

Monika was spoiling for a row and it showed. Lena was a chunky girl and in truth the necklace was far too delicate for her. But it wasn't the necklace that rankled with Monika, it was what it stood for. They were all aware of that. No one was going to bother cajoling Monika into switching pimps.

Lena was a laugh though, and said good-naturedly, 'Well, I'm sorry about that but I don't know Frank Bruno well enough to borrow his jewellery.'

Even Monika laughed, then said nastily, 'Here it comes, Miss fucking World!'

Lena shook her head.

'She's too young. I'm sorry, but he should draw the line.'

The young girl was more than aware of the stir she was causing. It was just getting dark so business would pick up soon and she knew the chances were she would get the next strike. She also knew it would cause aggravation. But she wasn't too bothered; she had good back up. At fourteen she thought she knew it all, and unfortunately already knew far too much about some things only she was too stupid to see that for herself. She was a runaway so that made it easy for the men who preyed on women to get her working the street.

Monika's tutting was so loud it made Joanie laugh.

'Leave her alone. She has to put up with Todd McArthur – she'll soon learn.'

Todd was a young pimp who concentrated on the new girls. He was good-looking, quietly spoken and vicious. All his girls were in love with him, even after he gave them the bad news. Unlike the older women who had no illusions about the men who lived off them, the younger girls had to experience the downside before they actually realised they were stuck there for the best part of their lives. A good pimp could track a girl who absconded within twenty-four hours, and frequently did that. The beating they then received and the fear of a repetition kept them on their toes or on their backs, whichever way you wanted to look at it.

A week in hospital was something to learn from and anyone too thick to toe the line afterwards was asking for all they got. Or that, at least, was the general consensus among the women.

A blue Escort pulled up by the side of the road and a small white man with a bad combover smiled at Monika. He was a regular and as she walked to the car she gave the younger girl a smirk that told her all she needed to know. Regulars were what they all wanted; they made life so much easier, gave you a chance to relax – something you could never do with a stranger, especially with the mad bastards they dealt with on a daily basis.

'Thank fuck she's gone, Joanie. Her drinking is getting worse!' Lena moaned.

Joanie sighed but didn't comment.

'That little girl's on crack. Look, she's fucking rocking.'

They watched her for a few moments before moving away.

'McArthur's a shitbag, ain't he?'

Joanie nodded before answering, 'Talking of shitbags . . .'

They laughed as their own pimp, Paulie Martin, chased the girl off, physically as well as verbally. He walked towards them then, his handsome face openly shocked.

'That McArthur will be opening a fucking crèche soon, eh?'

'That child was cracked out of her box.'

'She'll get a crack across the fucking head if she talks to me like that again!' He was smoothing down his designer suit. 'I want you in a parlour, Joanie.'

She smiled. It was better in the massage parlours though she was only asked if he was desperate and she knew that.

'Okey-doke, how long for?'

'Just get in the motor, will ya? It's like pimping for William G. Stewart. No questions, just move.'

One thing in Paulie's favour, he was funny and the girls appreciated his humour. It had lightened more than a few crap evenings.

He shouted over his shoulder, 'Lena, you tell that little cunt McArthur if I see any of his girls within pissing distance of mine again, I'll break his fucking neck.'

'All right, Mr Martin.'

As Joanie was driven to East Ham she relaxed. This was a bit of luck and she was going to enjoy it while it lasted.

'You look happy, Joanie.'

Paulie smiled at her and she melted. He was devastatingly handsome and knew it, from his thick black curly hair to his deep blue eyes. He was heavy-set and not as tall as he would have liked but he had something about him and whatever it was, it made women want him. In his game that was definitely a bonus. He had learned early in life that a smile and a well-timed compliment could get you anything you wanted from certain women.

Paulie rubbed her leg above the knee as he drove and Joanie smiled once more. He was a bastard but he was her bastard, so she forgave him anything. She knew he was giving her the scrapings but she was also wise enough to appreciate that that was about all she was going to get these days so she enjoyed it while she could.

She could still hack it with a certain type of punter, though. She had the cheap and cheerful look that appealed to the older men. Joanie was the pensioner's friend, and she was glad of it. You rarely got a tip but it was over in no time so that was a bonus. In fact, she was perfect for a massage parlour in many respects. The men who used them were lazy and frightened of being seen kerb crawling: locals who tended to use the one nearest the pub, or out-of-towners who worked nearby and came in flashing their money and their false smiles. It was cheap as well; none of the girls was ever going to be in the hundred-quid-a-fuck market anyway so all in all it worked out fine.

Paulie was clever enough to know the kind of girls who would make him money: not too good-looking but not complete dogs either – that was all right on the kerb, but not in the comfortable surroundings of a parlour. Equally if the girls were too good-looking they frightened the men off; he had noticed that over the years. As Paulie told anyone who'd listen, most men rented a bit of strange so they could feel in control. Men without money and prestige were easily intimidated by women who were too good-looking, they felt that they had to be nicer to them. His girls, and he used the term loosely, were just the right side of trollop to suit his clients' needs.

As they pulled up outside the parlour he yawned.

'Ask Jon Jon if he wants a job with me. I've heard he's making a bit of a name for himself around and about.'

Joanie nodded.

'Okay. How long am I working tonight?'

'One of the girls has gone on the missing list. Probably a few days.' Paulie yawned once again then said, 'Fucking real, ain't it?

All I done for her and she goes on the trot.'

Joanie kept her own counsel. She was more than aware of what he had done for the girl; he had done the same for her and look where it had got her.

'Don't hurt her when you find her . . .'

He didn't bother to answer. Instead he leaned across her and opened the car door.

'Be good, Joanie.'

She nodded.

'Oh, and do me a favour, will you? Keep your fucking opinions on my working practices to yourself in future. I own you, Joanie, like I own all my girls, and if I ever found I wanted you lot to have opinions, I'd book myself into the nearest mental institution sharpish just to teach meself a lesson, OK?'

She nodded once more. The anger in his voice was evident and she knew he could turn on a coin.

'Well?'

She nodded harder this time.

He rolled his eyes.

'I mean, fuck off, Joanie! Now!'

He was bellowing and his voice was loud enough to be heard above the traffic. Joanie jumped from the car as fast as she could and scurried into the massage parlour. She was humiliated and hurt, and the worst thing was, it showed.

Gaynor Coleman shook her head sadly and said, 'That man is a ponce.'

Joanie, as usual the joker, said, 'That man is everyone's ponce, ain't he? He *is* a pimp after all!'

All the older women laughed with her and she felt better. But it had hurt, the way he had spoken to her, had hurt her deeply considering all the years she had given him.

She sat down with the girls. The smell of baby oil and cigarette smoke was overpowering, but at least it was better than exhaust fumes and the drunken ranting of Monika.

She had her first punter ten minutes later.

Joanie's working night had begun.

Kira, Bethany and a little girl called Catriona who was only seven were playing as the sun went down. They were having a great time. Various mums were already outside, sitting on kitchen chairs and nattering about each other's lives. The atmosphere was good. The kids had been fed chips and Coke, and a few bottles of wine had been opened.

Jon Jon watched his little sister from the balcony as he rolled himself another joint. His mobile was ringing and he knew who was on the phone but didn't answer it. Instead he called over the balcony to his sister.

'Come on, Kira, time to come in.'

She heard her brother's voice and looked crushed.

'Oh, Jon Jon, five minutes, please.'

Her voice was a studied whine.

Her big eyes were open to their widest and Catriona's mother, a twenty-five-year-old brunette, laughed as she shouted: 'I'll watch her, Jon Jon, she can sleep at mine tonight.'

Catriona was having the time of her life and once Kira went inside would be moaning because none of the other kids gave her the time of day. She was too small for the majority of the girls but Kira loved the smaller kids.

'That's all right, thanks anyway. Get your arse up here, Kira.'

'Please, just five minutes, Jon Jon!'

His mobile was ringing once more and he called out, 'Five minutes and that is it!'

One of the neighbours whispered, 'Say what you like about him, he is good to those girls.'

The other women nodded their approval and Kira basked in the pleasure of someone being nice for once about her brother. Usually it was a case of raised eyebrows and knowing smirks, whispered conversations or outright abuse – though her brother's growing reputation had put paid to the latter these last few months. He was getting a reputation as a hard nut, a face, and was determined to cultivate that to the best of his ability.

Five minutes later she reluctantly said goodnight to her friends and thanked Catriona's mother for offering her a bed for the night. Kira ran up the four flights of stairs to the flat and let herself inside. After making herself a Marmite sandwich she sat with her brother on the balcony, waiting patiently until he had finished shouting down the phone.

'All right, Kira, get ready for bed now.'

'Can I eat me sandwich?'

He laughed.

''Course you can, but don't fuck me about tonight and I'll let you watch telly, OK?'

'Thanks, Jon Jon. You are the best brother in the world.'

'I must be to put up with you, eh?'

She was happy, she loved it when he was like this and chatted to her. He *was* nice, her brother, whatever anyone else said. He was nice to her.

'Can I have a story as well?'

'Don't push it, Kira!'

But his voice was warm as he spoke and she knew she was in with a chance. Jon Jon told great stories. Then his mobile rang again and she sighed. He was shouting and swearing once more and she knew her story was out of the window. She went inside and put on her pyjamas.

Settling herself in bed, she watched *Queer As Folk USA* on Sky until she fell asleep.

Chapter Two

Joanie had just got in from work and was making herself a cup of coffee when Jon Jon came into the kitchen.

'All right, Mum? Good night?'

She nodded. She was dog-tired and it showed. Her eyes had dark circles under them and her skin was grey. She looked like a woman who had spent the night with too many men, all strangers and all using her body. She had also had a screamer, a punter who had done the business and then tried to get out of paying. This was the last thing she'd needed as she wanted a regular place in the parlour. It was good money and much safer than the kerb.

She kept this pearl of wisdom to herself, though, because she knew her son would have other things on his mind, but still it rankled. She gave good service and she knew she did. She had been worried it might stop her from being used again, especially as she knew that Patsy, the head girl in the East Ham parlour, didn't really like her. That was due to the fact that Joanie had had a thing going with Paulie longer than any of the other girls when poor Patsy had once actually believed that *she* was going to be Mrs Paulie Martin. More fool her, though that was not what Patsy had wanted to believe. But who was Joanie to piss on her rival's firework? The truth was, Paulie was already married. Overweight and a pillar of the church, his wife Sylvia was respectability incarnate, and more to the point she was stupid – the perfect foil for his nefarious businesses and strings of other women. Paulie kept her and his two daughters in the manner to which they had become accustomed, and enjoyed keeping the two sides of his life separate. If his wife knew what he really did it would kill her, he believed. Though once or twice over the years

Joanie had seen her near the businesses she had never said so to anyone, least of all Paulie. She knew when to keep her trap shut; it was another prerequisite of her job.

Now she lightened her voice as she said: 'I ended up in the parlour so that was a touch.'

Jon Jon didn't answer her, but she had expected that. He never spoke directly about her job; it was always roundabout allusions, non-committal comments.

'How was me little Kira then?'

He smiled.

'Good as gold, Mum. She always is.'

He watched the lines of strain leave his mother's face for a second at the thought of her youngest daughter. Jon Jon was having trouble getting out the ironing board. In the cramped space of the kitchen it was a difficult job. Joanie knew he was going to iron Kira's school clothes. He was good like that.

'I'll have a coffee, Mum.'

She could smell the sleep on him still. He was handsome and he was kind; she shut her mind to everything else about him. She had to or she would never sleep another night – or day as the case invariably was with her job.

As he plugged the iron in Joanie said nonchalantly, 'Oh, by the way, Paulie told me to let you know that there's work with him if you want it.'

As his mother's words penetrated, Jon Jon stared at her in disbelief.

'He what?'

The boy's voice was high with incredulity.

'He wants you to work for him.'

Joanie knew what was coming next but she tried anyway. At least if he worked for Paulie she would know where he was and what he was doing.

'Hear him out, he ain't so bad . . .'

'You can tell him bollocks from me!'

Jon Jon's handsome face was completely devoid of expression as he tried to comprehend what had possessed the woman who had borne him to ask such a stupid thing of him.

'Don't talk to me like that! I was only telling you what he

asked me to. Anyway, he ain't such a bad bloke.'

'No, 'course he ain't, pimping me mother out for me! Fuck me, Mum, shall I go round and shake his hand then?'

Joanie closed her eyes in distress.

'Come on, son, I don't deserve that and you know it.'

Her voice was soft, eyes pained with the insult even if it was true.

'Think of the wedge, and the perks.'

Jon Jon slammed down the iron.

'Do I look like a fucking pimp then? Come on, Muvver, answer me!'

Joanie knew she had said the wrong thing and was regretting even mentioning it now.

''Course you don't. I only passed on the message, that's all.' She was shouting back at him now.

'Well, in future, don't bother.'

'You could go far with him. He needs someone with a bit of nous . . .'

'Well, he don't need me. Whatever you might think, I ain't no fucking woman-seller.'

'Piss off out of it, Jon Jon, you could earn a decent poke with—'

He interrupted her, savagely.

'I know I'm more black than white, Mum, but that doesn't make me a pimp. Or was me dad one? Is that it? Only no one seems to know anything about him, do they? Especially you.'

He knew he had gone too far and was immediately sorry.

'Oh, Mum, why do you wind me up like this? You know how I feel about men like Martin.'

Joanie left the kitchen quietly without answering.

Jon Jon carried on ironing Kira's school clothes but his heart wasn't in it any more. He was still reeling from the shock of what his mother had said. The fact she'd thought he might even consider the offer burned at him even as he understood her motives.

His mother's coffee was still side by side with his on the worktop. He took it into her bedroom for her.

'Here you are, Mum. Have a couple of hours' kip.'

She smiled at him sadly. She looked old, lost and haggard suddenly.

'I'm sorry, Jon Jon.'

He ruffled her hair as if she was the child and he was the adult.

'I know, Mum, I know.'

Both of them were aware he didn't apologise back.

'Move, you fat bastard!'

Joseph Thompson watched as his son struggled to make a pot of tea, his enormous bulk making it almost impossible for him in the confines of their kitchen. Tommy was sweating; already it was far too hot for someone of his size. He glanced out of the kitchen window and watched the kids going to school. He felt his father come up behind him and winced.

'Look at them, little girls dressed like fucking whores. That's what you're looking at, isn't it?'

Tommy was annoyed but kept his voice even as he said, 'I ain't looking at them like that and you know it. I just like to watch them chatting and having a nice time, that's all.'

Joseph sneered at him.

''Course you do! Now make the fucking tea, you fat nonce. I have to go to work in a minute. Have you done me sandwiches?'

'They're in the fridge.'

No more was said between the two men after that. Ten minutes later his father left the flat without even saying goodbye. Tommy waddled into his bedroom and pulled a box from under his bed with difficulty. Opening it, he smiled.

It was full of Barbies. Some were dressed, nearly all were missing their heads. Underneath them was a dazzling array of costumes and miniature items, everything Barbie needed to be the perfect girl about town, from shocking pink mini-dresses to perfect little handbags and boots. But these were wet, he discovered, and from the sudden stench of urine knew exactly what had happened to them. It wasn't the first time and he knew it wouldn't be the last.

Stifling a sob, Tommy set about putting the dolls back together again, setting the clothes to one side to be washed. Sweat was already pouring from his brow. Tommy wiped it away with one meaty fist to mingle with his tears.

As he replaced the heads he mumbled 'Bastard!' over and over again.

Kira and Bethany sat in the lobby of the flats and giggled. They were playing the hop and enjoying every second of it.

Unlike Bethany, this was Kira's first time and for her it was an exciting novelty. Bethany just wanted to sit, chill and smoke.

'I know, let's go up the library!' Kira suggested.

Her friend shook her head in disbelief and said sarcastically, 'Are you sure? Two school kids in the library on a school day?'

Kira saw the logic of this statement and giggled again.

'I never thought of that.'

As they sat there they could hear a radio playing the top ten. They swayed together and joked, both safe in the knowledge that none of the adults roundabouts would dare to grass them up to their respective mothers. It would be too much aggravation for them.

'Let's go over the park.'

Bethany shook her head and lit another Consulate, pulling the minty taste deep into her lungs and practising trying to make smoke rings.

'Wanna puff?'

Kira shook her head.

'No, ta, I hate smoking.'

Just then a door opened and Little Tommy's head poked out.

'What are you two doing?'

Bethany as usual was the one to answer.

'What's it look like?'

Tommy looked her over, it was not an attractive sight, but smiling brightly said, 'Want a cup of tea?'

The two girls looked at each other and grinned.

'Yes, please.'

Giggling together over this grown-up invitation, they walked into his flat.

Paulie saw Jon Jon's distinctive dreads and bibbed him as he drove past. Jon Jon ignored him and carried on walking to his friend's. He had a pocketful of Es and was looking forward to unloading them. Since the first craze for them in the nineties the price had been drastically reduced. Four or five years ago he could get good money knocking a few out at twenty-five quid apiece; now he was lucky to get five hundred quid for a thousand.

Still, he was earning from it and that was the main thing.

He also had another item on his agenda and was going to get that out of the way before he got down to business.

He opened the door of his friend Carty's squat and called out loudly, 'Only me.'

'Through here, mate.'

Carty was in the kitchen cooking up batches of crack. The smell was awful but that was mainly due to the overflowing bin and the blocked sink.

Carty was already off his face and this alone annoyed Jon Jon. He could understand people taking serotonin-based drugs like Es, but not crack with its dopamine-induced high followed by deep depression. It was such a selfish drug. At least Es or grass made you empathise with people, enjoy their company more. Want to be in the world of happiness, not the hell of loneliness which was how crack seemed to affect people.

In the past Jon Jon and Carty would snort a bit of coke at weekends and have long meaningless conversations that made perfect sense at the time but were in fact just the ramblings of two mates out of their nuts. But since he had started freebasing the drug Carty had changed. When they had just snorted it he had been a laugh, a *crack* even. Now his whole life revolved around rocks and that was what Jon Jon wanted to talk to him about today.

'Bit early even for you, ain't it?'

Carty sighed.

'Fuck off, Jon Jon. Get off me case, will you?'

He was annoyed.

'You're me mate, but have you had a fucking good luck at yourself lately? You look like a cunt and you are acting like one.'

Carty ignored him; instead he measured out the baking powder carefully, holding his breath in anticipation of what was to come. His crack pipe was lying idle on the worktop and Jon

Jon felt it. It was still warm so he knew his friend was already on his way to nowhere for the day.

'You got the Es?'

''Course I have. Who wants them anyway?'

'Marky Morgan. He left five hundred in the freezer. Wants you to drop them round his place.'

'He don't fucking want much, does he? Get him on the blower and tell him to get here or I leave with the wedge *and* the drugs.' Jon Jon pulled open a beer and drank deeply before saying, 'Fucking cheek of him, eh?'

But Carty was already away in his own world again and Jon Jon watched his friendly sadly. He looked around the dirty kitchen. It was full of crack paraphernalia and this annoyed him more. He knew he might get a capture for his dealing, and if he did would take it on the chin, but he would be ashamed to be associated with crack. To him it wasn't a recreational high, it was a death sentence. He wouldn't sell that shit even to the crack heads who deserved all they fucking got. You had to have standards and he felt his were high considering that his main job was dealing.

Taking a new bottle of beer from the fridge, he called Carty's name. As the other boy turned around Jon Jon crashed the bottle into his cheek. Carty collapsed under the blow, and when he hit the floor Jon Jon kicked him until he stopped moving. Then he systematically searched the flat and took every bit of money from the place along with some jewellery and class-A drugs. He pocketed the lot, but left the crack where it was. Carty would need a rock more than ever when he finally came to. Jon Jon had made his point though: the friendship was over.

'He's had more than enough warnings so fuck him.'

Calling a cab, Jon Jon whistled silently through his teeth as his mobile rang again and again. He guessed it was Marky wanting his Es. Well, he could get off his arse and come and collect them. Who the fuck did he think he was?

When the cab turned up Jon Jon walked jauntily from the squat, feeling lighter than he had in ages.

It was time for a spring clean and he had started with his best mate.

The cab driver knew him and without asking drove him back to his mother's flat in silence. Such was the reputation Jon Jon was earning for himself, and he enjoyed it.

'Where did you get them from?'

Tommy smiled with pride at the awe in Kira's voice.

'I've collected them for years.'

'But ain't they girls' toys?'

Bethany had no interest in the dolls; she was past all that. Kira however was in raptures.

'I love Barbie, Tommy, I think she's great.'

Kira, who loved glamour and clothes and makeup, had finally met a kindred spirit.

Tommy was over the moon with her reaction and it showed.

'You look a bit like her, you know, Kira.'

She was overwhelmed by the praise.

Bethany sighed. Already over nine stone, she was her mother's daughter and envied Kira her slim good looks even while she loved her as a friend.

'Do I? Do I really, Beth?'

Bethany nodded and grinned reluctantly.

'You do actually.'

Tommy lumbered from the room awkwardly to get them their teas.

'He's a right fucking weirdo, ain't he, Kira?'

She tutted.

'Don't be horrible. He's nice, just a bit . . .'

Bethany made a face and said helpfully, 'Fat?'

Kira laughed despite herself and said: 'No, sad.'

Bethany, her crinkly hair pulled back in a ponytail, giggled.

'He likes you anyway.'

Kira shivered.

'Stop it, I can hear him coming.'

Tommy came into the room and lowered his bulk on to a large chair by the bed; his pudgy hands held the three mugs easily.

'Here you are, girls, a nice cuppa.'

Tommy was in his element. He loved guests and these two were the kind of guest he'd dreamed of having. Girls, young girls, were his favourite. He loved the way they talked and sat and even moved their little hands. He wasn't too sure about Bethany yet; he had a feeling she could be a mare if the fancy took her. But Kira . . . well, she was a little lady. A Barbie in the making.

'I love the Sleeping Beauty Barbie, she's one of my favourites. And I love the Barbie air hostess as well. All her little lilac cases!'

Kira's voice was high with excitement.

Bethany lit another cigarette even though Tommy frowned.

She waved out the match and looked at him askance as if to say, 'Ashtray, now.'

He shook his head and said sadly, 'In the lounge.'

Bethany skipped from the room to search for the ashtray and used it as an excuse to have a good nose round.

'She don't mean it, Tommy. She thinks it makes her look grown up.'

'Well, it doesn't. It makes her look like a little tart.'

Kira didn't answer him; she didn't know what to say. Instead she picked up Malibu Barbie and sighed with complete happiness. This was turning into a really good day.

Joanie turned over another card. The woman before her was waiting with bated breath.

'Well, come on, Joanie!'

'King of Wands. It's him all right.'

The woman deflated.

'He'll be back then?'

Joanie nodded and they both laughed.

'You didn't need me to read your cards to tell you that – he always comes back anyway.'

'I know, but hopefully one day he won't. He'll stay with whoever he's shagging and leave me alone!'

Joanie really laughed now.

'If he did, no one would get a bigger shock than you, Suzy, and you know it.'

Her neighbour placed a ten-pound note on the table and then heaved her weight from the chair. She was heavily pregnant and her husband Dicky always went on the missing list when she got to seven months. This was her seventh child and he had gone again.

'Keep the money, Suzy, I don't want it.'

'Nah, that's all right, you been sitting there an hour telling me what I already knew. Fuck me, you deserve it for your patience.'

Joanie laughed.

'Thanks, love, but I'll take it off your club account, OK?'

Suzy hugged her awkwardly.

'Thanks, darlin'. I better get home and sort out the others.'

Joanie saw her out and then she went into her small front room and looked around. It was clean and tidy, and this made her smile. Turning on the TV she put on UK Style; *The House Doctor* had just started. It was one of her favourite programmes. One day when the kids were gone she was going to do this place up a treat. That was her dream.

Then, kneeling in front of a display unit that held a collection of photos and ornaments, she opened the large bottom drawer and took out her treasures. Over the years she had collected all sorts of things for her flat. These ranged from an espresso machine that was hidden in her wardrobe to a silver After Eight holder for her imaginary dinner parties.

In her wilder dreams Joanie had celebrities to dinner, and lovingly planned the menus and which wines to serve. She pictured the glassware – she had bought some lovely glassware over the years – and all the china and cutlery. She saw herself in a shimmering dress, looking years younger than she was of course, holding court over her table as banter and sparkling repartee abounded.

In her mind's eye she could see all this as if it was a recent memory, something she had already experienced.

The front door slammed and she put everything away quickly, but Jeanette came into the lounge and said loudly, 'Interrupting you, am I? Who's coming to dinner today – Sidney Poitier as usual?'

When the kids had been smaller Joanie had shared her dreams with them and they had joined her in her reveries, inviting their own celebrities and choosing the menu and décor. Now it was a joke between them all and inside Joanie this hurt, though as usual she laughed it off.

'You know me and Sid!'

'You're fucking mad, Muvver. Ding it all out or use it, for fuck's sake. Sitting in the drawer for years, it's a wonder it's not all ruined.'

Joanie closed her eyes and shouted, 'Will you stop fucking swearing, madam!'

They looked at one another and then both burst out laughing.

'Where's Kira?'

'How would I know that! With Bethany, I suppose.'

The mood was broken again. Kira made Jeanette jealous, had done since the day Joanie had given birth to her. Everyone had said Jeanette would grow out of it but she never had. If anything it had grown worse over the years.

'Make me a cuppa, love, while I sort this lot out.'

'Can't, going out.'

Jeanette walked from the room, her face in its usual surly expression.

Joanie sighed once more, whispering, 'Kids, who'd fucking have them?'

Bethany had already gone home but Kira was busy playing with all the dolls and their paraphernalia. In his wardrobe Tommy had everything Barbie had ever needed and Kira was in raptures once more as she went through it all.

'You are so lucky, Tommy!'

He was happy now Bethany had gone. He didn't like the streetwise girl half as much as he did Kira. She was a lot like him. Not physically, of course, but she had the same naivety and he responded well to that.

'I save up for what I want and then I send off for it.'

'That's what I want to do when I grow up. Buy things.'

Tommy smiled at her. She really was exquisite, her high cheekbones and blonde hair giving her an almost Nordic look. In a few years she would be a real stunner. She was gentle and ladylike too, which was something else that attracted him to her. Unlike a lot of the kids on the estate she didn't use bad language or feel an urge to look like the carbon copy of a pop star. She was a thoroughly nice kid.

They dressed the Barbies and chatted together. So engrossed

was Tommy that he nearly fainted with fright when he realised the time. It was a quarter past five and his father would be in within ten minutes. If he saw her here there would be ructions!

'You'll have to go, Kira love. You really must go.'

The urgency in his voice communicated itself to her and she jumped up from the floor.

'OK, Tommy. Can I come and see you again?'

His face softened and he grinned.

''Course you can.'

When she'd left he stood for a few seconds looking at the mess in the room, and even though he knew there would be murders – no tea cooking, no kettle boiled – he savoured the feeling of having found a friend. A kindred spirit.

Then he pulled himself together and rushed into the kitchen to start the evening meal. It occurred to him then that he hadn't eaten anything all afternoon. When his father's key turned in the lock a few moments later Tommy closed his eyes and waited for the tirade.

He wasn't disappointed.

The slaps he could take, it was the constant undermining of his self-esteem that he found hardest to bear.

But what else could he do?

'Where have you been, madam!'

Kira smiled timidly and as usual Joanie's heart melted. She often wondered where this child of hers had come from; she was like neither of her parents, thank God.

'I forgot the time, Mum. I was playing.'

'Come and get your dinner.'

As she tucked into her frozen lasagne and oven chips Kira reflected on her day with Tommy and decided that she liked him. He was fat and odd but she liked his quietness which reminded her of herself.

Jeanette sat at the kitchen table and attacked her own food. Jon Jon joined them and asked Kira about her day at school. The lies didn't come easily but thankfully he had a lot on his mind.

As she looked around her she felt warm inside. She had a new friend, and that new friend had a roomful of Barbies. What more could a little girl want?

Jeanette was ready. It was seven-thirty and she was dressed to kill. Kira, who for once had come indoors of her own volition after an argument with Bethany over S Club Seven, said sadly, 'Are you going out?'

Jeanette nodded.

'You tell Muvver or Jon Jon and I'll make your life a fucking misery, right?'

Kira nodded.

'Where you going?'

Jeanette didn't even bother to answer her.

Alone in the flat the little girl made herself a bowl of cornflakes and sat on the back balcony. For once there wasn't a lot of action out there. A big storyline was going on in *EastEnders* and the place was deserted until at least eight-thirty.

She watched as Tommy's dad walked towards the high street and the pub, then she waved at her friend who had come outside to try and cool down like she had herself. It was stiflingly hot.

Tommy mimed drinking a cup of tea and Kira nodded happily. Leaving the flat door open, she ran quickly over to her new friend's.

Unknown to her she had just missed meeting the police armed with a search warrant.

Inside the massage parlour it was just getting busy.

Joanie brought her punter into a tiny cubicle and smiled ingratiatingly. He was one ugly bloke, and even she felt her stomach turn at the thought of what she had to do. As he jumped happily on to the massage table, devoid of everything except a suspect pair of boxers, she sighed. Lifting up the crop top, she exposed her breasts as per usual.

'Give me a special, and take your time.'

She ripped open the condom packet and the man waved his hand decisively.

'Oh, no you don't! I ride bareback.'

'Well, you can ride on your own then, mate. No condom, no sex.'

He sat up abruptly. He was well into his fifties with that unkempt look about him of a man too long on his own, eating the wrong food, drinking too much, and never having had a relationship of any kind with a shower or bath. A real charmer.

'Listen here, cunt, you ever heard the expression "If I am paying then I am saying"?'

Joanie nodded.

'And have you ever heard the saying "Roll this on or the cunt is gone"?'

Sherry in the next room heard the exchange and started laughing, and Joanie, looking at the man sitting there with his face a mask of disbelief, started to laugh as well.

He was enraged.

'Anyone ever told you that you've got a big mouth and maybe someday a man might just shut it for you?'

Joanie threw the condom into the bin. Putting her boobs back into the little crop top, she said, 'Yeah, plenty of times. But you see, mate, you don't get a lot of your actual men in here, know what I mean? Now fuck off!'

He was depressing her and suddenly she saw her life for what it was. This happened periodically and she felt the self-loathing wash over her like a wave.

Throwing his clothes at him she said, 'What are you, mate? Deaf as well as ugly? Get out.'

'What about me blow job?'

'Use the Hoover, love. I'm sure you two are very well acquainted!'

It took a fifteen-minute talk, two rows and half a bottle of vodka to get her back to work. But seeing him off had cheered her up no end. She might be a brass but she was still a person, and as long as she believed that, she wouldn't sink into the mire like so many others before her.

Her next punter was in his early twenties and extremely nervous. She put him at his ease, gave him a good service and got a fiver-tip. Joanie was over her tantrum already.

Chapter Three

Jeanette finally walked up the stairs at twelve fifty-five to see the door to the flat closed and a large red Execution of Warrant notice staring her in the face.

She felt her heart stop in her chest as she realised what had happened. The warrant was bad enough, but when they found out she had left Kira alone there would be ructions. Her brother would rip her heart out over this. And that was without what her mother was going to say.

She ripped the notice from the door. It covered firearms and drugs which meant the filth could have a field day turning things upside down and it was all legal. She wondered briefly what her brother had done this time.

As she put her key into the lock a young PC opened the door.

'Are you the occupant of these premises?'

Jeanette ignored him and walked through the flat looking for Kira. She was nowhere to be seen.

'Where's me sister?'

The PC was radioing in and didn't answer her for a few moments.

'What sister?' he asked eventually.

'Me little sister – Kira.'

There was fear in her voice now.

'No one was here when the warrant was executed at seven thirty-nine. The property was empty though the door was open. Now where is your brother Jon Jon?'

She shrugged and walked from the flat.

'Where are you going?'

Jeanette blanked him, saying, 'You ain't got no warrant for me so mind your own fucking business!'

'Where's your brother, do you know?'

She carried on walking; she wouldn't even dignify that question with an answer. She tried ringing Kira's little pink mobile. Nothing but the message service. She sighed once more; this was all she needed. She talked angrily into the phone.

'Kira? It's me. Fucking ring, will you? And when Mum and Jon Jon find out that we've been raided without you letting anyone know, you are in deep trouble, lady!'

She turned off the phone feeling better for her outburst.

Maybe Kira was with one of the neighbours. As she walked down the stairs she texted her brother's mobile to alert him to the danger awaiting him; she also texted her mother. Each text omitted to say she had misplaced her sister.

But half an hour later she had to admit that 'misplace' was not exactly the right expression. Kira was literally nowhere to be seen.

Jeanette was actually starting to feel worried. No one had seen her sister, spoken to her or heard anything about her. They had seen the filth, though, that much was evident. But, she consoled herself, Kira was sensible enough to disappear if the police arrived. She *had* to be somewhere nearby. Bethany's phone was turned off so Jeanette began the walk to the girl's house a few streets away. It was the only other place Kira could be, and when she got her hands on her she would wring her neck for causing so much worry.

But there was that niggling fear still because her sister had not tried to contact her at all . . .

Fortunately no one had called her back since the texts so she knew she had a while yet to locate the missing child. Once the balloon went up there would be murders. She was beginning to wish she had stayed in as arranged. It would be tonight of all nights that it all fell out of bed.

Jon Jon was in a bed-sit in First Avenue, Manor Park, working out a scam to bring in drugs from Amsterdam with Sippy Marvell, a young Jamaican dealer from Brixton.

Sippy had rented this room for years and it was only ever used for business dealings. It was scruffy but clean and he had laid in a good stock of drink and puff; both essential requirements when doing any kind of planning. At least Sippy thought so anyway. Both of them had their phones turned off, another thing Sippy insisted on, and they were getting on like the proverbial house on fire.

Sippy was a bona-fide Rasta; he accepted Jon Jon for the half-white Rasta he was trying to be, and they understood each other.

Jon Jon was interested in the way Sippy incorporated his religion into his everyday life. He loved the Rasta philosophy even though his own line of work, drug dealing, didn't really match up to the beliefs he wanted to make his own. Then there was the problem of violence. Look at the morning he had had for a start. But he could listen to Sippy talking about Marcus Garvey and quoting the Scriptures for hours.

He wasn't disappointed now as Sippy whispered while building a joint, ' "And the earth brought forth grass and herb yielding seed after this kind, and trees yielding fruit whose seed was itself after this kind, and God saw that it was good." '

He grinned at Jon Jon as he said louder: '*Genesis*, man. The Bible, for fuck's sake.'

His thick Jamaican accent gave the words extra resonance so far as Jon Jon was concerned. Those words in a South London accent just didn't hold the same appeal.

'We need to sort out the finer points, Jon Jon, before we make any more plans. So ring me friend James Grey and ask him to pop over for a little chat.'

He loved the slow drawl that was Sippy's way of talking; it was quiet yet held far more authority than if he'd screamed out the words at the top of his voice.

'Knowing you, Sip, your ancestors were the first dealers then!'

Sippy laughed at the compliment.

'We smoke to meditate. Remember that if you is banged up in Brixton! It's a religious thing.'

Jon Jon laughed. He turned on his phone and the texts rang out loudly. Peter Tosh was playing quietly in the background and the sudden noise was an intrusion into the little world they were occupying.

He read the texts quickly before looking at Sippy and saying, 'I got big trouble.'

His friend shrugged.

'You sort it, I ain't going nowhere. The evening is young yet.'

Joanie cabbed it home as soon as she received the message from the parlour receptionist. Jeanette had phoned there in the end out of sheer desperation.

As she entered the flat she dimly registered the police's mess and swore under her breath. The Execution of Warrant notice was screwed up on the floor where as far as Joanie was concerned it could stay.

She aimed the PC out of the door in minutes and then, grabbing her eldest daughter by the front of her jacket, bellowed, 'Where is me baby?'

Jeanette shook her head.

'I don't know, Mum. I can't locate her.'

'Have the filth took her? I assume you'd left her on her Jacksy, they might have done. Was there anything here from Social Services?'

Jeanette shook her head.

'No, nothing, just the warrant notice. Let go of me, Mum!'

But Joanie was not listening; still grabbing her daughter's jacket, she closed her eyes and willed herself to calm down.

'What did Old Bill say?'

She shook Jeanette's jacket once more, nearly unbalancing the pair of them.

'Will you answer me!'

'She wasn't here, Mum. Now let me go!'

Joanie threw her daughter none too gently on the sofa. Then she punched her across the head, hurting her own hand in the process. It was a hard punch and it said a lot for her daughter that she didn't even wince with the pain.

The phone rang and Joanie made a dive for it.

'Hello.'

Her voice was strained.

'Yeah, who's this? Where the fuck is my baby . . .'

Jeanette watched the worry wiped from her mother's face.

'Oh, thank God! Yeah, thanks. I'm on me way over.'

She replaced the receiver and sank down on the floor in relief. Her legs had literally given way under her.

'Is she all right, Mum?'

Jeanette sounded genuinely concerned.

'No fucking thanks to you, you fucking little mare!'

Joanie lit a cigarette with shaking hands. It was taking all her will-power not to punch her daughter's lights out once and for all. Christ Himself knew she had been building Joanie up to it for a while now.

'I am going to pick her up. You better start clearing this place up, and when I get back I am going to fucking muller you! I ask you to do *one* thing for me and you can't even fucking do that. You wait till your brother gets in; he at least knows how to look after his little sisters. You included, you lazy, selfish bitch!'

'Where was she?'

But the words fell on deaf ears; Joanie was already walking out of the door.

One good thing as far as Jeanette was concerned: Jon Jon wasn't coming home tonight. Not while the warrant was still out on him anyway. So at least she had some respite there.

'She's been here all evening.'

Joanie was staring at the grotesquely fat man before her and smiling nervously. Kira was asleep on a dilapidated sofa behind him, but at least it looked clean. That was the first thought in her head.

He had placed a blanket over the sleeping child and now absent-mindedly pulled it up over her like a mother would. There were crisp packets and empty Coke cans on the battered table, also the remnants of a sandwich. He had obviously taken good care of her and Joanie was grateful for that.

His strange high-pitched voice was kept deliberately calm and slow as he explained the situation. He sounded like Dale Winton on helium.

'I sit on the balcony, see? It's the heat. I saw your other daughter go out, and then Kira was on her balcony, I mean your balcony, so I asked her over for a cup of tea. Then the police arrived and I didn't know what to do. She didn't have her phone and the only number she knew off by heart was her home one, but I didn't like to call that until I saw you were there, what with the police and everything. I mean, I can see in your front room if the curtains are open.'

He said the last bit rather nervously and Joanie grinned.

'Thanks, mate. I appreciate it. You did the right thing.'

He went out to the kitchen to make tea and Joanie thanked God for this man who had inadvertently staved off disaster. Social Services would have whipped Kira away if they had seen her alone in the flat. He clearly didn't know what a big favour he had done her.

Tommy came back in with the tea.

'Listen, if you're ever stuck, I'll come to yours and watch her. She's a good kid. Very polite and well-spoken. Her manners are impeccable, as my old mum would have said.'

For some strange reason, Joanie took to him.

'Thanks, mate, I'll bear that in mind.'

In fact she would never even contemplate it but she wouldn't say that to him. He had done her a favour tonight and so she could afford to be nice. Plus the tea and the tranquil atmosphere were doing her good.

She felt calmer than she had for a long while. It was his quietness. She guessed he had cultivated his calm, soft-spoken demeanour to compensate for his weight problem. In fact, he sounded like a queen, and not one that ruled any country she knew of.

Reading her mind, he said simply, 'It's glandular, but I also overeat so I don't help meself.'

His open face was so honest she felt a moment's sorrow for the hulk of a man before her.

'I get on very well with Kira, you know. You've done a wonderful job with her.'

Joanie smiled at the compliment. He was like a big kid himself. A *very* big kid.

'Well, I'd better carry her home. Thanks again, Tommy.'

'You're welcome, Mrs Brewer.'

'Call me Joanie, everyone does. By the way, where's your dad?'

Tommy looked uncomfortable for a split second.

'He stays out sometimes, I don't know where. Don't like to ask.'

He was clearly as green as grass, and Joanie smiled at him. She knew from the neighbours that his father treated this poor man like dirt. She had heard him going off herself at times. Suddenly she felt incredibly sorry for this overgrown boy before her.

'Pop over for a cuppa tomorrow, if you like?'

He grinned from ear to ear and she could see him swelling with pride.

'I would love to take you up on your invitation, thank you.'

She smiled again and then picked up her daughter easily. Kira was as light as a feather. She settled into her mother's body and Joanie could smell cheese and onion crisps mixed with butter. She hugged the child to her, happy now she had her back safe and sound.

Joanie walked home quickly and quietly. The less the neighbours knew the better. People only know what you tell them. Her mother had drummed that into her from a kid and it was true. It had stood Joanie in good stead all her life.

Especially since she'd lived round here.

Jon Jon was in the interview room at the police station.

'I don't know what you're talking about. What serious assault?'

He shook his head once more and settled back in his chair.

'Come off it! Your best mate is in intensive care, you were seen going into his squat and now you're trying to tell us you know nothing about it?'

Jon Jon grinned.

'Catches on quick, your mate, don't he? I said, I don't know what you're talking about and I'm telling the truth. I was with Cherise, one of me birds. So who exactly saw me there?'

The DC was getting annoyed.

'Never you mind.'

'If I had been seen there, which would have been a lie, you would have arrested me by now, wouldn't you? I know my rights, see.'

'You can also afford the best brief there is. Fuck me, Giros must be worth a fortune these days. Only as far as I know you ain't got a job, have you?'

Jon Jon's solicitor Jeffrey Callington raised his hand and said: 'You don't have to answer that, Jon Jon. They found nothing at your home, and they have nothing even to put you at the scene. Now, if it's all right with you gentlemen, I think it's about time we left. My client came here of his own volition . . .'

The DC blew out his lips noisily as he interrupted.

'With his solicitor in tow!'

Callington stared at the younger man disdainfully as he said, louder now: 'Is there a law against that then? Only if so, I have never heard of it. If you aren't careful we might be taking this further ourselves. This is the seventh occasion on which you have pulled my client in and each time you've wasted valuable hours of both his and my time.'

He smiled coldly.

'I take it we can leave?'

The DC smiled back sarcastically.

'Be my guest.'

Jon Jon grinned.

'No, ta, I'd rather go home, but thanks again for the offer.'

Callington was still smiling as they walked from the room.

When the door shut on them the DC said through gritted teeth, 'He was lying his head off.'

DI Baxter, a veteran of twenty years' standing, answered him sarcastically, 'No! You don't fucking say?'

'He's alibied, sir, it checks out. The girl and her parents are willing to make statements.'

The WPC was still green enough to give people the benefit of the doubt. She smiled as she said: 'Who do you think did attack the victim, sir?'

'Well, I think it was that lying little bastard who just left, but I suppose Professor Green in the library with a candlestick is a better bet at this particular moment in time. That is one slippery little fucker but I'll have him! One of these days I will have him bang to fucking rights. Black bastard he is.'

Baxter rubbed at his tired eyes.

'I hope the Carty kid dies. Hopefully we'll kill two birds with one stone then.'

The DC grinned once more, his young face hopeful at last.

'Be a touch, no doubt about that.'

Joanie tucked Kira in for the tenth time; she had never been so frightened in her life. Jeanette was still subdued after the massive clump she had distributed earlier. If Social Services got her younger daughter she would never see her again, Joanie was aware of that. Unlike the older two, Kira had never been in care, ever. In Joanie's younger days the courts had imprisoned prostitutes at the drop of a hat, and consequently her elder kids had paid a high price for their mother's way of earning a living. With so many counts against her already, they wouldn't hesitate to take Kira into care.

Well, it was never going to happen to her baby. This was one child she would do right by if it killed her.

Going into the front room again, she saw her elder daughter sitting forlornly smoking a cigarette and felt a moment's sorrow for her.

Jeanette, God love her, was her own worst enemy. Her attitude was always going to be her downfall. Even as a kid she had been a right stroppy little mare. Fight her own fingernails if the fancy took her. But if nothing else good had come of tonight, Joanie knew it had frightened her elder girl and so in that respect it wasn't a complete disaster.

Jon Jon was quite capable of taking care of himself; she didn't need to worry about him or Jeanette like she worried about Kira. Where they were naturally streetwise, her youngest wasn't. She was not backward exactly, but she had what were called learning difficulties. She went to a mainstream school but barely kept up with the other kids. Her naturally sunny personality made up for a lot, Joanie knew that, but Kira could not be left alone. She had no street sense whatsoever and that was what worried her mother so much.

'How could you leave her like that, Jen?'

Jeanette's face screwed up into a tight ball as she whined, 'Oh, Mum, be fair. I hate looking after her all the time. I'm fourteen,

I want to be out with me mates.'

'You mean, shagging. I hear everything, remember that.'

Jeanette looked so young, underneath the thick makeup, that her mother's heart went out to her. She had had a fright and it showed.

Joanie stared at her daughter's profile; she could be really pretty if she didn't look so much like a candidate for *The Trisha Show*.

She tried to hug the girl, but was shrugged off.

'Leave it out, Mum. Save it for your baby.'

They sat in silence for a moment before Jeanette said, 'Wanna drink?'

'Yeah, go on then, love.'

It was the nearest Jeanette would come to an outright apology. Joanie knew that and accepted it. One daughter knew too much, and the other daughter would never know enough. God played jokes, she was convinced of that. She only wished she could laugh at her own life.

Kira called out in her sleep then and she was catapulted from her seat, but Jeanette had got there first and was settling her down gently.

Joanie watched from the doorway and felt her heart lighten.

She realised she was close to tears as she watched the little tableau before her. She had really had enough of this life. It was hard to keep up a happy front when inside you were slowly dying.

Little Tommy was happy, or as near to happy as he had ever been. It was wonderful to wake up in the morning with an agenda. He had an actual appointment, not with the doctor or some other specialist but with another person. He hugged the knowledge to himself.

'What are you grinning about?'

His father broke into his reverie and he shrugged.

'Nothing, just enjoying the day.'

His father laughed at him as usual.

'What the fuck have you got to look forward to? More food?'

Tommy was crushed, but he didn't rise to the bait.

'Do you want another cuppa, Dad?'

'Go on then, son.'

For once Joseph felt a twinge of guilt. He was hard on the boy, but then living with Tommy was hard on him. His son was so *weird*, nothing to brag about, and Joseph needed to brag, it was in his nature. No one at work knew about Tommy, he had made sure of that.

Joseph had a girlfriend of sorts and now she wanted him full-time. It was such a bind. The fact he loathed his own son didn't help matters either. But this morning he didn't get in any more digs. When he left the atmosphere was neutral for once.

Tommy watched his father from the balcony until he disappeared round the corner and then he made his plans. Shower first, then he was going to put on his best clothes and at ten-thirty exactly he was going to walk over to visit his new friends. Oh, he was so happy! This was his first ever engagement and he didn't want it to go wrong.

He wished his mother was alive. She would have been so proud of him. The Brewers seemed like such nice people.

'Stop it, Jon Jon, please!'

Kira was terrified as her brother dragged Jeanette from her bed by the hair.

'Just keep out of it, Kira, OK?'

Jeanette was trying to prise her brother's fingers from her hair. She was already crying. He dragged her bodily into the front room then, throwing her roughly on the sofa, bellowed, 'What have you been told, eh?'

He was so angry his eyes were nearly popping out of his head. He was obviously on something and it wasn't cannabis.

'What have you been fucking told! You *never*, and I mean *never*, leave our Kira on her Jack Jones.'

Kira was terrified as she watched the scene unfold before her eyes.

'I didn't mind, Jon Jon, I had a lovely time! Tommy let me play with his Barbies, and I had lovely cups of tea and that.'

Jon Jon grabbed at his own dreads in anger and frustration.

'Can you hear her, Jen? Just listen to her. She spent the evening with a bloke who plays with fucking Barbies!'

'He's all right, Jon Jon. I think he's queer to be honest.'

Joanie was the voice of reason as usual. She knew her son was more than capable of half-killing the frightened girl before him.

He poked his face into his sister's as he shouted again: 'Fucking Barbies? What next? You'd leave her with Fred West if it got you out for a couple of hours.'

He was spitting with rage now.

'Do you realise she could have been taken away last night, spent the next few weeks in a fucking foster home? You know what the filth is capable of. It would make them laugh, knowing the aggravation they had wrought on us. And where was you, eh, while the house was getting torn apart? Come on, I want to know who he is so I can rip his fucking head off.'

'But she wasn't taken, was she? So get a fucking grip.'

Jon Jon took a step closer and Kira screamed. It was only this that stopped him from attacking the crying girl.

'Well, that's it now, Mum. She is grounded for the duration.'

He poked a finger at Jeanette.

'You ain't going out till the Second fucking Coming now.'

She jumped up and screamed, all fear gone at the thought of not being allowed out.

'It ain't up to you, it's up to Mum! Tell her to stop working for once. Selling her crump to all and sundry while I look after her kid. Or better still, if you're the man of the house, why don't *you* keep us then?'

Joanie answered her.

'I ain't took a penny off any of you and I won't, you know that. To all intents and purposes this is my house and I'll say what happens in it.'

Jeanette laughed nastily.

'You better tell him that then, because *he* thinks this is *his* house.'

She stormed into her bedroom, shouting, 'I have to get ready for school.'

Jon Jon laughed despite himself.

'That's a first, ain't it? *You* going to school?'

'Leave her, Jon Jon, she got the message. Come on, Kira. Stop crying, love. What do you want for breakfast?'

'Can I have anything I like?'

'Within reason!'

Kira grinned through her tears and Jon Jon closed his eyes in distress. She was beautiful. Blonde and blue-eyed, she was going to be absolutely stunning – and she would probably never be any older in her mind than she was now. It was such a frightening thought.

Even after this rigmarole all she was interested in was getting a bowl of Coco Pops. Her attention span was so short this upset would be forgotten after the first spoonful.

He followed them into the kitchen.

'Jeanette's right, Mum. Maybe you should quit working. I can see us through.'

Joanie poured out the bowl of Coco Pops without answering him. He knew how she felt about his drugs, and she knew how he felt about her own particular way of dealing. It was a no-win situation.

'She had a fright, she'll be OK now.' Joanie grinned suddenly. 'He ain't half a funny bloke. Nice enough, but so fat! I mean, honestly.'

Kira laughed.

'Can't I stay with Tommy, Mum? He has lovely things at his house, Barbies and treats.'

'What did you do last night, Kira?'

Jon Jon seemed genuinely interested.

She thought earnestly for a few moments, her little face screwed up in concentration.

'Er . . . we played Barbies, like I said, and then we watched *Sleeping Beauty*. Tommy has all the films – he loves princesses like I do. It was lovely. We had drinks of Coca-Cola and sandwiches and sweeties. It was fun.'

Joanie ruffled the child's hair.

'He seemed nice enough, bless him. And be fair, Jon Jon, he done us a right favour.'

'I suppose so. But we don't know anything about him, do we?'

Joanie shrugged.

'What's to know? He came up trumps for us and that's enough for me. He's a bit slow.' She nodded towards her daughter. 'That's why they get on so well, I think.'

Jon Jon nodded sadly.

'I see what you mean, Mum. Well, you suss him out, see what you think. He might be a touch with Miss Unreliable on the prowl.'

Joanie slipped an arm round her son's waist.

'Did you hurt Carty, son?'

He nodded.

'I had to, Mum, he's a fucking crack head. Caused me no end of grief.'

Joanie pushed her hair from her eyes and smiled.

'I heard he was really damaged.'

She kept her voice neutral.

Jon Jon shrugged.

'Should have thought of that, shouldn't he? I ain't got time for wasters, Mum. 'Specially not crack-head wasters.'

The subject was closed and Joanie wondered at a son who could be so caring and compassionate with his sisters and family and yet could physically maim a close personal friend.

She didn't want to think about any of it too much, so she did what she always did. She smiled and laughed and joked. Kira was in stitches as she left for school with her big brother. Then Joanie went straight for the Valium.

Just to take the edge off life. That's what she had been telling herself for years.

Chapter Four

Monika was staring at the huge man before her in absolute awe. He was bloody big. He was also a nice fella who tried so hard to be accommodating it was painful to watch him.

Being on the large side herself she knew the battle he faced daily, not just inside himself but with the outside world. Though she laughed about him with Joanie, they liked him a lot. Tommy was kind and compassionate.

Yet, for all his size, she saw that he was surprisingly light on his feet. That was another thing she had noticed about him: he managed to get about all right. Far better than you would think when you looked at him, though he did huff and puff more than most.

Tommy for his part was having the time of his life. Two women were sitting talking to him as if he was a real person. Someone who mattered, someone who actually belonged in their world. This was his third visit now and he felt welcome and respected. It was the latter that pleased him most. Joanie was a goddess to him now, and since she had welcomed him into her home, the neighbours had started to show him new respect, especially since Jon Jon too now gave him the time of day. Like his mother, he didn't judge books by their covers. Tommy had decided early on that he liked the boy. He certainly had his priorities right where his family was concerned. He was like a father to his sisters, watching them like a hawk.

Nowadays, thanks to the Brewers, people called out to Tommy as he sat on his balcony, and he had even started to take the long trek to the shops on a daily basis. That alone was hard work, but it was worth it because people spoke to him now. Were actually interested in him. He had his own niche in the life of the estate.

He also had unlimited access to Kira, which was the idea after all. He loved her, loved being with her. She was everything to him, and she loved him back. She had told him she did. She had also said she felt stifled by her family, but he had explained how lucky she was to have people who actually cared about her and he thought she had understood what he meant. He hoped so anyway.

Joanie grinned at him; she had a lovely face. She also had a dignity that wasn't apparent on first meeting her but which shone out like a beacon after a while. She had had a hard life, he knew that and could sympathise with it. More than most people, in fact.

'So do you want the job then?'

Tommy grinned from ear to ear.

'Oh, please. It would be my pleasure.'

He flapped one hand and sent Monika into gales of laughter once more. But it was friendly laughter, not vicious and at the expense of his pride. It was laughter to be shared, by him as well as everyone nearby. He was in his element, even camping it up a bit to please them all.

'Now all we need to sort out is the money.'

Tommy's face fell.

'Please, Joanie. I couldn't take money from a friend.'

She smiled at him. She knew he meant what he said and appreciated the fact, but he had to be paid. Fair dues.

'Listen to me – you will get a few quid, son. Now I don't want to hear no more about it, OK?'

He smiled and nodded, pleased that the decision had been taken out of his hands. Wait until he told his father he had a job! A real job. Not like the ones he had done before. Homework, boring soul-destroying homework. Hours and hours spent making boxes.

That would give his dad something to think about.

'Well, if you're sure, Joanie.'

He was thrilled with the way things had turned out. Joanie let him make the tea because she knew it pleased him so much. He wasn't a bad fella, just lonely. And if anyone knew about loneliness it was her.

Tommy's face clouded over then. Suppose his father put a block on the babysitting? So he said quietly, 'The only fly in the ointment is me dad.'

Monika laughed that hearty laugh of hers and said loudly, 'Fuck him, Tommy. Jon Jon will have a word if necessary. So stop worrying, mate.'

But even as he smiled they could see the fear on his open face. Then it vanished, as quickly as if a curtain had been lifted. Jon Jon would sort it out. Even his father wouldn't dare cross Jon Jon Brewer.

The two women saw his expression change and then happiness was glowing from him once more.

'I'll talk to him. Don't worry, Tommy.'

As she spoke Joanie made a face at Monika that sent her into stitches once more.

'Fucking miserable old bastard he is. Here, Joanie, tell you what – we'll Godfather him. He looks senile so we'll just make him an offer he can't remember!'

They all laughed again, except Tommy was laughing at the sheer scandalous audacity of the words and not because he thought they were funny.

If his father only *knew* he was the object of ridicule for a change! He broke into a cold sweat just thinking about it. But for all that it felt good to laugh at him, about him.

Tommy had friends, and his father could do nothing about it. Not without letting the cat out of the bag anyway.

He pushed that thought away as quickly as it had come into his head. That was all in the past now, like his father said. It was wonderful just to be in this kitchen with people who accepted him whatever he was and whatever he looked like.

For the first time since his mother had died Tommy felt valued, needed.

It was certainly a heady feeling.

Paulie was at home finishing his breakfast. He always ate a late breakfast and it was always served to him by his wife Sylvia.

She was a big girl, fleshy and raw-boned. She had a lovely face and no dress sense whatsoever, which suited Paulie down to the ground. She never stood out at Masonic dos and was a pillar of the local church. She was also an exemplary mother.

His two daughters, Pauline aged eleven and Jacqueline aged nine, were perfect little middle-class misses with the right hairstyles and suitably demure clothing and personalities. No chance of them going into the family business, not with the amount he was weighing out for their school fees anyway.

He liked his home life, it suited him. In fact he was loath to leave the bosom of his household today because he was dog-tired and fancied a bit of the other with old Sylvia. She was due a good seeing to and they both knew it.

Paulie felt lucky in his life. He was totally in control of everything and everyone around him. He poured himself another coffee and smiled at his wife.

Sylvia watched her husband and stifled the laughter that was spiralling up inside her body and threatening to burst out. He had to be the most smug, self-satisfied and ignorant man on the planet. She knew all about him, but wasn't going to let on, and if he thought he was going to touch her at any point today or in the future he had a big shock coming. She had loved him once, many years ago. Now she wasn't sure how she felt about him.

What she did know, though, was that he was a good provider and that was more important to her than anything. She was not going to end up like her own mother, living on past glories while scraping out her life in genteel poverty.

So Sylvia had made a separate life for herself, and Paulie had no idea that she was gradually manoeuvring him away from herself and their daughters.

She was spending more and more time at their 'country retreat'. This was actually a four-bedroomed mock-Georgian house in Kent, but it did the job as far as she was concerned. It kept her and the girls away from this cretin she called a husband, and that, as far as she was concerned, was a touch.

Nowadays they were like strangers who just happened to reside under the same roof. The roof he had paid for admittedly. She attended functions with him where she stood beside him like the good wife she was. And she *was* a good wife, even though he had not always been a good husband. In short, Sylvia knew which side her bread was buttered.

As he leered at her now she looked away. Men, she had always thought, were so predictable. Well, Paulie was in for a shock and no mistake!

Jeanette was with Jasper, the man of her dreams. As usual school was out of the question and she was truanting round a squat used by his friends. To her he was the be all and end all. His deep blue eyes were like magnets to this child-woman and he knew it. And used it.

Girls liked Jasper Copes. He was good-looking and he was hard. What more could any of them want?

The only thing that spoiled it was that Jasper and all his friends were racists. They belonged to the new breed of skinheads. Jeanette's having a brother with a Jamaican father was not really something that endeared her to the people around her in this squat. Even the girls looked at her askance, and talked about her and Jasper among themselves.

Jeanette secretly hated it here, but it was where Jasper wanted to be so she followed like the good little girl she was. She knew that when Jon Jon found out who she was seeing there would be murders, but Jasper had a hold over her and she felt if she wasn't with him her life would be worth nothing any more.

She prayed daily that Jon Jon and Jasper would meet and get on. But that was one miracle even Jesus would be hard pressed to perform.

Her eyes lingered on the BNP posters and she shut her ears to the racist banter all around her. She felt left out, and as much as she loved Jasper, she was glad. She wouldn't want to feel comfortable in a place like this. These people were ignorant and they were ugly, both inside and out.

She wished she knew what exactly it was about Jasper that made her so eager to overlook his lifestyle. True, he was the leader, the one they all looked up to and listened to. Sometimes when she saw him in this mode he frightened her. But alone with her he was softer, and made her feel good about herself. So he couldn't be all bad surely?

One of his friends, Polo Jenkins, said to her loudly, forcing her from her reverie, 'I said, did the filth get your brother yet?'

''Course not!'

She spoke to him as if he was stupid and this was noted by everyone there. One thing about being Jon Jon's sister: it made people wary of you. Being Jasper's bird helped a lot as well.

The atmosphere was charged for a few seconds and she saw Jasper grin. He liked it when Jeanette defended herself.

She sighed. They were talking once more about their god Nick Griffin and she went back on to autopilot. Ten minutes later she said, 'I'm off, Jasper.'

The conversation was now about the poor African immigrants in Northampton of all places, and how AIDS cases had increased by three hundred per cent since their arrival there.

Jasper smiled at her.

'Give me a minute, mate.'

She shook her head.

'I said, I'm off. And that means now.'

She stared him out and could see him debating his reaction with himself. Eventually he shrugged.

'Fair enough.'

She left the squat, and when she got outside and the fresh air hit her, took deep breaths as if to clean her lungs from the stench of their hatred. She also heard loud laughter from inside and was shrewd enough to know it was from a joke made at her expense.

Sad, but feeling strangely lighter, she made her way home. Those people were sick and she wanted nothing to do with them, Jasper included. She didn't really mean that, and she knew it, but it made her feel better to think she could act so tough. She didn't need him, she didn't need anyone. Her mother's neglect and the years spent in and out of care had seen to that. The sensible part of her was saying, 'Walk away from him.' Their lives were too different and all the scheming to see him was killing her. If Jon Jon only knew! She felt hot every time she thought about it.

However, when Jasper caught up with her five minutes later Jeanette felt inexplicably pleased. He had chased after her. That in itself was a first. It proved he really did care about her, she had to believe that. As he smiled down at her Jeanette felt her heart melt.

He wasn't all bad, not like he thought he was. If that was true he wouldn't be here with her now.

She had walked away and he had followed her. For once she held the power in their relationship and it felt good. She only hoped it lasted.

Twenty minutes later she was stretched out in his bed, the grubby sheets giving off their familiar rank smell. His mother as usual was nowhere to be seen. Karen Copes spent most afternoons in the local pub with her cronies.

The strange thing was, Jeanette didn't even enjoy this bit of it, but if it was what it took to keep him, then so be it.

She did what Jasper wanted and she did it willingly.

Kira and Tommy were now fast friends, and knowing that she had unlimited access to his Barbie collection was the icing on the cake as far as she was concerned. His dad was nice to her as well, though she often felt the atmosphere between him and Tommy. But Joseph Thompson always gave her a kind word and somehow she knew that life was easier for Tommy when she was there.

She went to the flat nearly every night after school just to peek at the dolls. Tommy would spend ages ironing the little outfits; they even had their own tiny hangers. As he watched Kira raptly rearrange the dolls' wardrobe he could not help but smile.

He made her a glass of orange and fished out a bag of plain crisps as a snack. He knew her likes and dislikes now, which was something else that pleased him.

His father watched them and shook his head.

'We've got to be careful, Tommy, you know that.'

He nodded.

He really wished his father would stop nagging. As he said himself, it was all in the past. This was a new start for them both.

Jon Jon heard Paulie before he saw him. Sighing, he finished his drink. Paulie was beside him in a second.

'What you doing in here, son?'

Paulie's voice was friendly yet wary. He knew he wasn't

Jon Jon's favourite person, but he could live with that. He had known him since he was a kid after all and had always liked him. He remembered when Jon Jon had liked him back, many moons ago. To give old Joanie her due, she had not done a bad job with him.

But word on the street was that he was a good little earner, and Paulie was always after the main chance.

Jon Jon answered him quietly.

'Having a drink.'

The sarcasm was not lost on either of them.

'You old enough now then?'

Jon Jon smiled despite himself.

'In here I am. Have been since I was fourteen.'

Paulie, like Jon Jon, couldn't resist looking at himself in the mirrored bar. He tidied his hair and said, 'What you drinking?'

Without waiting for an answer he said to the tall blonde with no bra and a permanent smile, 'Two large brandies, love.'

He gazed around the bar, clocked every female and rated every man in the place. He waved to one or two men and smiled at most of the women over sixteen and under thirty-five.

'So how is Haile Selassie these days then? Alive and well and living in South London?' He tugged Jon Jon's dreads as he said it.

'Fuck off, Paulie.'

The smile was gone now and Paulie answered in a serious voice: 'I've fucking killed for less and you should know that. But for the sake of your mother, I'll overlook it.' He paused before he said, 'This time anyway.'

It was a warning and Jon Jon knew it. He didn't answer. Whatever Paulie was or wasn't, he was classed as a bad man. Not a member of the heavy mob like local legend Big John McClellan, but a hard man nevertheless who could take care of his own interests and Jon Jon knew it would be wise for him to remember that fact.

The jukebox came on and Gareth Gates was singing in the background. The place was buzzing even this early in the day. By six it would be packed. Jon Jon picked up his drink and raised it to Paulie.

'Did your mum mention I wanted to see you?'

He shook his head. Paulie knew it was a lie. If he told one of his girls to run naked up Park Lane setting fire to her farts, she would do it.

Jon Jon stared ahead and for a second Paulie felt an urge to slap the boy across the face, give him a humiliating little tap. How dare the kid look down his nose at him? Because that was the message he was getting.

Instead he sipped his brandy before saying, 'Listen, cunt, I don't want your arse, I just want to know what you're involved in and if I am interested I might want a little slice, see? Now option two, which I must admit is far more in my favour than yours, is I find out on me Jack Jones and then I remove it from you for once and for all. Do you get my drift?'

Jon Jon felt the heat of humiliation sweep over his face and neck. Watching, Paulie felt almost sorry for him. He liked this kid's temerity. It reminded him of himself at the same age. He was running his first woman at sixteen – the fact it had been his own mother he kept well under wraps. She lived in Eastbourne these days and enjoyed the quiet life. He avoided her like the plague, but saw her all right for a few quid. He knew where his priorities lay.

'So, Jon Jon, shall we sit down and start this conversation again? Only this time you are more forthcoming and I am less aggressive. What do you say, eh?'

He was smiling and Jon Jon knew he was captured. But one day . . . one day he would be able to tip this man's bollocks, and he could wait for that. He was young yet, he could bide his time. So he would. But when the time came, he would enjoy wiping the smile off this man's face once and for all.

They picked up their drinks and went to a table that miraculously became vacant when they showed they wanted to sit there.

Even as he hated Paulie, Jon Jon loved the respect he got from everyone. It was what he was determined to win for himself and his family. His mother especially. He knew that whatever Joanie had done, she had done for the right reasons. He'd reminded himself of that fact since he was eight years old.

He talked to Paulie when they were finally settled. Really didn't have any choice in the matter.

Joanie was back on the kerb and she hated it. In fact, tonight she had meant to have a night off. A tooth was hurting and she was soaking cotton wool in brandy and cloves and pressing it into the hole.

She was also drinking large vodka and Cokes so that when she went to sit outside with the other women she was already drunk.

Kira was running round with Bethany and their laughter was loud in the summer air. A red-haired girl was sitting across from Joanie on the left-hand side of the drying area. She was very pretty and dressed nicely which was what made her stand out.

'Who's she?'

Joanie's voice was slurred.

'That's Caroline's sister. She's staying for a few days. Left her old man.'

'Oh, is it? She looks familiar.'

Barbara Moxon, Joanie's neighbour, raised her eyes to the ceiling and said, 'Don't you remember her? Her little girl was murdered last year. Or was it the year before . . .'

'*That's right.* I remember now. Poor girl, what a thing to have happen to your child.'

'Go off your head, wouldn't you?'

'Lovely-looking girl and all.'

Barbara nodded in agreement, as if being good-looking had ever warded off evil. They watched the girl as she collected her belongings and made her way up to her sister's flat. As she walked towards the lobby doorway she turned and looked back at them for a few seconds then she walked inside and was lost from sight.

The mood was flat now and Joanie took a deep gulp of her drink. Her mobile rang and she answered it.

'What? Oh, for fuck's sake . . .'

'What's the matter, girl?'

'Monika's been nicked, wants me to have Bethany tonight. She's beaten up a store detective. That bird gets steadily fucking worse.'

Her mobile rang again and she answered it with a curt, 'OK.'

She stood up and stretched. 'See you later.'

On her way upstairs she rang Jeanette and demanded she got herself home. Thanks to Monika she had to work tonight, toothache or no toothache.

But she could have done without it. She was already three sheets to the wind and it was going to be a long night, she already knew that much.

It was bad enough when you felt one hundred per cent, but when you felt wafty it was a bastard.

She wouldn't even bother having a bath.

Jasper was annoyed and it showed.

'Why do you have to look after her? Why can't Fatty have her?' They were in bed and they were stoned, but his voice was still angry. 'I wanted us to have a night in together, Jen.'

Jeanette made a decision.

'Fuck her. Fatty can have her. I just won't go home.'

She settled down once more and put her mother, brother and sister out of her mind completely. There would be ructions but she would sort it all out as and when. For the moment she was happy where she was.

Joanie knew after an hour that her daughter wasn't coming home and rang Tommy. While she waited for him, she cursed Jeanette under her breath. She didn't want to take the piss with Tommy in case he got the ache with coming over so often. Even though she knew he loved it, you could have too much of a good thing and she had done a deal with Jeanette that as long as she looked after her sister now and again, Joanie wouldn't be too hard on her.

Now Jeanette had let her down again and even though she knew her daughter was only being a typical teenager this complete lack of regard was starting to get on Joanie's nerves. Well, if Jen wanted any money this week she could whistle for it.

She wondered who it was her daughter was seeing, and what kind of person he might be. Jeanette was so secretive these days and Joanie was past trying to get anything out of the tight-lipped girl. She would ask Jon Jon to put his ear to the ground. See what he could come up with.

Kira was ready for bed and waiting with bated breath for Tommy. Joanie smiled as she looked at her younger daughter. She was a good kid, bless her. She knew she wouldn't have half the trouble with her that she'd had with the other girl.

That in itself was something to be glad about. She couldn't go through all this again, for all the money in the world.

Paulie and Jon Jon found their truce was working better than either of them had expected. In fact they had a lot in common, but then when Jon Jon had been a kid this man had been good to him. Jon Jon realised now that it was because Paulie had wanted his mother in his stable, but he accepted that. If he had a fight with everyone who had ever used her he would never have time to sleep. Anyway she'd gone willingly, though that still didn't mean he had to like it, did it?

But as much as he hated Paulie's main money-spinner, he admired his acumen and business sense. Jon Jon could learn a lot from this man. He could also, if he used his loaf, get his mother out of the life and into the know.

He realised early on in their conversation that with Paulie in his corner his profits could increase tenfold at least. And that was only at the rate he was dealing now. Once he hit the big time he would earn silly money.

'You done Carty, didn't you?'

Paulie's voice was low, conversational.

Jon Jon shrugged but didn't answer, his face completely devoid of expression.

Paulie laughed.

'Good lad. I heard through the grapevine that he was smoking the profits.'

Jon Jon scowled.

'Who told you that?'

He was annoyed to think he had been the topic of public conversation, and this fact showed in his face. He was fuming at the thought of his private business being common knowledge; it just made him even more glad he had unloaded that waster Carty. Because this had to have come from him, it certainly didn't originate from Jon Jon's own mouth. When Carty finally came out of hospital he was going to go straight back in there, Jon Jon would see to that himself.

Paulie was laughing once more.

'Easy, tiger!'

He finished his brandy before saying, 'Calm down, it was only an observation made by someone I trust.'

But the boy's reaction pleased him. He was proud, too proud really, but it showed he could keep his mouth shut and that was important as far as Paulie was concerned. Jon Jon forced his emotions under control and Paulie stopped himself from laughing again.

He liked this kid! For all his man's size and obvious intelligence, he had the temper of a five year old. But he would learn, and Paulie would teach. He knew the boy had a natural head for business, was already raking in a good wedge at only seventeen. Under expert guidance and tuition he would become a force to be reckoned with.

He also had the violent personality so important to their kind of business. Jon Jon could administer a slap if necessary, and he could garner himself additional respect while doing it.

Paulie threw a fifty-pound note on the table.

'Fill them up again, son, and keep the change.'

Jon Jon did as he was bidden.

Paulie watched as the boy pushed his way through the now crowded bar and he smiled again. Jon Jon had an arrogance about him that was evident even in his walk, his mannerisms. It was inbred. He wondered who the boy's father had been because he'd never got any hint of that from poor old Joanie. She was a victim waiting to happen, always had been and always would be.

As Jon Jon made his way back to the table Paulie saw one of his henchmen enter the bar with a small dark-haired girl. It was noisy and smoky now and he had to shout loudly to attract their attention. Jon Jon had just sat down when the man arrived at their table.

'All right, Paulie?'

He was big, heavyset, and clearly extremely nervous.

'I wasn't expecting to see you in here.'

'Obviously not. Have you got me money then?'

The man was opening his mouth to answer when Paulie's fist shot up and knocked him backwards. Getting out of his seat, he kicked the man over and over again in the face and chest. Then he dragged him off the floor and threw him towards the young girl he had entered with.

'You've got twenty-four hours, cunt.'

Jon Jon was impressed but as usual kept his face neutral.

Paulie went up further in his estimation when he sat down at the table and did not even mention what had taken place; instead he picked up their conversation from where they had left it.

He had made his point, though, and they both knew that. It said a lot for the public house they were in that no one even bothered to help the wounded man up from the floor. Even the little dark girl left him there.

'Now then, where were we?'

Paulie and Jon Jon, without realising it, became friends that night even though neither of them would admit that fact out loud.

To outsiders they had a finely calibrated truce.

Chapter Five

Carty had regained consciousness and after a visit from Jon Jon was suddenly willing to make a statement that completely exonerated his one-time friend. Carty did look rough, but in his heart of hearts Jon Jon could feel no regret for what he had done. It had been necessary, and it had been unavoidable.

He felt relieved once it was all over officially. It didn't matter what the police *thought* as long as they couldn't *prove* anything. That was something he had learned at a very early age.

Carty had even had the nerve to try and talk him round – as if he was stupid enough to enter into any kind of relationship with a crack head! Business or otherwise, he was now a liability and out of Jon Jon's sphere of friendship. He could drop dead. Jon Jon put the hard word on him about his big mouth and discussing their private business and Carty took the reprimand without a murmur. He was terrified and it showed.

The man was a joke, a shadow of his former self. Jon Jon only hoped the time in hospital helped him to kick his habit before the habit kicked him.

After all, he wasn't a vindictive person.

As he left the hospital he rang around and arranged a few meetings then made his way back to his mother's by his usual mode of transport, unlicensed taxi cab.

Jon Jon knew that he could only drive himself after he had passed his test. He was shrewd enough to realise that with his growing reputation he was a candidate for a tug at any moment, and driving without a licence would be such a stupid nicking he would never take that chance. He had no respect for people who went to prison for driving convictions; they were an embarrassment as far as he was concerned. Once he passed his test he would wear a seat belt and make sure the rent on the car, meaning the tax and insurance, was always up to date. Sometimes it paid to be legal. He wouldn't even drive over the speed limit because he would never open the door for Old Bill in any way.

And now he was in with Paulie the chances of a decent motor were getting better by the day.

He wondered how his mother would react to his having taken the job. After all his talk he felt as if he had let himself down, but it was too good an opportunity to miss. And knowing his mother like he did, he felt sure she would understand his motives.

All in all, he was finally getting somewhere in his life.

It was a good feeling.

Joanie was laughing as usual. Kira was dressed up in some of her old clothes and Jeanette, for once being a proper girlie girl, was helping her little sister to make herself up. As Joanie stirred the beef casserole she had cooked for dinner, she listened to their chatter. Jeanette had spent hours going through her wardrobe when she was little, dressing up, putting on her makeup and perfume. She had been a dear little thing once.

She missed them all small. Life had been so much easier then; she had been their world and they had been hers. Now only Kira still wanted her really. The others tolerated her haphazard affection, though in fairness to Jon Jon he hugged her when he knew she needed it. He had been the honorary man of the house for so long, he was like the husband she had never had!

She laughed once more at this thought. But deep inside she knew it wasn't funny in the least. None of the kids' fathers had stayed about long after their conception, let alone until the actual birth. But she had kept her kids and she was glad that she had. When all was said and done, they were all you had in the end. Joanie didn't remind herself that they were all she had had in the first place.

She was smiling as usual when she turned and looked at Kira, standing in the kitchen doorway.

The smile was wiped from her face in an instant.

Kira looked like a grown woman and it was frightening somehow. Her eyes were heavily made up, and her lips were lined in red and glossed and looked so full they were a permanent pout. Her blonde hair was backcombed and seemed fuller, even sexy. It was like looking at her child in ten years' time, except poor Kira would look like a babe outside then while inside she would still be a child.

Kira picked up on her mother's mood and her face dropped.

'Have I done wrong, Mum?'

Joanie hugged her and said loudly, more for her own benefit than her daughter's, 'No, love. It's just a shock, that's all, seeing you so grown-up.'

Kira relaxed and hugged her back.

'Can I keep it on, show Jon Jon and everyone?'

Joanie shook her head as she thought, I can just imagine his face if he was presented with this!

'No, sweetie, you wash it off. Your dinner will be ready soon.'

Kira nodded and walked back to the bedroom. Joanie could feel her heart racing in her chest. It had been almost surreal, seeing her like that. She'd looked so much like an adult, and a beautiful adult at that. The worst thing of all was that Kira had looked like a miniature version of Joanie herself at the same age.

She gulped at her glass of red wine and puffed deeply on her Benson. As she stared out of the kitchen window she noticed that the nights were drawing in and this pleased her. Darkness made her job easier. It also kept her young daughter where she could see her.

Inside the flat.

Jeanette walked into the kitchen also looking like a glamour puss and said to her mother gaily, 'Didn't she look fantastic, Mum?'

The pride in her voice made Joanie want to cry. But she nodded. It was so rare that Jeanette did anything with her sister, she didn't want to spoil it.

'Like a little woman. But do me a favour, Jen, don't get her up like that too often.'

Jeanette pushed her thick brown hair back as she said gently, 'Don't worry, Mum, I won't. It was really quite shocking to see her like that even though she loved it. Do you know what I mean?'

'I do, love. It scared me to be honest.'

'I took a few photos of her in the bedroom to keep her happy, then I washed it off her face. Before Jon Jon saw her. But you should have seen her posing on the bed, a right natural and all, grinning away one minute and looking all sultry the next. She's a case, eh?'

Joanie ruffled the girl's hair.

'You're an old softie really, ain't you?'

Jeanette laughed but she didn't push her mother away as usual and Joanie chanced giving her a hug. It was returned and soon Kira joined them and they were all still laughing and hugging when Jon Jon burst through the door.

'Can anyone join in this session or is it for members only?'

'What's a member?'

Kira's voice was high and interested and Joanie answered her with a quip.

'That depends on who you ask, my lovely.'

Everyone laughed except Kira but she enjoyed the happiness around her and then laughed anyway, even though she didn't know why.

Jon Jon was deliberately putting them all in a good mood and Joanie could have kissed him for it. Their laughter was loud and long. She had not felt so happy for a long time.

As Joanie served up the food later she looked at her kids and felt the swell of pride she always did when she saw them en masse. When they were all happy in each other's company it made it all seem worthwhile.

They weren't a bad family. At least they loved one another, cared for one another. Most of the time anyway.

The evening breeze was cool, and Monika and Joanie were chatting as they waited for the cars to stop.

One of Todd McArthur's young girls wandered towards them. She was as high as the proverbial kite and her smooth-skinned face was grey.

'You all right, love?' Joanie asked.

The girl stared at her glassy-eyed and barely managed a nod.

Her slow blinking gave the game away to the other women; she was seriously out of it. Looked like she had just come round from an anaesthetic.

Joanie sighed. The poor little mare didn't know what was going on. She wasn't capable of getting in any motors tonight.

'Come on, let's get you home.'

The girl shook her head, but it was obvious that was about as agile as she was going to get. Not that that would bother the punters at this end of the market. Romance they certainly didn't want.

'Leave her, Joanie, you'll only end up with McArthur on your back.'

Monika's voice was bored.

Joanie grabbed the girl's arm.

'Fuck him! She ain't in no fit state to do anything. She's a danger to herself.'

The girl was trying to struggle but she was so out of it that all she could manage was a few head shakes.

'Call a cab, Mon.'

Monika was shaking her own head now.

'No way, she ain't our responsibility.'

Joanie started to walk the girl towards the pub nearby. The young girl was stumbling along, and as she took her arm to steady her Joanie saw the line of track marks and sighed.

What a piece of work that McArthur was! Scum, he was, scum. She remembered his mother, a nice woman with a respectable way about her. Even his old man, who was still banged up on a twenty-five for murder, had disowned this son who sold young girls. As she helped the girl along a Mercedes screeched to a halt and Todd McArthur himself was standing on the pavement blocking their way.

'What the fuck you doing?'

His voice was high, angry and tinged with disbelief.

Joanie tried to push him out of her way, but he had planted himself firmly on the pavement. His hand-made shoes looked incongruous among the used condoms, syringes and discarded cigarette butts.

'I said, what the fuck you doing?'

He was strong, wiry, with the athletic look of a footballer. He prided himself on his physique, and also on being a force to be reckoned with in the female game while still so young. His arrogance got right up Joanie's nose.

Monika was watching warily and a few of the other women crowded round, all willing to take him on for Joanie. For the first time ever he felt nervous round his workforce.

'This child is out of her nut and I am putting her in a cab home. She ain't in no fit state to work tonight.'

McArthur's face wore the look of a man in a state of complete amazement before such sheer and utter brazenness. He looked around him at the ring of concerned faces. This had to be a joke. He half expected Jeremy Beadle to jump out from behind a car.

'I will be the fucking judge of that. Now take your fucking hands off her!'

The shock of seeing her pimp before her sent the girl into a sudden frenzy of fear. She was shaking, and Todd dragged her by the hair towards his car. The women all watched Joanie, waiting to take their cue from her. A lonely punter was reduced to whistling for their attention and Monika, always the selfish one, sloped off and jumped in the car as fast as possible.

Joanie felt a spurt of foolhardy anger.

'You better be taking her home, boy.'

All the women were nodding now as if in agreement and Todd looked around at the sea of faces and felt the first prickle of serious unease. But his street instinct told him he had to sort this out or he would lose the fear and respect he needed to ply his particular trade.

He bundled the girl towards his car and then, turning on Joanie, bellowed: 'Who the fuck are you to question me?'

She felt real rage flare inside her then. The girl was lying on the pavement completely oblivious to what was going on around her. Joanie poked McArthur none too gently in his chest and said in a low voice, 'I remember you, boy, when you ran the streets with your arse hanging out of your pants. You was a little ponce then and you're a little ponce now. I'm warning you, mate, the game is a hard life for a woman but it's even harder for a pimp when he loses the respect of his women. You bear that in fucking mind in future, because one of your girls will end up dead soon and then you'll see the darker side of me and the likes of me.'

Todd McArthur was in complete and utter shock.

This *had* to be a wind up.

The women were all staring at him, their heavily made-up faces and scanty clothing somehow sinister in the darkening night.

Then, his natural antagonism coming to the fore, he took back his fist and slammed it into Joanie's face. She went flying backwards and, pulling out his weapon of choice, a Stanley knife, he walked towards her.

The women were all terrified now. Then, as Joanie lay on the dirty pavement, her nose bleeding and her eyes already swelling, all hell broke loose. She was amazed to see her son dragging Todd McArthur along the pavement and then proceeding to give him the hammering of a lifetime.

One of the women helped her to her feet and they all watched in awe and sick fascination as her son meted out the punishment due to the prone figure on the ground.

Joanie was still trying to get over the shock of seeing her son in her workplace, something that had never happened before. Then as she saw Paulie Martin it all fell into place.

He sauntered over to her. Taking her hand, he grabbed her chin and stared closely at her face.

'You'll live, Joanie. I ain't so sure about McArthur though. Strong little fucker, that boy of yours.'

He smiled at her as he handed her a spotlessly clean handkerchief.

'By the way, after tonight you're in the parlour full-time.'

Joanie's face was a picture and the women all looked at one another as they realised just who this young Rasta was.

Paulie stopped the beating and Jon Jon and his mother made eye contact. She could see the confusion in his face and knew it was mirrored in her own.

She looked so small to him, her face battered and bleeding, her poor body dropping with the pain and humiliation of him seeing her like this. He understood her so well and in that second realised how much he loved this woman who had borne him. Whatever she was, she was all he had ever had or would want to have.

Going to her, he hugged her close.

'You all right, Mum?'

Paulie watched them and felt strangely sad before the obvious love between them. He realised it was years since his girls had hugged him without an ulterior motive, usually requests for money, horses or suchlike.

The police drove by slowly and Paulie waved at them in a friendly manner. They carried on driving.

'Let's get you home, girl.'

He helped Joanie into the back of his car and then, turning to the assembled women, said in a jokey manner, 'Call an ambulance for the girl. As for him, call a hearse. He'll fucking well be praying for one before the week's out.'

Monika was dropped back to the beat just as his car pulled away. She looked at Todd McArthur and then listened to the story, her big dark eyes as wide as they would go.

Wonders would never cease.

But she was gutted she had missed the spectacle. It would certainly have been worth more than a tenner to her to have seen something so extraordinary it would be the talk of the pavement for years to come.

Tommy was shocked to see Joanie home so soon especially with Jon Jon and a strange man in tow. Her obvious injuries made him very upset.

'Are you OK?'

Joanie smiled as best she could.

'Yeah, just a little accident.'

Paulie looked at the huge man in morbid fascination.

As usual Jon Jon went straight into Kira's room to check on her. She was soundo, tucked in and contented. He smiled as he leaned over and kissed her gently on her silky hair.

Then he pushed twenty pounds into Little Tommy's hand and he left quickly. He knew when he was not wanted.

'Who the fuck was that?' asked Paulie.

Joanie looked at him and started to laugh. It was a quiet giggle at first and then it gradually became a real rip-roarer of a laugh. Eventually Paulie joined in.

It was the light relief they all needed. In their world the worse things were, the more you laughed about them. It was the only way to survive.

Paulie sat on the sofa beside her. With his arm around Joanie's shoulders, they laughed together so hard they had tears in their eyes. Jon Jon watched them, knowing there was a private joke here of some sort and not understanding it.

What he did understand, though, was that his mother and this man had a relationship of sorts and whatever it was it excluded him. He made them all a drink and busied himself in the small kitchen.

As Kira walked into the room in her Tinkerbell pyjamas Joanie opened her arms to her, then remembering her face, said to her daughter, 'It's all right, sweetie, Mummy fell over in her high heels.'

Kira jumped on to her lap and gently kissed her mother's sore cheek.

Paulie watched in fascination as Jon Jon brought first a drink, then a cold compress, and finally some painkillers. He pushed the cushions behind Joanie and made her comfortable then took his little sister and put her back to bed, all the time talking to her gently and calming her fears before making her laugh.

Paulie was impressed despite himself. He also remembered the good times he had had in this flat over the years. It was still scruffy, but it was spotlessly clean.

'Here, Joanie, you still got all your old crap in the cupboards?'

She smiled even though it hurt and said: 'Yeah. Still buying it.'

'Are you all right, Joanie? Really?'

She could hear true concern in his voice and it made her happy. She had loved this man for so long. Now he had her son in his pay and it was this that made him give her the respect she needed, indeed craved, to get her through her harsh existence.

''Course I am. I just hope that little girl is OK. She was too young – much too fucking young.'

Jon Jon listened to them talking. His mother and Paulie spoke together naturally, like old friends, and he supposed in a funny sort of way that was what they were. He remembered waking up and seeing Paulie in his mum's bed years ago; remembered too how happy she had been when that happened. Paulie would cook them all big breakfasts and make them laugh. He was the only man who had ever acted like a father to them in any way.

But the visits to Joanie dwindled and then they had stopped happening altogether. In their own way they had all missed him, but not so much as their mother. Something inside her had died then. Now he saw them together again and knew that his mother still adored this man who had sold her to anyone with a tenner, and even took a percentage of *that* from her.

The world was mad but Jon Jon felt lucky to have known that from a very young age.

Like his mother, he made what he could out of life.

Paulie found that he was comfortable being back once more with Joanie, enjoying her funny talk and even funnier foibles. He remembered her and the kids all planning fantasy dinner parties with guests ranging from Batman to Elizabeth Taylor. He had gladly joined in the fun; could not in fact recall ever laughing so much at home.

She was kind was Joanie, had a big heart, and suddenly he missed the solace he had found between her legs and in her happy household. Her kids, unlike his own, found happiness in silly things and adored this woman who sold her arse to put food on the table and clothes on their backs.

He missed that feeling of belonging, and as mad as it seemed, he had belonged here once. Unlike in his own home where he had to take off his shoes and creep about like a fucking burglar in case he made any untoward noise or mess. He had loved that cup of tea in bed in the morning, the sound of the kids playing and arguing and Joanie's voice as she shouted at them good-naturedly. She could distribute a wallop across the arse or a kiss quite impartially. He missed the smell of this place: of children, of Joanie. His own house smelled sterile, of pot pourri and bleach, a bit like his wife.

He also missed the way Joanie used to hold him to her breasts and soothe him, the way he could relax safe in the knowledge that she would always be there for him, no matter what. He looked into her eyes and felt the pull of her once more. It was her kindness, the bigness of her, that had attracted him all those years ago and which he realised now still had the power to move him. She had offered him her whole life for the taking, and he *had* taken from her: he had taken her kids, her home, had taken what he wanted from her and then discarded her. And she really had not deserved that. She had given him far more than he had ever given her. Far, far more.

There had been other Joanies, younger, firmer, but none of them had had that definitive something she had always had. Whatever it was, it had rung his bells and it still did. And that had been the bug bear: because she was a brass when all was said and done, and Paulie was a man to be reckoned with. So why did he feel like this about someone who had been laid more times than a second-hand carpet? What was this attraction that was so strong he only felt complete while in her company, inside her, even enjoying being with her children who were a Heinz 57-variety pack.

Whatever it was, it still had the power to make him want her even though she was looking older these days, a little haggard. But her smile still had that crinkle at the sides and her eyes still sparkled even though one was closing rapidly from the blow she had taken earlier. Joanie grabbed what she could from life and took whatever it threw at her. It was her heightened survival instincts that made her seem doubly alive.

Could it be that he actually admired her? He didn't know, didn't want to know. It was suddenly too painful to contemplate.

He put his arm around her shoulders and pulled her gently towards him. She settled herself into his body and savoured listening to the beating of his heart. He held her to him tightly, enjoying the feel of her. He kissed her gently on the top of her head and then Jon Jon crept from the room, leaving them together.

He had his own agenda tonight and now that Paulie was here no one would question his departure. He wondered if they would even notice he was gone.

As the front door closed behind him, he wondered what was going to be the upshot of this night's work.

He hoped whatever it was it made his mother happy. She deserved to be happy, truly happy, for once in her life. And if her happiness revolved around Paulie, then so be it. He hoped she got what she wanted for once. Who was he to tell her what to do or how to live her life?

She had so little to make her happy, why would her son deny her this night with the man she craved? He only hoped Paulie didn't hurt her any more than she had been hurt in the past.

As Jon Jon walked through the chill night air he concentrated on the score he had to settle tonight.

A banging on the front door woke Jeanette and Jasper. They lay side by side, listening to his mother swearing and cursing as she went to answer the frantic knocking. Jasper was already pulling on his trousers when the bedroom door burst open and he and Jeanette saw her brother standing there.

'Fucking push your way in here, would you? You black bastard!'

Karen Copes's voice was loud and gravelly. Last night had obviously been spent in the pub and her son was actually ashamed of her.

Jasper closed his eyes as he bellowed, 'Get the fuck away, Mum!'

Then he pushed her from the room, sending her sprawling in the hallway. He stared into Jon Jon's eyes.

'So now you know, don't you?'

Jon Jon looked at his sister. She was naked and he shook his head sadly as he said: 'Get up and get dressed.'

He was embarrassed and so was she. It was excruciating for them both. He turned his back and went out into the hallway.

Jasper watched her scramble out of bed in terror. He threw her clothes at her and followed Jon Jon.

'Outside, now!'

He and Jon Jon walked from the flat, Jasper following the intruder down the stairs and out the back. The darkness outside was broken only by the bulkhead lights over the lobby doors. These were flickering and dim, but they could see each other perfectly, the same anger and animosity mirrored in each man's eyes.

Jasper had his cropped head signed; he actually had 'BNP' razored into one side. He looked like a reject from the Third

Reich. Then there was Jon Jon with his soft dreads and coffee-coloured skin. The only thing they had in common at this moment was their mutual hatred.

'She is fourteen years old and you are one dead ponce.'

Jasper shook his head.

'I care about her and there's nothing you can do about it. You don't own her.'

The arrogance in his voice was like a red rag to a bull.

'She is my sister, my flesh and blood, and scum like you will never get near her again.'

As Jon Jon raised his fist to take Jasper down once and for all, Jeanette came outside. Bursting through the door, she cried, 'Please, Jon Jon! Please . . . I'm sorry. Let's just go home.'

She was hanging on her brother's arm and Jasper watched her, feeling strangely detached. Devoid of her usual makeup, Jeanette looked what she was: a little girl. And a terrified little girl at that.

Jon Jon thought of his mother, how she had looked earlier, thought of her life and knew that if he didn't do something now this girl's would eventually run along the same lines. He fingered the knife in his pocket once more, caressed it gently before pulling it out.

Jeanette saw it and screamed.

Jon Jon grabbed Jasper quickly and efficiently. He felt the heat of shame as Jon Jon held the blade to his throat.

'I could take you out now but you ain't worth it. A fucking bullyboy ain't worth a life sentence. But I will tell you this much. Take a good look at my sister – her father was a Turk. He stayed around for a few weeks and then he went on the trot. So, Golden Boy, remember that when you pass her in the street. But don't talk to her, don't even acknowledge her existence, or I swear I will kill you stone fucking dead!'

Then Jon Jon threw him aside as if he was nothing. His strength lay in that contemptuous dismissal and they both knew it.

Jeanette was devastated that her own brother would make her sound like nothing.

'You bastard, Jon Jon! You'd do that to me?'

The hurt in her voice didn't affect him one iota.

'A fucking bullyboy. Look at him, Jen. Take a good fucking look at what you're throwing your life away on. He ain't even stuck up for you, girl! His life is talking shit and toy-fighting with the police. Get a grip before I murder over you – and I will, girl. I will cut this cunt into pieces before he uses you again. A bullyboy and a Turkish girl? He's laughing at you, him and all his mates, you stupid prat!'

Jeanette was mortified in case Jon Jon was telling the truth. She looked at Jasper and her heart sank. He couldn't even meet her eyes.

Jon Jon laughed.

'Fucking bullyboy! Go on, touch my sister again, I dare you.'

He grinned nastily.

'You smoke black weed, listen to reggae, and *still* you want to punch our heads in – you stupid sick fuck!'

Then he proceeded to give Jasper the biggest hiding he had ever had in his life and, without all his friends as back up, Jasper covered his head and took it. There was nothing else he could do. He knew in a one to one Jon Jon would always be the victor.

The beating was quick, brutal and humiliating. Afterwards Jon Jon dragged Jeanette away and she cried like she had never cried before.

Jasper lay on the ground, feeling he had actually got off lightly. He had expected Jon Jon to use the knife at any moment and the fear had been suffocating. He was in dire pain, felt as if his body was on fire, and knew his face would be unrecognisable by the morning. But he was alive.

In the darkness he lit a cigarette and felt the sting of tears. He was alive and completely humiliated.

Joanie lay in bed with Paulie and still couldn't believe he was actually beside her once more. The sex had been all she had remembered: he was the only man she had ever really enjoyed the act with, and she knew that would never change. The feel of him asleep on her breasts was so familiar, it felt like the last few years of neglect had never been.

She was holding him to her gently, savouring his deep snoring and making the most of the time he would allot her because she knew that this was a one off.

In the dimness she could make out his face. It still had the power to move her. She loved him so much; had once actually harboured dreams of being with him full-time. Had seen herself as his girl, of course, not his wife – she was not completely delusional. But still perhaps his number one bird. His main squeeze.

She smiled at the thought now. Once it had seemed possible, anything had. There was something she wanted to tell him but now, after all these years, she wondered if she should. It might make him stay around, see more of her, but it could also make him walk away from her for good.

But no. She had missed her chance years ago. She had to accept that, just take what she could from this man asleep beside her. Savour whatever crumbs he threw her way. Her trouble was she knew her own worth down to the last insult.

She hugged him to her once more and kissed the soft skin of his forehead, grateful for this time because in truth she had never thought to feel him this close ever again. She heard the kids come in, and heard their respective doors shut. Now she could try and sleep herself.

It was funny, but even though the kids lived their own lives and she was useless in her efforts to help them any more, she still couldn't sleep until they were all in. Safe and sound. That was how she liked to think of them, tucked up in their little beds. Safe and sound. And so was she tonight, safe in the arms of the man she had loved since she'd first clapped eyes on him all those years ago.

She savoured every memory of them together, enjoying the bittersweet recollections even though some of them made her want to cry.

Finally, after what seemed like hours, she slept.

Chapter Six

Karen Copes was still shouting when the hospital staff asked her to leave at five-thirty in the morning. She had been creating since they had reached the A & E unit, and her shouting, swearing and crying was wearing a bit thin now. She had so far threatened two nurses, a doctor and the hospital receptionist with physical harm. Even though everything possible was being done for her son, she didn't feel they were bothering enough. Finally it was decided she had to go and Karen declared she was not going without a fight.

The fact that it was her own son who had requested her removal only made her more angry. Her foul language could be heard all over the unit. It took three doctors, a security guard, and eventually her own son's wrath to finally remove her from the premises.

She only went home because she needed to get a drink inside her, even though she would never admit that out loud. Her drinking was getting to such a level even she was noticing it. Mornings were the worst; trying to get a quick snifter in when she was being watched like a hawk was difficult. She still argued that she was only a social drinker, but that argument was sounding hollow even to herself.

Now, with Jasper's injuries, she was convinced no one could say a bad word about her having a few drinks to take the edge off her concern for him. But she was still disgruntled about being made to leave. It rankled that her own son wanted nothing to do with her, and she was shrewd enough to know that he would have that calf-eyed child there before he would have her.

Still, now that her son had started the great fight, wouldn't she enjoy seeing it through to the finish? It never occurred to her that Jasper might have died, that he was now grievously ill after his body had taken a serious battering. She was more interested in the implications of it all. The fact that it had happened and now there'd be repercussions. In her heart of hearts she even felt he was being a bit of a nancy over it all, though she would never have said that. Once her son was back on his feet it would all be resolved. So he was pissing blood? Big deal! Been there, done that! Anyone would think he was the first person to get a good hiding. They had it too easy these days, that was the problem.

The mini-cab driver had to open the windows of the car because Karen smelt like a brewer's dray. She didn't take offence. She needed the fresh air herself.

Jasper was relieved to see the back of his mother, she was such a pain. He asked his sister Junie to phone Jeanette on her mobile and tell her what was happening; he also instructed her not to tell anyone else what had occurred. He knew that if this became common knowledge it would cause a small-scale war on their respective estates. The trouble was, he wasn't up to anything, let alone the kind of aggravation this would cause. It was worse for him because he knew he would have done the same in Jon Jon's shoes. This had been on the cards for a long time, but his own total capitulation had been a shock to him.

As he lay in bed he was a frightened boy inside, and this knowledge was harder to bear than anything.

Even the knowledge that Jeanette's father was a Turk didn't change the way he felt about her and that in itself was a surprise. Perhaps inside himself it was something he had always known. She looked foreign, and that was against everything he had been brought up to value. His mother had brought them up to hate everyone who wasn't English. She had made them feel that they were automatically top dogs because of their heritage.

But now he wasn't so sure. Apart from his friends in the ICF who had jobs, all his other so-called mates were on the jam roll and that was not the most enviable place to be. But who actually wanted to work for a living? Well, Jon Jon did by all accounts, worked his arse off, and whatever Jasper thought about him he'd had the edge last night because of that. In Jon Jon's line of work you had to be hard to survive.

But still he cared for Jeanette, and so did Jon Jon – that much had been proved to him last night. And he had to allow for that. He would have felt the same about things if his sister Junie had taken up with the likes of Jon Jon.

For once in his life Jasper Copes was starting to see someone else's point of view and the novelty was doing his head in.

Joanie caught a glimpse of herself in the bedroom mirror and knew she had seen better days than this one. Her eye was swollen and bruised, but at least her nose looked OK so that was something anyway.

She could hear Kira laughing in the kitchen with Paulie, his deep tones penetrating the walls. She knew he was laughing too.

Joanie lay in bed savouring the moment. She only wished the room had been tidier. She knew his own home was kept spotlessly clean and envied his wife with the means to have a cleaner and a gardener. She most envied her for having a garden, a luxury none of Joanie's children had ever known. Some people just didn't know they were born.

Jon Jon came into the room with a mug of strong sweet tea and two Paracetamols. Joanie smiled her thanks, and allowed him to scrutinise her face.

'Fucking piece of shit he is! He'll think twice before he raises his hand to a woman again.'

Joanie didn't answer him but clasped his hand and squeezed it gently.

'You're a good boy, Jon Jon.'

And he was, to her. He loved her and she felt that love, as he had felt her love all his life. It was what had given him the confidence that buoyed him up every day. He sat down on the bed and sighed.

'Paulie is cooking up a storm in the kitchen. Like old times, eh?'

She nodded happily.

He smiled at her gently.

'Are you OK with me backtracking like I did and going to work for him?'

She smiled.

''Course I am. At least he'll see you all right. If you're going to use the street to make money, son, you'd better make sure you're with someone who will watch your back. In all honesty, Jon Jon, I'm glad.'

She had put his mind at rest and they both knew it. There was so much between them that remained unspoken that sometimes they felt almost shy with one another. But the time would come when they would talk, and then they would resolve it all.

Just not while Paulie was in the flat; not until they could each concentrate on what the other was saying.

But Jon Jon knew he should warn her somehow about what might happen next. He was amazed his collar hadn't been felt already. Jasper was a shitter and shitters phoned Old Bill.

But his mother looked so happy, he didn't have the heart to ruin that. So he smiled and chatted and waited for the knock on the door. He didn't do a runner because he knew if Jasper grassed there would be literally nowhere *to* run. In his mind's eye he saw Paulie waving the filth on the night before. When Jon Jon had taken out McArthur, he'd hoped his newfound employer would have enough clout to smooth things over. But Jasper was another thing.

He took a mug of tea in to Jeanette and was not surprised to find her bedroom empty. For the first time in his life he was truly frightened of what she might get involved in.

Like Jasper, he didn't want his sister to make the mistake of her life.

Kira went to school full of bacon, eggs and bonhomie. Happiness shone from her face.

Tommy watched her from his balcony and she waved merrily at him.

He realised then that he loved her. Seeing her was like a drug to him. The more he was in her company, the lonelier he felt when she wasn't around.

He watched her until she was out of sight then, sighing, went back inside to wait the day out until he could see and talk to her again.

He looked at the photograph of her he kept on the windowsill in the kitchen. Kira was laughing, it was a lovely picture. Picking it up, he caressed her face with a pudgy finger.

His father looked at him, but he didn't say anything.

On a tour of the massage parlours, Paulie explained what he wanted Jon Jon to do. Paulie's current number one, Earl Jones, had to be given the hard word. In a tactful way, of course. He'd say he wanted Earl to take on wider responsibilities, learn other aspects of the businesses – or at least that was how he would describe things to him anyway. In reality Paulie just wanted him as a heavy and nothing else. Earl was a great lad but hardly the sharpest knife in the drawer. It was only his loyalty to Paulie that was keeping him employed. Jon Jon was a much better deal as a deputy. At least he could count without taking his socks off. He also had an innate cunning. The fact that he had always liked the boy Paulie didn't admit to himself. If you analysed things too much it could do your head in; he had learned that lesson at an early age.

'You have to learn the parlours' locations and pick the money up for me as and when I ask for it. I have never had a routine. Once you do you're fucked. Remember that, Jon Jon. Even with a rep you still get the little gangs who want easy money, so to stop the theft and the fucking embarrassment of getting robbed by a crowd of fucking ice creams, you never give anyone an insight into what you do. Right?'

Jon Jon nodded but his head was up his arse, as Paulie observed to himself. He said nastily, 'An I fucking boring you or something? Here I am, giving you the benefit of my considerable wisdom and experience, and you sit there like a taxidermist's latest conquest.'

Jon Jon wiped a hand over his face and answered him truthfully, 'I nearly killed someone again last night.'

Paulie laughed.

'Don't worry, Jon Jon, McArthur will live, more's the fucking pity!'

Jon Jon sighed, then lighting a Marlboro Red told his boss the story of Jeanette and Jasper.

Paulie drove for a while in silence and then he said seriously, 'I'd have done the same at your age. You're still fucking half-cracked. Let's see what occurs before we make any plans, OK? He wouldn't be stupid enough to go to Old Bill, would he? Not a bullyboy like him.'

This was said in a derisive manner, but like Jon Jon, Paulie privately wondered if Jasper was going to make a statement. If he still wanted Jeanette he would need to get her brother out of the way. Personal problems caused more hag than anything in their line of work. Many a good man was banged up on the say-so of the old woman when she wanted shot, they were all aware of that.

Joanie was happier than she had been for a long time. When Paulie had said she was to work full-time in one of the parlours, she had assumed it was still as a brass. But it seemed that thanks to her son's meteoric rise she was to be a receptionist. She would virtually run the place after a spot of training from a head girl known as Lazy Caroline.

Paulie had seemed genuinely benign when he had explained her new role and she felt the stirrings of hope once more. If she used her loaf she could maybe have things back like she'd had them before. But whatever happened she would run his business like it had never been run. This was her chance, a golden opportunity, and she would not waste it. As Joanie sipped her tea she felt she might just explode with happiness.

The first thing she was going to do today was get a good cut and colour, get her streaks done properly and her nails done. Maybe even treat herself to a new outfit, one befitting her new station in life as receptionist-manager of a massage parlour. It was like a fairytale.

Her eye wasn't half-bad, she'd had worse, and she could cover it up for the time being. Once she got her hair sorted out she would be fine.

When she heard a knock on the door she assumed it was Monika. Opening it, she was shocked to see Jeanette standing there.

'Where the fuck have you been all night? The school's been on the phone again . . .' Then something in her daughter's face registered and she said loudly, 'What? What is it? Is it Kira?'

Jeanette was upset and it came over in her voice as she bellowed, 'No, it's not your fucking precious Kira!'

Then the whole story tumbled out.

Jasper Copes? Of all the people in the world her daughter had to take up with! Jasper, the local bullyboy, the local racist.

It was laughable really, if Joanie had had a laugh left inside her.

Jasper stared at the two policemen warily.

'I don't know what you're on about. I was mugged.'

The older detective sighed heavily.

'Did this mugger have a white stick and a dog by any chance? Only they missed your wallet, keys, jewellery, *drugs*.'

Jasper shrugged.

The man leaned nearer the bed. Aware he was on a mixed ward he whispered now, 'Don't take me for a cunt, Jasper. Your mother has already filled me in on the details.'

Jasper tried to grin.

'Was she pissed as usual?' He laughed once more. It was painful and it sounded painful. 'She don't know what day of the week it is half the time; the other half she don't know her own fucking name. Now as I said, I was mugged. Or shall I rephrase that? It was an *attempted* mugging. Why don't you leave me alone?'

'So you're going to sort it out yourself then, are you?'

This was said derisively and duly taken on board by the battered boy lying in his hospital bed. Jasper beckoned with one finger and the policeman leaned towards him, his face suddenly alive with interest.

'Fuck off, filth.'

The officer shook his head sadly. His voice was resigned as he said, 'You never learn, do you? Next time he'll bury you, son, and he will have more witnesses than a bent filth on a bender. He'll bury you – and do you know what? I won't even bother to break sweat. You're not worth helping, you deserve all you're going to get. And knowing Jon Jon Brewer, you'll get plenty.'

They left Jasper then, but those words stayed with him. But he was not grassing anyone up; it was not in his nature. Plus he wouldn't last five minutes on the pavement if he even chanced it. He just wanted to go home, but was still in tremendous pain and at least he felt safe in hospital.

Jasper Copes knew he was in a nightmare of his own making.

Kira left school at lunchtime. She was walking alone to the chip shop when as she crossed the busy road she saw Jeanette and waved. Her sister blanked her completely. Crushed, Kira carried on walking to the chippie, but the sun had gone from her day now.

Then, waddling towards her, she saw Tommy, and his big welcoming smile made up for her sister's contempt. She found that now and again she bumped into him at lunchtimes and she was beginning to look forward to it. Bethany was playing the hop as usual but Kira was too frightened to keep it up. She knew her mother worried about her, and Joanie had explained that when Kira was in school she didn't have to worry because she knew where she was. It had been explained in such a way that the child was frightened to truant now in case she broke her mother's heart. Consequently she was often alone.

But today she was lucky. Not only did she see Tommy, but there inside the chip shop was Bethany. Her friend ran outside, her round face troubled.

'Have you heard?'

Kira shook her head.

'Heard what?'

'About Jon Jon!'

'What about Jon Jon!'

Kira was alarmed now. As Bethany explained yet another version of the events of the night before, Tommy made his goodbyes. No, he couldn't take to Bethany. He knew her sort and he wanted Kira to himself. Just him and her. That was enough for him *and* for her most of the time. Such was his disappointment, he didn't even stick around for the gossip about Jon Jon.

★ ★ ★

Jeanette looked lost as she waited for her brother. Her long hair was unbrushed and she had not bothered to apply any makeup since she only cried it off. It had taken her mother ten minutes to talk Jon Jon into meeting her. She sat in the local McDonald's, nervous and agitated. Luckily the staff were used to customers like her. This McDonald's was a meeting point for skagheads. More deals were done in here than in the City of London not ten minutes away.

As Jeanette stared out of the window at the car park, she watched the comings and goings around her. She saw small packages and rolled-up tenners exchanging hands at an alarming rate. She knew the majority of the dealers and their clients. Every now and again a smart BMW or ZX would pull up and replenish the dealers' pockets with plastic baggies full of crack, heroin or cocaine.

If you wanted grass or solid it was now more a street-corner thing; decriminalising it only made it easier for the dealers. They didn't have to travel far to work. Instead they just wandered around, chatting and being what Jon Jon called 'easy'.

She was surprised to see him pull up outside with Paulie's number two, Earl. If Jon Jon was bringing a fighter then he must be worried about reprisals. But who was he more worried about? Jasper and his crew or the police?

Jeanette sighed. It was useless speculating, she would know the score soon enough.

Earl had been given the hard word by Paulie, but was happy enough with his new duties. Inside he'd acknowledged that sometimes it had all got too much for him. He was great at the actual collecting, it was working the money out and counting it up that he had the problems with. If he was in the middle of counting and a bird walked by or his mobile rang he was fucked, would have to start the whole process over again. It was time-consuming and boring.

Now he was babysitting Wonder Boy as he privately called Jon Jon. He had heard about his escapades the night before and grudgingly admired him for it. He was a hard little fucker and still only seventeen. Paulie, though, was good at picking out the movers. Hadn't he picked out Earl himself? Plus he liked

Jon Jon. Earl was black, both his parents were too. Jon Jon, although a mongrel, was a good kid.

He was also mates with Sippy, so that alone guaranteed him entry into any company he chose. Sippy was Earl's cousin and they were tight. He had told Earl to watch Jon Jon who was going to be big on their circuit before the year was out, and already the prophecy was coming true.

The heavy gave Jon Jon a friendly wink as they entered the Mackie D's. Jon Jon was pleased. He had been worried about Earl's reaction to him usurping the number one position, but he had taken it well.

Now he concentrated all his energy on his sister who looked so young and so appealing with her tear-ravaged face that he felt the urge to muller Jasper Copes all over again.

Karen Copes was so drunk she couldn't grasp what was being said to her. So she smiled and nodded and wondered when the fuck the police would leave her house.

Her daughter Junie was doing the talking as usual. She had been primed by Jasper and knew exactly how to word it and in what context to put it.

The police left none the wiser and extremely frustrated because they knew that this was as far as it was all going to go. They didn't give a toss about Jasper, he was just another young gun they wanted off the pavement. But they would have liked Jon Jon Brewer on a plate and this time it wasn't going to happen.

He had more lives than the fucking X Men, and he was a slippery little sod. But they would wait. Wait and listen.

He would be theirs in the end.

Joseph Thompson was thrilled with his day. As he parked outside his girlfriend Della's house he saw her wave to him from the front garden. He'd been hoping she would make it home for lunch. Inside she put the kettle on and chatted as she unpacked her shopping. He loved it here, it was bright and sunny and friendly.

Della was in her early fifties, heavy-breasted and plump. Her grey hair was cut short and she tended to dress in track-suit bottoms and T-shirts. But she was always smiling, and always happy to see him.

'Have you considered what we talked about, Joe?'

She was staring at him quizzically, but he knew she wasn't the type to push it. He smiled easily, hoping she would not go on when she heard what he had to say.

'It's hard, Della, you know the score with Tommy.'

She sighed.

'I understand, of course I do. But from what I hear he will be OK on his own.'

Joseph frowned.

'What have you heard then?'

She caught the undercurrent in his voice. She knew he was touchy about his boy and thought she understood why. Joseph didn't know but she had already seen Tommy. Her friend from Bingo had pointed him out to her up the shops. She lived on the same estate and said to Della that everyone there liked Tommy, or Little Tommy as he was called. But when Della had seen him for herself she had understood Joseph's feelings. His son was cruelly obese, and she felt that for a man of Joseph's temperament it must be hard to live with someone who was so far from perfect.

He'd been so secretive about his boy, for a long time refusing even to discuss him. That alone proved how he felt about things. She had also heard vague rumours that Joseph was not kind to his son but wasn't sure whether to believe those stories; he was so kind to her and her children, and he doted on her granddaughters. He said it was so nice to be part of a *real* family, and she had understood what he meant.

'I heard nothing specific,' she said now. 'You old silly! I mean, he seems to have got a little niche for himself where you live, that's all.'

Joseph visibly relaxed.

'I don't know, Della. I can't just leave him on his own like.'

She smiled gently.

'Well, the offer's there when you feel ready.'

She changed the subject then. She wasn't getting deeper into a conversation where she was going to be asked to have his freak of a son living in her house, or more to the point where she had to explain outright that *that* was something that was *never* going to happen. Della wasn't as sweet and nice as people thought. She could argue her end when she needed to. Her dead husband had found that out and changed his attitude accordingly. She was sure Joseph Thompson would do the same.

First things first, though. She had to get him through the door.

She smiled as she said, 'How about a nice bit of egg and bacon for your lunch?'

Joseph grinned.

'Sounds lovely.'

She opened the fridge and took out some bubble and squeak.

'I cooked extra cabbage and mash yesterday. This will go down a treat with it, eh?'

She also took out tomatoes, mushrooms and sausages. She knew how to make a man feel wanted, did Della. And she was a fantastic cook, a great little housewife, and wasn't after the old how's your father morning, noon and night.

Joseph could do a lot worse, he knew that. He would work on giving Tommy the bad news.

Jasper was feeling better, but his heart wasn't in the conversation he was having with his crony Dessie.

He looked at his mate as if for the first time; saw the looks from the nurses at his tattoos. His neck had *Cut Here* written across it and small blue lines to indicate exactly where. Someone would one day, and Jasper felt tired once more at the thought. A black nurse with a bright smile and an easy manner walked towards the bed, but one look at Dessie and his cold eyes and she retreated. Jasper felt embarrassed all over again. It was getting to be a habit these days. She had been a star while looking after him; sensing his fear she had gone about her business efficiently and kindly. He was in pain now and the injection she'd been going to administer would have been welcome. He wished Dessie would go away, but of course he wasn't going to say that.

'Need her, don't you!'

'She's a fucking nurse and, yeah, I need one at the moment.'

Dessie nodded but he wasn't happy and it showed. Something

wasn't right, he could feel it. He was waiting to be told the whole score and Jasper kept evading the issue.

Eventually Dessie lost any sympathy he might have had and said aggressively, 'Look, Jasper, I ain't fucking about all day. What happened? Your mother reckons it was fucking Jon Jon Brewer.'

He looked slyly at his mate as he spoke but not a flicker showed on Jasper's face.

'That's bollocks.'

'Not according to your muvver.'

'What is she then? Mrs Reliable all of a sudden? Don't tell me she's sober for a change – they even threw her out of here. She hates poor Jeanette and wants me to aim her out the door. Get a fucking grip!'

His voice was so dismissive that Dessie relaxed. For all his big talk he had not been looking forward to any real confrontation there if he could help it. Jon Jon was an anomaly. He was liked for a start, which was more than they were. But he was also unpredictable. Look what he had done to Carty.

'Were they coons?'

Jasper shook his head.

'Nah. Skinheads like you.'

Dessie frowned, his big open face puzzled.

'Don't you mean us?'

'No, Dessie. I mean they were like *you*. Big, pig ignorant and mob-handed.'

Dessie was offended and it showed. It wasn't the first time it had been pointed out to him that he was not the bravest soul in Christendom when he was on his own. He was purely a mob fighter.

'That's nice, ain't it?'

Jasper smiled.

'You are such an easy wind up.'

Dessie laughed, but he didn't think it was funny. The truth never was. They both knew the damage had been done.

'Where do you reckon they were from then?'

They often fought other skinheads, it was the nature of their particular beast.

Jasper shrugged.

'Fuck knows. They didn't exactly introduce themselves.'

Jasper relaxed slightly. Dessie believed him and the others would follow suit. He had started off the lie, now he had to carry on with it. He hoped Jeanette was faring as well as he was.

He liked her, loved her in fact, but would never say that out loud, of course. He was too hard for that.

'Please, Jon Jon.'

He drank his coffee and studied his sister's face. She was pretty and she was shrewd – and she was mental over a fucking bullyboy who spent his Saturdays fighting at football matches with the ICF, and the rest of the time preaching about keeping Britain white.

How had that happened to Jeanette?

Whatever else they were, they were a multi-racial family. Her long dark hair came from a Turkish bloke their mother had taken up with for a while. He had left after five months with the telly, the video, and Joanie's purse. His parting gift to her had been a belly full of arms and legs.

Jeanette was white-skinned enough, but the Turkish side was there if you looked. It gave her that unusual look she had. Her striking eyes were hazel, a greeny-brown. But then his mum was naturally dark-haired too, she streaked hers to get the blonde look she craved. Jeanette did the same except she had low lights, browny-reds that made her strong features look softer.

Jon Jon wiped a hand across his face. He was tired out.

Jeanette tried again.

'He told the filth *nothing*. To everyone else he is going to say it was a gang of skins, a rival gang. He ain't grassed you.'

Still Jon Jon didn't answer her.

'Everyone else' was Copes's skinhead mates.

'If I go along with this you'll have to stop seeing him, you know that, don't you?'

She nodded and he couldn't look her in the eye. He saw it was what she had expected.

He spoke once more, gently and with emphasis.

'I mean it, Jeanette. No talking for the sake of it. I mean *stop*, *finished*, once and for all. Or next time I *will* fucking kill him and go down for it with a smile on me face.'

She nodded once more, tears closer than ever now as he said gently, 'Let me think about it, OK?'

She wiped her eyes. It was more than she had hoped for.

Chapter Seven

Joanie looked good and she felt good.

Her hair was perfect, streaked to within an inch of its life, and her makeup was tastefully subdued, having been carefully applied by a pretty girl in Debenham's Lakeside. She was wearing a tailored black trouser suit with a white shirt underneath. She looked sexy, but also businesslike and smart. Her nails were long and French manicured, her shoes high and open-toed.

She looked at herself in the mirror and was amazed at the transformation. She looked like a woman who was going to work, real work, and the thought of not having to flash her clout for a living any more made her happier than she could have believed possible.

Jon Jon's look of admiration when he came in was balm to her soul.

'You look great, Mum.'

Joanie hugged him. He was a handsome man, her son. Even dreads looked good on him. He had an aquiline face that made him look artistic and intelligent, which he was. Jon Jon was as bright as a button. His school, when he had deigned to go, had wanted him to make something of himself. And he could have. Still could – only not in any legal way.

Joanie pushed these thoughts from her mind. This was a good day and she was not going to let anything or anyone spoil it.

'I feel like I'm starting a whole new life, and it's because of you, Jon Jon.'

He grinned.

'Nah, it ain't because of me, Mum. You just needed the push to get a proper job. Paulie says you may even have to go on the cards.'

She smiled once more.

'Me having a proper job, eh! I wish I knew where me mother was, that would tickle her no end.'

They both laughed.

'Knowing me nan, she'd be so drunk she wouldn't know what you were talking about anyway.'

Joanie nodded her agreement.

'Kira's late.'

They both automatically looked at the clock on the wall; it was a market copy of the Taj Mahal, all gold plastic and glitter. A real Brick Lane special. Kira had bought it one Christmas. No one had had the heart to tell her what they really thought of it and it had been on the wall ever since.

Everyone's eyes were automatically drawn to it as soon as they entered the room. Now they both stared at it, worry clouding their faces. It was nearly five o'clock and she should have been in an hour since.

'Perhaps she's gone over Tommy's.'

'I'll go and see, Mum. You make a cuppa, eh?'

Jon Jon slipped from the flat, glad of the respite. He felt stoned, had been puffing all afternoon and he knew he had to clear his head as they had a bit of work on later that needed sensible behaviour.

He was paranoid over Jasper. Had heard that he had nearly split the skinhead's liver and that Copes was still very ill in hospital. It was funny: Jon Jon could be vicious and he knew it, but wounding Jasper was a different kettle of fish. This was over family and that made it all the more emotive as far as he was concerned.

It wasn't like clumping someone over work or money – that kind of upset he could put out of his mind. But with the worry over his sister his violence wasn't calculated any more. He had lost control, that was what bothered Jon Jon.

Kira was drunk.

Thanks to Bethany and another girl called Alana, she was paralytic. It was terrible to see her. Bethany was frightened because what had started as a joke was now out of hand.

Slipping a bottle of her mother's Bacardi under her jacket had been exciting at first, and making themselves a playhouse in the bushes of the park had been great as well. But the Bacardi and Cokes, which had tasted so sweet and nice, had rapidly made them sick. And Kira had carried on drinking. Now she was vomiting everywhere and her face was deathly white one minute and a blazing red the next. The sweet smell of the sick was making Bethany retch herself and Alana had already done a runner home.

Bethany was also aware of the rift between her mother and Kira's. She knew her mother was not impressed with Joanie's new job. Bethany wasn't sure why, all she knew was that her mother's oldest friend was no longer flavour of the month at home and she had been told to keep away from Kira.

Now she had all this on her plate.

Kira lay back on the grass. It was cool and she felt so hot and feverish. If only she could focus her eyes she would be OK. But every time she tried there were too many Bethanys and they made her want to laugh. Her hair was all over the place and she looked like a demented Dalek.

Bethany was near to tears. She'd been sick herself from what she had drunk, but watching Kira pumping out vile black vomit started her off again and they both retched until their throats hurt.

That was when the park keeper found them.

Twenty minutes later the police were there and Bethany was crying and Kira was once more laughing her head off.

The WPC shook her head at the park attendant, disgusted by what she was witnessing. Kira was still retching, and her clothes were stained with sick. It was in her hair and all over her hands.

The policewoman called an ambulance.

Jon Jon had never seen anyone Tommy's size move so fast in his life. As soon as he heard that Kira was not home from school he was pulling on his jacket and getting ready to scour the streets for her. Jon Jon was impressed by the man's obvious concern for his little sister. It had taken him a while really to trust Tommy but now he saw him as his mother did – as a nice man, a caring man.

When Tommy picked up the phone and asked his father if he had seen Kira, the urgency in his voice was contagious. Even Jon Jon was getting worried now. The big man kept saying, 'Are you *sure* you haven't seen her?'

When Jon Jon told him to calm down he finally replaced the receiver and said, 'That's the only number I have apart from yours. And she can't be far, can she? Kira wouldn't go missing, she knows how we all worry.'

He was near to tears.

'I'd better get back to me mum, OK? We'll keep you posted.'

Jon Jon was glad to get out of the flat. Tommy's nervousness was rapidly communicating itself to him and he was getting really worried himself.

Joanie got to the hospital at just after eight-fifteen. Bethany had eventually given the game away about who they were and Joanie arrived at the same time as Monika. Neither woman spoke until the doctor had explained the situation to them.

Kira had had a minor epileptic fit and was suffering from alcoholic poisoning; Bethany was none the worse for her ordeal and could go home immediately.

'That bloody Bethany!'

Joanie spoke her mind without a second thought. Monika, however, was not having her daughter blamed for this fiasco, as she described it to herself.

'Look here, Joanie Brewer, your Kira was as much to blame. She drank the fucking stuff, no one forced her.'

Joanie shook her head angrily.

'Piss off! You know she wouldn't have dreamed of doing anything like that by herself, Mon. Bethany is the one who thinks up these kind of pranks.'

Monika, still smarting from Joanie's newfound promotion, was not in the mood for arguments. She was going to go straight in for the kill.

'Who the fucking hell do you think you are, eh?'

Everyone could hear her and Joanie closed her eyes in distress at what she knew was to come.

'You waltz in here dressed like mutton and fucking start on

about my little Bethany! Like Kira is whiter than fucking white. Just because you ain't flogging your arse no more don't make you better than me, mate. I know all about you, love, remember that.'

'You know my Kira wouldn't do something like this, Mon, not unless she was told to. You know what she's like.'

Joanie was trying hard to keep her temper but it was difficult.

Monika put her hands on her ample hips as she yelled, 'Why don't you just say it, Joanie? She's six seconds behind everyone else, thick as shit, is *that* what you're telling me at last? Only most people have already sussed that much out for themselves.'

She saw the look on Joanie's face and regretted her words immediately.

'My child is ill, Monika. She has alcoholic poisoning, she's had a fucking fit. She might be a lot of things but she ain't *thick*, right!'

Joanie's hand was clenching into a fist and Monika remembered just in time what Joanie was capable of if upset enough.

They were both being observed by a large woman with long red hair and designer glasses. She wore a print trouser suit and black boots. They assumed she was a fellow visitor until she said in a carefully professional voice, 'I am Tammy Jones, the social worker for this hospital. When you are finished perhaps we can have a word?'

Both women looked at her in utter shock.

It was Jon Jon who saved the day. Taking Monika firmly by the arm he marched her away, leaving Joanie to talk to the woman in peace.

Monika was terrified. Jon Jon must have heard the tail end of their row and she regretted her words big-time. But he had other fish to fry. Pushing her none too gently out of the hospital doorway, he barked, 'Just fuck off, Monika. Get yourself and Bethany home.'

She didn't need telling twice.

Jeanette used the respite from being watched to text Jasper. They had been texting each other since the incident and their love, as they saw it, was stronger than ever. As she received yet another declaration of his total devotion she felt as if she would burst with happiness.

There had to be a way . . . She was determined that there had to be some way they could build bridges and get back together. It was just a matter of seizing their opportunity.

Jon Jon thought he had it all sorted but she was not going to let him or anyone else dictate what she was going to do with her life.

She texted Jasper about the latest débâcle with Kira, beloved daughter – and pain in the arse most of the time. Though she didn't write that down, naturally. She was just grateful the spotlight had been taken off her for a while.

Tammy Jones smiled at the well-dressed woman in front of her. Ensconced in her untidy little office with mugs of bitter coffee, she questioned Joanie about the incident.

'My Kira is not stupid as such, in some ways she is as bright as a button, but she has learning difficulties, you see.'

Tammy Jones saw all right. Joanie was desperate to get herself out of this office and away from someone she saw as on a par with the police.

'She's just easily led, that's all.'

Joanie was getting desperate now.

'I want to go back to my daughter – she needs me. She can't function without me and I need to be with her.'

That Joanie was earnest Tammy had no doubt. That she herself also had to deal with a baby with two broken legs and an elderly woman staff suspected was being sexually abused by her own son, meant Kira rated quite low on Tammy's scale. She would write up a report and leave it at that. There'd be a follow-up visit in a week or two just to be on the safe side, but it seemed they had all learned a valuable lesson.

The fact that Joanie was a prostitute didn't bother her; the child was well fed and well nurtured. There were no visible signs of abuse. This really did seem like a childish prank gone wrong.

Joanie left thankfully a little while later and made her way back to Kira. She was shaking inside and out, and when she got her hands on Bethany there was going to be hell to pay.

Monika could thank God that Kira was not being placed on an At Risk register or subject to visits from a social worker, turning up all hours of the day and night. Because if that had happened Joanie would have had to sort Monika out once and for all, and the mood she was in now that would have been something the police really would have had a field day with.

Jon Jon was sitting with his sister. Joanie watched him carefully giving her sips of water. She looked awful. Seconds later Tommy bustled in, and the three of them sat beside Kira as she lay there, feeling ill and sick but more loved than she had ever been in her life.

When Paulie came in a while later it seemed natural for them all to be there together, though to outsiders they made for a strange-looking tableau.

Bethany was a worried child. Her mother had half murdered her over the drinking business and she was sore and upset. She liked Kira, loved her even, and knew deep inside that she should never have given her the drink.

Now Bethany had a hangover, and her stomach hurt. Everyone was annoyed with her so she bunked off school and went back home where she put on makeup in her mother's bedroom and sipped from the glass of Bacardi and Coke she had poured herself from Monika's drink stash. Hair of the dog was what her mother always said sorted her out after a drinking binge. And as Monika had a drinking binge every day Bethany knew what she was talking about.

The house was dirty, but that was her fault as her mother had handed the housework over to her a few years earlier. Clothes and bedding were always slightly soiled here; Monika only did things like that for them when she was sober and lucid enough to get her head together. Now that her daytime hours were not taken up with going to Joanie's since the quarrel she had started to go to the pub so Bethany knew she had the house to herself. Unlike Kira, she enjoyed the feeling that alcohol gave her though she was determined not to drink too much ever again, just enough to make her feel like laughing. To take away the pain she felt inside.

Kira had a whole network of people taking care of her. Bethany had no one really except Monika who at best was a haphazard mother, whose sporadic affection for her daughter was outweighed by her own need to drink to blot out the life she lived.

Today the alcohol made Bethany cry, but even that felt better than nothing. She stared desolately round the unkempt room and the tears flowed even faster. And as she cried she sipped at the glass of Bacardi and Coke more and more often. Like it did for her mother, it deadened the pain.

Tommy was still in mortal fear over what had happened to Kira. Joseph listened to him going on and on until finally he had had enough. It was bad enough having to endure him lumbering around the place, knocking things over with his bulk and wittering on about that bloody Brewer family. Joseph wanted out. He wanted to be with his girlfriend and her family, to enjoy all the benefits that they could offer him.

And the benefits were legion. The house was Della's, he had found out that much. She had a few quid from her old man's insurance, she was a lovely cook and enjoyed a few drinks with her game of Bingo.

She was also a prude and the few times they had had sex it had been over quickly with the minimum of fuss. She was a fit mate for him all right; the last one he had acquired had been after it all the time. She had worn him out. Sex was over-rated if you asked him, especially at their age.

Della's house was bright and cheerful, she had Sky TV and her grandchildren kept the house full of laughter.

What was he waiting for?

He stared once more at his son and felt the loathing rise up inside him. He had to get out of here. He felt like he was in jail, trapped.

'Shut up for a minute and listen to me, will you!'

Little Tommy faced his father. His pudgy hands were occupied drying a teacup and it looked incongruous in his meaty fist, like a child's toy.

'I'm moving out, Tommy.'

His son stared at him for long seconds before saying, 'What do you mean, moving out?'

Joseph sighed.

'It's time you learned to look after yourself. I'm moving in with me girlfriend.'

Joseph waited for a reaction but was amazed when Little Tommy merely grinned and said, 'Good for you. When do you think you'll be going?'

Joseph couldn't answer him for a moment. Of all the things he had expected, his son's obvious joy and genuine happiness were not among them. What the hell would the boy do without Joseph to order him around?

'Will you be OK, Tommy?'

His father had never asked him that question before and he felt a terrible loneliness settle on him as it occurred to him that they had been stuck with each other for too long.

Far too long.

He smiled brightly.

''Course I will, silly. When do I get to meet the lucky lady?'

Joseph stalled him then, backtracking slightly.

'All in good time. Let me get out of here first.'

Tommy guessed that his father had not mentioned him much, if at all, and was sad again at two lives spent so closely linked and yet so far apart. It was laughable really.

'Well, your washing is nearly done, and I'll have the ironing out of the way in the blink of an eye. I assume you're eager to get going. Is she nice?'

Joseph shrugged.

'She's all right. Nice enough, I suppose.'

'Any family?'

The question was innocent enough so Little Tommy was not ready for the answer when it came.

'Mind your own fucking business, you nosy fucker! Any little girls, you mean. I know you and how your mind works.'

Tommy shook his head.

'I never meant anything like that and you know it.'

He could hear the strain in his own voice.

'I am happy for you, just for *you*. I think it would be good for you to be with someone else.'

He was nearly crying now as he bellowed, 'Why do you hate

me so bloody much! What have I ever done to you?'

It said a lot for Tommy and his new relationship with his father that he felt he could challenge him like this. Before Kira and Joanie had come into his life he had taken whatever came his way, whether it was abuse or his father's complete indifference. Now he stared at this man who had given him life and wondered how the hell they could be related. But his father was ignoring him, something he could keep up for days, weeks even.

Joseph carried on drinking his tea oblivious to his son's hurt. He had said what he had to say, now he would make his arrangements. He looked round the poky little kitchen and thought of the comfortable home he would soon be ensconced in.

The promise of a new life brought a rare smile to Joseph's face.

Paulie watched the young girl as she sauntered into his massage parlour. Of medium height, plump, with natural blonde hair and large blue eyes, she would be a magnet for some of his customers. She smiled at him and said quietly, 'Can I speak to whoever is in charge, please?'

She was polite, he would give her that.

'What do you want, love?'

She smiled again.

'I need a job.'

He could feel the confidence coming off her in waves.

'And how old are you then?'

He was smiling now. The girl smiled back as if expecting the question.

'I know I don't look it but I'm nearly twenty. I have me birth certificate with me.'

She was disarming in her semblance of honesty. She also had a slight accent, but he couldn't place where it was from.

'Come through to the office.'

She sat opposite his desk without being asked and crossed her legs. It was the childish plumpness that was her attraction and she knew it. Her dress code was simple and sexy. She looked like a sixth-former. Black skirt, a tad too short, and a white blouse unbuttoned to show creamy flesh. Tanned legs and high platform shoes.

But it was her eyes that held the real key to her personality. She looked like she knew too much, and Paulie knew those eyes would attract the punters in droves. She looked far too innocent . . . until you looked into those eyes. He had a feeling she better than anyone knew the effect she had on men.

She was literally sitting on a gold mine.

'What's your name – and I mean your real name, not the name you are using today, do you get my drift?'

She nodded.

'Liz Parker, but I go under the name of Angel.'

'I'm sure you do. Now, have you any idea what this job actually entails?'

She smiled, unabashed.

'I know exactly what the job entails – I've been doing it since I was thirteen. Would you like me to give you a taster, free like?'

Those eyes were harder now. He could see her calculating the main chance. She must want the job badly to offer to audition for it. Yet he knew a lot of the other owners made girls audition for them. It was a free blowjob, and most men wouldn't turn one down.

She was still smiling that smile of hers. Now it was his turn. But it was a nasty smile, and she picked up on it immediately.

'I wouldn't touch you, love, with a barge pole. Now show me your birth certificate and some other form of identification and you and me might come to some arrangement. But it will not be any arrangement that means bodily contact, OK?'

Her child-like good looks were marred now by the hard expression on her face. She opened her bag, a snide Burberry, and placed the required documentation on the desk. They didn't speak again until she saw him going to photocopy the documents.

'Here, what do you think you're doing?'

He laughed at the temerity of her.

'Saving me own arse, darling. Anyone questions me about you, I need some kind of back up.'

'You won't get questioned, Mr Martin.'

He smiled once more. It was 'Mr Martin' now. She knew who he was after initially misreading the situation. He admired the way she changed her approach so quickly. She was the good girl now, all polite and looking for a job. A real job as opposed to a blowjob.

He wanted to laugh but he didn't.

'Empty your handbag.'

She clutched the bag to her chest.

'What for?'

He had thrown her completely and he was enjoying himself.

'Just empty the bag out. Now.'

She was still clutching it to her chest.

'My bag is private!'

'Not in my parlour it ain't, love, and you better get used to that fact.'

He took the bag from her forcibly and tipped the contents on to his desk. She was vocal in her anger and he turned on her quickly.

'Shut the fuck up!'

The usual makeup, condoms and assorted pens fell out of the bag, as did a crack pipe and a few rocks in an HSBC moneybag. There was also ecstasy and what he judged to be amyl nitrate. But it was the six-inch switchblade that annoyed him most.

'Quite the little pharmacist.'

She was deadly white now.

'Who were you going to stab, love, anyone I know?'

He was holding the knife in his hand now as if he was weighing it.

'It's for protection. I've been working the pavement. You know what that's like.'

Her voice was normal now and he almost felt sorry for her. All her bravado gone, she was just a young girl who was terrified.

'Not personally, I don't. Now listen to me, love. Your first mistake was offering me a blowjob. I could swallow that one, if you'll pardon the pun, but there is no way drugs or weapons make their way in here. Not that kind of junk anyway. Now sling your fucking hook.'

She didn't move. Instead she looked at him and for the first time he saw a spark of the girl she could have been if she hadn't embraced the life so early. She had similar eyes to his younger daughter. That knowing, childish look of an adolescent girl practising her charms on the nearest available male, usually their father.

'Please, Mr Martin, I really need this job. I would *never* have brought anything into work with me. I've been in the know for a long time and I swear that nothing would have made its way in here. *Nothing.*'

'What about the crack? You won't go the night without it. There's a bit of coke knocking around here but that's about it. The odd joint maybe, but crack is a complete no-no, darling.'

'It's not mine. It's my boyfriend's.'

'You just scored it for him?'

She nodded.

'Nice bloke he is. I suppose you earned the money for it as well?'

She nodded once more.

'You want a bit of advice, love? Change the boyfriend and change him soon. You'll be on it within three months. Seen it time and time again.'

She sighed, and he could see she was near to tears.

'I need this job. I can't take another night on the pavement. I want the job to get meself a proper place and that.'

He sat back down and stared at her for a while. She had something about her. He knew she would do things for the business. Joanie would have given her a chance but she wasn't here due to Kira's foray into alcohol abuse. Lazy Caroline was off gallivanting with her new squeeze and he was left to hold the fort.

'Who's your boyfriend?'

She was startled by the question.

'Why do you want to know that?'

'Because I am a fucking nosy bastard! So come on, who is he?'

She sighed once more, and he could see she was going to lie to him so he said abruptly, 'I can find out in two hours, love. I can find out his name, address and his fucking cock size so tell me the truth.'

'Pippy Light.'

She saw his eyebrows rise.

'Pippy! Jesus, love, you really have started at the bottom, ain't you? Working your way down the ladder by any chance?'

She shrugged.

'Where you from?'

She shrugged once more then thought better of her attitude and said gently, 'Cardiff originally, but I was in care all over the place for most of me life.'

'Train them well in care. I get a lot of you girls in and out.'

She smiled then, a friendly smile.

'I need this start, Mr Martin, and I will literally work my arse off if you give me the chance.'

'What about Pippy? He's a poxy useless pimp, violent and arrogant. I don't want him here causing fucking aggravation.'

'He won't be. Look, can I be straight with you?'

He nodded.

'That will be a first but carry on, love.'

'I picked this parlour because of Pippy. I know you have the required rep to keep him off me back while I work me trade. Last night he rolled another punter and I don't work like that. I want to go on the trot but it's hard when someone takes every penny you earn.'

He believed her, and finally felt sorry for her. He had seen girls in this position time and time again. Then he glanced at his watch. He was late and already fed up with the conversation and the company. Pippy wouldn't come after him, he knew that much.

'Start tonight, six prompt. You work till two, OK?'

'Thank you, Mr Martin, you won't regret it.'

'I'd better not, love, or you'll know about it.'

As they left the office Liz was happier than she had been in weeks and it showed. Jon Jon was waiting outside. He looked at the girl and smiled. She smiled back and Paulie noticed it was a real smile, not a punter smile. It made her look even younger and prettier than she was.

In the car he looked at Jon Jon and said caustically, 'Fell in love, have we?'

Jon Jon didn't answer him and Paulie laughed.

'She's been round the turf more times than Red Rum, son, and her current squeeze is mad Pippy Light so I wish you luck, Jon Jon – you are going to need it.'

Jon Jon just smiled.

He liked the girl and that was all that concerned him.

Chapter Eight

Kira felt ill, and she looked ill.

Like many before her she vowed she was never going to drink alcohol again. Her head was still pounding, and her thirst was way out of proportion. It was a week since the incident and she was still feeling the after effects. But more than anything she was missing Bethany. She knew that her mother and Monika were at war but was unable to understand why Bethany was now banned from here as well. She consoled herself with the thought that once she was back at school the row could be cleared up. At least, she hoped so. Her mother and Monika had never fallen out for so long before and she was getting worried.

As she lay on the sofa watching *Coronation Street* she looked small and vulnerable. Even Jeanette felt sorry for her. With her own problems forced to take second place for once, she made her sister cups of tea and generally fussed around her. Seeing her looking so ill had really brought home to Jeanette just how much she loved Kira. Yet the loyalty so abundant in the other members of the family still eluded her. She was on the verge of doing something so fundamentally wrong in the Brewers' scheme of things that she should by rights be terrified even to think about it, let alone plan it.

Now that her mother was finally going back to work Jeanette had offered to take care of her sister, but with an ulterior motive. Jon Jon was watching her like a hawk so she was going to let him and Joanie think she was indoors with her sister when in reality she was going out to see Jasper. He was home now though still fragile.

It was two weeks since the attack and physically he was getting stronger by the hour. It was mentally that he was still weak. Jeanette was determined to see him. Tonight Karen was going up the pub with her mates, and Junie was going with her to keep watch and alert them if she was on her way home. Jasper was to all intents and purposes on his own. Though still ill, he had healed better than anyone could have hoped. The doctor had said he was always amazed by the resilience of the human body, and Jasper had made a marvellous recovery.

But he was different now; nervous, thin and gaunt. Jeanette felt that all that had happened to him was her fault. It was her brother who had attacked him, after all.

For that she hated Jon Jon with a vengeance even as she loved him. She knew that Jasper's racism was at the heart of the bad feeling between the men, but even as she understood that, the pull of him made her disregard any lingering feelings of loyalty to her family she might have had. She wanted Jasper and that was enough for her.

They had been texting each other all afternoon and she was going to visit him if it was the last thing she did. Even if it meant doing something so outrageous, just knowing she was contemplating it frightened her. But she was going to do it, no matter what.

She watched Kira drink the last of her sweet tea and waited for her eyelids to droop. The sleeping pill should knock her out for the night. Her friend had told her that she gave them to her little daughter all the time so she could shoot out to take care of business, which meant in their speak to score drugs or work a while to pay for them.

The girl in question was even lower down the food chain than Jeanette's own family. At nineteen she had a five year old and another child on the way. She was the Queen of her Maisonettes and all the young girls thought she was fabulous. She was a fount of wisdom on everything from sexual matters (give them what they want and you will get what you want) to school (don't fucking go, no matter what they say or do, and eventually they will give you the hard word and leave you to your own devices). All good advice that had proved correct. Lorna was a popular girl.

And if her daughter had felt no side effects then Jeanette was willing to take the chance with her own sister. Plus, after what had just happened to Kira no one would think Jeanette would be stupid enough to leave her on her own. It was perfect. When they all came back she would be sitting on the sofa watching TV as if nothing untoward had happened.

Little Tommy deserved a night off, especially as he was washing and ironing all his father's clothes ready for the big move. It had all worked out perfectly really, almost like fate was taking a hand.

Jon Jon was out scrumping a new bird from the parlour and her mother was out with Paulie – going through the books, she said.

Jeanette smiled. That was the first time she had heard it called *that* before!

Lately he was never off the doorstep, and her mother was glowing with all the attention. In one way Jeanette was pleased for her; in another way she was waiting for the bombshell because she knew it would fall. Paulie would disappear like he always had before and then her mother would be left devastated again.

But, like Joanie, she was going to grab at her own chance of happiness while she could. Jasper was everything to her, and though she didn't understand why this was, she accepted it as her mother had accepted the same feeling many years before.

Kira's eyes were drooping now and Jeanette took the empty mug from her gently and placed it on the coffee table. Her excitement was such she felt as if she would burst with the prospect of seeing Jasper, of touching him, loving him.

Ten minutes later she took one last look at her little sister sleeping soundly and then slipped out of the front door.

Jon Jon was in lust and he knew it.

Liz Parker was like a magnet to him. Even as he despised her weaknesses, he loved the idea of having sex with her.

But once it was over, he wanted shot of her as fast as possible.

The fact she was a brass bothered him not one iota; he only wanted to fuck her, not commit to her for the rest of his life. Yet he went through the rigmarole of taking her out, and no matter how often he asked himself the question he could not understand the logic behind his own actions. He was part of Paulie Martin's firm, and as such he had the pick of the brasses. It was a perk of the job. He wondered briefly if it was because of his mother. Could that be why he treated this girl with a respect she certainly did not deserve?

He didn't know. All he knew was he wanted shot of her now, and he wanted shot of her quickly.

As she pulled on her knickers he said nonchalantly, 'Is that the time? I better get going, I have to meet Paulie in twenty minutes.'

She didn't answer him and he knew she knew he was lying. He slipped her a tenner for a cab, not for payment just transport fees, and then left the little flat near his home where she was renting a bed until she sorted herself out. He was going home to shower before starting work for the night. After he had been with her he always felt the urge to scrub himself clean.

That was another anomaly he was trying to work out in his head. He was giving her one three times a day. That meant three showers a day. He only hoped it would burn out with her soon so he could get back to normal.

Bethany was inside Joanie's flat and staring at the doped-up girl on the sofa. She had opened the door with the key Joanie kept hidden in the coalhole that stood beside every flat's front door. All the coalholes were used to store junk now, from old paint tins to empty beer bottles and Christmas decorations. Most people hid their spare keys in them somewhere and Joanie was no different. Bethany had only come in for a look round, she had not expected to see Kira on her own and asleep. Kira was never left alone, unlike Bethany of course who had brought herself up in the absence of anyone else to do the job.

She tried to wake her little friend and, failing to do so, helped herself to a few things, among them a ring from Joanie's dressing table and fifty pounds in fivers from Jon Jon's wardrobe. She left the flat as quietly as she'd entered it, unsure of what she was going to do with the money and the ring but pleased nevertheless that she had acquired them. Like her mother, she always had her eye on the main chance.

★ ★ ★

Paulie and Joanie were in a pub in Essex. They had ordered a bar meal and were chatting together about the parlour. He was glad she was on her way back to work because he was getting fed up with policing the place himself. The girls were nervous of him for a start, which was how it should be, of course. But it didn't make for a good atmosphere in the place itself. Plus he was a great believer in the old adage, you don't have a dog and bark yourself. As he privately and sometimes publicly referred to his girls as dogs, he thought it was rather fitting.

He was loath to put anyone else in because it would have caused ructions when Joanie returned. Once a girl had a taste of power it sent her off her head, and as most of them already were off their heads it did not make matters any easier.

Lazy Caroline was due back at work this week as well, after her sojourn in the Greek Islands with a young girl she'd flipped her lid for. He shrugged; it took all sorts, he supposed.

But Joanie was looking so well these days even with all the aggravation she had had. He still wanted her, and for him still to want someone after all this time both amazed and worried him.

He suspected he was getting old. The younger girls these days were determined to give the blokes a good time and pulled out all the stops to ensure they had one. It was bloody wearing at times, especially when a quick dip and a cuddle were his only real requirements. If he wanted sexual gymnastics he would go Up West and pay for them. But the younger brasses all wanted just the one man to shag and would do anything to achieve that end.

It was like being caught in a blue film and he was long past all that poncing around, plus he knew they didn't really enjoy it, why would they? He was just a means to an end to them.

He was a face and he had a few quid – he was like the *Mirror* pension scheme to them when all *he* wanted was a quick fuck and a goodbye. Was that too much to ask?

He watched Joanie tuck into her steak and chips. She ate nicely did old Joanie, and he saw the looks she was getting from the other men in the bar. She was oblivious to them and for some reason this pleased him.

She was looking well enough, old Joanie, he couldn't take that away from her. Still, they were supposed to be talking business so they did. He could see how much she was enjoying herself, and watched as the lines of strain gradually left her face. She had had to put up with a lot over the last few weeks and had as usual handled it far better than most people would have done.

She was a survivor was Joanie, and in his heart of hearts he knew that it was just as well. Her life could not have been lived by anyone else. At least not as well as she had lived it.

Later he was going to take her in the car. He liked doing it in the back of a car; it was cramped but it made for a laugh.

And one thing he would give old Joanie: she was always game for a laugh.

She had had to be.

Jean Best was knocking on the door of Joanie's flat when Jon Jon walked up the stairs. She was small, dark, and obviously not from the flats.

He smiled at her disarmingly.

'Can I help you?'

Jean smiled back at this polite young man and said casually, 'I am looking for a Ms Brewer, Joan Brewer?'

Jon Jon nodded.

'That's my mother. I'm afraid she's out. Will I do?'

One part of his mind was registering the fact that she was obviously here on some kind of mission, the other half was eyeing the folder underneath her arm. She was Social Services or probation, there was no doubt about that.

He opened the door with his key and invited her inside. He assumed Jeanette hadn't answered the door to this unknown woman and was pleased with her acumen for once.

'This is purely a routine follow-up after your sister's little mishap recently.'

Jean Best was marking her territory and he appreciated that. She was telling him in a nice way that she was only here to observe that his sister was OK and then she would be off. Her voice was soothing and sounded friendly enough to Jon Jon to be believable.

As they walked into the lounge the smile was wiped from both their faces. Kira had rolled over in her sleep and was lying at a crooked angle on the floor. She had taken the contents of the coffee table with her when she had fallen and it was obvious to anyone that this child was out for the count.

Jean Best saw the look of shock on the boy's face and knew it was mirrored on her own.

'Jeanette?'

The boy was hollering out the name as he picked his sister up from the floor. She opened one eye and immediately closed it. It was obvious she had been given or had taken something to make her sleep.

'What is going on here?'

Jean Best's voice was different now, the authority of years coming to thc forc. Jon Jon, nonplussed for once in his life, didn't answer her. All he could see was how it looked, and he wanted to know where his sister Jeanette was and he wanted to know now.

He stood up and looked at the woman before him. Her face was set and her eyes were like flint. Even her thinning brown hair bristled. She was bending over Kira, taking her pulse and feeling her forehead. The girl slept on through her ministrations.

Jon Jon, taking a decision, asked the woman to leave, explaining that his other sister should have been here with Kira and that he would ascertain where she had got to. It was probable she had gone to look for him, but he made it plain to the social worker that he had only been gone twenty minutes. He knew she didn't believe him but he also knew she would have trouble proving otherwise.

She finally left, but he knew she would be back and when she was it would mean trouble. Big trouble. But not as bad as the trouble Jeanette was going to find herself in when he got his hands on her.

He rang his mother on her mobile first, and then he rang his sister. Neither of them answered, which did not come as any surprise. He rang up Little Tommy and asked him to come over and watch Kira.

Then he made his way to Jasper's.

★ ★ ★

Joanie and Paulie were entwined in the back of his Jag, laughing their heads off.

'Here, Joanie, do you remember years ago when we went in the woods that time and the filth shone a light in the car and you shouted out, "I ain't getting out of this car until I get paid"?'

She burst out laughing again.

'Their faces! They were a picture.'

He hugged her to him, feeling her skin against his hand. The warmth of it. The softness. In the half-light she looked younger, and he saw the girl she had been all those years ago when she had first come to work for him. Even then she had had something about her, though he had never ascertained exactly what that something was. All he knew was he liked her, liked being with her.

'We better get moving, girl.'

He didn't attempt to move as he said the words so Joanie stayed put. She loved the feel of him as much as he loved the feel of her.

'Thanks, Paulie.'

He grinned down at her.

'What for?'

She smiled.

'For being here this last few weeks.'

He kissed her gently on the forehead.

'We're mates, ain't we, Joanie? That's what friends are for.'

He was telling her not to take any of it too seriously; distancing himself verbally and physically. It was what he had always done and she wondered why she didn't just leave it.

As he let go of her he pretended to stretch. The pretence did not fool either of them. Joanie got dressed in silence; the atmosphere in the car had changed again.

She sighed deeply.

She should have kept her mouth shut and then they would still be lying here enjoying the quiet and each other's company. Now they were speeding back to reality and it was all her fault.

Her own big mouth would always be her downfall.

★ ★ ★

Bethany was asleep when Monika came into the house. She was crashed out on the sofa, looking very young. Monika, feeling an unaccustomed twinge of guilt, decided to carry her to bed. As she picked her up she clocked the ring and the fifty pounds underneath the cushion the girl was using as a pillow.

Bethany was woken roughly then the whole sorry tale was told. Monika, however, wasn't interested in her daughter's foray into thieving, she was more interested in the fact that Kira the wonder child had been left in the house alone. Miracles would never cease.

Still smarting from previous events, she set the rumour mill running almost immediately. Joanie had left her Kira, the one with the learning difficulties, alone.

It was, for Monika, sweet revenge.

Joanie had her kids, her job, now she even had that fat ponce at her beck and call. Her, Joanie, a brass who was no better than Monika was herself. Yet everyone liked her, had always liked her.

Well, Monika had found a chink in her armour and she would use it, let people know that Joanie wasn't as snow white as she made herself out to be.

After all, who the hell did Joanie Brewer think she was?

The sad part was, Monika knew that whatever else Joanie Brewer might be, she was ten times the mother she herself could ever hope to be and that was what rankled the most.

Monika's elder daughter had nothing to do with her and soon Bethany would follow suit. It was a hard life for women like her, and she had made it harder still by taking absolutely no interest in anything other than herself. That, unfortunately, was how it had always been. Her kids raised themselves and Monika sat back with a drink in her hand and left them to it.

Joanie walked into the block of flats feeling happy with her evening out. Even though it had been slightly marred by her own silly comment, she had still enjoyed herself. She could smell Paulie all over her and was loath to bathe it away. She loved being with him, and knowing that a few words out of place had brought things to an abrupt end hurt her. She should remember that to be close to Paulie, you pretended you were anything but.

He liked her to act as if she was just a mate. A good mate admittedly, but a mate nonetheless.

As she let herself in she was smiling broadly. He had told her to come back to work tomorrow night bright and early. He thought she was doing a good job with the parlour and she was pleased that she was doing so well. If she could sort out the kids and her private life as well she would be truly happy. But until then she would concentrate on work, on getting in there tomorrow and making a go of the place, once and for all. In fact, she was looking forward to it.

Jon Jon's face as she walked into the lounge told her that things had just taken a turn for the worse.

'What's going on?'

His mother's voice was resigned. Looking at her, Jon Jon felt sad for what he had to say.

'Jeanette left her on her own. I think she's given Kira some kind of pills, I can barely wake her up.'

Joanie was struggling to comprehend what was being said to her.

'Jeanette what?'

Jon Jon sighed as he explained once more.

'Jeanette, our Jeanette, has drugged our Kira?'

The disbelief was there again, along with devastation at what she was hearing. Jon Jon explained it all in greater detail.

'Where is she?'

Joanie's voice was flat-sounding, almost muffled by anger.

'She's gone, Mum.'

Joanie looked puzzled.

'What do you mean, gone?'

He shrugged and said harshly, 'Gone. I threw her out.'

Joanie screwed up her eyes as she said incredulously, 'You what?'

Jon Jon sat down beside her.

'She is out, Mum, and she ain't coming back here. Not now, not ever. She stepped over the line tonight, the two-faced little bitch! A social worker came . . .'

He saw his mother's face blanch. She was shaking her head.

'No, Jon Jon, they didn't see Kira had been left on her Jack

Jones? That's all we fucking need!'

He explained how he had told the woman he had only been gone twenty minutes, that he was the responsible adult who was taking care of his sister. He tried to settle his mother down with reassurances but the truth couldn't be disguised.

'She *drugged* Kira?'

He nodded.

'That's what it looks like, Mum. I found four Temazepam in her bedroom drawer. I assume she got them off her piece-of-shit mate over in the maisonettes. Another cunt who'll be getting a visit from me.'

His words made Joanie think of where her daughter must have gone.

'Jasper?'

It was a question but the fear she felt was in her voice as she uttered his name.

'Don't worry, Mum, he's OK. If he wants her that bad, he can have her. I'm taking all her gear over there in a minute.'

Joanie walked into Kira's bedroom and stared down at her youngest child who didn't seem any the worse for her latest ordeal. She was dogged by bad luck, this child. If poor Kira ever did anything it turned into a three-ring circus. Joanie only hoped her child's life was not to be plagued by bad luck for ever.

As she pushed her daughter's hair back from her forehead and looked at her beautiful face, she wondered at a sister who could drug and leave someone so small and vulnerable – and all for a worthless bullyboy like Jasper Copes.

Joanie would have forgiven her eldest daughter a lot, but feeding Kira Temazepam was the final blow. If she wanted Jasper Copes so much, so be it. Jeanette could live with him and all it entailed, including his drunk of a mother and all his racist mates. The only decent member of the family was his sister Junie, and she had had to live her mother down all her life. But then, Joanie had had to live her own mother down so she could sympathise with the child on that score. But the Copeses' filthy house and the mother's drunkenness were Jeanette's problem now and Joanie felt she never wanted to lay eyes on her again.

Was the girl so stupid she didn't see her own heritage would always be there between them? Her father had been a Muslim, a nice enough fellow but a Berserk all the same. And that Turkish blood was in Jeanette whether she liked it or not.

But Jon Jon was right: let them have her because Joanie had taken just about all she could. Jeanette was fifteen soon and was already out of control; always had been if her mother was honest. She was selfish, arrogant and ignorant, and she was never going to change. Jealous too of this poor child who needed all the help she could get. But then, that was Jeanette all over: self, self, fucking self.

Joanie put her hands over her face and cried like she had never cried before. All night she had had an inexplicable conviction that hr life was at a turning point. Out with Paulie she'd thought it was for the better; now though she was not so sure.

It was as if a dark cloud was hanging over them all. As stupid as it was to believe in such things, it felt more real to her at this moment than every punter who had ever passed between her legs, and they were legion.

If Jeanette stood in front of her now Joanie would rip her to pieces so it was just as well she wasn't. She only hoped Jasper Copes was worth the hurt he had caused because she had a feeling he wasn't worth the proverbial wank.

She sobbed all night until in the end Jon Jon shouted at her, but she could hear frustration and fear in his voice rather than anger.

Joanie did a lot of things when she was upset. She shouted, screamed, threw things, even cried. But this deep endless sobbing was a first. And Jon Jon didn't know how to cope with it. With any of it.

Paulie sat in the dark in his own lounge and sipped brandy poured from an antique crystal decanter. He stared around him. In the gloom the room looked eerie. Yet he knew that to most people, even if they did not consider it a comfortable room, this would be a place to admire. It was most definitely not a room to sit and relax in. He had never relaxed in his own home, not really. He always felt like an outsider here. It was mad because he'd provided all this for his wife and daughters. But they were separate from him somehow; existed beside him, not with him. He paid for everything and they smiled at him and occasionally thanked him. He knew no more about his girls now than he had when they were newborn babies.

They were in the country again. They were always in the country these days and Paulie didn't mind. He knew he should mind, but he didn't. He never knew what to say to them when they were around. In the past he had gone down there for weekends; now he left them to it, only speaking occasionally on the phone to one or other of them. Of course, it normally was because they needed something. Usually something to do with the horses or a trip they were planning. He knew they called him Barclays behind his back and it had made him smile once. Not any more, though. It rang far too true these days.

He thought of Joanie's mad house, and then considered his own home with its three en-suite bathrooms and a garden you could lose a circus in. Yet it felt sterile, unused. Even his mother, on the few occasions she had been allowed through the front door, had observed that the Borgias would be better hosts.

She had a point and all. Even he felt like an unwanted fart in a packed lift, and it was his fucking house, all bought and paid for by him!

He poured more brandy and turned on one of the lights. The room took on a rosier hue, and suddenly he decided he was going to turn on every light in the house. He was laughing as he ran around, flooding the place with light.

'Might as well have a fucking party!'

He was hollering out into the empty rooms, seeing them all lit up for the first time ever. Lamps, overhead lights, even the garden and outside lights were turned on. He ran out on to the drive and looked at his house. It looked really welcoming for the first time he could remember.

Inside once more, he drank the brandy in one large gulp, coughing with the after-burn as it made its way into his stomach.

He wondered what Joanie would think of his house. She would love it, he knew that much. But he wondered what she would think if he told her he actually preferred to be round her flat with her mad dinner-party collection and her noisy kids who, although bastards, were also a lot like their mother: what you saw was what you got.

He was sorry he had left her so early. He had been going to a club owned by a mate in King's Cross but at the last minute had not fancied it. He wished she was here now so they could have a laugh and reminisce about the old days.

It was crazy really, he had everything everyone else wanted: money, prestige, he was a face known to all and sundry. He commanded the best tables in restaurants, the respect of all his peers. Yet he would rather spend his time in the company of a small-time hustler and brass who had three kids by three different men and who sold her crump for a few quid to whoever cared to request it.

He felt the sting of tears.

What had his life come to when Joanie's son meant more to him than his own flesh and blood, was like the son he had never had? Yet even if Paulie had been given a son, he knew the boy would have grown up as indifferent to his father as his daughters were. Sylvia would have seen to that.

There was no love left on either side, and now he was being honest with himself he admitted that his daughters didn't really love him either.

Paulie sighed.

What was there to love anyway? As someone had once pointed out, he was a deceiving, conniving whoremonger. How many times had he been called that before? Too many times really. Years ago it had made him laugh. Now he was reaping what he had sowed and it hurt. Sometimes, like tonight, it hurt so much it was almost a physical pain.

He buried his head in the arm of the chair and said one word over and over: 'Joanie.'

Chapter Nine

'Something was going on over there last night, I can tell you.'

Joseph listened half-heartedly to his son's chatter, glad that this was his last day here and consequently the last time he had to hear the saga of his son's newfound mates the Brewers.

It still rankled that because of them Joseph's own behaviour was curtailed. He couldn't do or say what he wanted any more. His vitriolic attacks on his son had become fewer because Jon Jon Brewer was liable to give him a dig if he upset their babysitter. Joseph couldn't wait to get away. His son couldn't wait for him to go. Each had a hidden agenda and each knew what the other's was.

But they had called a truce and so far it was working.

'I think that Jeanette is a little mare – know the kind I mean, don't you, Dad? Trouble, that is all that girl causes.'

Joseph had tuned out his son's chatter, only coming back to reality when he heard his plans for Kira.

'You be careful with that girl . . . remember last time, the trouble?'

His son gazed at him, that dead, unblinking stare that Little Tommy had had since he was a baby. It was unnerving, as if he was an empty vessel.

Tommy moved then, walked over to his father and, leaning on the kitchen table, looked into his face as he said casually, 'No. *You* remember it much better than I do, you go on about it all the time! Kira and me have something special. I love her, *really* love her. But not in a bad way. I leave that kind of love to the perverts.'

'You don't know what love is.'

Tommy grinned.

'What are you telling me? That *you* do?'

His father dropped his eyes first and this did not go unnoticed by either of them. Joseph just wanted to get out of this place once and for all.

There had been a subtle shifting of power here and his son was now the decision-maker. That fact alone made Joseph feel inadequate. It had taken him a long time to subdue his wife, but his son had been easy prey. Now, it was as if he was coming out of a cocoon and what had emerged was a strong-minded individual with a nasty streak.

It was definitely time for Joseph to move on.

'By the way, tell your lady love that I will pop over once you are both settled in properly.'

It was said as a threat and both men were aware of that fact. They fell silent then, a hard unyielding silence that jangled the nerves.

Heidi Marks read the report before her carefully. It seemed this child Kira Brewer had been in hospital for alcoholic poisoning but staff there had believed it to be a prank, a one off. However, a follow-up had revealed the child to be possibly drugged and undoubtedly left alone. A brother who she now knew had a file the size of a phone book had said the girl had been left with an older sister, who also had a large file devoted to her, and that he had only been gone twenty minutes. He thought the older sister, Jeanette, had possibly gone out to look for him.

It was feasible except for the child being knocked out. She saw that the social worker had written in red pen that the child 'looked drugged or maybe drunk, possibly both?' Alcohol had played a part before, as they well knew.

The older children had both been in and out of care while small due to the mother's convictions for prostitution. But she was, it seemed, a good mother in her own way. The anomaly was, most prostitutes' children were well dressed and well fed as this was one of the main reasons women went on the game in the first place.

The older children were typical of their age and background.

Truants, petty thieves, yet seemingly adult enough to survive in their world. Jeanette Brewer had run away from home and from council care on many occasions. She had been in homes up and down the country, and had left during the night and refused to go back once collared. Same with the boy, Jon Jon. What kind of name was that anyway?

The youngest child, however, had never been near them. Never been in care, and until now had never even come to their attention. The school said the girl was very well behaved, slow due to her learning disabilities but well nourished and cared for. In fact, she was better fed and dressed than many of her contemporaries. She tried hard, attended regularly, and was a well-liked and balanced little girl. In fact, the school went to great pains to maintain that she was one of their more privileged pupils, having a good family network looking out for her. She was almost always escorted to and from school, and her mother was a caring parent, interested in her daughter's education.

So what was the score?

Heidi would think carefully about this before rushing in, but if the other children were anything to go by maybe this one had slipped the net? She read and reread the case notes on all three children. There was something wrong here but she could not for the life of her put her finger on it. She had a twenty-four-carat shit detector in her brain and it was working over-time as she tried to piece together exactly what it was that was bothering her here.

The mother she understood was now going into full-time paid employment – another no-no for prostitutes who almost never seemed to get out of the quagmire that easy money led them into. Money easily earned was easily spent, that had been proved over and over to her. She had visited women who earned hundreds of pounds a night and yet still didn't have a slice of bread in the house for their children or else failed to put decent shoes on their feet.

But then, that was generally after the drink or the drugs got to them. Most took up past-times like that in order to carry on doing the job that paid them so well.

It was a vicious circle.

Men were lucky really; she had always thought so. Look at this poor woman: three kids and no man on the horizon so she had sole responsibility for their care while their fathers went through life impregnating women and then moving on to the next one without a second's thought for the children they had abandoned. Often not even knowing they had left anything behind other than an odd sock or maybe a shirt. Yet the end result of their lust became a living, thinking, breathing person who would have to deal with the fact their own father was an unknown quantity. Life had kicked these poor children in the teeth before they had even drawn breath on their own.

Heidi Marks felt sad for them, but then she often felt sad.

She had that kind of job.

Joanie was back at work and enjoying it as much as she could considering all she had to contend with. But what was bothering her most was that she had lost all desire to see Jeanette. Had lost all interest in her, in fact.

The flat was quieter without her, and the rowing had all but stopped. It was amazing what a vacuum one person could leave in the space of twenty-four hours. But although no one said it out loud, since Jeanette had gone their lives were all the better without her constant upset.

So Joanie now felt guilty about this even as she struggled to put her emotions regarding her elder daughter on hold. It was funny but in some ways she could finally sympathise with her own mother. Joanie herself had been a Jeanette, but then she'd had every reason to be. She knew that the succession of men trailing through her young life thanks to her mother's haphazard dating system had been reproduced in her own life and the lives of her kids. One-night stands, occasional week-long associations, and always the inevitable hurt and betrayal after they had left, usually with her purse and/or some electrical items. She cast these thoughts from her mind. Paulie had stayed longer, he had been the only one to do so. Yes, he had left her in the end, but he always came back. This last lot had proved that to her.

That was then and this was now.

Unlike her mother Joanie had tried to mend her ways and this showed in Kira. She had had all the things Joanie had never had, and neither of her other children had had. She was going to be all right, Joanie's youngest child, she was determined on that much. And she had firm plans for the future now and would be putting them into operation as soon as she could. Once the cloud of Social Services' interest had passed she was going to look at renting a nicer place in a better area.

That would ensure Kira had a good chance as she grew up of meeting regular people. People with proper jobs and proper lives. Jon Jon was going to help as well. He was even talking about buying somewhere in the future, a thought that made Joanie feel almost dizzy with delight.

And he would do it as well. He was capable of doing anything he wanted, that boy. Even Paulie was impressed by him and took him everywhere now. The fact her son had not harmed Jasper again spoke volumes as well. He was learning to keep himself under control. That was Paulie's influence, she was sure.

So, other than Jeanette, all in the garden was looking decidedly rosy. But every time Joanie thought of her giving that precious child Temazepam her heart hardened even more against her elder daughter.

Jeanette had made her own bed. Now she could lie in it as long as she wanted. Let her have a bellyful of Karen Copes. That should be punishment enough for anyone.

Liz Parker was just leaving her flat to go to work when she saw Pippy Light leaning against a garden wall a few houses down.

She sighed.

This was all she needed; she was already late.

He was smiling lazily at her and she marvelled at a man who could look so innocent and even handsome in a rough and ready kind of way yet who was as mad as the proverbial hatter. And Pippy was mad. Not mental, not touched, but bona-fide mad. In fact, he was responsible for more vicious assaults than Saddam Hussein and all his henchmen put together. He wasn't big, he wasn't physically powerful, but what Pippy had was a total disregard for human life, his own included, that bordered on mania. He would attempt to kill anyone and die in the attempt if that was what it took to achieve his end.

So Liz was understandably wary as she approached him.

'Please, Pippy . . .'

He grinned, holding up a well-manicured hand. He had recently smoked a couple of tabs so he looked reasonably relaxed. She was grateful for that much anyway.

'It's OK, Liz. I know you're working for Martin and I can only applaud your choice of pimp.'

The sarcasm was evident in his voice.

'All I want is a little favour, and you owe me, girl.'

She nodded her assent because she had no other choice and they both knew it.

He smiled again.

'I have been asked to provide the entertainment for a few businessmen who come to town every so often.'

She nodded once more even though she felt sick with apprehension because she knew that she was to be the entertainment for them all. It was one of the corporate gang bangs that were so popular at the moment. This was Pippy's way of punishing her without having to touch her himself. She consoled herself with the fact that with his temper she had actually got off quite lightly.

'There will be between seven and ten blokes and you do whatever you are asked. I want you at Jesmond's by nine tonight, OK?'

She nodded again.

He was giggling now as he watched her face.

Jesmond was a large black man who dealt in literally everything. You wanted it then Jesmond would find a way to provide it. Pippy and Jesmond were kindred spirits where any kind of deviation was concerned. It was why they got on so well. The only person who had any real rapport with Pippy was Jesmond and that was because he was nearly as mad as his friend was. In Jesmond's favour, however, was the fact he had a long-term girlfriend and two children, all of whom he adored.

Pippy, on the other hand, had no one he cared about or who cared about him. Liz had known she would not get off lightly when she left his employment but as long as this was a one-off she would swallow it. After all, she had done these kinds of shows before.

Once, they had been her stock in trade. Fresh from her children's home, she had run away at thirteen and swiftly become immersed in the seedy world of child prostitution. A world she had initially embraced because the money gave her freedom and the men she dealt with treated her like a queen. However, after a while they had not been so kind and the money had become less.

She was not to know that what had happened to her was part of the usual pattern. Give the little girls and boys love and affection, money and a certain status, then when they're feeling secure for once start to treat them badly, make them worry that their positions could be usurped by other, prettier girls and boys. And there you have the perfect recipe for a grand-scale but very lucrative disaster.

Liz had believed once that she was in the know when all this time later she finally realised she actually knew nothing. Except of course how to manipulate men for money, and how to use her body to its best advantage.

She had no real sexual feelings, and emotionally had confused sex with love on the few occasions a man had shown any kind of normal healthy interest in her. But she was a survivor and so she battled on, wondering how she found herself continually on the receiving end of the cruelty of the Pippys and Jesmonds of this world even while she accepted that this was her life, the one she had inadvertently chosen. Telling herself continually that she ought to get used to it and accept it.

Still, at least Pippy would soon be in the past so she would grit her teeth and smile until this last show was over.

If it got him off her back and stopped her ever having to do another show then it was worth every second.

Tommy was showing Kira the bedroom that had been his father's. He had bought new paint for the walls, a bright pink, and a paler shade for the cupboard doors. It was going to be the Barbie room and Kira was in raptures over it.

He had always bought *Barbie* magazine and had kept every edition and its centre-page poster. These were going to adorn the walls. In proper frames, as he pointed out, not stuck on with Blu-tack.

Kira could see it all in her mind's eye and made comments to Tommy about where to put the dolls and their accoutrements.

To her, as for Little Tommy, this was a dream come true.

'How are you feeling, petal?'

She smiled.

'Better than I was, Tommy.'

He stared into her blue eyes and the breath caught in his throat. She really was exquisite. He held up Cinderella Barbie against her and said sadly, 'It's like looking in a mirror.'

He hugged her to him tightly, and she hugged him back.

'Now then, how about I go down the offie and get us some treats, and then when I get back you can help me plan her office space. I mean, Barbie must have an office, eh?'

Kira nodded.

'Also I thought, if it's all right with you, Tommy, that we could put all her clothes in the wardrobe over there, and all her little shoes and bags can be put with whatever outfits they belong to.'

'You are so clever, Kira. You can start the sorting if you like while I nip out for our sustenance, eh?'

She grinned happily.

'OK.'

He left her kneeling on the floor of the bedroom pouring the contents of the shoeboxes on to the floor. He almost skipped to the shops. Now his father was gone life was fantastic. Absolutely fantastic. He had free rein in his own home. No more worries about his beloved Barbies being pissed on, no more worries about having to hide them from his father's sight.

Little Tommy was almost dizzy with joy.

DI Baxter was drinking tea in the police canteen, thinking about Jon Jon Brewer and his latest little escapade. As usual they had nothing on him, or nothing concrete anyway. And now he was bosom buddies with Martin he was almost untouchable. Paulie Martin was a pillar of the community in some respects, always in the paper for his charitable works even though he had more girls on the game than all the pimps in Sodom and Gomorrah put together.

It galled Baxter even as he admitted that he himself had been on the receiving end of Martin's generosity on a few occasions. Everyone had at one time or another. If you wanted tickets to the boxing he was the man to get them for you, at a fair price and all. He could also, for a favour, arrange for you to meet the fighters in the dressing room and have a photo done with them. He was good like that, was Martin. But it didn't mean they had to like him or swallow his outrageous behaviour any more.

But fuck Martin, it was Jon Jon Brewer he was after. That slippery little sod was getting a name for himself so bad the stench was making its way into every station this side of the river.

Baxter would wait. Watch and wait. Carty was out of hospital now, and so was Jasper Copes. Something would occur; it was the law of the street.

'Well? I said, clean the cubicle.'

The girl was high, but not so high she didn't know what was going on around her.

'I cleaned it earlier, Joanie.'

It was said in a friendly way but the undertone of defiance was there nonetheless. Joanie kept the place much cleaner than Lazy Caroline ever had and most of the girls went along with it. But one or two couldn't be bothered even though since she had introduced the new regime the place smelled much better.

Joanie grinned and disarmed the girl in front of her.

'Don't be a prat. Just give the place a once-over with the spray. It ain't a lot to ask and I ain't sending no more punters in until you do, Deirdre, all right?'

Deirdre sighed but nodded.

'OK then. But it's stupid because it will be full of oil and God knows what again in a minute.'

Joanie shrugged.

'And pick up the condom wrappers and wipe the floor over before someone goes flying and sues us for a broken cock or something!'

Deirdre rolled up then. Say what you like about Joanie, she was a laugh. She cleaned the cubicle and Joanie went back to her office.

The phone was ringing and she picked it up. She loved this job so much. It was just like being a real secretary.

Jon Jon and Sippy were having a beer in the Mad Hatter on the South Bank. It was a nice pub and they were guaranteed not to see anyone who knew them there. As they exchanged details of their different livelihoods and sorted out their usual business they made a strange pair. Two Swedish girls were giving them the come on and they were trying to ignore them until business was out of the way.

Sippy was pleased with Jon Jon's newfound status, especially as he had predicted it himself. Men were getting the big jobs younger and younger nowadays because the heavy sentences handed down by judges took people out of their ballpark quickly and efficiently. Consequently, they both had friends just a bit older than them who were away for the duration and this made them take their own businesses far more seriously. If caught they knew they would be finished once and for all. Sippy had a wide network of people that the police would have to get through before they could finger him, and he was advising Jon Jon to do the same. He was listening avidly to everything his friend and mentor was telling him.

'How's that Liz?'

Jon Jon shrugged.

'Don't know. Don't care.'

Sippy didn't believe him and it showed.

'I hear she's still doing a bit of work for that Pippy. Watch out for that bastard – he's one mad boy.'

Jon Jon shrugged.

'It's a free country.'

Sippy laughed.

'Watch Liz too. She is one of them girls who can't or won't be loyal. Whores can be like that, or they can be so loyal it would break your heart. Especially to their pimp. Just watch your back with her. Pippy is in with that Jesmond and he is bad news for women, especially white ones.'

Sippy realised then what he had said. Jon Jon's mother was a brass and she was white, but he often forgot that and knew that

from him Jon Jon would not take the words as an insult.
Jon Jon shrugged again, an exaggerated display.
'Pippy don't fucking scare me.'
Sippy laughed loudly.
'No? Then he fucking should, because he scares me, man. You took what he had and he will go all out to teach you a lesson, Paulie Martin or no Paulie Martin.'
'Let him. I like a challenge.'
They both laughed then because Sippy knew that the more faces Jon Jon took out, the bigger deal he would be. Their business was all about reputation. That was what earned you the big bucks and the loyalty.

Paulie and his wife were eating dinner. He watched her as she dished up. The table as always looked fantastic. The dinner service had cost him a small fortune, he had got it for her one Christmas and the expense had seemed worth it at the time just to see the look of joy on her face.
Things made Sylvia happy.
Nice things.
Tonight they had grilled steak with mushrooms, tomatoes and home-made thick-cut chips. There was also salad, corn on the cob dripping butter, and three other vegetables: broccoli and cauliflower in rich and creamy cheese sauce, and mangetout. There was enough here to feed a small army. The girls were at their friends' so all this food was a waste really.
One plate was heaped much higher than the other. It made him smile because he knew that was her plate. She could eat for England, could Sylvia.
'Got enough there, Sylv? Can't have you dying of starvation, can we?'
He was joking and she knew it but it annoyed her just the same. Her name was Sylvia, it was a nice name and she wondered why he always had such trouble saying it.
'I was Christened *Sylvia*, married as *Sylvia*. My name is *Sylvia*.'
It was the way she said it more than the words themselves. The sarcasm was almost palpable. It really annoyed him, as it was meant to.

Paulie sat back in his chair and surveyed her. As she shovelled food into herself he stared as if seeing his wife for the first time. Her slack mouth almost lunged at the fork. Joanie ate with more finesse than Sylvia. For all his wife's airs and graces she ate like an animal. She glanced at him as he observed her and stopped eating, fork piled high with food halfway to her mouth.

'What's wrong now?'

It was spoken as if to a recalcitrant child.

'You having a laugh, Sylvia?'

He always got more Cockney when she was playing the lady of the manor. He made himself laugh now as he said seriously, 'Slow down. Anyone would think the food was going to be whipped away from you at any second.'

They stared at each other for long moments.

Sylvia was good at giving the evil eye. Once it had made him laugh, long ago when they had still pretended to like each other.

She replaced the fork on her plate and said conversationally, 'Do you really want to know why I rush my food, Paul?'

He nodded. He had a feeling that there was something going on here he wasn't aware of. There was a hidden agenda, he would lay money on it. It was in her voice, in every nuance of her words.

She took a deep breath as if she needed to summon up courage before saying quietly, 'I rush my food so I don't have to sit in your company any longer than I have to. I have not enjoyed your company for many years and we both know that, don't we? I spend an inordinate amount of time at our country retreat so I don't have to see you, smell you, or engage in conversation with you. In short, any time spent with you is under duress.'

She sat back in her seat triumphant at the effect her words were having.

Paulie didn't answer for a while and then he said, 'And the girls, do they feel the same?'

She smiled as she nodded.

'What do you think, Paul? That they enjoy having a Cockney pimp for a father? What do you think they could possibly have in common with a man who sells women for his own personal gain?'

That was one in the eye for Paulie. He'd had no idea she even knew how he made his money – 'wheeling and dealing' was the way he'd always described it to her. But it seemed she had his measure after all.

He licked his lips before saying, 'What's brought all this on?'

She shrugged.

'I have had enough of this pretence of a marriage, that's all. I want out.'

He was quiet for a moment and she assumed he was devastated.

'I suppose you want the houses and a settlement?'

'It's the least you can do. And the school fees, of course, plus the upkeep of the horses.'

Paulie shook his head, considering this.

'I suppose that's fair enough.'

Sylvia nodded vehemently. If she had known it was going to be this easy she would have done it years ago.

'What about the villa in Marbella, Sylv? Sorry, Sylvia. Do you want that and all?'

She nodded again.

Now he was laughing. She sat very still, beginning to feel uneasy.

'Don't want fucking much, do you, Sylv? Do you know how many blowjobs my girls had to do to buy all this stuff?'

He shoved his plate violently across the table. It crashed to the floor and shattered into pieces. The noise was deafening as every piece of crockery fell after it when Paulie picked the table up and shoved it towards his wife.

He leaned towards her.

'Do I look like a cunt to you?'

She didn't answer him so he grabbed her face and forced her to look at him.

'Answer me, you fat bitch, or I'll wipe the floor with you.'

Sylvia shook her head.

'I said, answer me!'

'No . . . No, Paul. Please stop!'

Her panic and fear were evident now.

'*You* look down your nose at *me*? Your old man was a fucking bank clerk! You think you're some kind of queen? You're nothing, just a self-satisfied snob. Well, you ain't going to be one on my money, love. Whatever you think of my girls, at least they're out there earning. And you can do the same in future because you, lady, are out on your fucking arse!'

He threw her from him and she grabbed at the table to stop herself from falling over. He was like a lunatic now and she watched in terror as he systematically tore the dining room apart, all the time shouting and screaming.

The police arrived twenty minutes later. She was cowering in the corner of the room, crying.

Yes, she would press charges. She also wanted a restraining order imposed as soon as possible, she sobbed.

It was only when she smiled complacently at him as they took him away that Paulie Martin realised he had played straight into her hands.

Chapter Ten

Kira and Tommy were covered in pink paint. When they looked at each other they laughed loudly.

'Good job it's washable or your mother would skin me alive!'

They surveyed the transformed bedroom and both agreed it looked wonderful. Every inch of space was pink except the ceiling and the floor. Even the skirting boards and the door were deep pink.

Tommy looked around him with pride. This was a dream he had had for so many years and now he was seeing it through to fruition. Something he had never thought to do. And best of all he had a little helper beside him, a pretty and hardworking helper he had all to himself. Something else he'd never thought would happen to him.

Kira sipped at her Diet Coke while he brushed out any runs or smudges on the paintwork. It was amateur work but neither of them could see that. To them it was a room fit for Barbie.

'Jump in the bath, Kira, and I'll make us something to eat.'

She ran from the room happily. As he listened to the water running he was once more overwhelmed with sheer happiness.

Kira was in his bathroom.

She was such a big part of his life now he worried in case something happened to take her from him. But nothing would happen, he would make sure of that.

Since his father had moved in with Della, Tommy's life had become what he had always wanted it to be: full of people and friends.

And little Kira, of course, she was the most important person of all.

As she sang and splashed he felt a serenity he had not felt since his mother was alive. He banged on the bathroom door and shouted, 'A good scrub now, remember.'

She shouted back at him and he could hear the happiness in her voice that was mirrored in his own.

Paulie was like a bear with a sore arse. Joanie noticed it immediately. No one could do right for doing wrong. Even she was getting fed up with him which spoke volumes considering what she had put up with from him over the years.

'Can't you lot just try and fucking keep this place tidier? It smells like a whore's fucking handbag!'

The girls all stared at him then at each other.

They were baffled. The place had never been so clean. He knew it and they all knew it. Joanie was now going under the nickname of Madam Domestos and she loved it. It lightened the atmosphere around the place and it also proved to the girls that she still had a sense of humour.

'Can you come and look at this please, Paulie?'

Joanie had trouble keeping her voice under control. He followed her into the office, his face dark with anger and his mumbling and swearing audible to all.

Joanie shut the door and then said quietly, 'Who the fuck has rattled your cage?'

He knew it was a fair question; inside he knew he was not being fair to anyone. But he was so angry he exploded.

'Don't you dare question me on my own premises!'

There was a warning in his voice, even the girls gathered around the door outside could hear that much.

But Joanie wasn't having any of it. Who did he think he was? She was not having any of his posturing today, and she also had to prove to the listening girls that she could hold her end up whatever.

'I'll question you where I like, mate. You come in here with the manners of a fucking rent man and shout at my girls . . .'

'*Whose* girls! Whose fucking girls, Joanie Brewer . . .'

He was livid, eyes bulging from his head now.

Joanie stared at him for long moments before she bellowed, 'I *run* this fucking place, not you. And if you are going to undermine my authority then you can stick the job up your arse!'

'I beg your pardon?'

He was in complete shock at her words.

'You heard. I ain't listening to this every time you have the hump. I ain't no one's fucking whipping boy, mate, especially not yours.'

He knew in his heart she was making a fair comment but he also knew everyone would be outside listening for his retort. If he backed down now they would walk all over him.

'Suit yourself.'

Joanie laughed then.

'Oh, I will, Paulie. Don't you worry about that.'

Her reply angered him even more.

'Where are you going, Joanie? Back to the pavement?'

It was unfair and he knew it. More to the point, she knew it. She was blinking back tears as she shouted, 'If I do, mate, I won't be working for you so at least I'll have that much to look forward to.'

She pushed past him and picked up her handbag. He grabbed her arm, contrite now. How had this got so out of hand? What was he doing, taking it out on her?

'I'm sorry, Joanie. Honest to God, I am so sorry.'

She looked into his blue eyes and for once they didn't move her in any way.

'What's the matter, Paulie? What's happened?'

Her natural niceness was to the fore once more. She genuinely wanted to know what ailed him.

'It's Sylvia, she aimed me out the door.'

Joanie smiled. All this over a marital argument? It was laughable, surely he could see that much?

'Is that all, Paulie! It won't last. You and her have been together for yonks . . .'

He shook his head.

'She got an injunction out and everything.'

Joanie was non-plussed. Now she didn't know what to say to him. An injunction? What was Sylvia Martin thinking of?

'Did you have a row then?'

He was sarcastic in his reply.

'No, 'course not, we was tight me and Sylv. Of course we had a fucking row!' His voice was rising once more. He was so childish sometimes she felt like she was talking with Jeanette when she couldn't get her own way.

'If you don't calm yourself down you can just go home until you're ready to talk properly to people. Now, politely, what was it about?'

He slumped into the office chair.

'She wants out, wants the lot, and wants me to roll over like one of Pavlov's dogs.'

Joanie poured them both a drink. Then, walking to the door, she opened it and stared at the girls gathered round as if she'd had no idea they had been standing there.

'Did you lot want something?'

They all moved away quickly.

She winked at them before closing the door once more.

'Thanks, Joanie. You think of everything, don't you?'

She smiled, sorry to see him brought so low.

'What about your kids?'

He shrugged.

'What about them? They're more her daughters than mine, she's seen to that.'

He gulped at his drink.

'I am so sorry, Paulie. Did you have any inkling this was coming?'

He shook his head.

''Course not. If I had I would have made arrangements.'

She had never seen him like this before and a small part of her was jealous of a woman who could provoke such a reaction from him.

'This injunction . . . you haven't given her a clump, have you?'

He shook his head but he couldn't look her in the eye, which spoke volumes as far as she was concerned.

'Where are you staying?'

'I slept at a mate's last night.'

She knew that meant a bird's and was annoyed he had not come to her. Yet why should he?

'You could have come to us, you know.'

He was on his high horse again.

'That would look good in the divorce if she finds out I was at yours and you a . . .'

He didn't finish so she finished for him.

'A brass?'

She laughed nastily.

'Well, by the time the briefs have finished delving into your business interests I think that will be pretty low on a scale of one to ten, don't you?'

She saw his face blanch, and realised that the thought had not occurred to him yet. Now he suddenly saw what was really going on. If Sylvia got a brief and they did start delving into his businesses . . . He felt the anger welling up once more.

The sneaky bitch!

He thought of all his bank accounts, all the offshore monies he could not account for legally. All his nefarious businesses that were in reality fronts for other even less legal practices from drug dealing to loan sharking. There was hardly a pie he didn't have a finger in and Sylvia could blow the lot if she wanted to.

'Oh, fuck, Joanie, what am I going to do?'

She shrugged.

'That's what people have briefs for, ain't it? Advice. So get some. See where you stand.'

He nodded.

She poured him another drink then and placed a hand gently on his shoulder while he drank it. Eventually he slid his own hand over hers and smiled at her.

'Sensible old Joanie, eh?'

'It's only money and you have loads of it. Give her a settlement or whatever they call it and get it over with sooner rather than later.'

He nodded but she knew it would be hard for him to give away money he saw as rightfully his. Money he had worked for.

'Be cheaper to get her fucking wiped out!'

Joanie wasn't sure if he was joking or not. She hoped he was.

She went outside and remembered the women had probably all been listening to the exchange as soon as the door was shut once more. They had always liked her but now, after the way she had spoken to Paulie Martin and got away with it, they also admired her.

Lorna Bright was sitting with her little schoolgirl friends and regaling them with stories of her exploits. Her daughter Laeticia was off school as usual and the School Board had been round. She was telling all the little teenagers what she had said. This consisted mainly of expletives.

They were both scandalised and excited, and wished they could all live at Lorna's instead of their own houses where they couldn't smoke, swear or take drugs.

In Lorna's you did what you liked.

The house was filthy. Piled-up dishes and cat urine and unwashed clothes and bodies made for a sour smell that hit you as you walked through the front door. The curtains were never opened and the living room was in perpetual darkness, lit only by the flickering of the TV which was never turned off even when the music was blaring out, which it was for nearly fifteen hours a day.

Lorna was in her element when the banging started on the front door. She opened it wide, expecting more young friends. Her heavily pregnant belly was escaping from a crop top and hipster jeans. Her dirty feet were encased in plastic flip-flops and her makeup was applied in a haphazard fashion that left her looking permanently startled.

It was the track marks all up her arm that people noticed the most; that and her belly hanging out like the fashion accessory it was.

The wide smile was wiped off her face when she saw Jon Jon Brewer.

'All right, Lorna.'

He walked into the maisonette as if he owned the place. His wrinkled nose told her what he thought of his surroundings and Lorna felt embarrassed for the first time in her life. She would love to bag someone like Jon Jon. He would guarantee her an easy life in every way.

In the kitchen the young girls looked frightened and excited in turn. Bethany, who was sitting on the work surface, looked absolutely terrified. That fifty pounds and the ring still loomed large in her mind.

'Get out.'

His voice was quiet and brooked no arguments. None of them needed to be told twice. The scramble to escape was noisy and overlong.

'I said, get the fuck out!'

Lorna watched the exodus with wide eyes. Alone, he looked at her little girl and smiled at her.

'Go and watch TV and shut the door, OK?'

She nodded, unaware and uncaring about what was going on around her. Jon Jon saw her skinny little stick-like arms and felt the anger welling up inside him. She had blue bruises, obviously fingermarks, and her eyes looked dead in her head. She was filthy, her pyjamas had obviously been on her for days.

When she went into the other room Lorna tried to smile as she said, 'What's the matter, Jon Jon?'

The bravado of earlier was long gone. He stared at her, knowing it made her uncomfortable. Eventually, after what seemed like hours to Lorna, he said gently, 'Did you give Temazepam to my sister Jeanette?'

She didn't answer but at least she now knew what the call was about. He could see her mind turning over as she tried to think of a way out of her predicament. Then, taking a deep breath, he said, 'This is your last chance before I shove that baby up into your ribcage with my fist. Now, one last time. Did you give my sister Jeanette Temazepam or not?'

He had no intention of carrying out his threat but she wasn't to know that.

Lorna nodded.

'Did you know what it was for? Now answer me carefully because I know the truth.'

She nodded once more, her fear almost tangible now. He could smell it coming off her in waves. She jumped as he walked towards her and he laughed.

'It wouldn't hurt her, Jon Jon. Honest! I do it all the time.'

He spat on to the floor, a sign of disrespect and also because the smell in here was so overpowering he could taste it. He raised his hand to push his dreads from his eyes and she stumbled backwards in fright, thinking he was going to attack her.

'Don't worry, I ain't going to do anything now, Lorna. But if I find out that you have had any more kids in here, spinning them your shit, then I will be back. Do you understand me?'

She was nodding again, her face devoid of any natural colour now.

'If you see any of my family you fucking run, and I mean *run*. You cause me hag big-time and me and you will have a score to settle after this little one is shit into the world, right?'

She nodded again.

He left her then but he had achieved his objective. She would think twice before she handed out any more jellies to kids.

It annoyed him, though. If anyone's kids should be removed from them it was Lorna. But she would get all the help in the world, heroin addicts always did.

It was all wrong.

His poor mother had moved heaven and earth to keep them clothed and fed, and none of the social workers could give a shit about that. They'd had everything they'd needed as kids: love, warmth and food in abundance. Yet because Joanie was in the know she was classed as the lowest of the low. It was very wrong, he knew that at first hand.

Jeanette heard about Lorna and broke into a sweat. Jasper seemed to think that Jon Jon had a point, which didn't help. She wanted Jasper to hate her brother as much as she did.

After all, he had aimed her out of her own home!

In consequence she was lumbered with Jasper's mother whose idea of an evening meal meant opening a tin or going to the chippy. Who had recently sold the washing machine for cash and who couldn't find the iron under the piles of unwashed clothes. Joanie's cleanliness and cooking had all gone unappreciated until now. Her mother's scruffy but welcoming home seemed like Blenheim Palace in comparison with the way the Copeses lived.

Now Lorna would have the hard word out on her and that would cause repercussions all over the place. No one was going to give Jeanette anything, were they? Not if they thought Jon Jon would jump on them over it. So he had curtailed nearly all her activities, and knowing him, he knew that. He had been round and threatened anyone and everyone she had ever dealt with in any way.

Jasper was not half as exciting now she saw him morning, noon and night and her guilt over what her brother had done was wearing thin. She was too young to be lumbered like this, it just wasn't fair! She loathed Jon Jon for it even as she loved him as a brother.

And to cap it all, she was missing her family big-time. Her mum's silly carry on; Jon Jon's hard-nosed rules and regulations. She even missed Kira, the instrument of her downfall.

And the worst thing of all was she had brought it on herself.

Bethany saw Kira walking to the shop and hurried to catch up with her. As they stood together at the kerb waiting for a break in the traffic on the A13 they chatted. It was a still day. The exhaust fumes hung heavy and the dirt in the air was visible as the cars rushed past on this busy Saturday afternoon.

Kira was well aware Bethany was not supposed to be talking to her, but her own mother had not imposed any such ban. Joanie would never involve her daughter in her own squabbles. Kira had merely been told not to get into any more scrapes with Bethany; those were her mother's exact words. Meaning, be nice and friendly but don't dare to join in Bethany's hare-brained schemes.

But on this sunny Saturday she was so pleased to see her friend that her mother's words were forgotten. They linked arms and walked to the shops, oblivious to the traffic noise and the dirt. As they walked they talked and laughed.

Bethany was on her best behaviour; she knew she had to be. They shared secrets, and Bethany was especially interested to hear that Tommy was going to meet his father's girlfriend that afternoon.

Bethany was older in years than her friend and some of her caustic comments went over Kira's head. Bethany was of course parroting her mother but Kira didn't know that.

'He's nice, though, Tommy.'

Bethany was jealous of this and replied, 'My mum says he's a nonce and she wouldn't leave me with him for all the money in the world.'

Both girls knew this was not true. Her mother did not even bother with a babysitter. It had caused arguments between Joanie and Monika on many occasions.

'Well, I like him and so does my mum.'

Bethany knew how loyal Kira was; she had stood by her friend enough times. But today her jealousy was getting the better of her.

'He's a nonce. My mum says he's been done for it before.'

Her mother had said that but they had both known it was just anger talking. No truth in it as far as they knew.

Kira snatched her arm from Bethany's and shouted, 'He is not a nonce!'

'He is!'

Bethany was adamant.

'Look at him, Kira, he looks so weird.'

'He does not. He's just fat, that's all.'

'A fat git!'

Bethany wanted to cry. She had been determined to get back friends with Kira and now look what had happened.

Kira was angry herself, something that was rarely seen, and shouted loud enough for the passers-by to hear: 'Your mum leaves you on your own because she don't give a monkey's about you! *My* mum has always said that. She says it's a disgrace the way she treats you, and you know that's true.'

Bethany knew very well that Joanie had argued with her mother on many occasions about the way she treated her daughters, but misplaced loyalty and the urge for a row made her flare up.

'Well, at least she don't leave me with a fucking child molester like yours does.'

A neighbour of Joanie's, passing by, raised her eyebrows at these words.

'He is not a child . . . whatever.' Kira couldn't pronounce the word so she shouted, 'He's just fat! Like your mum is!'

Bethany had taken all she could; she slapped Kira hard across the face. Then they were both crying but the damage had been done.

'I'm sorry, Kira, I'm so sorry . . .'

Kira ran off and Bethany, crying her eyes out, ran after her.

'What do you think then, Joanie?'

Verna Obadiah, a West Indian girl married to a Nigerian, was breathless with anticipation over what Joanie was going to say.

She turned over another card.

'The hanged man! Will he die, Joanie?'

Joanie grinned.

'No, you silly cow. This denotes all sorts of things. But I can tell you now, he ain't going to leave his wife for you.'

Verna's boyfriend was a bus driver called Roger with startling blue eyes and sandy-red hair. Her husband had no idea she was seeing him and even the advent of a light-skinned child had not alerted him to anything going on. But Verna lived in hope, and hope, as Joanie had always maintained, was all people like them had most of the time.

'Your old man finds out what you've been up to and *you'll* be hanged, girl!'

Verna laughed.

'He wouldn't notice if I was missing until he went to the fridge and the beer had run out!'

Joanie laughed with her.

'What do you want to do, Verna?'

It was a fair question and Verna was honest in return. Joanie gave great advice. Everyone knew that.

'I want to get away from the old man and I hoped me bloke would help me to do that.'

Joanie shook her head and then got up to put the kettle on.

'Your husband'll kill you, Verna, and then he'll kill Roger.'

The woman smiled sadly.

'I know. Roger's trying to get rid of me an' all. I think his wife has got a whiff of something going on.'

She stretched and yawned loudly.

'Just tell me that things will pan out, eh?'

Joanie spooned sugar into cups as she said wearily, 'Things always do pan out – that's the trouble. You don't need the cards to tell you that, Verna. No matter what happens, you get over it eventually.'

It was advice she'd given over the years to countless women, from her mates on the street to visiting royalty like Kathy McClellan, the wife of Big John, who'd visited her regularly all the time her old man did his lump. He was out now and chasing everything in a skirt apparently, but Kathy still thought Joanie was marvellous for telling her things would pan out.

Other people saw Joanie as a tower of strength. She only wished she felt like one too.

Della was surprised by Joseph's son. He was huge, yes, but he was also very well-mannered and so helpful. She was amazed to find she liked him. He had complimented her on her home, her décor and her cooking. He had admired her family photographs and had eaten only small amounts of food while obviously enjoying what he had had.

Now he was telling her about his little job childminding a neighbour's daughter. Della knew Joanie and liked her as much as she could like anyone. She had a good reputation roundabouts did Joanie Brewer, that her children had not wrecked no matter what they did. If Joanie saw fit to let him take care of her child, and she was an exemplary mother there was no doubt about that, then Della would see him in the same light.

She could feel Joseph's nervousness. It was coming off him in waves. He had hardly spoken and yet his son had ignored that fact, filling the silence with his easy chatter and even making Della laugh. When he got up to leave she was disappointed.

'Are you sure you wouldn't like another cup of tea?'

He smiled at her.

'No, really. I have to get back. My job. You know what it's like.'

She smiled back and nodded.

'Thank you for a wonderful afternoon, I can see why my father wanted to come here. It really is a lovely home and you were a most gracious hostess.'

Della was beaming at him as he walked down the path. She nudged Joseph and he waved half-heartedly as his only child waddled off up the road.

'What a nice boy, Joseph.'

He nodded but she was aware that he didn't answer her verbally. Men were so strange at times.

Tommy walked home in the darkening evening. He actually had enjoyed the visit, but he admitted to himself that he had enjoyed his father's discomfiture more.

His face when Tommy had gone into raptures about how pretty Della's grand-daughters were! It had been worth going for that alone.

God paid back debts without money, all right.

Tommy was in his element.

As he walked home he thought about the evening ahead. They were going to frame the posters tonight, and Kira wanted to put glitter on the wood to make them look more glamorous. He had bought the glitter glue that day and knew she would go into raptures over it.

Then, later, they would walk over to her own home where he would put her to bed and give her a cuddle as he told her a story. That was the best part of the night as far as he was concerned: her little body pressed close to his as he whispered stories into her ear.

Chapter Eleven

Jon Jon picked up the money from the parlours as usual. He was in a good mood; life was getting better by the day. All he had to do was sort out Jeanette and everything would fall into place.

He walked into the new parlour in Barking. It was quiet inside, restful. He smiled at the girls and walked through to the office.

Ginger Carvey, a fifty-year-old prostitute whose hair gave her the nickname, grinned at him. Her good looks were marred by the black teeth that were displayed every time she opened her mouth. Jon Jon shuddered at the sight of them.

'You get better looking every time I see you, boy!'

He laughed.

'Pity I can't say the same for you, Ginge!'

She grinned again.

'Cheeky little fucker.'

She poured him a drink and he swallowed the whisky quickly, picked up the money and left. The girls all smiled at him. Since the news had gone round he was seeing a brass they were all hoping the next one would be them. Anything to make life easier.

Plus he was good-looking, Jon Jon Brewer, and looked older than his years. He gave them all a collective wink as he walked from the building. That was when he heard the shouting start.

Back inside, he ran to the source of all the noise. A woman was cowering in her booth, a large man bending over her. He had her by the hair. She was nearly naked and he was without trousers or underpants. He was a big old boy, all hanging belly and hairy legs.

Jon Jon grabbed him by the hair and forced him on to the

ground. Letting go of the girl, the man started swearing and shouting.

'What you fucking doing, man? What you beating on the girl for?' Jon Jon roared.

The man was on his knees now and it was uncomfortable.

'Let me fucking go, you little bastard!'

Jon Jon kicked him in the gut as he let go of his hair. By the time the man had lumbered to his feet Jon Jon had the Stanley knife in his hand. He was not taking any chances.

'You lairy old fucker, what's your problem?'

The girl was outside the cubicle now, surrounded by the other brasses.

'She owes me! Tell him, you ugly bitch. Go on then, fucking tell him!'

The girl was crying and Jon Jon felt a moment's sorrow for her.

'No, big boy. *You* tell me.'

'She owes me money. I work for a debt collector and this is how she pays the debt off.'

'Not any more she don't.'

This from Ginger.

'You are making a fucking meal of this two hundred quid. She's repaid it ten times over. You're never out of this fucking place.'

Jon Jon picked up the man's trousers and threw them at him.

'Get dressed and fuck off. The debt is paid.'

'Oh, no, it ain't!'

Jon Jon squared up to him.

'Are you up for a real row then? Me and you?'

There was something in Jon Jon's voice that alerted everyone to danger. His eyes were like slits and his mouth was set in a grim line. His stance was solid. Jon Jon was up for a row. A serious row.

The big man was not up for anything and it showed. He was a coward and he had proved it by picking on the girl in the first place. He put his trousers on and left but as he walked out he spat in the girl's face.

Jon Jon took him down then full force. The Stanley knife

opened up the man's head, and as he grabbed at it the blade was pulled once more across his fingers. Then Jon Jon kicked and pummelled him until he was spent. Finally he half pulled and half dragged the man out the back of the building and left him in the car park behind the parade of shops.

He locked the door once he was inside, washed his hands, and the blade and then said to Ginger, 'If he comes back, you ring me, right?'

She nodded.

'You're a good boy, Jon Jon.'

'Who's he work for?'

'Jesmond.'

Jon Jon laughed.

'I can expect a call from him then, can't I?'

Ginger laughed.

'You're not even bothered, are you?'

He shrugged with the arrogance of youth.

'Well, you should be. He's a hard nut to crack.'

Jon Jon winked at her.

'Ah, Ginger, but so am I.'

He walked from the building and as he got into the car Earl said, 'Your phone has been going like the clappers.'

'Why don't you answer it?'

Earl shrugged.

'It was flashing up *Mum*. So it wasn't a work call.'

As they pulled away from the kerb a police car passed them and Earl cut it up by the traffic lights. He was laughing as the filth pulled them over.

'You stupid prick!'

Earl was not laughing now he realised what he had done. Jon Jon was not in the mood for any more aggravation, especially as he had over forty grand sitting under the passenger seat. He'd have to ring his mother back later.

Joanie was worried. She had not seen hide nor hair of Kira all afternoon. As she walked up to Tommy's, she smiled. Kira was still so entranced with the painting of the Barbie room she was probably sitting there now discussing it.

Tommy opened the door and looked surprised to see Joanie there. He was in a dressing gown and had obviously just had a bath.

'Hello, Joanie.'

He didn't invite her in and she felt awkward for a second.

'I just got out of the bath.'

She nodded at his explanation.

'It wouldn't take Einstein to work that out, Tommy. Have you seen Kira, by any chance?'

He was immediately concerned.

'No. She was supposed to pop up but I haven't seen her yet.'

He was pulling the dressing gown around him, no mean feat since it was two sizes too small.

'Did she say she was going anywhere to you at all?'

He could hear the fear in Joanie's voice.

He shook his head.

'Not a word. Have you tried all her little friends?'

'It's getting on for seven o'clock, Tommy. She wouldn't stay that long.'

He shook his head, looking puzzled.

'Look, Joanie, let me get dressed and I'll come over, OK?'

She nodded. He watched her walk away. Then, closing the door, he threw off the dressing gown and struggled into his clothes.

Monika nearly fainted when she saw Joanie on her doorstep. It didn't help that she was sober and had just woken up.

'All right, Mon?'

Joanie sounded friendly so Monika smiled as best she could and invited her in. In her heart she couldn't wait to make things up. No one else put up with her like Joanie did.

Joanie meanwhile could smell Monika's last takeaway over the acrid smell of ingrained dirt. She wondered how she had ever let it bother her before. Monika had often let Bethany sleep at hers but Joanie had never once let Kira sleep in this house. It had been a bone of contention once. Now she was getting so worried she wouldn't care if she found Kira ensconced in Bethany's bed, filthy sheets included.

'Is Bethany in? Only I'm looking for Kira.'

Monika blinked a few times before she bellowed out her daughter's name then shrugged. She walked through to the kitchen with Joanie following her.

'It's only half-seven, Joanie, she's probably out with her mates.' Monika's voice sounded bored. 'You worry too fucking much. You should let her have a bit of independence now and again. Do her the world of good.'

'Like you do Bethany, you mean?'

It was out before Joanie thought what she was saying and Monika turned on her.

'What's that supposed to mean?'

There was belligerence in her voice and her stance.

Joanie took a deep breath.

'I'm sorry, Mon, but I'm worried.'

Monika was appeased by the apology.

'Look, kids like a wander. That's natural. She's probably playing out and forgot the time. Bethany's always doing it.'

Because Bethany knows there is never anyone at home. No one who cares anyway. But Joanie stopped herself from saying that out loud.

'Ain't she with that Tommy?'

It was said slyly and Joanie replied quietly, 'Monika, do me a favour, mate, and don't wind me up today. I know what you've been saying and I really don't want a row, OK?'

Monika blew out her lips and sighed.

'There's something wrong there, Joanie. A grown man with all them dolls . . . it ain't natural.'

Her voice was friendly but all-knowing and Joanie decided to go before she lost her temper once and for all.

'If you see your Bethany, ask her to let me know if she has seen Kira, OK?'

'Where are you going?'

Joanie sighed sadly.

'I'm going to look for my child, Mon. By the way, exactly *where* is Bethany?'

Monika didn't answer her.

'You have no idea, do you? She could be anywhere and you couldn't give a toss, could you?'

'She can look after herself.'

It was said flatly, with no emotion. Joanie stared at her one-time friend and then, looking round the dilapidated room, she answered her caustically: 'Well, she's always had to, ain't she?'

As she walked down the overgrown path she wondered at her friend's complete indifference to her own children. Poor Bethany, no wonder she was like she was.

When Joanie located Kira she was going to give her a telling off she wouldn't forget in a hurry. Then she was going to get her a bowl of treats and hug her all night long.

Paulie and Jon Jon were giving out to Earl who was taking it very well.

'I can't believe you did that, Earl. Are you fucking stupid? If plod had searched the car and found that money, you two would have been banged up by now. How would you have explained it away?'

Earl didn't answer.

Paulie was fuming. This was all he needed today.

He had had his first letter from Sylvia's solicitor and the name on the letterhead alone had stunned him. They cost a fortune and he had the feeling he was going to be footing the bill for his own divorce.

Now he had Wonder Boy sitting here like a brain-dead amoeba after nearly bringing the filth down on them like a ton of bricks.

'The tax man would have been bad enough but how exactly was you going to explain over forty grand in cash to Old Bill?'

Still Earl didn't answer. Jon Jon felt sorry for him but he could see Paulie's point. Earl needed to be brought to book.

His phone beeped a text and he read it quickly.

'What's the time?'

'Why? Are we keeping you, Jon Jon? Got a hot date with your bird?'

He shook his head.

'Me little sister is missing, if you must fucking know.'

Earl looked at his watch.

'It's after nine, Jon Jon.'

He was grateful to have the heat taken off him.

'She's probably with that fat geezer.'

Paulie's voice was dismissive, but Jon Jon was already walking out of the door with Earl following him.

'Sorry, Paulie, I have to go.'

He got up from his chair.

'What about the rest of the money?'

'I'll collect it later.'

Jon Jon was gone and Earl was following him like a lost sheep. Paulie was annoyed but he swallowed. He knew what Jon Jon was like about his sisters.

Bethany was outside her friend's block of flats when she heard the news about Kira. It seemed she had been missing since early afternoon. All the mothers were talking about it and she listened as they discussed it.

'Say what you like, that girl was well taken care of.'

The other women murmured agreement. They had all joined in the search of the flats and the surrounding streets: husbands, partners and children. But no one had come up with anything. It was nearly eleven at night.

Bethany had not yet been home and it occurred to her that no one was out looking for *her*. Her mother would have gone to work without even checking she was at home. She felt a great wave of self-pity wash over her.

As she cried one of the women said sadly, 'Come on, Beth love, she'll turn up.'

And those words made Bethany cry even more. All the women made a fuss of her but it was no compensation because she knew that Kira was missing because of her.

'I've called the police, Jon Jon.'

He nodded.

It was gone midnight and still there was no sign of Kira. They had searched everywhere, been to every house and flat and looked in every outhouse and shed on their estate. They had visited the park, the waste ground, and even the pubs round and about. Jon Jon had looked in the rubbish shutes and bins though he didn't tell his mother that. It was as if Kira had disappeared off the face of the earth.

Joanie was getting seriously worried now, more so because she knew her youngest wouldn't voluntarily go missing. She knew not to go anywhere without one or other of them being told where she was.

There was a knock at the door and Joanie let in a neighbour. Mary Brannagh was a small dumpy woman with straggly grey hair and dark glittering eyes; the gypsy in her was evident. Joanie and Mary had always had a certain rivalry because Mary did Tarot cards as well.

'All right, Joanie?'

She nodded.

'She'll turn up, Mary love. And when she does, I am going to muller her.'

Joanie kept her voice as light as she could.

Mary answered her ominously.

'She is with someone she knows, Joanie. A dark-haired person.'

Her voice was hushed and Joanie, even though she knew Mary meant well, wanted to strangle her and sling her out of the front door. Instead she was saved from answering by Jon Jon doing the deed for her.

'Come on, Mary. Out, love. No more of this talk, me mum's worried enough as it is. We have the filth coming in a minute.'

He hustled her out of the door and she was not happy about it. But there was nothing she could do.

When the door closed behind her Joanie looked at her son and said plaintively, 'Where the fuck is she, Jon Jon?'

Mary had frightened her now. Joanie believed in the cards and what they said.

Jon Jon sighed.

'I don't know, Mum. Now calm down, she's probably just forgot the time.'

Joanie was not to be placated.

'She ain't forgot the time, she can hardly *tell* the fucking time! She's gone. But at least she's with someone she knows. That's what Mary said, ain't it? Who does she know who would keep her out this late? Who do we know who's got dark hair?'

Jon Jon sat on the sofa with his head in his hands.

'Leave it out, Mum. If you start listening to Mary Brannagh you might as well sign yourself in fucking Runwell and be done with it.'

'Well, where is she then!'

Joanie was hysterical now, screaming out the words.

'How the fucking hell should I know? You're the one who let her go up the fucking shops, Muvver, not me!'

Joanie knew that she was being unfair even as she shouted, 'Are you blaming me then?'

Jon Jon tried to hug her. He knew how upset she was and felt powerless because he didn't know how to make it all better. She threw him away from her.

'Leave off, Jon Jon. I want Kira. Not you or anyone else. I want me fucking baby!'

Then the crying really started. By the time the police arrived an hour later Joanie was on the verge of a nervous breakdown. She could not stop crying.

Jon Jon explained everything to the policemen as she sat in a chair chain smoking and drinking tea laced with vodka.

Tommy was tireless in his searching. Everyone remarked on it. By the time dawn had broken most people had given up to go home for a few hours' sleep before going to work.

The whole estate had been out looking. Even Sippy Marvell and his henchmen were driving round searching. Paulie had all of his male workforce on it and Jasper's cronies were roped in as well.

Jeanette was devastated. She had arrived at her mother's at one in the morning, crying her eyes out. Now she sat with Tommy and Joanie as they waited for news. She was warming more and more to Little Tommy, especially when she saw him holding her mother gently as she cried. The pain in his face was raw.

The police were searching Kira's room for anything that might give them a clue as to where she had gone. Joanie was getting impatient with them and it showed.

She lurched over to the room and said loudly, 'She ain't run away! How many times do I have to tell you that?'

The WPC smiled gently.

'Kids often have people in their lives they don't tell their parents about. We have to make sure she isn't writing to someone or phoning someone secretly. Does she use a computer at school? Internet cafés?'

Joanie shook her head.

'I told you, she has learning difficulties. She can't barely write her own name, bless her. And computers are out of her fucking league. Look at her room, she's nearly twelve and it's like a four year old's! Someone's got her, took her off the street, and you lot are fucking around here!'

'Stop it, Mum! Stop it. She could just be lost.'

Joanie looked at her son in incredulity.

'The whole of this estate is out looking for her and you think she might still be lost? It wouldn't surprise me if they found Lord fucking Lucan, they've looked so bloody hard! Everyone knows her so where the fuck is she? Where is my baby!'

She was pulling her hair and screaming now.

The WPC took Jon Jon aside and said, 'I'm sorry, mate, but it's time to call in a doctor.'

He nodded sadly. His mother's fear was communicating itself to them all now.

Joanie was sedated at eight thirty-five in the morning. It took them over an hour to talk her into having the injection. Jon Jon was glad they had done it. The local news was carrying the story and the way it was worded there was no doubt in anyone's mind that Kira Brewer was not coming home. There were even frogmen dragging the river.

He went into his own room and cried like a baby.

Paulie Martin watched the news in his girlfriend's flat. She was young and pretty with thick blonde hair and pale blue eyes. She was slim to the point of emaciation but she had boobs to die for. She made him a mug of strong coffee and then joined him in the large leather chair as he watched the news.

'Poor Joanie, eh?'

He nodded.

'If anything's happened to that child she'll go off her head, she loves her so much.'

He nodded again, not at all happy with the way this girl was talking about Joanie. Joanie was his private friend. He wondered how much Jenny knew about the two of them, and how much she was trying to find out. He knew how whores gossiped.

'She was so good to me when I had my abortion.'

Paulie's ears pricked up at her words.

'What abortion?'

He had one eye on the TV now and one on Jenny.

She laughed.

'Don't worry, it wasn't yours! No stray Martins went AWOL.'

And none would in the future. She had just seen the last of him but he wasn't about to tell her that.

'I was pregnant last year, by me bloke. Anyway he didn't want to know and neither did I to be honest. So I had it taken away, and the funny thing was I felt really bad afterwards, crying and all. Anyway, Joanie helped me out, explained about hormones and that.'

She looked sad for a few moments.

'Joanie said she considered it when she found out about Kira but couldn't do it. Said she loved the father too much and it was probably all she would ever get from him.'

Jenny laughed.

'I don't think he was exactly Mr Reliable, know what I mean? But she said she had been with him off and on for years.'

She got up, stretched then said innocently, 'I like Joanie, I wish she was my mother. Those kids of hers are her world, and that youngest one . . .'

She sighed.

'Well, if anything's happened to her, it'll kill Joanie, won't it?'

'Did she say who the father was?'

The girl shook her head.

'Nah. I'm going for a bath. I might pop round later and see how she is. You can let yourself out.'

He nodded.

In his heart he had always wondered if Kira was his. It had kept him away from Joanie at the time because of Sylvia. If she'd thought he had fathered a child there would have been hell to pay and he had waited for Joanie to put the hard word on him. But she hadn't and he had breathed a sigh of relief and picked up where he'd left off.

Now he shook his head thoughtfully. She would have told him, wouldn't she? He'd thought it had been a punter, like the other kids' dads. Some men picked up brass and lived off them for a few months then went back to their real lives.

Paulie didn't put himself into that category, of course.

The picture of Kira was on the screen again. He remembered her laughing face; remembered her sitting on his lap as a toddler and smiling up at him. Remembered how much Joanie and the others had loved her. He saw her again with her bright eyes when he had cooked her breakfast a few weeks earlier. Remembered her concern when Joanie had been clumped by Todd McArthur.

She was a nice kid.

The picture on the screen was a school photograph and he had seen it many times in Joanie's without really taking it in until now. He had known this child since she was a baby. He could see her in his mind's eye, with the other two, helping to plan the fantasy dinner parties and laughing at her mother's mad schemes.

Joanie was a good mother. He had always known that it was part of her attraction as far as he was concerned. Her house had been the antithesis of his own home.

The kids had always come first in his house, which meant they came before him. Sylvia had used them that way. Whereas in Joanie's they had always come first, but *he* had joint first with them. Because the kids had liked him there for the simple reason he made their mother happy. They loved her so much they wanted what she wanted.

If Kira had been his, Joanie would have told him, surely?

But common sense was telling him she wouldn't, because if she had, she would have lost him.

When Jenny got out of the bath he was still sitting in the chair and he had obviously been crying. He was also on the phone arranging a meet for eleven that morning. When she came out of the kitchen he was gone.

No goodbye, no nothing.

More to the point, no bloody money either! But that was Paulie Martin all over.

Chapter Twelve

DI Baxter looked at Joanie and felt a pity for her he didn't know he had inside him. She had aged twenty years overnight; she was grey-faced and her eyes looked dead. But looking at her closely he saw the same terror he had seen in the eyes of every victim he had dealt with throughout his long career as a policeman.

He had never liked her, or any of her family for that matter, but even that natural antipathy couldn't stop him feeling sorry for her now. She was already defeated; already the hope was draining from her. He could see it in her eyes, in her whole demeanour.

He had until now loathed them all, the Brewers. Joanie had given birth over the years to a one-family crime wave. Jon Jon was a drug-dealing violent waster, and Jeanette had been a pain in the arse since she'd first started shop-lifting. Her name was also a byword for running away. 'Doing a Brewer' was the local station joke. Only now it wasn't funny at all. Jeanette had been a pain all right, but Joanie had never looked like this when her elder daughter had gone on the trot.

When he had first heard Kira's name Baxter had assumed she was just another one ripe for trouble. How wrong could you be? It seemed this girl was not all the ticket and was taken care of devotedly by the whole family.

Now he felt a terrible sadness for Joanie and even for Jon Jon. He could see the devastation in their faces. Knew, without experiencing it, exactly what they were going through.

'Will you be all right doing the appeal, Joanie?'

She nodded.

They were going national, hoping that someone had seen Kira. Or more to the point, hoping that if someone had her they would let her go. But he didn't say that to Joanie, of course.

''Course I'll be all right.'

She would do anything to help find her daughter.

'Do you think someone might have taken her, Mr Baxter?'

He didn't answer her question. Instead he said, 'Let's not speculate, Joanie, eh? You get yourself off, love.'

She looked at him sadly.

'I appreciate all you've done. You know that, don't you?'

He nodded, feeling worse than ever now.

As she left the room he saw the drooping of her shoulders and the way she shuffled her feet as if she was an old woman already.

Baxter had had the Chief Constable on the phone and realised then that this was serious, more serious than anyone had first thought. The Chief had told him in no uncertain terms that this was a priority on a par with the Queen going on the missing list. He had wondered at first who Joanie was shagging to get a reaction like that from his boss but eventually assumed it was Paulie Martin who had rattled his cage.

Because it was a Brewer missing they had all assumed at first it was just another runaway. They had had so many of them with Jeanette that they had lost count – not that anyone was going to admit that up front. Now, though, Baxter was worried himself and also feeling guilty. If they had got out earlier maybe the child would have been found.

But it was a Brewer!

They were all streetwise. Always had been. Only it turned out this one was thick as two short planks. Just missed being in the mong house, but how was he supposed to know *that*?

If Jeanette and Jon Jon were anything to go by it would have been fair to assume she was on the bash with her mother. Or else shacked up with one of the local rogues, like the other sister was. Jeanette was already shagging for England with a local vagabond, causing no end of aggravation for the force. Jon Jon was in the frame for trying to maim the fucker, and that was without all the other people he had attacked over the years, his best mate Carty included. He had even had a tug the night his sister disappeared.

Jon Jon's room had been an eye opener as well. It was just books, books and more books. Who would ever have thought that Jon Jon Brewer had a real brain rattling round in his head? Baxter already knew he was streetwise, but those books had been something else. Classics by Russian authors with names that were unpronounceable. One of the other blokes said that as they had gone through them they had seen Jon Jon had written things in the margins, his own thoughts on what he had read.

Now they would watch him more closely than ever because people who had real brains thought up good scams and Jon Jon was going to take this place over one day, Baxter would lay money on that. He was Paulie Martin's blue-eyed boy. Well, brown-eyed, same difference. If he was also a contender for fucking *Mastermind*, what else was he capable of dreaming up?

Social Services were sending over the Brewers' records this morning. Hopefully Baxter could save his own arse with what they contained. But whatever he told himself, however he publicly justified his actions, inside he felt guilty.

Kira Brewer looked like a nice little kid.

From what he had heard, she *was* a nice little kid.

But even if she had been a bastard in more than name only she should still have been given the courtesy of a full-scale police search as soon as she was reported missing.

He lit another cigarette and smoked it quickly. He had actually given up the habit two years previously but he needed a fag big-time this morning because if his Chief Constable was in on this they were all in big trouble. Especially as it seemed he was taking a personal interest in the case.

Baxter hoped the television appeal would bring forward some clues. It was going nationwide. Maybe, *hopefully*, she was sitting in a McDonald's somewhere, lost or in the company of a friend. It had been known before now. Runaways had turned up not even realising that their disappearance had caused so much trouble. Kids didn't watch the news after all.

But he was clutching at straws and he knew it.

No one had seen her. It was as if she had just disappeared off the face of the earth, and it was this that was worrying him.

Here was a child who had been watched like a hawk so the chances were whoever had taken her, and he had no real doubt in his mind that she *had* been taken, knew her like she knew them.

But with Joanie's track record who was to say it wasn't a punter, a likely lad, an ex-boyfriend? Somebody could have followed Joanie from her place of work. Her whole lifestyle would have to be looked into. They were also looking into the lives of friends and relations, especially that fat fuck who was the resident babysitter. He was suspect from the moment you clapped eyes on him. Was he a nonce or a raving poof? It was hard to tell but Baxter would find out.

Kira Brewer had been missing for over twenty hours. If missing kids weren't found in the first twenty-four it was assumed they would not be coming back.

Because that, unfortunately, was usually the case.

The police had finished with Kira's room and Joanie was cleaning it up again. She had changed the bed and put on Kira's new Barbie quilt cover. When she came home that would really please her. The tiny room looked bigger since Jeanette had gone to Jasper's. Kira had missed her sister but had loved the freedom of being able to do what she wanted in there.

Tommy was helping Joanie. They didn't talk but his company made her feel better. They placed all Kira's teddies on the bed the way she liked.

As Joanie looked round the room at her daughter's pictures and toys she wanted to scream with fear but held herself in check. She was still convinced that Kira would come strolling back in, or else would be found lost and bewildered somewhere.

She was *not* dead.

Even though she knew very well that nothing good would stop her daughter from coming home to her, she hoped against hope that Kira was with someone she knew. Someone with dark hair, Mary had said. Joanie held on to that hope. She was with someone who knew her, and anyone who knew Kira loved her. God would not take her child from her. He wouldn't be that vindictive. However she had lived her life, she didn't deserve this. He knew that.

Tommy smiled at her kindly.

'I thought you came across really well on telly, Joanie.'

'Thanks, Tommy. I hope someone sees her, recognises her like and brings her home.'

He polished the small dressing table as he said gently, 'So do I, love. So do I.'

Joanie knew that like everyone else he didn't hold out much hope.

If Kira wasn't coming home Joanie prayed that it would be an accident that had taken her baby away. The alternative was so terrifying she daren't even think about it. She had to keep forcing it from her mind.

In her trade she'd seen better than most what men were capable of. Some of the punters she had had over the years had shocked her with their wants and so-called needs so she was under no illusions about what men were capable of with women, girls or indeed little children.

She knew deep inside herself, they all knew, that Kira would never intentionally leave her or her family. So where was she? Who was she with? Was she with someone with dark hair? Mary Brannagh had told her that much and Joanie believed her.

It was precious little but all she had to hold on to. The knowledge made her want to scream out at the world. Instead she cleaned her daughter's room and got everything ready for her homecoming.

Picking up a nightdress, she held it to her face and breathed in the scent of her child, seeing her little smiling face and hearing her happy laugh. The baby sweat smelled so sweet, the pain in Joanie's chest felt as if her whole body was being torn asunder.

'For Christ's sakes, Paulie, I *have* stuck a bullet up their arses. What more can I do?' Chief Constable David Smith was annoyed and it showed.

'All right, keep your fucking hair on.'

Smith was angry and forgot for a moment who he was talking to.

'We could have sorted this over the phone.'

Paulie was fast losing patience.

'No, we could not. Now stop talking shite and listen to what I'm saying. I want this sorted and I want her home sooner rather than later. Do you get my drift?'

Smith nodded. It had suddenly occurred to him exactly who he was dealing with here. All his past associations with Paulie Martin were now in the forefront of his mind and he had a terrible feeling Paulie was going to use them against him.

Of course, in this he was right.

Paulie had been his Christmas box since he had set his foot on the first rung of a very high and quickly scaled ladder. Paulie had asked for a few favours over the years and Smith had seen that he got them. Nothing really big, only guaranteed licences for his parlours, a few quashed charges. Hardly major league.

What worried Smith now was what he had accepted in return. Money, obviously, and holidays. A car once, a new Jaguar, for helping out one of Paulie's business associates who was having trouble with the banks due to some previous convictions that then somehow miraculously disappeared from the national database.

Smith had later accepted the car and ten grand cash, only weighing out two grand to the girl who had actually wiped the man's name from the records. He had thought he was so clever at the time. Now he wondered if Paulie had been aware that he would keep the lion's share of the money through greed and an inflated sense of his own importance.

It was all coming back to haunt him and Smith was mortified at the thought of his skulduggery becoming public knowledge. Like all men of his ilk he was most worried about the ignominy of being caught, the public shaming. Worried about how he'd be perceived then by friends and colleagues.

Paulie knew all that was going through his mind and wanted to laugh at him. It was always about Smithy and his standing in the community. Well, he should have thought about that when he was up to his skulduggery! No one had forced him into this situation, he had chosen it. Loved being in the company of faces, loved feeling like a million dollars in front of his mates.

Did Smith think Paulie Martin had actually liked him or something? Did he think they were mates? Did he not know they were using each other? Was he that fucking stupid? He really was a prick, but Paulie was going to lean on him and get that child every bit of help he could. This bloke was a joke. All he thought about was himself. Even the brasses laughed at him, and he liked a brass, did David Smith. Liked them young as well. Legal, but not so's you'd notice.

Young and vulnerable-looking . . . look great on the front page of the *Sun* that would. And that was where Paulie would put him if he didn't toe the fucking line! Paulie owned him, had done from the first second he had taken a drink for services rendered.

Paulie had no personal allegiance to him. He was a filth, and worse than that he was a bent filth. At least with the others you knew where you were and they afforded you a bit of respect. Whereas this ponce thought he was something special? Well, Paulie was about to disabuse him of that notion once and for all.

'Look, Dave, you get on their case and you tell them it's because if you don't help out a friend he is going to tell the world about all your little schemes and scams. I also want you to tell Baxter that Joanie Brewer is to be treated like fucking visiting royalty. It's bad enough what's happened without him acting like he's doing her a favour by even listening to her.'

Smith nodded almost imperceptibly.

'You have got to come through for me now, Davie boy, like I have come through for you over the years. This is called a deal, see, and I kept my end of the bargain, didn't I? Well, now it's your turn. You shit bubbles of pink chewing gum if I tell you to, right?'

The Chief Constable nodded once more, his face white and strained, all bravado gone.

'I said, *right*?'

Paulie was bellowing now and Smith started babbling with fright.

'OK, Paulie. OK.'

'Don't try and cunt me about, Davie boy, because I am on the verge of killing someone meself and we don't want that dead body to be yours, do we?'

He nodded once more and Paulie knew he had said enough for the time being. Smith was clearly not happy with the situation but knew he could do nothing about it. This would teach him to keep himself inside the law in future. So at least some good had come out of it.

It was getting rid of Paulie once and for all after this that was going to be the poser. The Chief Constable knew now that he had to distance himself from Martin as soon as possible. This little lot could blow up in his face if he wasn't careful. It had just come home to him exactly what he was up against.

The first time he had taken a gift from Paulie it had been given so discreetly that it had not felt as if he was actually doing anything wrong. Plus it was his boss at the time who had encouraged him. In fact, he had been the one who had introduced Smith to Paulie in the first place so it hadn't seemed half as bad as it should have done. If his boss was up for it, why shouldn't he do the same?

His wife had loved it, the extra money and the lifestyle, and if he was honest he had loved it all himself. Women when he wanted them, on tap twenty-four hours a day. He had even arranged for women for his friends and watched their incredulity as they saw what he could command by a simple phone call. He had loved showing off his power.

He had pretended that Paulie was in awe of him, and wondered now if he had actually believed that himself. Until this moment his veneer of respectability had never been challenged. Now it had been he was regretting everything he had ever said or done with Paulie Martin. Every boast, every promise, was standing out in his mind amplified one hundredfold.

'Be sure your sins will find you out.'

His mother had had no idea how true that saying really was.

Penny Cross had worked in Supa Snaps for five years and she loved her job. She loved watching the photos when they flicked into view and she could garner a glimpse into other people's lives. She was a gossip and consequently loved the little insights she got into people's holidays or birthdays or just days out.

Kira's face was on the front page of the local paper. The little girl's disappearance was the talk of the place at the moment, especially as she was known to them all. Penny had been miffed that the photo was a school one and not one of the ones she had developed over the years. Joanie loved a photo of the kids, Penny knew that better than anyone.

It was Joanie who had told her that her husband was having an affair. Like most of the local people Penny had her cards done every now and again. Joanie had been kind to her afterwards, but Penny knew her husband had gone because the bird, a certain Pauline Garston, had been able to have babies. She had already had two by him when Penny had found out about her.

Pauline had been ten years younger and a lot more fertile. Penny could laugh about it now but at the time it had crippled her.

But that was in the past.

It was Monday morning and she had a backlog from Saturday to get out so she'd better move her arse up a gear.

As she sipped at her coffee she suddenly saw pictures of Kira Brewer coming out of the machine and her heart skipped a beat.

Kira must have dropped the film in on Saturday though Penny hadn't seen her. Who had been working here with Penny then? The young school leaver, Maurice, it must have been. Funny, there didn't seem to be any envelope with customer details in the rack.

Penny picked up the photographs and stared at them. She didn't like what she was seeing, especially after what had just happened. The girl going missing and everyone looking for her.

Then she was frightened; she was not sure what to do. Should she give the photographs to the police or to Joanie? She didn't want any trouble.

She stared down at the disturbing pictures again for a full five minutes before she dialled 999. She would give them to the police, see what they made of them. But the fear stayed with her as she placed them in a brown envelope and put them in a locked drawer ready for the police when they arrived.

Della could hear the shouting before she even got inside her house. As she slid the key into the lock she was scandalised at the thought that her neighbours could hear this noise.

It was Joseph and his son arguing but it was Joseph who was

shouting. She couldn't imagine Little Tommy doing that somehow. He was always so quietly spoken. She pushed her way into the lounge and saw Tommy cowering on the sofa, Joseph standing over him, one fist raised.

'What the hell is going on here?'

The two men looked at her for long seconds before Joseph lowered his arm.

'What are you doing back so early?'

It was the way he said it – as if she had done something wrong, something sneaky. She had only come back into her own house!

'I beg your pardon? Do I have to get permission to come into me own home now then?'

Tommy watched for his father's reaction, expecting him to fell her with one blow as he had Tommy's mother if she had ever dared to answer him back like that.

Instead Joseph smiled, actually smiled as he said, 'You came in while we were having a family argument, love. Sit yourself down while I make us a cuppa, eh?'

Della was slightly appeased by his tone but she was still wondering what was going on.

'Were you going to hit him?'

She turned to Tommy.

'Was he going to hit you?'

Tommy didn't answer her, but he liked her more and more as her voice mounted in volume.

'I am talking to you, Joseph Thompson, so you had better answer me!'

Joseph walked from the room and went into the kitchen. It was obvious to everyone that he was not going to say a word.

Della turned her attention to Little Tommy.

'What the hell is going on here?'

Tommy pulled himself up with difficulty; it was obvious he had been crying.

'You'd better ask him, Della. I am sorry you had to witness all this. Truly sorry.'

'I think I should be told what occurred. Tommy?'

He shook his head sadly.

'You really need to talk to my father.'

Joseph came back into the room then.

'Get out, you useless bastard! Get out of this house and keep out of my life. If I ever clap eyes on you again, I'll kill you.'

Della was shocked to the core. She would never have believed that Joseph was capable of talking like that to anyone, let alone his own son. Tommy stared at his father and she could see the hatred in his eyes, the same hatred that was mirrored in his father's.

'Go on, tell her, Tommy. Go on, I dare you.'

Joseph was nearly laughing now for some reason.

'It's you who'll be in trouble, son, remember, not me.'

Tommy walked from the room slowly and heavily. Each step felt as if he was walking through water.

'You thought you had it over my head, didn't you? Well, think about it, boy, and think about it hard. I done nothing, remember? Nothing. It was to all intents and purposes *you*, not me. It was your mother who saw to that, mate. Remember that when you next get the urge to open that fat trap of yours. It was your mother's doing, not mine.'

Della watched Tommy leave and for once in her life was struck dumb. When he had gone she said quietly, 'What the hell is going on here?'

Joseph shook his head sadly as he answered her.

'He never got over his mother's going and he drags up the past all the time. I admit I wasn't always kind to her, Della, but it's hard on a man to have a bedridden wife nearly all his married life. And then on top of it all I was lumbered with *him* and all.'

He shook his head again and opened his arms wide to encompass her and the room.

'You don't know what all this means to me, Della. This life I have with you. No cooking and cleaning for a sick woman and a child who listened to every bad word she said about me. She put a gulf between me and him that Jesus Himself would be hard pushed to cross. She was jealous, and he is like her in that way. He knows I'm really happy for once in my life. Hates the fact that I have a good-looking real woman who I adore. He can't stand it so he came here and dragged up the past again. A past best left dead and buried.'

He looked defeated, shrunken, and Della's heart went out to him.

The compliments helped as well.

She was adored, was she?

Well, that was a first. Her misgivings forgotten, she put her arms around him and hugged him close.

'You've got me now, mate.'

He smiled as he said, 'I know that, Della, and I thank God for the fact every day of my life.'

As Tommy made his way home he felt the sickness rising inside him. He would not tolerate his mother being mentioned by that thug of a man. His mother had been good even if she was weak, and she had had to put up with that man and his bullying until she had died.

Well, there was more than one way to skin a cat and he would see to it that his father paid for those words and for what he had done in the past.

He had always watched Tommy like a hawk. Even today still reminded him of certain things so that he could keep him in his place.

Now, though, that was all out of the window. This was war. And if it were left to Tommy, he would win this war outright. Della was going to find out exactly what she had taken on.

The WPC looked at the photographs and sighed. This did not look good; it did not look good at all. In fact, it put a different complexion on everything.

She bagged up the photos and took Maurice Delray's phone number and address. Then, clutching the bag tightly to her chest, she left Supa Snaps.

Penny Cross watched her leave and wondered if she had done the right thing. Joanie was a good mate in her way, and Penny was sure that those terrible photographs could not have had anything to do with her. But then her natural gossipy ways came to the fore. Plus, she reasoned, Joanie *was* on the game. That type of thing was probably her stock in trade.

She picked up the phone and started to ring around her cronies to see what they made of it all.

After all, the photographs would soon be common knowledge anyway.

Chapter Thirteen

Maurice Delray was nervous. His mother Oleta was staring at him like he had just grown another head. Her shock was absolute. She felt a wave of hot fear wash over her, and it was all because of the policeman in their front room. He looked so incongruous standing there in his uniform in their clean and tidy home. Oleta was terrified that her Maurice was in some kind of trouble.

As she looked at her son she saw the strain in his face and the terror in his eyes. If he was going down the same road as his brother Wendell then she was going to have to be harder than she had ever been before but she would save this child of hers from the path of wrongdoing.

Wendell was doing eighteen years for armed robbery, as lost to her now as if she was still in St Lucia and he back living with a father who had never done an honest day's work in his life.

She had tried to make a good life for them all once she'd reached England but it had been hard. Wendell had never been one to take orders from anybody. He was his father's son in that respect.

Now she worked twelve hours a day in the canteen of a factory in Barking and she was buying her little flat and sending her youngest son Maurice to college. She had turned them around, made a decent life for them separate from the one her husband had chosen. And she was reaping the benefits of her hard-won lifestyle in her son Maurice. So what was all this about? She was practically wringing her hands with terror and disappointment.

'What do you want?'

Maurice's voice was quivering with fear and tension. The West

Indian inflection was there, barely discernible but there nonetheless. The policeman guessed it was due to nerves.

'We want to talk to you about Kira Brewer.'

Maurice saw his mother's face blanch.

He didn't know who the girl was, he said, had never seen her in his life. The policeman showed him her picture then.

'She's the little girl who went missing. You must have seen it on the news or in the newspapers?'

It was then that the PC realised there was no TV in this room, only a small portable radio. The place was pristine, so clean it was shining. The sofa and chairs still had the original plastic covers on them and the carpet had a runner going round it to keep it clean.

All the walls had religious prints on them, beautifully tinted in pastel shades. They each showed Jesus looking handsome and blond, His eyes looking up towards the heavens.

The boy nodded slightly.

'Did you see her in Supa Snaps on Saturday?'

The boy pondered for a moment, aware that this was an important question and giving it his full attention.

He shook his head.

'No, I didn't see her in there. I would have remembered. But the name of the person who brought the film in to be developed would be on the envelope.'

The policeman nodded.

'But there was no envelope, you see. We wondered if maybe you had done the photographs as a favour for a friend or relative?'

Maurice shook his head once more.

'No. I wouldn't do anything like that. I could lose my job.'

The policeman believed him; there was an innate honesty in this boy which shone through. Either that or he was a very good actor but the PC didn't think that was the case. The boy had nearly had a heart attack on seeing him there.

Most of the kids he dealt with lied as a matter of course, and lied well. He saw the boy's mother relax as he answered the questions in his clear and concise way. He was glad she wouldn't have any trouble, she looked a nice woman.

'Can you come down to the station with me, son? Just to eliminate you, fingerprints and that.'

The boy nodded, but he clearly wasn't happy about it.

'We can send an unmarked car for him, if you want?'

The PC realised that the mother had no idea what he meant.

'I mean, Mrs Delray, we can send a normal-looking car instead of the police car. That way no one will know where he's going.'

He saw the thanks in her face. The neighbours were all important to her and he understood that. This woman was still trying to live down Wendell. The copper knew all about him but was shrewd enough not to let on about it.

Maurice smiled at his mother and she smiled back.

Sometimes the PC hated his job, but he tried to make it as easy as possible for the people he had to deal with. He was in the minority at his station and not the most popular guy on the block. Most of his colleagues saw it as their mission in life to make life as hard as possible for everyone and anyone who was not Old Bill.

But seeing this woman's face now it was worth every second of the aggravation not to be that sort of policeman.

Della was worried by the way she had seen Joseph behave to his own son. When she had thought about it later, she concluded that she had not been told the whole story. He had not even given her the bare bones of what had happened between them. He had bullshitted her with that love and adore bit. She wanted to know what it was really about.

Now she was pestering him, though, he was getting upset once more. She could see the anger build in him.

'Just leave it, Della. It's family business.'

'I am your family now, aren't I?'

He sighed and wiped his large hand across his sweating face. He looked nervous and angry, a lethal combination with Joseph Thompson but she wasn't to know that. She still pushed the issue, unaware of what she was risking.

'But what did you mean when you said, "Tell her, Tommy. Go on, I dare you"?' She was determined to get to the bottom of it all.

'I didn't mean anything.'

Della was not to be put off.

'Well, it must have meant *something*. That's not a statement you make unless there is something to tell.'

Joseph grabbed her arm and shoved her towards the sofa.

'It didn't mean anything! I was just upset. Now can we drop the fucking subject? Fuck me, girl, what was your last job? Giving out the food parcels in Auschwitz?'

She had never in her life been spoken to like this before. As she lay on the sofa it occurred to her that Joseph wasn't so amenable as she had first thought. In fact, he was dangerous, looked capable of really harming her.

As she stared up at him her eldest daughter came in at the back door. Della had never been so glad to see anyone in her life.

Della's eldest daughter Patricia was her father's girl: short, dumpy and very meek. Her own three daughters were like their grandmother: outgoing and loud enough to be heard when it mattered.

'What's going on, Mum?'

Joseph was beseeching her with his eyes and against her better judgement Della covered things up. She didn't want anyone to know that all in the garden was anything other than lovely.

'Nothing, love. Put the kettle on.'

Pat did as she was told, but there was something not right here and she knew it. More to the point so did the girls.

They all stared at their new granddad with wide eyes except the youngest, Aurora, who jumped straight on his lap for a cuddle.

Only today the sight didn't fill Della with happiness; it made her uneasy and she wasn't sure why.

Joseph's temper was bubbling away under the surface and that worried her.

It worried her a great deal.

Lorna was outside Jon Jon's block of flats when he walked past without seeing her. Her heavy belly seemed to be weighing her down and she puffed as she tried to catch up with him.

'Jon Jon!'

He stopped deliberately by the kerb and waited for her to catch him up.

'What?'

It was a question and also a dismissal. She was not at all sure she was doing the right thing now. He looked down into the face that had just missed being pretty.

'I ain't got all fucking day, Lorna.'

She bit on her lip before answering him and it made her look very young. He had a glimpse of the girl under the makeup and veneer of hardness for a few seconds. He saw his own sister if she wasn't careful. Jeanette was going the same way as this piece of filth only she was too stupid to see it.

'I heard a bit of gossip . . . I thought you should be told.'

He laughed at her.

'What am I now then, a fucking fishwife? Do I look like you?'

She shook her head as she said, 'It's to do with your sister. Your sister Kira, I mean.'

Jon Jon was all ears now.

'What about her?'

Lorna was still not sure if she was doing the right thing. She wanted brownie points with Jon Jon but maybe this was not the way to go about it. Earl was bibbing from the car and she knew Jon Jon was in a hurry. She needed to state her case as quickly as she could.

She kept telling herself that her cousin wasn't a spinner so what she had told Lorna was as near the truth as to make no difference.

'Well, out with it then?'

She was frightened as she said, 'It's Little Tommy Thompson.'

Jon Jon sighed as he said pointedly, 'And?'

'He's been done for noncing before.'

Jon Jon wiped a hand over his face.

'You been talking to Monica?'

She shook her head.

'No. Jon Jon, I heard this from me cousin, Carly Lanesborough. She knows him from when they lived over in Bermondsey.'

He grabbed her arm.

'Get in the car!'

He pushed her inside and she landed in the back awkwardly, her huge belly making her movements clumsy.

'Drive! We're going to Bermondsey.'

Earl drove.

He didn't even question what was going on, he would know soon enough. That was the good thing with Jon Jon. There were no long drawn-out discussions, you just went and did what you had to do.

Carly lived in a nice little flat with her husband Colin. She was the antithesis of her cousin and Jon Jon was glad about that. If he had had to endure another Lorna he might not have hung on to his precarious patience. As she made them all coffee, Carly filled him in on what she knew.

'I was over your way visiting when I saw about your sister like. Everyone knows about it anyway, with the news and all.'

He nodded.

She was trying to justify gossiping, he could understand that.

'Anyway, I heard about this Tommy, and if it's the same bloke as the one I knew, he was accused of noncing a young girl. Nothing came of it, I'd better state that now.' She put up her hands as she said it. 'But he was accused by the girl's family and moved away afterwards with his father. No one knew where, they just disappeared like. But if it is him then it's a big coincidence, ain't it?'

Jon Jon nodded.

'Tell me what you know about him, Carly. What did he look like?'

'He was a big fat geezer, and he lived with his dad. They weren't around here that long. He used to have a load of dolls and that, and some of the kids used to go in his flat and play with them.'

Jon Jon could feel his heart racing at her words.

'Anyway, one little girl said she was touched and that was that. As you can imagine the neighbours were all out for them then, but the next thing we knew the complaint was withdrawn and they fucked off and no one thought any more about it until this all happened.'

'Do you know why the complaint was dropped?'

She shook her head.

'I did hear tell it was because it was the dad's girlfriend's grand-daughter or niece or something, but you know what gossip's like. Anyway, they live over by Canary Wharf now in the council flats. The name was Rowe, and that's about all I know.'

Baxter stared at the photographs and felt his heart lurch. Of all the things he had anticipated, these had never figured.

He looked down at them once more and saw a Kira he had never expected to see. She looked so far removed from the child in the school picture it was unbelievable. Plastered in makeup, she looked like a grown woman but it was the eyes that commanded his attention.

She looked all-knowing.

She looked like she was offering a good time, looked like an eleven-year-old ancient.

She looked like her mother.

This was a born-again Joanie and that was the real shock. He felt as if he had been punched in the stomach, as if the breath had been forced from his body. No way was he expecting anything like this. But it was the thought of talking to Joanie that was worrying him most.

If these denoted what he thought they did then Joanie was either very much in the dark or she was a better actress than any Academy Award winner.

He stared at the photos once more. He could not believe what he was seeing.

Jeanette was packing up her few bits and pieces and going home to her mother. She was glad to be going back, truth be told. Jasper knew how she felt and in fairness to him he understood. If he could have, he would have lived somewhere else as well. Karen was not someone you would choose to spend any time with. Now that the drink had got her she was a nightmare.

As Jeanette packed, Jasper's mother gave her a running commentary on everyone's opinion about her sister's disappearance.

Not sparing a second's thought for Jeanette's feelings, she said, 'She's dead, love, sure as sure.'

The girl closed her eyes for a moment in distress.

'Do you mind, Karen? That's my little sister you are talking about.'

The words were clipped, rude, and this did not go unnoticed by Karen Copes who was at the stage of drunkenness where she was just looking for something like this to happen.

'I'm only telling you what I heard.'

The words were slurred and barely intelligible. Karen was having trouble focusing her eyes and blinked as she tried to front up to Jeanette. She noticed inconsequentially how tidy the room was now. Jeanette had cleaned it from top to bottom and this annoyed Karen for some reason. It was like a slur on her and her house.

'Too good for us these days, ain't you?'

Jeanette didn't answer her, she knew it was pointless.

'Think your shit don't stink? Well, I heard your mother is for the high jump, lady. That little sister was being abused and she knew all about it.'

In one part of her brain Jeanette knew that it was just the drink talking, knew that this was Karen all over, spoiling for a fight. She always wanted to fight when she had had a drink and it was usually poor Junie who bore the brunt of it.

But she also knew that there was probably a grain of truth in the fact that there was a rumour. The rumours on the estate were always over the top, that was why people loved them so much. She had loved them herself when they were not about her family. Now, though, her honour was at stake but for Jasper she was willing to let the slur go. So she carried on packing even though the urge to fell this woman was foremost in her mind.

Karen took this for proof of what she had said.

'Nothing to say then? The truth hurt, does it?'

'Why don't you shut the fuck up, Karen?'

She laughed so hard she had to support herself against the doorjamb.

'Going home to Mother of the Year, are we? Joanie the brass.'

Jeanette closed her eyes and attempted to hold on to her temper. She could say what she liked about her own mother but no one else was going to. Not in Jeanette's hearing anyway.

'If you were half the mother mine is you'd be all right, Karen.'

The bait had been taken and Karen was over the moon. She had been determined to get a reaction and now she had got one.

They stared at each other for long moments, the air heavy with animosity.

'I might have my faults but at least I'm there for my kids.'

'Your kids loathe you! You are a joke, the local drunk. On a man it's bad enough but on a woman it's disgusting.'

Jeanette's words were spoken low and vehemently. Karen knew the girl really meant what she was saying.

'My mother, for all her faults, is a good woman, a decent person. And do you know something? Unlike your kids we love our mother. Anything she's ever done was for us, for our benefit, and we know that even if you don't!'

'If your mother is so fucking marvellous then why is your sister on the missing list?'

In part of her mind Karen knew she was being unfair, knew that what she was saying was evil, hateful, but still she said it. This girl was not leaving without a row, Karen was determined on that much. She was like everyone else. They all thought that they were so clever, so fucking great, when they were no better than she was.

They all lived on this poxy council estate and they all barely survived, dreaming of the day the council moved them somewhere better, although by then the damage had already been done. The kids were out of hand and the parents had split up or grown too used to this environment to survive anywhere else.

It was laughable the way some of them still put on their airs and graces, with their fucking flat-screen TVs and their gardening programmes. This was the arsehole of the world and the sooner they realised it the better.

She had heard about Jon Jon talking of buying a house. Who the fuck did he think he was? Who the fuck did any of the Brewers think they were, this one included?

'You'd better take that back, Karen.'

She laughed.

'The truth hurts, don't it? Your sister is missing, ain't she? Or have I missed something? Perhaps she was just mislaid, is that it?'

Jeanette licked her lips as she watched the harridan before her spew out her malice. It was as if she had burst a canker and all the vile putrid pus was running out of this woman's mouth in hateful words.

Jeanette realised that she could have been anyone. That Karen was ready to blow and she was merely today's unlucky target. But it was so spiteful what she was saying, and so unfair to her mother who, whatever Jeanette thought of her privately, had taken good care of them in her own way.

'Ain't the cards told your mother where the little girl is then? She makes a fortune off everyone else with her readings. Can't she consult the Tarot and get the address where that poor child actually is?'

Jeanette was holding on to herself but it was taking every scrap of effort she possessed. Jasper's mother was still standing only *because* she was Jasper's mother. No other reason. If she had been anyone else Jeanette would have wiped the floor with her by now.

But Karen Copes wasn't finished yet. In fact, she was just getting started.

'I'm amazed *you* ain't been collared for a stint on the pavement. I mean, it runs in the family, don't it? Whoring is the family business – even your granny was flashing her clout to all and sundry. Yet you put yourself above me and mine? Not one of you knows who your father was. Not one of you has any idea where you come from. You're all fucking mongrels, scum, the lot of you!'

She picked up her cigarettes and lit herself one, pulling on it heavily before she said in a conversational tone, 'Is that what happened to Kira then? Been bashed out, has she, and didn't come home?'

It wasn't just the words that sent Jeanette over the top, it was the smirk that accompanied them. The blow when it landed was harder than anything Karen had experienced in her life.

Karen Copes had been clumped by everyone within her orbit at some time or other. Husband, children, friends and family had all been driven to hit her at some point because of her bad mouth. But she had never taken what she was taking now off anyone.

It was as if Jeanette was possessed. All her worry and fear and hurt lay behind every blow and every kick. All the words that had just been spoken were in her mind as she attacked this woman who had inadvertently given her an excuse to vent her emotions. When Jeanette had finished she looked at the bloody body on the floor and started to cry. What had she done? How could she go home to Joanie now with more trouble to lay at her door? She couldn't, it wouldn't be fair to her mother. Not now. Jeanette had just set the seal on her own continued exile and she hated herself for it.

Then she saw Junie watching her and held out her hands in supplication. She hadn't even known the girl was in the house.

'She pushed me, Junie, she pushed me too far.'

Jasper's sister nodded nonchalantly. She had seen it all before.

'She'll survive. Get yourself out of here for a bit while I call an ambulance. I'll look after her, don't worry.'

In fact, Junie hated her mother more at this moment than she had ever hated her before. But then, she had heard every vicious word Karen had said.

Sylvia had all the records of Paulie's businesses. She had been through the three safes he kept at home and was perusing these pieces of paper as if they were gold dust. Which, of course, to her they were.

She had had him followed for months, and now knew everything about him. The association with the Brewer woman had amazed her, though. Knowing his penchant for younger women she had actually felt a moment's jealousy of this prostitute who, it seemed, had her husband's ear. Even her son worked for him.

Now the woman's child was missing and that was terrible.

Whatever Sylvia was she was still a mother.

She saw her own children as an investment in the future. All the time she had them she was safe. It meant she had something over Paulie's head. Something to keep the money rolling in.

She knew everything there was to know about her husband, and the old saying that knowledge is power had never seemed so true. If he played ball, as she was sure he would, then she would accept a settlement and agree to take a back seat and forget what she knew. If he wouldn't then she would give all her information to the relevant authorities and take her chances.

But she wasn't too worried about that prospect. Paulie knew which side his bread was buttered and so did she. Sylvia shook her head as she glanced through the papers then she put them all away. The girls were at her mother's for a few weeks until everything calmed down.

Sylvia ran herself a bath and lay in the hot water, luxuriating in the solitude and the aroma of ylang-ylang.

As she lay there she closed her eyes and hummed a little tune. She loved this house, but she loved it most when she was alone in it. That was something Paul had never understood, her need for solitude sometimes, her need to be alone.

He had learned, though. She had made a point of teaching him manners, as she put it to herself. If it had been left to him she would have ended up like one of those dreadful women his business associates were married to – over-the-hill blonde bimbos whose husbands had women all over the place and who could only talk about their villas and their sun beds and their stupid children.

Well, that was not for Sylvia. She was not going to end her days with a man who had no social graces and even less personality than the Labrador dog he had thankfully buried in the garden two years previously. It was the only time he had ever gone against her, when the girls had wanted a dog. They had plagued her, and she had said no, and then one day he had come back from a friend's scrapyard with the puppy in a cardboard box.

The girls had been all over him that day and Sylvia had learned a valuable lesson. Never let them believe he had their best interests at heart, it must all seem to come from her. Consequently, the girls had always believed that he'd had no intention of getting them horses, that their mother had had to talk him into it.

She smiled as she thought of it.

'All right, Sylv?'

Her eyes flew open as she heard her husband's voice. For a split second she thought she was hallucinating. But there he was in the doorway of the en-suite, looking quite at ease in these surroundings despite the injunction banning him from the house. She sat up, the force of her movement making water slosh all over the floor.

'Oh, Sylv, that's not like you, making a mess, is it?'

She was stunned.

'Now get your fat arse out of the bath and get it down those stairs so we can have a talk.'

Her face was all lines now, her consternation evident.

He looked her body over as she sat there and made sure she realised what he thought.

'Fuck me, Sylv, you do look rough in the buff!'

He laughed at his own silly rhyme, knowing he was annoying the life out of her and enjoying every second.

Chapter Fourteen

The old woman answered the door and stared at her visitor with naked animosity. Jon Jon knew instinctively that this was someone who had had more fights than Mike Tyson and probably won most of them.

'Excuse me, I'm looking for the Rowe family and someone said they lived here.'

Jon Jon was smiling his best smile, but he could tell by the way that she was looking back at him that his bright friendly expression might not be enough. He had a feeling she was not into political correctness. She saw a black man and that was it. She probably thought muggers were touting for business on the knocker these days.

'Who wants to know?'

It was a deep voice, a real Cockney voice, and coming as it did from this tiny woman in front of him it made him want to smile. She was real old school Cockney and proud of it.

Jon Jon knew the best thing to do was to treat her like she was treating him so he said without preamble, '*I* want to know, Mrs Rowe.'

That was the law of the street round this way and he understood it. Then he said, more quietly and respectfully, 'I am Jon Jon Brewer. My little sister is missing, Kira, it's been on the news and that.'

She nodded slowly, still eyeing him up and obviously finding him lacking.

'What has that got to do with us?'

She was so suspicious Jon Jon wondered how the fuck she ever got her meters read. He had a feeling he would have a better chance of getting into the Bank of England on a Sunday afternoon than he did of setting his foot across this old dear's front doorstep. He also had a feeling that it was because of the colour of his skin. He was used to that now, but it still annoyed him.

He tried again in his best voice.

'I was told you had had dealings with a certain Little Tommy . . .'

The door was shutting in his face now and he pushed out an arm and a foot to stop her.

'Please, Mrs Rowe, this is important.'

'Get your bleeding foot out of my door, Sonny Jim.'

She was game and he admired her for that much anyway. But she was also starting to annoy him.

If she knew what could have happened to Kira then she was going to tell him even if he had to beat it out of her. And he would do that and all, old woman or no old woman. He wanted to know and he wanted to know now. He had been keeping a lid on his emotions but it was getting harder and harder by the hour. Jon Jon sighed and forced the door open as he did so.

Earl came into view and she looked him up and down aggressively. Jon Jon could not help liking her. He would lay money that in her day she'd been a force to be reckoned with. Probably still was.

'Open the door, lady, please.'

Jon Jon's voice was low, almost pleading with her.

'I ain't got nothing to tell you.'

She planted herself in front of him, arms crossed, her body language speaking volumes.

He sighed once more. This time his voice was louder and far more authoritative.

'Well, I think you have. Your daughter or grand-daughter or whatever was supposedly nonced by that cunt and I want to know what happened. I ain't going nowhere until I find that out.'

He had made his point, he knew there was no sense in labouring it. They stared each other out. Mrs Rowe was small, almost birdlike. She had grey hair which had once been black scraped into a bun, and wore large gold hoops in her ears. She was wearing enough tomfoolery to open a jeweller's shop, rings, bangles, and necklaces – so many necklaces she looked like Mr T's little sister.

She wore an overall pinafore, the type that fastened at the side to keep her clothes clean while she worked. But it was her face that fascinated Jon Jon most: it was wrinkled up in all the wrong places. She looked like a little spider monkey, her brown eyes filled with either cunning or intelligence. He wasn't sure which yet but he was going to find out.

'Now we can do this the nice way or the nasty way, Mrs Rowe. It's up to you.'

He looked aggressive enough to make her think twice about what she was doing. She stared him out for a few seconds more before grudgingly opening the door wide enough for him to pass her.

'*He* ain't coming in.'

She nodded at Earl who grinned.

'Don't want to, love.' He looked at Jon Jon. 'I'll be in the car, OK?'

Jon Jon nodded.

'Sure you'll be all right? The woman looks vicious.'

'Fucking smart arse!'

She was annoyed but it was a friendly animosity now. She had taken what Earl had said as a compliment. Mrs Rowe walked into the flat without another word, her back stiff and her manner still unfriendly.

Jon Jon followed her, wiping his feet on the mat and shutting the door gently behind him. Inside he could smell scones cooking, a homely smell that suited the surroundings.

In the tiny front room there was a two-seater sofa and an easy chair, a tiled fireplace with an ancient gas fire, and a hand-built red-brick shelving unit to one side that held an old portable TV and an ancient radio.

It also held photographs of three smiling girls, all blonde and blue-eyed. He guessed one of them was the child in question.

Above the fireplace was a painting of a crying boy. The walls were papered in burgundy flock and the dado rail was chipped and yellowed from the gas fire.

Jon Jon felt the powerlessness of old age in this room and it made him upset. The poor old bag had lived through a world war for *this* – a poxy flat that was damp, dilapidated and overdue for knocking down while warehouses along from here were being stripped out and sold for hundreds of thousands as yuppy 'lofts'.

He smiled at her with an effort. Fear for his sister was overriding everything else in his life. He had been keeping it together for his mother's sake but he was on the edge and no amount of cannabis would change that.

The old woman stared at him again and he could practically feel her sizing him up, but the funny thing was he liked her more every time she blanked him. She had heart and he knew that whatever she said would be the truth.

'Want a cup of tea?'

It was said grudgingly, good manners overtaking her innate racism. He nodded. Anything to get her talking without having to resort to violent language or behaviour. He had the distinct feeling he was the first black person to step across her doorstep in the whole of her long life.

'Sugar and milk?'

He nodded again, and when finally she was settled by her fireside with a mug of tea he spoke once more.

'I really need your help, Mrs Rowe. You must know about me sister – Kira Baxter? She's only eleven and she's missing. Well, I heard off one of your old neighbours that some bloke who lives near me now was accused of noncing by someone in your family. This is really important, Mrs Rowe, because he might know what's happened to Kira . . . might know where she is.'

She looked him over, her natural animosity coming to the fore once more. Finally, after what seemed an age, she spoke.

'My big boy, my eldest, is doing thirty years: drugs and armed robbery. His wife Leigh, a trollop of the first water, lived nearby.'

She sipped her tea to give herself time to phrase this carefully.

'She started to leave the girls with this Little Tommy Thompson. Anyway, the next thing we knew she had taken up with his old man, Joseph.'

She sipped at her tea again, playing for time once more. Jon Jon guessed it was hard for this woman to talk about her family to a stranger.

'Her middle girl, Caitlin, was always round there – she loved it, you couldn't keep her away. Then she said that she had been touched like, physically. But we never got to the bottom of it, see. She never said who it was, the father or the son, all we knew was she said it had happened. Leigh kept us out of it all. Didn't want anyone to know, see, because of me boy. He was well banged up by then but Leigh knew he would still want answers so she went on the trot with the kids. He loved them girls . . . whatever *he* was, he loved them. But their mum – he hadn't long got sentenced and already she was out more often than the local tom. It was fear of him finding out how careless she'd been with the kids that sent her on her way. She was gone overnight and so was they, the Thompsons. They knew once it got out they couldn't stay round here. Shit sticks, don't it? And I ain't seen none of them since. They all went on the trot, mate.'

Mrs Rowe sighed heavily.

'No one knows where Leigh and me grandkids went. It's my guess someone gave her a wedge to go, and believe me, son, she wanted to. She wanted out of it all. I can understand that in some ways. My boy wasn't the easiest of husbands, a violent sadistic bastard like his old man, but like I said, we never got to the bottom of any of it, see. The only people who know what really happened are Leigh, her daughter and the blokes concerned. And let's face it, they ain't going to say anything, are they?'

She sat back in the chair as if tired out from all the talking. He guessed rightly that visitors were few and far between for her. She spent her days visiting her son or waiting for letters from him. It was a terrible existence for anyone, especially a proud woman like her.

'And you have no idea where Leigh is?'

The old woman shook her head.

'What I can tell you, though, is I never liked the father or the son, but out of the two give me the boy every time. He was treated like shit and he swallowed all that he was given. I couldn't say much, see, about the situation because my daughter-in-law was already trying to get out of my son's life and that meant getting out of mine as well. I had to be careful what I said like because I knew she wanted shot. I'd lost me son, and then I lost me grandkids as well. What's left for me now, eh?'

She could see the answering fear in this boy's eyes and offered him a crumb of comfort.

'I have her mother's address. I don't know if she's still living there but if she is she'll know where her daughter is. Closer than close, them two. She won't tell me fuck all and I have given up trying. Thinks I'll tell me son, which in fairness I probably would. But if you find out anything for sure, let me know, would you?'

He nodded.

''Course I will, mate. How are you coping without your son?'

She shrugged.

'Best I can, what else can you do?'

'Are his mates seeing you all right?'

It was the law of the street: you looked after the family of friends banged up. They had lost a wedge and you provided it for them.

'Look around you, son, what do you think?'

She went into the bedroom and came back with an envelope, the address written neatly on it.

'I ain't got no phone number for them and I don't know if they're still here but you can give it a try.' She sat back down before saying quietly, 'If you find me grandkids, let me know how they are, OK?'

His heart went out to her. She was obviously missing them.

'I promise I will.'

He stood up. Taking both her hands in his, he said: 'Thank you, Mrs Rowe. I really appreciate your help.'

She smiled then, for the first time, and he knew he had finally won her over.

'I was no help really, son. But I hope you find your little sister.'

He took out a wad of money and peeled off five hundred quid. She eyed the notes hungrily.

'Treat yourself, mate.'

She seized the money in her claw-like hands.

'I won't knock it back, son, I appreciate it.'

He wrote down his mobile number and gave it to her.

'If you hear anything, Mrs Rowe, give me a bell.'

She nodded.

'And if you ever need anything, you use that number, you hear?'

She nodded once more, knowing that he meant what he said.

'I wish you luck with your search.'

He sighed.

'If it was left to the filth we'd still be none the wiser.'

'Always the way with them.'

Spoken with the voice of experience.

She saw him out of the flat and he shook her hand once more.

'Take care, Mrs Rowe.'

'And you, son, best of British.'

She didn't shut the door straight away but watched him to his car, waved and finally went inside. He was a nice boy. Respectful. She would tell her Harold all about him on the next visit.

She hugged the money to her chest then looked at the clock. If she got a move on she could still make the bookie's before the last race.

Paulie was enjoying the look of fear on his wife's face. It was years since he had even remotely felt that he had the upper hand. Virtually all their married life Sylvia had been the mother of his children. He had respected her for that much, if for nothing else.

Now, though, he hated her. Whatever he was, he had always taken care of her and she should have known he would have taken care of her and his kids for ever. If she had wanted to leave that badly, he would have got over it. He would have seen them all OK, kept up the school fees and everything else. But instead she had caused trouble. Serious aggravation. Did she think he was so stupid he'd swallow that?

He saw the table set for one. She was going to have a marathon lunch as usual. Sylvia got through more food in the course of a day than most women did in a week. He opened the fridge. It was stacked with grub; just looking at it made him laugh.

When she finally came into the kitchen he was still laughing. She was wearing a thick dressing gown, belted tightly at the waist. The only thing missing was a No Entry sign. But that was hardly unusual for her. Her face was scrubbed, oily skin shiny in the daylight.

Paulie looked at her and wondered how she had ever come to belong to him. He must have had shit in his eyes. She felt as far from his life now as the Man in the Moon, but he was determined to stop her getting all her so-called rights.

'All belted up, are we, Sylv?'

'What do you want?'

So she had regained her voice, had she? She was speaking to him as if he was a servant or a shop assistant. Someone beneath her notice.

Paulie leaned back against the granite work surface and crossed his arms nonchalantly.

'Who you fucking talking to?'

She didn't answer. She knew by his voice that he was going to lose it at any moment. She kept quiet, just stared at him and waited for him to talk once more.

He knew the signs; she was good at this, was Sylvia. In the end you believed it was you who was in the wrong. She could keep up the silent treatment for days on end. She even did it to the girls.

'You'd better start talking, Sylv, because I ain't got all day. Me and you are going to sort this out, once and for all.'

He moved towards the sink and the action made her jump. It pleased him that he had frightened her. She needed a good scare did Sylvia. She needed a good hiding as far as he was concerned and if she wound him up today she was going to get one.

He put the kettle on.

She moved slowly towards the back door and he said quietly, without looking at her, 'You go near that panic button and I will rip your fucking tits off, you hear me?'

He turned to face her then and she nodded.

'Now you sit down and you talk to me properly, and if you attempt to talk down to me or try any of your tricks, me and you are going to fall out big-time, do you understand me?'

She nodded once more and sat at the table.

He placed a pot of tea there and two cups. As he poured the tea out, he said, 'Where are my daughters?'

'At the country house.'

He smiled sarcastically.

'It ain't a country house, Sylv, it's a mock-Tudor that happens to be in the country. Who's with them – your mother?'

She nodded.

'Oh, great. And is Morticia doing her usual good job of turning them against me – against all men, for that matter? Like she did with you?'

She didn't answer and he decided to leave it. He didn't care anyway.

'Now,' he sipped his tea noisily, 'you are going to get this house and the dump in the country, you are going to get a nice little earner to keep you in the manner to which you are accustomed, and you are going to accept the figure I decide. 'Cos if you don't, Sylv, I am going to make sure you end your days holding up a section of motorway somewhere near here. I ain't joking. You've pushed me to the limit this time. It's the sneaky underhanded way you pushed me out of my own home – and this *is* my home – and out of the girls' lives that really rankles. And do you know something, Sylv? I don't even like them girls. I love them but I don't like them. Pair of fucking madams, they are, but then you saw to that, didn't you?'

He slopped his tea as he picked it up, his anger evident.

'I've wanted shot for years, Sylv. You only had to ask, mate, and I'd have gone gladly.'

She was hurt now and didn't know why. His words cut her to the quick.

'What are you going to do – go to one of your whores?'

She was actually jealous! It amazed him even as it made him sad.

'Is that what all this is about? I went to them, Sylv, because you stopped any contact between us years ago. And I need a bit of affection, love, even if you don't. I provided for you and I provided well.'

'You provided for yourself, for your needs. What about mine?'

He was laughing at her words.

'*Your* needs? Your needs consist of a fridge full of grub, a cupboard full of sweets and crisps, and two children you can manipulate and dress up. You wanted a fuck-off house and you got one. You wanted a top-of-the-range Merc and you got one. You wanted a bespoke kitchen and you got one. That's your needs catered for, Sylv, and I provided it all, love. And what did I get out of it? I'll tell you what I got, shall I? Sweet fuck all as usual. Not even a bit of a leg over now and again. Not so much as a kind word off me kids – and they *are* my kids. Whatever you try and tell them, they are mine.'

She closed her eyes at his words and he almost felt sorry for her. The truth was a powerful weapon and he knew she couldn't cope with it.

'I ain't your fucking father, to be nagged to an early grave, poor old fucker. Your mother passed her own disappointment on to you, and you will pass it on to those girls, God help them. But I digress as usual.

'I will provide for you all, but if you ever pull a fucking stunt like this again, Sylv, I will see you with nix, fuck all. And I can do that. You should know me well enough by now.'

She had never seen him like this before, not with her anyway. He had always treated her with respect. But she'd hated him at times, hated his easy way with people and his easy acceptance of everything. People liked Paulie. At masonic dos or at parties she'd watched her friends come on to him. It was something about him.

She knew that they wondered what he saw in her, and the more overlooked she felt, the more she ate and the more she pushed him away until finally she grew to hate her own husband. She couldn't compete with the girls he slept with. How could she? They would do all the things she had never wanted to do. Why couldn't he just hold her sometimes? Why did every touch have to lead to sex? Sometimes she felt that as far as he was concerned she could have been anyone. All he needed was a hole to shove it in and he was happy.

Those women of his slept with men all day, it was how they made their money and he knew that, earned money off it, and yet still he could touch them intimately. Could still kiss them, want them. And now he dared to ask why she didn't want him touching her!

He was watching the changing expressions on her face and said tartly, 'What's the matter, Sylv? Am I taking up good eating time? It's about ten minutes since you stuck something in your gob, ain't it? You must be getting withdrawal symptoms by now.'

He knew he was hurting her deeply and yet couldn't stop himself. When she had had the police remove him from his own house any feelings he had had for her had disappeared. Now it was payback time and he was enjoying himself.

'My life is the girls . . .'

She was being sanctimonious once more; the old Sylv was back.

'The girls are all right and you know it! Fuck me, you just left them with the female equivalent of fucking Frankenstein. You think you're such a great mother, Sylv. Well, I know someone who has had none of the advantages you've had and her kids have turned out fine. Nice people who love her dearly. Now one of them is missing and she is going out of her mind and you couldn't even comprehend what her life is like. How it has affected her. Your idea of a problem is if one of the girls doesn't finish their homework. You should get out in the fucking real world, Sylv, with everyone else.'

'Go on the game, you mean?'

He laughed out loud at the words. Coming from her they sounded outrageous.

'It would be a fucking start, Sylv. At least then you would know what it was like to earn your own fucking money.'

He saw the tears in her eyes and still he didn't relent. He wanted out now, even more than she did.

'Don't you even care that a child is missing? You haven't asked if they've found her or wondered if she's all right. You're a mother, you should care about things like that. Fuck me, even I care!'

She shrugged then, her tone dismissive as usual.

'She'll turn up. Those kind of kids always do.'

'What do you mean, *those* kind of kids?'

His voice was low now and she was annoyed that he cared so much for a prostitute's child. She had heard about the mother. Who hadn't?

Her voice rising with each word, she said nastily, 'The kind of kids whose mother sleeps with men for remuneration. The kind of kids who drag themselves up. The kind of kids who are used to running the streets at all hours of the day and night. The kind of kids you so obviously prefer to your own daughters. And if she doesn't come back her mother can just have another one, can't she? That's what those type of people do, isn't it?'

He was still reeling from the word 'remuneration'. Only Sylvia could talk like that as if it was normal. How everyone spoke.

'You are fucking *sick*, Sylv, do you know that? The child could be dead and your own snobbery stops you from caring. Well, Joanie Brewer is a good woman, a better person than you could ever hope to be, and a better mother and all. Those children are a credit to her. And you know something else? I feel more at home round there in her council flat than I ever felt here.'

He stood up then. He had to get out before he physically hurt her.

'You can get back to your hobby now.'

He opened the fridge and threw all the food on to the floor, enjoying the mess, enjoying seeing her brought so low.

'Stuff your boatrace, girl, go for it. Have a cake on me. But remember what I said, Sylv: you push me and I'll see you with fuck all.'

He left her then and as he slammed the front door felt lighter than he had in years.

Joanie was listening to DI Baxter as he explained that they needed to ask her some more questions about her daughter. She nodded, her face devoid of expression as she concentrated on what he was going to say.

'Have you found her, Mr Baxter?'

She was terrified of the answer.

He shook his head.

'I need to ask you about some photographs we were given. We want you to tell us who took them if you can, and also tell us why they were taken.'

She nodded once more, not sure what he was talking about.

He placed the photographs on the table, laying them down

one by one. Joanie stared at the images of her baby, remembered when they had been taken, the fun they had had. Remembered her sudden fear at seeing Kira look so grown-up, so adult. It occurred to her then in a sickening moment of comprehension that this was why she was being questioned about them. They thought she was noncing her own child!

'My daughter Jeanette took them ages ago – months it was. She had dressed Kira up and put makeup on her. As you can see, she looked a lot older than her years.'

In her confusion and surprise she was babbling and knew that Baxter thought there was something sinister about the pictures. That there was some kind of a hidden agenda here she was not talking about.

'Mr Baxter, Jeanette took these pictures as a joke. You can't honestly think they were taken for any other reason?'

He didn't answer her. These were all he had to go on, and who was to say that the other daughter wasn't involved?

Joanie was a brass, ergo she would do anything for a few quid. Who was to say she herself hadn't rented this child out? She rented herself out often enough. He had to take this very easy, try to find a common ground. The pictures were also being looked at by a psychologist who specialised in this type of thing, though he privately wondered at a man who could look at this shit all day. It made Baxter feel sick just seeing Kira's smiling painted face. The child was clearly having the time of her life.

'You have to believe me, Mr Baxter, these were taken as a joke, no more. My Kira loved dressing up. Loved makeup and clothes, glittery girlie things. I was shocked when I saw her, after the photos were taken. She looked so grown-up like.'

Joanie was crying again and Baxter watched her carefully.

'Who took them into Supa Snaps on Saturday?'

She shook her head.

'I have no idea. Maybe Kira took them in herself?'

He shook his head as he said, 'It wasn't her. The film wasn't even in an envelope. No name, address, nothing.'

She looked non-plussed. Either Joanie was a good actress or she had no idea what was going on. He couldn't make up his mind which but he was going to find out.

Was she in such a state because her child was missing or because she'd had a hand in it? He had seen it time and time again. When you killed someone, deliberately or accidentally, guilt ate at you, and if the person you'd killed was a close relative you hid behind the tears people expected you to shed. Even felt you deserved the sympathy.

Now these pictures had put a different complexion on things. Children were unlikely to be murdered by a stranger. Statistically the chances were low, though it still happened. But they were usually killed by a relative or friend, someone they knew and trusted.

And he was sure now that Kira Brewer was dead. It was just a matter of finding her body and fingering the culprit. Which could very well turn out to be her grieving mother.

Chapter Fifteen

'They think we had something to do with her disappearance, Jon Jon.'

Joanie's voice was incredulous.

'Don't be stupid, Mum.'

She shook her head sadly.

'You weren't there. I had to sit through that ponce Baxter questioning me about photographs of Kira that were taken months ago. Jeanette put some makeup on her while she was dressing up one night and took a few photos. You wait until you see them, Kira looks about twenty. Anyway, Baxter and all his cronies think they were taken to titillate. Even got a psychologist on the band wagon.'

She sipped at her cup of tea.

'I'm on the game so to filth that means I have no morals whatsoever. It means I am capable of noncing me own daughter. What the fuck do they know? I told him straight – maybe if they had come out when I first rang they'd have located her by now. Over two hours I had to wait for them fuckers to finally come round here.'

She was crying again. Jon Jon felt the pain his mother was going through as if it was his own.

'They don't even know how the photos got in Supa Snaps, see. They weren't put in normal like, by all accounts. No name with them, nothing. But I said to him, if we was up to something like that we would hardly take the fucking things in there to get developed, would we? And do you know what he said, the cheeky fucker? He said, where would I have taken them then?'

'They have to ask, Mum.'

Jon Jon slumped on the sofa, his handsome face grey with worry.

'You'll be next to be questioned.'

He sighed.

'Well, we ain't got nothing to worry about, have we? If Jeanette took them as a joke they'll have to accept it eventually.'

Joanie finished her tea and lit up yet another cigarette.

'How could they even think we had something to do with her going missing, Jon Jon?'

He placed an arm around her shoulders.

'They have to look at every angle. It's what they do.'

He didn't mention that he was doing some investigating of his own. He would wait and see what he found out first. No need to worry her until he knew the score. He had been to Leigh's mother's house twice and found no one in so he was going back later this evening to catch them on the hop – always the best way to get information from people. Strike when they least expect it.

It didn't occur to him to share any of his knowledge with the police. This was personal, he wasn't about to let them fuck it up for him. If they caught whoever it was they would just lock them up, and what good was that to Jon Jon? He wanted retribution, and he was going to get it. That was why he had not mentioned anything to his mother. 'Sufficient to the time thereof.' He knew his Bible, he read it often enough thanks to Sippy and his teachings. 'An eye for an eye.' Yeah, he'd take the fucker's eyes out all right. The Bible gave good retribution, he liked the easiness of it. You fucked up, you paid the price. You covet my ox and I'll stamp on your head. It was, after all, still the law of the street. Two thousand years later he felt the Bible had more relevance to people like him than all the clergy and politicians in the world.

'Let me make you a sandwich, Mum, you must eat something.'

She shook her head.

'You have one, I couldn't eat a thing.'

He made her a sandwich anyway and tried to encourage her to eat it. Then he waited with her until Paulie came round to take over for the night. He had been a brick the last few days and Jon Jon knew his mother felt better when Paulie was around. He couldn't leave her with anyone else because she wouldn't take notice of anyone else.

Paulie kept her occupied. He had heard them having sex, and was glad. If it took her mind off what was going on, Jon Jon wouldn't mind if she took men on by the dozen. And Paulie cared about her. He tried to act like he didn't but it was clear for anyone to see who bothered to look. Jon Jon was sorry for them both really. In another life they would have settled down together and been happy.

He looked at Kira's photo once more and prayed to God to bring her home. He didn't hold out much hope that his prayers would be answered.

He left them a little later, his mother lying on the sofa and Paulie Martin waiting on her hand and foot.

It was a sight to see.

Jasper Copes and his friends were still searching for Kira. It was as if they were on a mission, Jasper feeling honour bound to help find Jeanette's sister.

Sippy and his friends were all still looking as well, and the number of BMWs out on the streets had doubled over the last twenty-four hours as other friends of Jon Jon's joined the search. The police were pleased with the turnout, giving them all designated areas to search, and for the first time ever they did as Old Bill asked.

The news crews loved it. Skinheads and Rastas working together with rude boys and casuals made for wonderful footage; everyone set their differences aside to look for the little girl. Kira Brewer had done more for race relations locally in a few short hours than any government could have accomplished in years.

But by now the searchers were aware that they were looking for a body as opposed to a living, breathing girl.

No one said that out loud, though.

When Sippy lit a joint while he helped search Victoria Park painstakingly the police didn't bat an eyelid. Everyone was working together for a common goal. Nothing else mattered.

Clubbers had joined in, pubs emptied as the news had gone round. And outside Joanie's flats people had laid flowers and messages of hope. But now time had run out and that was the hardest part for everyone concerned.

Leigh Rowe's mother was a big woman with bleached blonde hair and a cigarette permanently dangling from her lip. When she heard the knock on her door she assumed it was kids. The ones where she lived were bastards and saw it as their aim in life to hassle the fuck out of everyone around them. Knock Down Ginger was practically the only game round these parts.

She opened the door in a short black lace dressing gown and a scowl, cigarette still hanging from her lip, and when she saw Earl and Jon Jon was not in the least fazed. It was twelve at night and she answered the door as if it was the early afternoon.

'What?'

Her face was hard and closed.

Earl looked at Jon Jon and shrugged.

'Well? Is this a social call or what?'

She removed the cigarette from her lip and flicked it expertly into the road.

'Are you Mandy Costner?'

She looked Jon Jon over as if it was a rat standing on her doorstep.

'Who wants to fucking know?'

Jon Jon had had enough of East End hard nuts. Pushing her back into the hallway he bellowed, '*Me!* I want to fucking know.'

Earl followed him into the house, laughing gently to himself.

'Well, he ain't in!'

She was trying to push them back outside. Jon Jon and Earl realised she thought they were debt collectors after her old man.

'We ain't here for money, we're just trying to locate your daughter . . .'

She was panting with exertion now.

'What do you want her for? Did that Harold send you? Only if he did, I don't know where she is.'

The front room door opened and a big man with a bald head, large shoulders and an even larger belly stepped into the narrow hallway.

'What the fuck is going on here?'

Jon Jon had had enough of it all.

'Get back in there! Earl, shut the fucking door. And you . . .' he pointed at the woman . . . 'shut the fuck up and go in the lounge and let me get to the bastard point.'

They stared at him stupidly until Earl said gently, 'Do what he says. He really ain't in the mood for being fucked about.'

'You come in my house and start ordering us about . . .'

The big man was annoyed and Earl and Jon Jon understood that. Jon Jon, however, had wasted enough time. He pushed and prodded both of them into the lounge. Earl followed him and turned the key. They knew now they were locked in here with two apparent madmen. It was all part of gaining the psychological advantage.

Inside the room the couple stared at them in trepidation. Jon Jon sighed heavily.

'I'm not here on Harold's behalf, though I do want to find your daughter.'

The man and woman looked at each other sceptically.

'Is that right?' Mandy's voice was flat now, all fear gone. 'And is that a pig flying over the top of the house?'

She lit another cigarette slowly, pulling in the smoke before she spoke once more. 'It's always to do with Harold. He beat the shit out of her and he enjoyed it. What that girl had to put up with . . .'

She pulled on the cigarette again.

'I don't care if you've got guns, you can shoot me and I still ain't telling you fuck all. So you are wasting your time.'

It was her final word.

The man sat back in a chair by the fireside and started to roll a cigarette for himself.

'She's right, mate, my daughter had enough from him while he was on the out. We ain't telling you nothing about her, no matter what.'

Jon Jon sat down on the sofa and said in his friendliest voice, 'I swear, mate, I don't even know Harold.'

'What do you want then?'

The man licked the Rizla as he asked this. It was evident he was completely uninterested in the answer.

'My sister is called Kira Brewer. She's missing.'

He saw them exchange glances.

'We're sorry about it but what has that got to do with us?'

It was Mandy talking now and her voice was gentler.

Jon Jon took a deep breath before saying, 'Your daughter accused a bloke of noncing her daughter Caitlin. Well, this same bloke, Little Tommy Thompson, used to look after my sister.'

They looked at one another again. The man barked at his wife, 'Make a cup of tea, Mandy.'

She nodded and left the room, Earl following her. They weren't stupid, no one was going anywhere on their Jacksy tonight.

'So what have you got to say then?'

Jon Jon waited as the man eyed him up. He understood this caution. He had heard all about Harold Rowe and he was a nasty piece of work. Jon Jon knew he needed to gain their trust but all this piss-balling about was starting to irritate him.

'Caitlin was nine when she accused him. She used to go round there with the other kids, see. Leigh had taken up with the father, though what she saw in him I don't know – he was as old as me! But after Harold I suppose anyone seemed a better bet. Cunt he was – broke her nose, her arm, punctured a lung once. Accused her of all sorts he did – jealous bastard. But Harold was also shrewd and when he got banged up it got worse. She had calls at all hours of the day and night, from so-called friends of his. You know the score. Keep the grass widow company – whether she wants it or not.'

Jon Jon nodded.

'Anyway, he had a few quid this Joseph – compensation or something, I don't know – and he was gonna take them all away. Then that all fell out of bed, don't ask me why, and that's when it came out about Caitlin. They didn't go to plod or nothing. There was a few rows, I clumped the old man naturally. Then Leigh got a place and she went, and the Thompsons had to leave because it was too hot for them round here.'

Jon Jon nodded.

'So who exactly did she accuse?'

'First the father and then the son, as I remember, and then it turned out they were both at it, see. What a fucking pair of scumbags, eh? And that fat geezer like butter wouldn't melt, though I must admit I had me reservations about him from the off. Fucking dolls! What geezer plays with fucking dolls unless they're a bit doolally tap?' He pointed at his temple to emphasise what he said.

'We never really got to the bottom of it. Leigh only told us the bare bones as and when she found out about it. Only natural really when you think about it. Who wants people to know their kids have been nonced?'

'And where is she now?'

The man grinned.

'Sorry, son, I ain't telling you fuck all about her whereabouts. She had a right old time off Harold Rowe and I ain't ever taking the chance of his finding her. He'd kill her – or get someone to do for her anyway. Sorry.'

Jon Jon understood; he would be protective of his own sister or daughter.

Mandy came back in with the teas and she was laughing; she and Earl had obviously got along fine.

'What was this money Joseph was supposed to have?'

Jon Jon was wondering if it had come from child porn or some such skulduggery.

'He gave our Leigh a wedge to stop her involving Old Bill and I told her to take it. I said, "You take it, girl, and fuck off out of it all." And that's what she did. Right or wrong, that's what she did.'

Earl could see the logic but it was Jon Jon who hit the nail on the head when he said, 'But if he was a nonce, why didn't she stop him from being able to do it again? My sister is missing, maybe even dead, because your daughter didn't tell anyone. She let him get away.'

Mandy had the grace to look ashamed but said unrepentantly, 'You don't know Harold. When Joseph offered her that money it was like a gift from God. She needed it to get shut of her husband once and for all.'

Jon Jon was appalled and it showed.

'So she used her own daughter's abuse to do that, did she?'

He shook his head in disgust.

'Do you know something? People like you make me sick. If your daughter had taken this to the authorities, my sister might still be around.'

He could feel violent anger bubbling up inside him at the injustice of the situation.

'We weren't to know that, were we?'

'If he did it once, chances were he would do it again or had done it before. You don't do deals with people like that. She should have took the wedge and still tumbled him.'

Mandy was annoyed as well now and said caustically, 'Well, she didn't. How was she to know he'd go after someone else?'

Jon Jon bellowed: 'He went after her girl so I think that might have given her a hint, don't you? Or do you think your grand-daughter has the fucking edge on noncing? Once a nonce, always a fucking nonce. It's like an illness, ain't it?'

No one spoke.

Leigh's father rolled another cigarette but his hands were shaking.

'No one thought beyond getting her away from Harold and his family,' he growled.

Mandy took up his words.

'You don't know what it was like – even we had to move away, that's why we came over here. He had us hassled all the time: fucking dog shit through the letterbox, taxis at all times of the day and night, abuse when we walked the streets from his bleeding mother . . . another mad old hag, her. It was a living nightmare. My girl was like a fucking corpse – couldn't eat, sleep. Even from prison he still controlled her life. He didn't care about those girls, just used them to get to her. She took the money and run, and who can blame her?'

Jon Jon felt sick.

'No one is blaming her for that, but she should have fingered the Thompsons.'

'And involve the filth? Harold would have got her address easier from them than anywhere else. You should know that, son. Most of that lot would do anything for a drink, and what's an address, eh? No, Harold would have seen my girl dead. We did what we thought was best at the time.'

Jon Jon laughed cynically.

'Best for you anyway.'

He stood up.

'Come on, Earl, this place is doing my head in.'

Jon Jon knew they'd get no more about Leigh's whereabouts. Not by asking anyway. Outside they turned on the scanner they kept in the car and fiddled about with it until they heard Mandy's voice speaking on a land line. They could have listened in on a mobile too. They had assumed she would let her daughter know what had occurred and they were right.

The scanner was a boon in their job. You could listen to anything: police radios, mobile phones and land lines, providing they had a walk-around phone which like most people these days Mandy clearly did.

Asylum seekers used these to listen in on cab firms' wavelengths and nick their fares. They were a great little tool.

Mandy explained the situation to her daughter who sounded frightened by recent events. Her mother quickly put her mind to rest.

'They were nice enough lads, love. I don't think your Harold would have had any truck with soots anyway, you know what he was like. And the big one, Earl . . . well, I tell you, girl, I wouldn't kick him out of bed!'

The two women laughed and Earl rolled his eyes in embarrassment.

'You've pulled anyway, Earl.'

He just shrugged.

'Mum, you're terrible.'

The two women laughed once more.

'No, I mean it, he was lovely.'

Mandy laughed again.

'That little Kira . . . do you think they'll find her, Mum?'

'Who knows, girl? I hope they do. Bless her little heart, she looks like Caitlin. All that blonde hair and those blue eyes.'

'Poor little cow.'

'And if those two Thompson bastards are involved! Well, I wouldn't want to be them if the two blokes who came here tonight get hold of them.'

She didn't say that Kira's brother was blaming Leigh for not speaking up but it hung between them unspoken. Leigh changed the subject quickly.

'You and Dad all right?'

'Yeah, fine. How's things your end?'

'OK. We're still in Pevensey Bay, catching the last of the summer. I'm going back on Sunday. They love it here, Mum, and so do I.'

'How's the caravan?'

'It was a bit messy. Whoever you rented it to last time wasn't too fussy, but I've spring cleaned it so don't worry. By the way, I've replanted them terracotta pots outside for you.'

'All right, love, thanks. I'll talk to you tomorrow.'

'Thanks, Mum. For everything. 'Bye.'

Leigh's words were loaded and Mandy said sadly, 'I love you, girl.'

But her daughter had gone.

Earl was already looking up Pevensey Bay in his *A to Z*.

'Don't bother, I've heard enough.'

'We going there now?'

Jon Jon shook his head.

'No, we are going to get ourselves an alibi.'

Earl shrugged.

'Whatever.'

'Do you want me to get the mother's mobile number for you?'

Earl grinned.

'Fuck off, Brewer!'

As they drove away Jon Jon said, 'How could they have taken money, Earl, knowing they were letting them nonces go out to do it again? My little Kira . . .'

Earl slowed the car.

'I know about Rowe and, believe me, he is one dangerous cunt. They were trying to protect their own. We all would in their position. And they're right about the filth – how many addresses have we got off them over the last few months? He could have found Leigh through court transcripts or local court papers. Use your loaf, Jon Jon.'

'But it's not your little sister they went on to nonce, is it?'

'My little sister looks like Ms Dynamite on amphetamines with twice the mouth. No nonce in their right mind would approach her.'

Jon Jon didn't smile even though he had met Renee many times. She was thirteen going on twenty-nine.

'And without being funny, Jon Jon, you don't know for sure it was the Thompsons, do you?'

'It was them all right.'

'You think they would nonce your sister, knowing all about you?'

Jon Jon sighed.

'Well, that makes no sense, does it, because they nonced a Rowe and Harold wasn't exactly the nicest bank robber on the fucking block, was he?'

Earl nodded.

'Point taken.'

Jon Jon started to roll a spliff as they drove along, something he had never done before in public.

'Drive back! I forgot to do something,' he ordered.

Earl turned the car round.

Mandy was watching a film and her husband was pouring them both large brandies. It had been an eventful night.

'I feel bad, don't you, Mandy?'

She nodded.

'But how could we have known that was going to happen?'

She couldn't bear the thought of them having anything to do with the disappearance of a child.

'How much did Thompson give Leigh?'

'Twenty-five grand.'

Her husband choked on his brandy with shock.

'Fuck me! That was a good few quid, weren't it? I didn't realise it was that much.'

Mandy nodded.

'He had an easy let off though, Mandy. I'll be honest, I wondered for a while if she had made it all up. You know what our Leigh could be like . . .'

His wife interrupted him.

'Not this time. And anyway, that was years ago when she was a kid.'

He sipped at his brandy before he said, 'I never believed it, you know, Mandy, none of it.'

His wife turned in her chair to look at her husband properly, the film forgotten.

'What are you saying?'

He shrugged, his large belly rippling with the movement.

'I asked Caitlin and she said Leigh had told her what to say to people.'

'*Of course* she told her what to say to people! You don't want your own kid talking about God knows what to all and sundry. Your own fucking daughter and you still can't believe a word she says.'

'All right, keep your bleeding hair on. But be fair, Mandy, she has told a few pork pies over the years, ain't she? I never saw anything untoward, that's all I'm saying.'

'So?' Mandy snorted with anger. 'You expected to see them do it in front of you, did you? Is that what you're saying?'

'All I'm saying is, when did either of them have the chance? Leigh wasn't living there, was she? I mean, it was just visits over, and trips to the park with the kids and that . . .'

Mandy shook her head in consternation.

'Why didn't you tell that geezer that then? If you're so sure they were innocent and your own daughter is a fucking bare-faced liar!'

'Because she *is* me daughter, that's why.'

That was when the paving slab came through the front-room window. Mandy and her husband watched helplessly as their car was trashed by an irate Jon Jon wielding a baseball bat.

'Call the filth, go on! Oh, but you people don't call the filth, do you? Not even for fucking child molesters and murderers,' he yelled through the broken window.

They didn't answer him.

There was nothing to say.

'Happy now, are you, Mandy?' her husband murmured.

She sat on the sofa and surveyed the state of her front room and cried. But like Jon Jon said, they didn't call the police. They weren't that stupid.

★ ★ ★

Joanie was awake as usual. She crept from her bed as quietly as possible so as not to disturb Paulie. In the kitchen she made herself a cup of tea and laced it heavily with Scotch. Mary Brannagh had brought the bottle over earlier in the day and as it was the only alcohol in the house she drank it gratefully.

Joanie took out her Tarot cards and shuffled them lazily, then she placed them on the table in front of her. She stared at the cards as if they were an enemy, which at this moment in time she felt they were. Night after night she had wanted to give a reading for her daughter, see what the cards told her. Since Mary had said Kira was with a dark-haired person it had caused Joanie to swing between hope and despair.

She already knew everyone thought Kira was dead. Now she was terrified of seeing it written in the cards. She gulped at the lukewarm tea, the Scotch reviving her even as she loathed the taste. Then, placing her head on the table, she started to cry again. It was a quiet sound, not the noisy sobbing she had given way to earlier. These were tears of fear and self-recrimination.

She should never have let Kira go out that day, but she'd had so much to do she had not been her usual vigilant self. Since the tear up with Monika poor Kira had been wandering around like a lost sheep unless she was over Tommy's. But he had been out that day as well.

What on earth had Joanie been thinking of to let her go to the shops on her own? Was her baby cold and tired somewhere now? Did someone have her imprisoned? Was she trapped in a fridge, gasping for breath?

The possibilities were endless and Joanie knew it was doing her no good at all to speculate. She groaned, the sound startling in the quiet flat. Even the loud music that was par for the course on the estate was not blaring out tonight, perhaps in deference to her mourning.

Was that what she was doing? she wondered. Mourning her child?

Then she was vomiting, holding her hand over her mouth to stop the foul spray from spattering the kitchen. She staggered to the sink and retched until her sides ached.

Then she felt a hand softly stroking her back.

It was Paulie.

She retched again and he carried on stroking her back as he whispered words of comfort into her ear.

But Joanie didn't really hear him.

All she was hearing was her little Kira calling out for her mummy, and her mummy wasn't there.

Chapter Sixteen

Little Tommy was outside the flats talking to a crowd of women and men; the search for Kira was still going strong but three days on, the heart had gone out of it. Everyone, including the police, was now looking for a body.

Still, the search had brought everyone together in a way that no one had thought possible. They all had a common goal and that goal was a child called Kira Brewer. Journalists were still all over the place though the news cameras were gone thanks to a bomb exploding in central London. The estate was alive with expectation, and even though hope of finding Kira alive was waning, it was still exciting for the residents to be front-page news.

As they read out their own words quoted in the newspapers they didn't find it at all incongruous that Kira's disappearance had brought them all together. This was a community who knew each other's lives intimately. They could see into each other's homes. They knew each other's families, everyone's foibles, exactly who was on drugs and who wasn't. Who was sleeping with whom; who was banged up and who had just got out. They knew the names and ages of each other's children and grandchildren. They lived in each other's pockets thanks to the way their homes had been designed. When the planners had built them in the sixties they had not allowed people any privacy. This estate had been built to house the overflow from the East End slums. It was old GLC and it looked it – crumbling buildings that were so long overdue for renovation they were only fit now to be pulled down and replaced.

But this place was their home and in their own ways they made the best they could of it. The council put them here and left them to their own devices. There were unwritten laws on how to behave in this neighbourhood.

Monika was nowhere to be seen. No one remarked on it until someone opened the *Sun*. There was a picture of her, all sad-faced and demure, along with the headline: 'I was on the game with missing girl's mother'.

The two-page article explained how she had met Joanie, what Kira was like, and how Joanie had worked the pavements and the parlours.

None of it was lies, but no one felt that Monika should have used Joanie's personal business to line her own pockets, which was exactly what she had done. It was a betrayal so heinous to them that Monika would never be able to walk these streets again. Not without taking abuse from everyone around her anyway. This was a tight-knit community and she had overstepped the line.

'The fucking bitch! Like poor Joanie ain't got enough on her plate.' This from a neighbour who had systematically rowed with Joanie over the years, usually about the kids, but that was forgotten in the face of this tragedy.

'She'll get her comeuppance. No one will give her the time of day after this.'

There was murmured agreement and finally everyone dispersed to go and buy their own copy of the paper and discuss its contents with other friends and family. Monika's name would be dirt from now on.

Joanie was a lot of things but she had been a good mother, an exemplary one even, and this was remembered by everyone. She was liked and that was important to all the people in this neighbourhood. They looked after their own and would pay Monika back for this.

Little Tommy walked slowly back up to his flat. Inside he put the kettle on and made a mug of coffee. He had all the day's papers and laid them out on the table to peruse them, his eyes lingering on the photograph of Kira.

'My pretty little princess.'

He said the words out loud and looked around him as if

expecting to see her there. The kettle finished boiling as there was a knock on his front door. He shuffled down the hallway to answer it.

His feet were swollen today. He had been walking so much the last few days that he was paying the price. He was so sad about what had happened it showed in his drooping face and whole demeanour as he opened the door.

Jeanette was already at the police station. She had been brought in for her assault on Karen Copes. Karen had not pressed charges, but they had kept Jeanette overnight to see a social worker. The girl was out of control and they all knew it but there was nothing anyone could do about it.

Jeanette had told the social worker to go forth and multiply and the woman had left. After adding another note to her file. She was fourteen years old and living with an eighteen-year-old man who had criminal convictions. His mother was an alcoholic and between her and her son they had more form than the Mafia.

Yet legally Jeanette was able to do what she wanted with her life and if that meant she decided to live with them then that was fine with everyone concerned. Even if Joanie had attempted to bring her home, it wouldn't have been possible. The Children's Charter had given her these rights and Jeanette used them in her own favour so as to do exactly what she wanted to do.

Baxter marvelled at a girl who could still get herself into trouble when her own sister was probably lying murdered somewhere.

He didn't allow for the fact that she had been on the edge and Karen Copes had pushed her over it. All he saw was a tart, and to him Jeanette was as much of one as her mother. The family were all scum. Those pictures of a little child plastered in makeup had finally woken him up to what he was dealing with here. In his mind Kira Brewer had been part of the family business and he didn't care how many times the Chief Constable rang him up, he would not change that opinion.

'Did you take those pictures in to be developed?' he asked now.

Jeanette shook her head.

'Nope. Why would I do that and not give me name and

address? Use your loaf, you must know who brought them in.'

Her voice indicated one of them was stupid and it certainly wasn't her. She sighed heavily as if bored by his questions.

'Look, like I said before, they were just a joke. I dressed her up and took a few photos of her, big fucking deal. No law against that, is there?'

She sat back in the chair and he stared at her. From her short black skirt to her cropped top she was every inch the bullyboy's girlfriend. Her hair was covered in some kind of shiny gel that made it look like it needed a good wash. Her little skinny legs were nicked with shaving cuts and her heavy shoes looked like clogs on her feet.

She was covered in makeup: foundation and blusher caked on her skin; vivid colours on her eyes; bright pink lipstick that made her look all-knowing. Like the other girl had, like Kira Brewer looked in her photographs.

Baxter despaired as he looked at Jeanette. If she wasn't in the family business now, she soon would be. He had seen it over and over again, girls following their mothers on to the street. It was like a vocation with them.

'So you admit to taking these photographs of your sister?'

She nodded.

''Course I do. But what's to admit? Like I said, there's no law against taking photos, is there?'

'These kind of photos there is.'

He pointed at the pictures, practically stabbing them with his finger.

Jeanette rolled her eyes to the ceiling.

'You're the one who thinks there's something bad about them. It's *you* that's making them into something they ain't. I took them to please Kira. She liked dressing up, and she liked makeup and clothes. All little girls do. Now can I go, please?'

'Where was the film when you last saw it?'

Jeanette thought for a moment.

'In the bedroom, Kira's bedroom. She must have taken it in to the shop, no one else had access to it. Now can I go, please?'

She was dismissing him and he knew it. Her arrogance knew no bounds. It was as if it was in the water supply and all the youngsters hereabouts absorbed it at birth.

But he had to let her go, there was nothing to charge her with.

Tommy opened the door to Jon Jon and Earl.

The smile on his face was replaced by an expression of terror when Jon Jon seized him by the scruff of the neck and battered him against the hall walls as he manhandled him into the lounge. He pushed him to the floor.

'You know why we're here, don't you?'

Tommy didn't answer. He was still heaving from exertion but his eyes said he had a pretty good idea.

'What did you do to my sister, you fucking nonce!'

Jon Jon's voice was low, no shouting just pure intimidation. He kicked at the man a few times, feeling the softness of that flabby flesh against his boot. Just the feel of Tommy enraged him; he was convinced the fat useless bastard was laughing at him. As he looked into that moonlike face he felt it, felt the fat freak's contempt.

'You must have thought you'd got away with it, you and your fucking father! I know all about Caitlin, I saw her granny and she told me about you.'

At the mention of the girl Tommy blanched.

'It wasn't true, Jon Jon, I swear! She was a liar, that girl. I never touched her.'

Tommy was terrified and it showed.

Jon Jon hauled him up with difficulty and spat into Tommy's face.

'I will kill you if you don't tell me exactly what happened, do you hear me?'

Earl watched then said quietly, 'Do it, Jon Jon. Stab him up. Fucking take him out now.'

Jon Jon half turned his head, listening to his friend. Then he saw that Tommy was out cold. He had passed out with fright.

'Fear will do it every time.'

Earl's voice was all-knowing.

Jon Jon went out into the kitchen. Seeing the kettle still steaming he turned it on again. When it had boiled once more he walked back into the lounge with it and poured it all over

Tommy's stomach and between his legs.

Tommy had on cotton trousers and a thin shirt. The water burned straight through. His eyes flew open and a scream escaped his lips.

'Now tell me what I want to know.'

Jon Jon held the kettle out to Earl.

'Boil that fucker up again. I'm going to cook him.'

Tommy's eyes were glazed with pain.

'Please, Jon Jon, I'm begging you . . .'

'Hurt, does it, you fat nonce? What have you done with her! Was she begging you to stop hurting her? Was she?'

Tommy was shaking his head, too paralysed with fear to talk.

'She's dead, ain't she?'

Jon Jon punched him in the head again.

'Where is my sister! Tell me where she is?'

Tommy was crying, fat globules of snot and spit all over his face.

'I don't know, I swear . . . Ask me father . . . He was the one . . . Not me . . .' He was rambling now the pain had overtaken him. 'He liked the little girls . . . not me. Not like that! Not me . . .'

He was groaning in pain and distress but still trying to convince Jon Jon.

'Where is my sister? What did you do with her?'

Tommy was nearly delirious now.

'I don't know anything. I swear on my mother's grave.'

He was crying, great heaving sobs that made his words almost unintelligible. Jon Jon stared down at him dispassionately.

'She was so sweet, so sweet. My Kira . . .'

The unearthly crying was reaching a crescendo now.

'I loved her . . . loved her. I never wanted her to get hurt.'

The words penetrated Jon Jon's brain and then the kicking started in earnest. All reason was gone now; he kicked until he was spent.

'You loved her, did you?'

He was panting from the exertion.

'I'll kill you, you cunt, and your father!'

But it was too late to talk to Tommy now.

Tommy couldn't hear anything.

Before he left, Jon Jon poured the newly boiled kettle of water over his face. Then, after spitting on him, he left.

They drove straight round to the father's girlfriend's house, Jon Jon riding shotgun in the car as they cursed the child's killers. He was crying his eyes out because now they knew she was gone; it just remained to find what was left of her. He was almost hysterical with grief; it was as if now the floodgates had opened he would never stop crying again.

He pictured her, her terror, the pain of what had happened to her. It was like a film playing in his head.

And he had welcomed her betrayer into his home.

Jon Jon felt it was all his fault.

It didn't occur to him to call the police. This was personal, he would deal with it himself.

Tommy's neighbour, Mrs Carling, waited for them to leave before she phoned the police. Even then she did it anonymously. No way was she getting involved when Jon Jon Brewer was on the warpath. She'd decided that on Saturday and she was sticking to it.

Della and Joseph had been to Patricia's house. On the way back they had stopped for lunch in Upminster. Della was happier than she had been. Joseph had convinced her that his argument with Little Tommy was strictly family business. His son was jealous of the fact he had moved out, apparently, though in fairness to him he had not seemed that kind of person. In fact, as she kept pointing out, he seemed to like his father living somewhere else.

Now that Kira Brewer was missing Della was worried about how it would affect them. The police had already been to her house and interviewed Joseph. Even though she knew it was only natural, anyone who knew the child would be questioned, it still bothered her. She couldn't leave it alone and knew this was annoying Joseph. But what had happened was so outrageous it was natural to keep talking about it, surely?

'Do you think Kira knew whoever it was who took her?'

Joseph sipped his pint and didn't answer her. Even at her daughter's he had refused to discuss it, and Patricia was as interested as everyone else. They had first-hand knowledge of a national news event and he was just sitting there like a stuffed toy. Joseph's son, as Patricia had pointed out, knew the girl better than anyone else. He was her babysitter, for crying out loud. But still Joseph would not be drawn.

Instead he had taken Della's grand-daughters to the park and left them to discuss it between them. Now he was sitting there sipping his pint for all the world like nothing out of the ordinary had happened.

He was strange that way.

'Are you going to answer me, Joe?'

He shook his head.

'I don't want to keep going over it. It's a terrible thing to keep thinking about.'

It sounded like fair comment but she was still not satisfied. Like her husband before him, Joseph was about to find out exactly what his new girlfriend could be like when the fancy took her.

'Anyone would think you had something to hide.'

He stared at her, his pint halfway to his mouth.

'What is that supposed to mean?'

Della shrugged nonchalantly then said sarcastically, 'Whatever you want it to mean. Only anyone else, any *normal* person, would be interested in what was going on. But not you.'

He was sneering now.

'So because I'm not a gossip, that makes me suspicious, does it?'

He was trying to keep some semblance of friendliness in his voice but it was getting harder by the second. He wanted to slap her across her fat-cheeked, smug-looking face.

Della shrugged once more.

'Take it how you like.'

She was spoiling for a fight now, a real row. She wanted to let him know just who he was dealing with.

He gulped at his beer.

'Do me a favour, would you, Della?'

His voice was friendly and calm.

She nodded.

'Shut the fuck up.'

Her face was a picture and Joseph felt it was worth the hag just to see that look of shock on it.

'How dare you!'

Her voice was low. After all, they were in a pub and she didn't want them showing themselves up.

'Right, let's go, Della. I ain't arguing here.'

He said it as if to imply he would be more than willing to argue in the privacy of the car. This was a new one for Della. Until now she had always been in complete control.

In the car she picked up where she had left off before he had even reversed out of the parking space.

'I can't put my finger on it but there's something not right with the lot of it . . .'

He didn't answer her because he was negotiating the car out into a country lane. Once he was on the road he said, 'Is that right, Della? It must be great being you, knowing everything. Being the only woman on earth to have psychic fucking tendencies.'

This was a Joseph she had never heard before and she wasn't sure how to handle him until he said, 'What did your husband die of again? Terminal fucking boredom I'd guess, listening to your trap going morning, noon and night.'

The barb hit home.

'How dare you, Joseph Thompson . . .'

He held up his hand for quiet and miraculously got it.

'I dare, I fucking dare, because you just couldn't leave it, could you? Do you know what I am going through? I knew that child, knew her well. She came in my home with me and my son. I liked her.'

His voice was drenched with emotion now and Della was wondering just what she had started. His tone had the ring of truth to it.

'Look, Joe . . .'

'Oh, no, you don't, Della. You don't talk me round this time. *You* are a fucking bully.'

He knew it was the pot calling the kettle black but this didn't bother him one iota. 'Well, that's it now, girl. I'm off home to my own place and my poor son.'

Her mobile rang and saved her from answering. She listened to the caller and he saw out of the corner of one eye her look of shocked bemusement.

'Oh, my God!'

Her voice was high-pitched.

'What's wrong, Della?'

'Little Tommy was attacked at home. He's in hospital, Joe, really bad by all accounts.'

He slowed down, much to the annoyance of the cars behind.

'Who done it?'

He stopped in a driveway to allow the other cars to pass them by and stared ahead of him for a few minutes. Then, leaning over her, he opened the car door.

'Get out.'

'What!'

'You heard, Della, get out of the car.'

Something in his voice and manner penetrated her anger. She got out of the car. He drove off then, leaving her stranded.

Della started sobbing into her mobile as her daughter struggled to understand what the hell was going on.

Baxter was considering early retirement. This latest attack on Little Tommy Thompson had caused uproar once more and the press was loving it. Worst of all, everyone knew who had done it but Jon Jon Brewer had a pub full of people who put him there at the time the attack took place.

Baxter was following up on the rumour that Tommy had been accused of noncing. They had put him through the national database and found nothing. They had looked at him every way but which, and still found nothing. But a rumour had been heard and now he was at death's door in the burns unit of Billericay Hospital, and Baxter was left to sort out the flak.

Joseph Thompson had gone on the trot as well. Was that because he had had a hand in something sinister, or because he was frightened of being accused along with his son? They wouldn't know until they found him.

Jon Jon the vigilante had done no one any favours but to the people round here he was a hero.

Baxter was going to pull him in anyway. See what occurred.

Joanie didn't want to believe what her son was telling her. Didn't want to believe that she had brought the instrument of her daughter's destruction into their home.

'Listen to me, Mum, he's a fucking nonce – him *and* his father. They were accused and gave a bird money to shut her trap. She had an old man banged up, a violent cunt who she wanted shot of once and for all. The money gave her the means to do that. I'm still trying to track her down, the whore, and when I do, I will find out exactly what went down. But one of them Thompsons knows where Kira is, where she's b—'

He stopped himself from saying 'buried' but Joanie guessed anyway. It was funny but she couldn't cry any more. It was as if all the tears had been shed. She was dry, inside and out.

She poured a neat vodka and gulped it. Then, picking up the bottle, she walked into her bedroom and shut the door.

'That ain't going to fucking help, is it, Mother!'

Jon Jon was crying.

She opened the door and looked at him before saying sadly, 'You got any better ideas?'

She had given up and Jon Jon knew that. He looked round the flat. All her stuff from the cupboards was on the floor. She had been looking at it before he had come home. She had been remembering happy times with the kids, her fantasy parties that they had loved so much. She had retreated into them as she always did to cheer herself up. It was all she had to show for her life and he suddenly saw it as overwhelmingly pitiful that a woman could have three children and a long life and all that was left at the end of the day was a few hundred quid's worth of memories.

He knelt on the floor and picked up a silver cake knife. Cradling it to his chest, he cried like a baby.

Little Tommy Thompson was in a critical condition. He was badly burned and had taken a severe beating. It was common knowledge now that he was a sex offender and even the nurses who had previously shown compassion found it difficult to touch him without seeing a mental picture of Kira Brewer.

Her face was etched into everyone's mind.

As they looked down at the man thought to be responsible for her disappearance they couldn't help but wonder if they were restoring a murderer to health.

The policeman who sat by his bed took a different view. As far as he was concerned, if Jon Jon Brewer or any of his cronies turned up at the hospital to finish the job he would be conveniently looking the other way. That huge mountain of flab that passed for a human being could die in agony as far as he was concerned. It was all he was fit for.

From the rumours going the rounds there was no doubt that Little Tommy, his father, or indeed both of them were the culprits.

The newspapers were investigating how the police had failed Kira Brewer and her family by not following up on paedophile allegations made by neighbours. Joseph Thompson had conveniently vanished, adding to public belief that there was indeed something suspect about the whole family.

For Little Tommy, horribly scarred, there was only morphine; he was out of it all now. If he survived this the only thing he could look forward to was prison and a life sentence.

If, of course, the other cons let him live to serve it.

Chapter Seventeen

Baxter read the news reports over and over. He sighed heavily. He hated this case. The papers were having a field day, and he was getting it in the neck from every angle.

Fuck Jon Jon Brewer.

Fuck him to hell.

He was a national hero now. Everyone knew he had done it, but no one could prove it. Supposition, the great British past-time. All Baxter could do now was damage limitation. If they did charge Jon Jon it would cause a public furore. The memory of Kira's sweet face was enough to see to that.

He felt as if all he wanted to do was go home and sleep and never wake up.

He had a feeling Joanie Brewer felt the same, but for different reasons.

Monika was in her element. Her nasty allegations had proved correct and Jon Jon had finally taken the law into his own hands and battered that fat bastard once and for all.

As she sipped her coffee there was a knock on the door.

'Answer that, Bethany.'

She was not worried about the neighbours any more. Thanks to Jon Jon she had been proved right. She was the next thing to a heroine, in her own mind. Monika's utter self-absorption knew no bounds.

Bethany saw who the caller was and wanted to run. She could not look her in the face.

'It's Joanie Brewer, Mum.'

Monika felt as if her cup was really running over now. Joanie had probably come to apologise, and she would accept the apology with good grace. After all, they had been friends for years and even Joanie could make a mistake.

'Well, open the door then, or are you waiting for her to walk through it?'

Normally a quip like that would have made Bethany laugh but the child had been in a deep depression since Kira had disappeared. Unlike Monika herself, Bethany had taken it badly. Almost personally. She sat glued to Sky News day and night. Morbid little cow she was.

Bethany let Joanie in and was saddened by the sight of her. She had aged overnight and now she looked dilapidated. Unkempt and untidy, she was a shadow of her former self.

'Hello, Joanie love. All right?'

Monika's voice was full of friendship and camaraderie. As if nothing untoward had ever happened between them. As if she had never betrayed her best and in reality only friend.

Joanie nodded almost imperceptibly.

'Want a cup of tea?'

Joanie shook her head slowly.

'Got any of the hard?'

Even her voice sounded dead, gravelly, as if it hadn't been used for months. Monika poured her out a large Bacardi and added a dash of Coke.

'Here you are, girl, get your lips round that.'

Joanie took a deep swig of the drink and then perched herself on the edge of the sofa.

'You look so skinny, Joanie!'

She stared back with indifference.

'It suits you, mate, you look years younger . . .'

Joanie interrupted her idiotic chatter. Only Monika would waffle on about weight and looks at a time like this. But then, Monika would be asking if her bum looked big if someone had a gun to her head.

'Were you lying when you said all that about Tommy?'

Whatever Monika was expecting it wasn't that. It was obvious from the look of astonishment on her face.

'What do you mean?'

She sounded offended.

'I *mean*, were you making up what you said about Tommy being a nonce?'

Joanie's eyes were hard and it occurred to Monika that she was walking on eggshells here.

'I want the truth.'

Monika was mortally offended now and it showed.

''Course I wasn't. Anyway, even if I was exaggerating a little bit, I was still right, weren't I?'

She was all self-righteous now, all wounded pride.

'Do you know what you've done, Monika? Do you realise what you have caused?'

Monika was not at all happy with the way this conversation was going.

'They've pulled my boy in and they will tie him to this if it's the last thing they do.' Joanie drained the glass. 'You know how they feel about him, and thanks to you they have a good excuse to bang him up.'

Joanie was nearly crying.

When they had asked Jon Jon to go to the station with them her heart nearly stopped beating with fright. She was convinced he was going to be put away. Baxter had wanted him for so long that his time had to be running out. His luck couldn't last for ever.

Her entire family had fallen apart since Kira's disappearance. She pointed a finger at her one-time friend.

'I swallowed the newspaper stories about us on the game, I didn't care because they were true anyway. But I can't forgive you for this. If they take my baby boy away I will have no one, and then I'll be coming for *you*. Do you understand what I'm saying? Jon Jon won't be in it once I get started.'

Monika understood all right. This was the old Joanie, the one people avoided if they upset her too much. The Joanie who could turn on a coin for a friend, a child or for herself. Monika needed to talk her way out of this one and quickly.

'But it *was* Tommy, everyone knows that now.'

Joanie shrugged once more.

'Do they? I wouldn't believe Lorna or her cousin any more

than I believe you. Lying bastards, the lot of you.'

Joanie stared at her.

'You talk shit, Monika. You lie constantly and now you've dropped my boy in it. He could be put away for years. If that happens I will make it my one aim in life to see you suffer. And you'll fucking suffer like you never thought possible.'

She stood up.

'I've lost one baby, Monika, and if I lose another . . .'

She left the sentence unfinished.

'But you won't, Joanie. Jon Jon is a hero. No one would dare nick him now. He's done the filth a favour; they hate nonces as much as we do.'

Joanie sighed.

'We catered to nonces our whole working life, we were just too stupid to see it. Look at all the young girls we've seen come and go over the years. We were as bad as the pimps because we should never have got involved in any of it. Sex is behind everything bad that ever happens in this country. Me and you were just at the bottom of the pile when it came to getting paid for it.'

Monika could not see any logic in what Joanie was saying. Grief was making her blame herself for something she'd had no control over. Joanie had lost it for good and all.

'This ain't got nothing to do with us and what we do, mate.'

Monika was trying in her own way to calm her friend down, make her see that it wasn't down to them.

'No? Then why are we plagued by bad luck? All us working girls are. It's one fucking drama after another. Use your loaf, Monika. For once in your life, look at the big picture.'

'But, Joanie, listen to yourself . . .'

'Oh, fuck off, Monika. Stop trying to be me mate, you wouldn't know one if they fell out of a tree and hit you on the head. Look after your own family for once. Look after that little girl there, overweight and unhappy, your Bethany. She's a born again Monika and she'll end up just like you, God help her. You are fucking scum, Mon, scum. You ain't worth a wank and you know it. But I tell you again, girl, you watch your fucking back and you watch it well.'

She left then and Bethany stared dully at her mother as Monika went ballistic at the unfairness of her so-called friend.

Bethany kept her own counsel but her guilt knew no bounds. She had lied to the police, she had lied to everyone.

But who ever took any notice of her anyway? Certainly not her mother, who should have guessed something was up. Joanie would have guessed if it had been Kira keeping something secret.

She went into her bedroom and sneaked a drink from her own bottle of Bacardi and Coke. She made a bottle up every morning from her mother's stash and Monika assumed she herself had drunk it the night before. The feeling it gave her was nice, made Bethany feel warm inside. Took away some of the loneliness and guilt for a while.

When she came back out her mother had left the house without even bothering to say goodbye.

Mrs Carling was in a quandary.

She had seen Kira Brewer at the shops on the Saturday she'd disappeared but she had not told a soul. She had seen her with that brazen little strap Bethany, but never a woman to get involved in anyone else's business unless it was gossiping about it, she had kept this nugget of information to herself.

Assuming the child would turn up eventually, she had decided to keep out of it. Especially as it involved the Brewers. She did not want any of them on her doorstep, no one in their right mind would. Just look at what had happened to Tommy. Though Joanie wasn't a bad sort in fairness to her. She did her best, and that was no easy task with the burden God had placed on her shoulders. Her washing was whiter than white anyway, and Mrs Carling judged people by their washing and how clean they kept their passages.

Now, though, it seemed the child was gone for good and she was getting a guilty conscience. Poor Tommy was in hospital and it was all such a mess. But she couldn't go to the police, could she? Not this late in the day. And Tommy and his father were the most likely suspects. Nothing she said or did would change that, surely? She wasn't one hundred per cent certain she'd seen the girls getting into that car . . .

So she kept her knowledge to herself, convinced she was doing the right thing. Tommy and his father would be charged, and that would be an end to it. What possible good could it do to involve herself in what could only be an explosive situation?

She made herself another cup of tea and decided to go to Bingo that night, just to take her mind off everything.

Jon Jon looked terrible as he sat opposite Baxter. He had the look of someone with a secret that no one was going to get at.

'I was in the Ship and Shovel all day long, Mr Baxter, you know that. Thirty people have sworn to it. What do you want – a statement from a judge to prove where I was? Only you don't get many judges in there, know what I mean?'

He was smiling and Baxter felt the urge to wipe that expression off the boy's face once and for all.

'How did you get on with Tommy?'

Jon Jon shrugged but he was finding it harder and harder to keep up his veneer of innocence.

'All right. But then, I had no idea he was a nonce, did I?'

'Who told you he was a nonce? We did stringent checks and found nothing.'

Jon Jon smiled.

'With respect, Mr Baxter, you lot couldn't find the fucking Hubble telescope if it landed on Roman Road Market.'

'Now listen to me, Jon Jon . . .'

The boy shook his head, dreads quivering with indignation.

'No, you fucking listen to me! My sister is out there somewhere probably dead by now, and you have the nerve to question *me* about an assault on a fucking nonce! Are you having a laugh or what? Pity you didn't put in as much time finding her, ain't it? Your lot never even bothered to come out for ages. It was just a Brewer and who gives a fuck about them? They're scum.'

He ran a hand over his face, which was sweating slightly.

'The newspapers are after our story and we won't talk to them. Fucking carrion they are. But I will if you don't get off my fucking back and do the job the taxpayers expect from you. That means finding out where my little sister is and what happened to her. She is eleven years old and she is gone. Every paper and every TV station is carrying her story as you know, yet not one fucking person has seen her. Are you looking for Joseph Thompson by any chance or are you just hassling my family?'

Baxter sighed. His ulcer was playing him up. The pain was like a knife stabbing him repeatedly, and to make it worse, in his heart of hearts he knew that what the boy said was true.

'You can't take the law into your own hands, Jon Jon.'

'But I didn't, did I? Someone did that for me. Let's face it, Mr Baxter, if it was left to you lot he'd still be sitting around enjoying his poxy little life.'

Jon Jon wiped a hand across his face once more, his agitation clear.

'And don't you fucking dare talk to me about taking the law into my own hands. You lot have tried to fit me up enough times over the last few years. Whatever happened to him he had it coming, and I hope his father gets some of the same.'

Baxter sat back in the chair and surveyed Jon Jon for long seconds then he said slowly, 'Can I trust you with something, Jon Jon?'

Jon Jon wasn't sure where this was going so he didn't answer. Baxter knew that what he was doing was wrong but he had to let this boy know what was happening. He was an intelligent sort, and in his own way he was fair.

He placed a file on the table opposite Jon Jon and then said quietly, 'I am going to get you a cup of tea and if you look in that file while I am gone there is nothing I can do about it, is there? Because I don't know you've looked, do I? I won't be in the room.'

'Why should I want to look at it?'

Baxter shrugged.

'Curiosity?'

'Killed the cat, didn't it?'

'I think you'll survive a peep, Jon Jon.'

He stood up.

'Milk and sugar?'

Jon Jon nodded and watched him leave the room. He stared at the file before him for a while, wondering what to do. He wouldn't put it past Baxter to try and fit him up even now. But curiosity got the better of him and he opened the file and all there was inside it was one piece of paper. He saw that it was from Little Tommy's medical records.

Jon Jon read it slowly twice then put it back in the folder. Getting up, he walked quickly from the room. Baxter came back with the tea and when he saw the room was empty, he smiled. He glanced at the report himself once more.

It seemed Little Tommy Thompson was incapable of having sex with anyone. His genitalia had never fully developed and the drugs he took to stabilise his obesity had shrunk away the little that was there.

That wasn't to say the thoughts weren't in his head, of course, but it proved that physically there was little he could have done. All the psychiatric reports said the same thing: he had no interest in or real knowledge of sex.

Poor beaten and burned Little Tommy Thompson was a virtual eunuch.

Della had been to the police to tell them what had happened to her. She was more upset about being dinged out of the car than anything else. But the fact Joseph had taken all his belongings from her house spoke volumes as far as she was concerned.

It never occurred to her that he might have been frightened away; she had him guilty of everything under the sun. And she was vocal about it as well.

The news hit the pavements by five-thirty that afternoon. Joseph Thompson was finished now; anyone who saw him would know who he was. His photo was on every news channel and in every paper. Within twenty-four hours there had been sightings of him by vigilant English tourists all over Europe.

But, like Kira Brewer, it seemed he had disappeared into thin air.

Liz Parker was lying beside Jon Jon and enjoying the feel of him. He had come to her earlier in the day and they had enjoyed brief but frantic sex. Then, instead of his usual disappearing act, he had stayed, lying with her and smoking joint after joint.

'Do you want a beer, Jon Jon?'

He nodded.

She opened them both a Bud Ice from her little fridge and they sipped them together. He passed her the joint.

'You all right, Jon Jon?'

He laughed then.

'Yeah, great. Me little sister's missing presumed dead, but other than that I'm fucking blinding. Yourself?'

She sighed.

'I was only asking, no need to be sarcastic.'

He had upset her, something he had never suspected could happen. As he looked at her little-girlie face he felt bad suddenly.

'I'm sorry, Liz.'

It was said quietly and neither of them could tell who was the more shocked by his words, her or him.

She smiled then, a real smile not the usual professional one that somehow never reached her eyes.

'*I'm* sorry. Your little sister seemed nice.'

She took a long toke on the joint then as he asked her, 'When did you ever see my sister?'

She turned to face him properly. 'I saw her a few times, with you and your mum. Just around, you know.'

He nodded then.

She settled against him once more and the plumpness of her body was reassuring to him. She felt good, she felt safe.

He stared round her little room which was clean for a change though the bedding had not been washed for a few weeks. It was the same each time he came, he was sure no other men shared it.

It was silly bedding, childlike. *Groovy chick*, it said on the duvet cover, in bright Dayglo colours, a picture of an adolescent girl sketched on bright pink cotton. Kira would have loved it.

The room had horrific flowered wallpaper on the walls and a deep green and orange carpet. It was like a flop house.

But then, in many respects that was just what it was. Somewhere to lay a weary head. Where had he read that? It came and left his mind in nanoseconds. He couldn't keep anything in his head lately. He guessed it was the circumstances and didn't try to analyse the reason why.

Liz laid a plump white leg over his brown ones and he watched the contrast, liked the contrast. She rubbed his stomach with a well-manicured hand, slipping it down between his legs, caressing him once more.

'More life in a music video at the moment, girl.'

But he could feel the first stirrings himself and knew she could feel them too from the triumphant smile on her face. What was it about her that made him feel as he did? She was servicing up to ten men a day and yet it didn't bother him. Was there something wrong with him?

He kissed her full on the lips, sucking her tongue into his mouth, the first time he had ever kissed her properly.

Then visions of her sucking other men's cocks made him throw her away from him swiftly. She hit the wall heavily and sat there nursing her shoulder which had taken the full force of the blow.

'What the fuck is the matter, Jon Jon? What have I done?'

He lay back against the pillows.

'It's my birthday today.'

Then he started crying. Really crying. He was sobbing and Liz took him awkwardly in her arms and hugged him as best she could.

Paulie and Joanie were in her bedroom. He had laid her down and now he was running her a nice bath.

'I don't want one!'

Paulie ignored her.

'You stink like a fucking polecat, you are having a bath.'

'Am I fuck!'

He still ran the bath and poured in some sweet-smelling salts.

'Get your gear off and get in that bath.'

His voice brooked no argument. Still she didn't move. He went out to the kitchen and started to unpack the groceries he had brought with him. The wine was cold so he opened it and poured two glasses. It wasn't the greatest wine but it was the best on sale in the chiller cabinet.

'Are you in that bath yet?'

He was walking into the bedroom as he spoke, listening for the tell-tale sounds of Joanie in the water. She was still on her bed and ignoring him.

He pulled the duvet off her. She sat up then, all indignation and grubby white underwear. He picked her up bodily and carried her, struggling, through to the bathroom. Then he unceremoniously dropped her into the scented water.

Her head went under a little bit and she emerged spitting out water and expletives, but he just walked from the room and came back with the glasses of wine. Joanie was lying in the water now, accepting of her fate.

He passed her a glass. She took it gratefully, sipped it and sighed.

'Are you going to take your drawers off?'

Suddenly she was laughing her head off. It wasn't a normal laugh but high-pitched, tinged with hysteria.

He put the toilet lid down and sat on it. Let her laugh. If it got it all out of her system so much the better. She was literally rocking with laughter now, the wine slopping all over her body. He leaned forward and took the glass from her then he stood up and locked the bathroom door.

He stripped down to his boxers and she watched him, laughing harder. He stepped into the bath and this made her laugh even more.

'Aren't you going to take your boxers off?'

This set her off again and he slipped behind her in the bath, hugging her to him as best he could as she coughed and spluttered with the force of her merriment. Then the laughter stopped as quickly as it had begun and she was leaning against him, turning slightly so she could bury her face in his chest.

She was crying now, sobbing, and he gently kissed her and held her to him tightly. He whispered words of love to her that she had never heard from him before and that he had never thought he would say.

'I love you, Joanie Brewer. I always have, girl.'

She basked in his attention, knowing he was only telling her this because she was hurting so much. She really felt the pain could kill her. Hoped it would so she would not have to experience another day without her baby. Wished for the release of death even as she wished for her baby back.

But Kira wasn't coming back, she knew that now.

It had settled on her in the night, this realisation that her child was gone from her for good.

Now her fear was for the others.

Jeanette, she knew, would always go her own road and this terrified Joanie more now than it ever had before. But it was Jon Jon, her first-born, who would bear the brunt of her concern from now on.

He was the only one of the three who had been a constant for her. He would always be there for her, no matter what. He had been her honorary man and had played that part in her life happily. Sometimes she felt guilty about the way she had treated him and wished she could have done it all differently. Why couldn't she just have met one man and settled with him like normal people? Why had she lived this life of indiscriminate sexual favours and money-gathering? She blamed herself and her work for what had happened to her youngest daughter.

And now Paulie, the man she had loved for so long, was telling her that he loved her and it meant nothing.

It was too late.

She was empty of love, could neither give nor receive it. But his arms felt good around her. She needed someone to make it all better. No one could really. But at least his arms around her made her feel less lonely.

When he unhooked her bra she didn't stop him. Paulie was like most men. Every display of emotion led to sex. He took her quickly and gently as he usually did and afterwards they lay in the rapidly cooling water without speaking. Enjoying the feel of each other's skins. The slippery feel of their bodies as they hugged in their watery bed.

Finally he kissed the top of her head.

'I love you, Joanie.'

And he meant it. She knew he meant it. It was what she had waited for all these years and yet now he had said it she didn't answer him. She just nodded her head and, closing her eyes, lay against him, listening to the beating of his heart.

It was too late and they both knew that.

They dozed together then. Paulie held her as if she was precious porcelain. The knowledge that he actually loved this woman overwhelmed him. Whatever she was or had been, there was a connection with her that he had never experienced with anyone else in his life. Not even his own children.

She opened her eyes and looked up at him. She looked younger somehow. The lines had disappeared for a few minutes as she relaxed against him and dozed.

'Was Kira my child, Joanie?'

She looked into his eyes and nodded her head.

Both of them were aware he had said *was*, not *is*.

It was like the final seal on Kira's fate.

They cried together then.

Book Two

Life for life,
Eye for eye, tooth for tooth, hand for hand, foot for foot,
Burning for burning, wound for wound, stripe for stripe.

– *Exodus*, 21:23

Chapter Eighteen

It was amazing what you learned to live with. Joanie felt at times as if Kira had never been alive, that her daughter was just a dream she had had many years ago.

Other days she felt as if she was buckling under the sheer weight of her sorrow, and the nightmares where she saw her daughter begging for her life were so vivid, so realistic, she awoke bathed in sweat convinced they were true.

But it was three months since she'd gone and there was still no news. The papers had forgotten her daughter. Everyone seemed to have forgotten Kira outside this little community Joanie called home. She saw the pitying looks of friends and neighbours, felt the sorrow inside them even as she felt it inside herself.

There were no news crews these days, no more running the gauntlet of the national papers. Kira was just a photograph in the police files now, though one of Jasper's friends had set up the Kira Brewer web-site, which Joanie had been grateful for even as she'd wondered what the fuck use it was going to be. Her daughter was gone from her. She was rotting away somewhere. She was dead. Otherwise she would have been home by now, her cheery little voice chattering away, her beautiful smile there for everyone to see. But the hurt, the hurt inside her mother, was not gone and neither was the anger.

There was a knock on the door and Joanie answered it, the falseness of her smile evident to her if not to the recipient. She had got over feeling excited at every knock on the door; didn't expect to see Kira standing there any more, telling her how she had got lost and found her way home.

Joanie opened the door to DI Baxter and despite herself the

hope was once more evident in her eyes as she looked at him.

He smiled sadly.

'Can I come in, Joanie?'

She knew by his voice there was no news, at least not any she wanted to hear.

He followed her inside.

'It's about Tommy Thompson.'

She sighed heavily now. Tommy was the arch enemy as far as she was concerned. Jon Jon had convinced her of that.

'What about him?'

She signalled to Baxter to sit down and he perched precariously on the edge of the sofa. She could almost feel how uncomfortable this was for him.

This was definitely not good news.

'Is he dead?'

There was hope in her voice again.

The DI shook his head.

'Joanie, listen to me, love. We have done everything possible to find out what happened but we can't see that he did anything wrong.'

He waited for her to digest this piece of information before he continued.

'In fact, we can't find any previous convictions, for him or his father. The girl who you say accused him, this Caitlin Rowe, has denied it outright. Said it was just a rumour. Her mother has now requested she be moved by the council to stop her being tracked down again. The mother is terrified Caitlin's going to be dragged into something she has no connection with.'

He looked at her drawn face, at the new lines around her eyes and mouth. Lines put there through sleepless nights and too much booze.

'So that's it then, he walks away? What about the money Joseph gave them? Can't you prove that he did so? Find out how he came by it?'

Baxter sighed heavily.

'Any chance of a cup of tea, Joanie?'

She went into the kitchen and put the kettle on. He followed her, his heart as heavy as hers.

'We found nothing, Joanie, nothing we can use. The Thompsons' flat was clean of everything, love. We searched it twice. Not a thing that shouldn't be there.'

'Why did the father go on the trot then?'

She wanted a row now.

'Maybe he was frightened, Joanie. Wouldn't you be?'

She conceded the point but not with words.

He pushed his case.

'I know I would be if I had your Jon Jon after me.'

'You didn't find a thing? What about the girl's mother, this Leigh Rowe?'

'Denied the lot of it, and if she don't open her trap then our hands are tied. We can't nick someone on rumours, Joanie, we need proof.'

She laughed derisively.

'That's a new one! It's never stopped you before.'

'That's unfair, Joanie, and you know it. This is different.'

She poured water over the tea bags when in reality all she wanted to do was throw the kettle at Baxter.

Hurt him as she was hurting.

A voice whispered to her, 'as Little Tommy was hurt'.

'He done it, I know he done it. Him and his father. Pair of perverted cunts they are.'

The barely suppressed violence was there in her voice and he knew Little Tommy would never be safe again.

'Without evidence, Joanie . . .'

She laughed once more. A hollow sound.

'Without a body, you mean. That *is* what you mean, ain't it?'

It was but he wasn't about to say it out loud.

'Look, I'm heart sorry for you and yours, I really am, but we can find no reason to charge Tommy Thompson. Rumour just ain't enough, love, even if it seems plausible. I need rock solid evidence.'

'You never needed that when you was after me and mine, did you? I waited hours for you lot to arrive the night she went missing.'

Joanie was near to tears. He put out a hand in sympathy but she slapped it away.

'Fucking hours I waited in here.'

She looked around the flat as if seeing it as she had that night.

'Not a fucking dicky bird from you lot. But that didn't matter, did it? It was only a Brewer on the missing list. Why give a flying fuck about one of them?'

He could see the anguish in her face and had never in his life felt so badly for someone before.

'They ain't nothing – scum of the earth, the Brewers. The mother's on the bash, the kids are like animals . . . Do you honestly think I don't know what was going through all your minds that night?'

He couldn't look at her. He knew what she was saying was true and he had been as guilty as everyone else. But he denied it anyway. He had to.

'That's not true, Joanie. We did all we could, are still doing everything possible . . .'

'Oh, blow it out of your arse, Mr Baxter.'

He decided he had to tell her the truth.

'Joanie, Tommy Thompson is incapable of any kind of sexual activity. Jon Jon knows that. He saw his medical records.'

'He told me, but like him I don't believe it. Tommy might not have been capable but that don't mean he wasn't thinking about it, does it?'

Baxter sighed once more.

'You're just making it harder for yourself. You don't know anything sexual happened to her, Joanie. She might have fallen in the river . . . anything. You're assuming the worst.'

Joanie rolled her eyes to the ceiling.

'Get a grip, Mr Baxter, you think the same as I do. You think it's that ponce and his father as much as I do.'

She was trying to make him share her guilt as well as her hurt.

'I had him in my home! I was his friend. I cared about him . . . trusted him.' She was near to tears again.

'I read up on nonces. "Grooming" they call it. Getting in with the family. And let's face it, with Jon Jon and me, who'd have thought anyone would have had the guts to pull a stunt like that? I know she didn't fall in no river. If she had she would have turned up by now. No one saw her, no one! So she was local, *is* still local. It's just finding her. Or what's left of her.

'Nothing happened to her that wasn't planned by that piece of shit and his father. Where is the father anyway? How can he disappear like this if he ain't dodgy? Even criminals have a hard job going on the trot for any length of time.'

Baxter had thought exactly the same thing but he didn't say it. Instead he suggested, 'Perhaps he's topped himself, Joanie. We have to consider all the options.'

She nodded, looking happier for a second, more relaxed.

'I hope you're right, Mr Baxter, and I hope Little Tommy follows in his father's footsteps. Until they are wiped off the face of the earth I will not sleep another night properly in my bed.'

'You shouldn't say things like that in front of me, Joanie . . .'

She blew out her lips.

'Like I give a fuck what happens to me.'

Baxter left a while later and Joanie sat on her own and smoked, as was her habit these days.

Paulie grabbed the girl's arse and she squealed with delight.

'Paulie!'

He laughed, and getting out of bed started to pull on his clothes. She was a new one, a girl called Linette. She had blonde hair, natural, and green eyes. If she had not been on the game from an early age she would probably have been married by now and treasured for her good looks. Instead she was being used by a man old enough to be her father. Because Paulie used her as he used all the women in his life.

'So, am I in the new parlour then?'

He nodded. He'd been going to put her in there anyway. The new parlour was specialising in young, good-looking girls. That was reflected in its prices and name: Angel Girls. It was situated in King's Cross, near Spearmint Rhino, and would cater for the City types. He was giving it six months. If the profits didn't match the overheads he would out it. But Jon Jon had done his homework and Paulie was glad to see him taking an interest in things once more. If only the boy could keep his mind on work all the time.

But he had changed so much in the last three months as to be virtually unrecognisable from the lad Paulie had taken on. He looked older and he looked harder. The boyish good looks had long gone, swamped overnight by grief.

Jon Jon was vicious, but it was a controlled viciousness. Whereas before he had been subject to quick flashes of temper, now he was constantly looking for a fight and he was finding them – and winning.

Paulie sighed as he thought about it. But on the plus side at least he had thrown himself into work and that had paid dividends for the business.

It was Joanie he worried about most.

She seemed to have caved in on herself, as if she was alive but not living. That was the only way he could describe the change in her. She walked, talked and sometimes she ate, but it was as if it was all in slow motion. All pretend. She wanted to be with her daughter, and was only carrying on until she knew for certain the child was dead. Then he had no doubt she would soon follow.

He himself was frightened to think of what might have become of Kira. Bad enough for that to happen to a child he knew. But to hear the child was actually his had thrown him. Paulie pushed the thought once more from his mind; he couldn't think about it. Besides, he only had Joanie's word for it anyway. And, he reasoned, how could she be sure?

She had been through more blokes than Dockyard Dolly, the stevedores' friend, so he was not sure if Kira really was his child or if Joanie merely wanted her to be his. He knew she believed it, but he wasn't sure he did. Either way, he didn't want to think about it.

As Linette left the flat he smiled at her tightly. Once she was dressed he had no real interest in her any more. He was strange like that and he knew it.

But he had an ear out and a bounty on the Thompsons' heads. If they could be found he would find them, it was the least he could do.

Little Tommy was still in constant pain, but it was getting easier by the day. He was in a nursing home in Sheffield, paid for by the government because he was in danger of retaliatory attacks in prison. No one here knew who he was, and he answered to the name of Jeffrey Palmer. He liked the name in some ways, it had an edge to it.

He wondered for the hundredth time what his father was doing and where he could have gone to. Joseph had a lot of cronies from the old days, and so Tommy assumed he must have looked some up. He had given various names to the police but they had come up with nothing. But then, they wouldn't, would they?

He had not given them all the names, he wasn't *that* stupid. He didn't want his father turning up again.

His face looked awful. They had made sure he had no mirrors in the room, but he saw his reflection in the window sometimes and he knew how bad he looked. But, he had decided, he had not looked that great to start with.

It was the only way he could cope.

He dreamed of his mother most nights, felt her hold him as she had when he was a little boy. If she had still been alive none of this would have happened, he was sure of that much.

He was eating again, comfort eating.

He wished he had never clapped eyes on Kira Brewer. His father had been right all along. It would only cause trouble, he had said, and he was proved right once more. Why hadn't Tommy listened to him?

The nurse brought him a carafe of fresh water and he ignored her. Actually, of course, she was ignoring him. None of the nurses really spoke to him, and he knew they didn't enjoy touching him. But then again, that had been true for most of his life.

No one ever wanted to be near him.

Except Kira, of course.

And look at the trouble that had caused.

He sighed and opened up another Mars bar. As he chewed on it aimlessly he wondered how long he would be here before he was moved once more. They were moving him constantly.

Was he on the run? He supposed he was in a way. That was food for thought, as his mother used to say.

Jon Jon was meeting a bloke from North London. He was a Rasta, originally from Jamaica and then from Newcastle upon Tyne. The man smiled at him and they shook hands, mutual respect evident in their stance and in their faces.

'Good to meet you at last.'

Sippy smiled at the two of them. He was glad he had brought them together. Sippy loved Jon Jon. There was a natural affinity, both business and personal, between them. Since his sister's disappearance they had become even closer. Sippy had a sister who had been caught in a gang shoot-out in Jamaica. She was still a child in her mind even now she was a woman in her body. He paid a substantial amount each month for her to be taken care of in a clean and caring environment in Surrey. At the end of the day she was blood and that was all that mattered. The fact he didn't advertise her existence was his business. But he had confided in Jon Jon to help him understand how you got over things.

Even the worst things.

Now as he watched Errol and Jon Jon he was glad that he had arranged this meet. It anyone could find this Tommy it was Errol. He had all the filth in his pocket, could get literally anything about anyone. Now he was tracking down the man they believed to be responsible for Kira's demise, and demise was the right word.

She was dead, they all knew it.

It was how she'd died they wanted to find out.

Sippy leaned forward in his chair and said quietly, 'If Jon Jon had a body he could bury her, and half the hurt would be gone, Errol. It's the not knowing.'

Errol nodded his huge head. He was handsome and knew it. Much taken to wearing white vests with blue jeans, he looked the epitome of the Rastaman – until, that is, he stepped into his limited edition Mercedes Sports.

He rarely wore shoes, favouring Reef sandals, and his body was well pumped up from weight training.

Errol sat back in his chair and sipped gladly at his pint of Guinness.

'Well, we might have some good news. I have two possibles for you. One's in Sheffield and the other in Birmingham, both suffering from burns, both under assumed names. I got this from a boy I own in the Met. Good lad. He works for the CPS – and for me as well.'

He threw back his head and laughed as he added, 'I always said he would go far.'

Sippy and Jon Jon laughed with him even though Jon Jon couldn't think what the fuck he had to laugh about, but he knew how to play the game and he liked Errol. Under different circumstances he would have roared his head off.

Errol slipped him a piece of paper with the addresses on.

'There are two numbers there. You ring them and you'll have specialised back-up to go with you, OK?'

Jon Jon nodded.

'Thank you, Errol, I appreciate it.'

He shrugged, embarrassed.

'I hope you find him and I hope you find your sister. It must be hard, man, very hard.'

Jon Jon nodded.

Sippy sat quietly, 'He need revenge, know what I'm saying?'

Errol nodded once more.

'Of course he does, and we'll see that he gets it.'

They chatted then about nothing, just chilling, all of them aware that Jon Jon couldn't wait to leave and follow up the information. But he stayed a while out of politeness because Errol had done him the favour of a lifetime.

Jeanette was talking to Liz Parker. The two girls got on like a house on fire.

'So, how much do you earn in an average night?' Jeanette asked.

Liz sighed and put her head on one side, thinking. The action made her look much younger than usual.

'About three hundred quid usually. If I do the special parties I can earn much more, of course.'

Jeanette was intrigued.

'What are the special parties?'

'Well, it's when you look really young like, no makeup, a gymslip and ankle socks!' She was laughing. 'Some geezers pay a fortune for all that, see, and you can get three bar just for a couple of hours' work. You have to act all shy like, unless they tell you different. Some of the blokes like you to be all virginal and others like you to be a right little slapper, it depends, but they all pay well. Plus, you're round their house, see?'

Jeanette saw and liked what she saw.

'Once, I was round this bloke's house and his wife come home . . .'

Jeanette's eyes were like saucers now.

'No! What did you do?'

'I run out the back door, had to take the baby oil and me uniform and everything with me. He pushed me out that house like I was on fire or something. Anyway, I was up the road when I realised I hadn't been paid.'

Jeanette's eyes were now stretched to their utmost.

'You never went back there?'

Liz grinned.

'Nah, but me pimp did and he got the money quick smart, I can tell you.'

'Does Paulie Martin do all that too then?'

Liz was careful how she answered this. She knew Jeanette's mother and Paulie were an item that went back years. There was no way she was going to fuck herself with a few words out of place now. Men like Paulie Martin had a way of knowing exactly what was said about them.

'Oh, Paulie's Mr Smooth these days, love,' she laughed. 'Why the big interest anyway?'

Jeanette shrugged.

'No reason. Just interested, that's all.'

Which she was – because she was thinking of doing it herself. Jeanette wanted a place of her own, somewhere she and Jasper could be alone together without Karen's motor mouth going round the clock.

'Who did you do these parties for then?'

Liz was quiet for a few seconds.

'Why do you want to know?'

'Just curious.'

'A bloke called Pippy Light, and he's a piece of shit. Your brother hates him.'

'Does he? Why?'

Liz was getting in over her head here and she knew it. Jon Jon would not take kindly to her telling his business to all and sundry, especially not his sister.

'He just hates nasty pimps, that's all.'

'Where does this Pippy hang out then?'

Liz laughed.

'Are you thinking of going on the bash or something?'

Jeanette laughed with her.

''Course not! I'm just wondering, that's all. A healthy curiosity, nothing more. That's what Jon Jon always says when he questions me about where I've been and what I'm doing. He thinks I don't know he's trying to keep tabs on me.'

'He cares about you, Jeanette.'

The girl flicked back her long brown hair in a gesture of contempt.

'He wants to live my life for me, you mean.'

Her face was dark now as she thought of how hemmed in she was these days. Her mother was as bad. Didn't want Jeanette back home – not full-time anyway. Kept saying she needed her space, time to mourn her loss. Kira again. It was always about Kira even now she was gone for ever. But Joanie still nagged Jeanette, got on her case about the bits of thieving she did, and the girl had had enough of it. She wanted her own life.

'Don't knock it, love. I wish someone had ever cared that much about me. Even once,' Liz said wistfully.

Jeanette grimaced.

'Well, you wouldn't if they did. It's a pain in the fucking arse.'

'After what happened to your sister . . .'

Jeanette jumped up then and said brusquely, 'Is that the time? I must get going, me mother's waiting for me to visit her.'

She always changed the subject when people mentioned her sister. Couldn't bear to think about Kira, feel once more her own scalding guilt for the way she had treated the child.

As she walked to Joanie's flat she wondered once more what had happened to her little sister. It was all she thought about when she was alone. She had a strong urge to be with someone else, not to suffer this pain alone. Jasper was good to her but the person she really wanted was her mum. This was happening more and more lately to Jeanette, though no one seeing that hard little painted face would ever have guessed at the desolation behind it.

Jon Jon watched the changing expressions on his mother's face and his heart went out to her.

'Do you think he's really up there?' she asked eagerly.

Jon Jon nodded.

'Meself I think he's in Sheffield. I don't know why, just a feeling, but I'm going to visit the Birmingham address first, and then if I have no joy I'll carry on up North. This Errol was a right nice fella. He's still looking for us and wouldn't take a penny for his trouble, you know.'

Joanie nodded.

'People come up trumps at times like this.'

She was pouring out yet another drink as she spoke and Jon Jon sighed, trying hard not to say anything to her about it and avoid another row. But her drinking was out of hand these days. Even though he felt he should try and stop her, he knew her circumstances were hardly normal and she needed something to bolster her through each and every empty day. Maybe when he'd sorted Tommy for good his mum would start pulling herself together.

She looked painfully pleased by his news and the thought that this was the only pleasure she was likely to feel for a long time, hearing the whereabouts of the beast who had murdered her child, almost made him weep. Instead he hugged her. Joanie hugged him back, enjoying the comforting smell of him, wondering what life was going to throw at them all next.

He left the flat fifteen minutes later and when he'd gone Joanie made a quick phone call. Then she ran around quickly sorting her stuff out. She had her coat on ready to go when the mini-cab bibbed her. She ran straight down the stairs and shoved her overnight bag into the car ahead of her. She told the driver to take her to the station as quickly as possible.

'You're in a rush, love.'

'And you are a nosy bastard!'

The tone of her voice told the cab driver to keep schtumm and he did.

Joanie opened the holdall and checked she had everything she needed.

She was smiling.

Jon Jon would do his crust when he realised she had gone to Sheffield ahead of him. He was arranging to go up to Birmingham the next day but first he had to cover himself for work, and the new parlour was opening tonight so he had to be there.

She, though, had both addresses and if she didn't find the fucker in Sheffield she would make her way down to Birmingham, pop in on her way home so to speak.

Joanie felt elated.

If she could she was going to find out where her daughter was, but whatever happened she was going to make Little Tommy pay for what he had done to her and her family. As she had waved her son off she'd wanted to laugh with joy and excitement. He wouldn't be home until the morning and by then she would be long gone. This was something she wanted to sort out for herself.

Jeanette came home to a dark deserted flat. No sign of Joanie apart from a near-empty bottle of vodka and the overflowing ashtrays. She made herself something to eat and went back out again. She was miffed and it showed.

No one bothered with her these days. Her mother, she knew, still blamed her for her sister's disappearance. More to the point, Jeanette blamed herself.

Disconsolately, she made her way round to Jasper's. She didn't know where else to go.

Chapter Nineteen

Jon Jon was enjoying the opening night of Angel Girls, something he hadn't thought would be possible, considering all that had happened in the last few months.

Starting up this place had taken his mind off his sister when he had most needed it and for that he would be forever grateful.

Tonight it was buzzing, had a great atmosphere. The new parlour was going to be a real money-spinner, and it was all down to him. He was proud of what he had achieved in such a short time.

Unlike the other parlours this one was getting a proper opening night. Normally they opened quietly and discreetly to allay the usual protests from housewives and do-gooders who were actually more worried about their husbands using the place than they were about seeing the neighbourhood go downhill.

As long as they kept it low-key they were in with a chance. The licences were acquired by a reputable legal firm and they would do their best to keep a low profile. No fighting in the street, whether between the girls, or girls and punters, was permitted. No foul language, and definitely no drunkenness.

Tonight, though, they had champagne and wine. They also had music. Jon Jon was crossing his fingers that everything would go like clockwork because he had almost made Paulie sink his money into this place.

It had been like a passion with him for the last seven weeks and he had opened this place in record time. Which was something he knew would score him brownie points if nothing else did. Paulie always wanted everything yesterday, and Jon Jon was a bit like that himself.

Angel Girls had everything: state-of-the-art booths for the workers containing the best massage oils and perfumed candles. The towels and sheets were top quality; they had skimped on nothing. Every wall was mirrored so the clients could observe themselves performing from any angle, and the booths were soundproofed too so they could also make as much noise as they liked. Each had its own CD and DVD player for soft porn or music, whichever was preferred. The place rocked and Jon Jon was proud to have been the instigator of it.

He and Paulie had sent out personalised invitations to all the big businesses hereabouts and tonight they had seen a really wonderful turnout. Their prospective clientele had money to burn and the handpicked girls were all very good-looking. They'd been briefed to talk to the prospective punters in a sincere and intelligent fashion – or as intelligent as they could manage anyway. As long as the subject stayed on them they should be all right. This was far more upmarket than anything Paulie had attempted before.

Jon Jon studied his boss's face as he smiled smugly around the crowded room, and felt himself relax. Paulie was weighing up exactly what this had cost him, doing his accounts as he assessed their client base. They'd decided they were charging four hundred quid for half an hour here. Serious money would soon be rolling in.

The place would pay for itself in just under three months, everything else was bunce.

This was going to work; the City gents already had lap-dancing clubs but this was to cater to the more *stressed* businessmen. The girls here actually had proper qualifications for aromatherapy, Reiki, even first aid. One was a qualified sports therapist, or at least Jon Jon had bought her the diploma. Her sports were more active movement than football, but she had the piece of paper nonetheless.

You name it, they had it, and this was to be the blind. To all intents and purposes this place was a legitimate spa which just happened to have extra good-looking therapists.

There was more than a smattering of women guests too. Jon Jon had allowed for this and had a couple of fit-looking boys milling around that he had pulled from a discreet escort agency. If things worked out they would go full-time here and make much more money than they were now. If any of the male customers preferred men then they were willing to cater for them as well.

As Paulie was convinced that all upper-class men were shirt lifters, as he so succinctly put it, no request would surprise him and Angel Girls could just as easily turn out to be Boys. All his workforce could take on punters of either sex, quickly and efficiently. In fact, Jon Jon's research had shown that many women were willing to pay for sex these days and Paulie was willing to bankroll anything if he thought it would bring a hefty return.

As Jon Jon pushed his way through the throng of people he saw himself reflected in the glass wall opposite. He was wearing a black Versace suit, white ruffled shirt open at the neck, and hand-made shoes. He looked the business and he knew it.

Kira would have loved seeing him like this. She used to love seeing people 'sparkle'. Unconsciously he straightened his dreads and as he did so caught Paulie's eye. He made a foppish movement with his hand, making Jon Jon grin. Then his boss motioned him into the office with a movement of his head and Jon Jon followed him up the thickly carpeted stairs, the R&B music pumping out behind him.

The office was austere and functional; steel-fronted filing cabinets, a glass-topped desk and polished oak floorboards. It was as up-to-the-minute as it could be, air-conditioned, sound-proofed. A monastic retreat from the spurious 'luxury' of the working booths below.

Paulie grinned.

'It's a hit, son, you done me proud.'

Jon Jon was thrilled by the praise. It was sincere and it was heartfelt.

'I'm glad to hear it, Paulie. I've been shitting bricks all week.'

Paulie laughed.

'I know the feeling, mate! But I can tell you, this lot love it. Something a bit naughty for them to do and talk about after to their mates. Regale the whole pub with stories of the good-looking bird they humped. And all the time they're actually paying for it! I could understand them bragging if it was free. Complete cunts, the lot of them.'

Thus Paulie contemptuously dismissed his clientele. He hated the men who frequented his parlours, saw them as inadequate, born losers. No matter how much money this lot might have they were still useless as far as he was concerned.

'You know what the next step will be, don't you?'

Jon Jon shook his head.

'What?'

Paulie pursed his lips and answered tartly, 'We'll lose some of our girls to the punters. *That's* the kind of dicks we'll be dealing with here. They'll fall in fucking love! Seen it time and time again though I've never understood a man who'll marry a whore. She'll give it to anyone, it's the nature of them. Why they flog their arses in the first place.'

Jon Jon didn't answer, just stared at Paulie until he realised exactly what he had said. He wasn't about to apologise, especially not to someone he employed, but it took the shine off the night for both of them.

There was a heavy silence. Eventually Paulie put his hand out and said gently, 'Congratulations anyway. You did good, kid.'

Jon Jon hesitated for a moment before he clasped the hand offered to him. He looked up to Paulie, even understood what he had meant, but Jon Jon's main loyalty was to his mother and he knew that Paulie respected him for that.

It was a strange relationship, and in many ways a loving one. Jon Jon was like a son to Paulie, and they both accepted that too without labouring the point.

Linette came into the office then without knocking and looked askance at Jon Jon, fully expecting him to leave because she was there.

'I want to talk to Paulie . . .'

She put on a baby voice, as irritating as it was false. She was also out of her box and still had white powder underneath her nose – not something that would endear her to Paulie Martin but Jon Jon decided to let her find that out for herself.

She paused before she said huskily: 'Alone.'

Jon Jon smiled at Paulie and cocked an eyebrow, taking the piss as he said loudly, 'Is she fucking sure about that?'

Paulie walked over to the scantily clad girl who smiled at him, her best professional smile, which was her second mistake of the night.

He said in a low, level voice that was far more terrifying than if he'd yelled at her: 'If you ever pull a stunt like this again I'll make sure no man would fuck you for free, let alone pay good money for it! You fucking cheeky mare.'

Her whole demeanour changed. She looked shell-shocked as indeed she was. She'd believed she had Paulie Martin under her thumb, but now like many a woman before her she was finding out different.

Then he bellowed in her face, one finger pointing to the door as if she was an errant schoolgirl.

'Out! Out now, and don't come back without my express fucking say-so.'

She rushed from the room near to tears. Paulie looked at Jon Jon, holding up his hands as he said in jokey fashion, 'You give them eight inches and they take the piss.'

Jon Jon started to laugh and then they were both at it, roaring with mirth. It put them back on the right footing somehow. They went down to the party together and watched the money rolling in.

Joanie was in a safe cab. She had got in touch with an old friend-cum-customer and he had sorted her out with a minicab from King's Cross to Sheffield, no questions asked. The man driving was a Bosnian with little command of English and this suited her right down to the ground. He shouldn't have been driving at all so there was no fear of him turning lippy after the event.

He had been refused asylum and was in effect on the run. Joanie liked him for that fact if nothing else.

She lay back in the seat as they drove up the M1 and tried to get a few hours' sleep, but she already knew it would not be possible. She was far too excited about the coming event. She checked inside her holdall and smiled once more.

Joanie was equipped for any eventuality. She was actually looking forward to getting the dirty deed over with once and for all.

She had always protected her children as best she could. Now she must teach Little Tommy exactly what a good mother did if anyone dared harm her child. It had to come from *her*, Joanie Brewer, not from Jon Jon or the police. From her, Joanie Brewer, the mother of the child he had destroyed. She wanted retribution and she was going to get it.

If she left it to the police – that is, if they could even tie him to Kira's disappearance, of course – Tommy would go to prison and be stuck on a VPU unit. And there he'd be laughing, his life hardly changed in fact; he would have access to computers, cups of tea as and when he wanted them. Such prisoners were classed as passive. Passive? After what he'd done?

She had asked around her friends and neighbours, talked to men who had been banged up and found out exactly what happened to the scumbags on Rule 43. It actually meant they could do what the fuck they liked all day because they were classed as passive! That word again.

Every other fucker was locked up for twenty-three hours a day, but not them. Oh, no, the nonces had the time of their fucking lives. The stories she had been told were unbelievable!

She was goading herself into feeling angry; she was going to need all that anger to help her do what she had to do. She was nurturing her anger now, making sure she didn't bottle out of what she had planned.

She knew what the general prison population thought of nonces, and rightly so, which made it worse to hear that the Vulnerable Prisoners' Units were veritable havens for like-minded individuals. By the very nature of their offences they were an abomination to everyone else so in the VPUs they flocked together for safety.

Most of them had never met another sex offender in their lives until they got banged up. Then, suddenly, it was like all their Christmases and birthdays rolled into one. They didn't have to hide what they were any more, and they didn't feel isolated or alone. Suddenly they were surrounded by people just like themselves. It made them feel *normal*. They were over the moon to discover that their hitherto clandestine activities were in fact as routine as making a cup of tea to the people surrounding them now. Or so they told each other anyway.

Well, she was going to see to it that Little Tommy paid for what he had done, and she was going to make sure he never had the opportunity to do it to anyone else. Joanie was humming under her breath as she lay back against the seat and tried to relax. The cab driver looked in the mirror and smiled at her. She smiled back. Then, lighting yet another cigarette, she let her mind drift back to the job in hand.

Jeanette had asked around about Pippy Light and had been told the same thing, by Karen Copes and even by Jasper. The best person to ask, it seemed, was Lorna Bright who had known him for years. In fact, she had once been his girlfriend. But Lorna was terrified of Jeanette these days, thanks to Jon Jon and his threats. Didn't even talk to her any more if she saw her up the shops.

Still, Jeanette was determined to find out what she wanted to know and she was willing to run the gauntlet to do it.

She walked up the stairs to Lorna's maisonette and knocked on the door. It was dark and it was late so she felt safe enough for the moment. She only hoped the place wasn't full of wasters as usual. Someone or other would want to get into Jon Jon's good books and grass her up to him to do just that. He was like a god round here now. Everyone revered him, especially since he had taken the law into his own hands with Little Tommy.

The burning of the nonce had made him a big man in the community; he had always been hard, even as a little kid, but now he was hard and respected – something everyone in their world strived to become.

Lorna opened the door, and the smell of skunk wafted out into the lobby. Jeanette could see that she was stoned out of her mind. Smiling tentatively, she said, 'All right, Lorna? How's the baby?'

Lorna did not find it in the least strange to have someone knock late at night and enquire about her child. This was par for the course for her and her so-called friends.

'Ain't you going to ask me in then?'

Lorna stepped aside and Jeanette walked past her into the sour-smelling dimness. In the lounge the only light was from the TV which was on as usual, and the new baby was lying on the floor. It had soiled itself and the smell was ripe. On the settee a man lay snoring, his naked body glistening with sweat.

The baby started to cry and Lorna jabbed at her with a dirty foot. Then, kneeling down on the carpet, she said gaily, 'Who's Mummy's little fucker, eh?'

Jeanette sighed.

'Shall I change her for you?'

She saw the gleam of calculation in the junkie's eyes. Yet another unpleasant task avoided. Lorna really was a piece of shit.

'Social Services are coming for her tomorrow. They already have the other bugger, Laeticia. She got so jealous of the new baby she tried to give her a clump!'

Lorna laughed.

'Anyway, I need a break. She can go for a few weeks and then I'll get some sleep.'

A few weeks would turn to months and they both knew that. When she had had her first daughter, the child had been born with a club foot and was very underweight. The story was that when Lorna went to the hospital eventually to bring her home, the child was already four months old and the nurses had refused to hand her over because they didn't know who Lorna was. She had not visited her baby once.

Lorna's own mum admitted how embarrassed she had been when the nurses had said, 'We've never seen you before, you could be anyone.'

It had taken two social workers and a court order to get the baby home with its far from doting mother. She had kept it long enough to draw benefits and family allowance before the frequent sojourns in care started. Laeticia was now a pretty if nervous child, and this one would be the same as she grew up.

'What did you call her?'

Lorna sighed.

'Trelayne Sioux.'

Jeanette smiled.

'Jerry Springer again?'

She laughed.

'Spot on! Those Americans have great names, don't you think? I wanted her to be different like, you know. A name is important, ain't it?'

The sad thing was, Lorna really meant what she said.

'She'll be different, all right!'

Jeanette wasn't sure whether Lorna was too stoned or too thick to take the insult for what it was.

'What brings you here anyway?'

Lorna was watching her changing the baby quickly and efficiently.

'I'll tell you in a minute.'

Jeanette cleaned Trelayne up and dressed her, then cradled the baby in her arms and nursed her.

'She's starving, any chance of a feed?'

Lorna jumped up.

'I always forget they need feeding all the time . . . that's why it's best she goes away for a while. You know, until she's easier to handle.'

She came back with some baby feed that had obviously been given to her in the hospital, and equally obviously had just come from the fridge. The baby took it anyway, grabbing at it and sucking hungrily, the noise loud in the room. The child's nails were already ingrained with dirt and she had a small bruise on her cheekbone. Courtesy of Laeticia, Jeanette supposed, though it wouldn't surprise her if Lorna had done it herself and blamed the poor child.

She remembered her own mother feeding Kira, who had always smelled sweet, and was always clean and tidy. It was strange but Jeanette was only just learning to appreciate how good a mother Joanie was.

'You're a natural, you should have one yourself.'

It was meant as a compliment and Jeanette knew that. But it still annoyed her. Lorna had no other ambition but this, having kids and getting the benefits. What a life! Not only for Lorna but for her poor children who would be in and out of care their whole lives, and then carry on the family business. Get what you could off the State, what you were *entitled* to.

It was that word *entitled* that always annoyed Jeanette's mother when she spoke to Monika about it. Monika couldn't take on board that you should have paid some tax in your life before you got handouts. She didn't see Joanie's logic: that the dole and benefits should be there only until you got on your feet, got yourself work, that they were never meant to be a lifestyle.

Now, watching Lorna, Jeanette understood why her mother had always been on at her to get herself an education.

Well, it was too late for that now.

Lorna opened a couple of cans of Red Stripe and placed one in front of Jeanette. She gulped deeply from her own can and burped loudly.

The man on the sofa groaned and turned over. Lorna didn't even look in his direction. He had a half-erection and it was pushing through his grubby underpants, Jeanette felt her skin crawling.

'Who's that?'

Lorna shrugged.

'Peter something or other, I met him in the pub yesterday. He'd had a win at the bookie's. I ain't supposed to you know what yet, but I was pissed as usual.'

She laughed loudly at her own wit.

'What do you want, Jeanette? Only your brother ain't exactly my biggest fan, is he?'

'Listen, Lorna, he can't tell me who to be friends with.'

'So he ain't sent you here then?'

She shook her head and saw the relief in Lorna's eyes.

''Course not! He don't fucking own me, girl.'

It was the right approach.

'Where can I lay the baby down?'

Jeanette followed Lorna through to a small bedroom; it held a mattress with a quilt thrown over it and a small Moses basket. Nothing else, not even a toy. There were a couple of dirty nappies on the mattress and the smell was ripe once more. Jeanette guessed that the mattress was probably wet anyway from the other little girl.

As she laid the baby down she said gently, 'She's beautiful. Is it true that Pippy Light's the father?'

Lorna shrugged.

'Could be, I suppose. At least she's come out white so I know who *ain't* the bleeding father!'

She was laughing now and the baby stirred in her basket.

Jeanette couldn't help grimacing with distaste at Lorna's words. Fortunately she misunderstood and nodded conspiratorially.

'Last thing we want is her up again, eh?'

They tiptoed from the room. Jeanette was so sorry for the baby she had just had to leave in her basket on a dirty bare floor, her clothes and bedding stained and bedraggled. She consoled herself that at least the child was clean and fed, even if it had been done by Jeanette and not her mother. Presumably Lorna would have got around to it eventually. At least, she hoped so anyway. It went against the grain for people like them to phone either the police or Social Services, but for the first time ever Jeanette realised what those agencies were actually for.

She had seen kids out playing till all hours, scruffy and dirty. But she also knew they had been fed and loved, if only in haphazard fashion. Lorna's child, though, would haunt her dreams. She knew that as surely as she knew her own name.

In the kitchen Jeanette sipped her Red Stripe as she watched Lorna ineffectually attempt to clean up around her.

'So what's the sudden interest in Pippy Light?'

'Just asking, you know.'

'Does your brother know you're interested?'

Jeanette grinned.

'He don't know everything, just likes to think he does.'

Lorna opened her eyes wide at this blasphemy.

'You're a cow, ain't you? Well, Pippy can be found at his flat most days. But I warn you, Jeanette, don't get in over your head. If you want to score I can give you names of people who aren't as heavy as him, you know what I mean?'

She scratched aimlessly at her head.

'I scout for him sometimes, see. He likes me, old Pippy. Sees me all right for a bit of gear now and again. I have to put out for him, but he ain't the worst. Just be careful. He'll take one look and want you out earning for him. You're jail bait and that's his favourite pastime. Schoolgirls . . .'

'Does he pay well?'

Lorna stared into her eyes.

'You ain't seriously considering it, are you?'

Jeanette shrugged once more.

'He'd probably be too scared of me brother anyway!'

Lorna shook her head.

'Not Pippy Light, love, he'd love it. Him and Jesmond would find it amusing. Them two ain't scared of no one.'

The last bit was said with bravado. After all, they were her friends.

'Where's his flat then?'

'You serious?'

Jeanette nodded.

''Course.'

'I'll ring him for you, hang on.'

Lorna could get a drink off Pippy for this and her own back on Jon Jon in one fell swoop. What with the social worker taking the baby in the morning, and the money for the introduction from Pippy, she could be out of her brains and quids in by lunchtime tomorrow.

Life was just getting better and better.

Joanie hit Sheffield at just after ten at night. She rang the mobile number Errol had given them and was directed to a council estate on the edge of Sheffield town centre. As she walked up the concrete steps to the flat of the person who was going to take her to Tommy she looked around her. This place could be anywhere. Other than the accent she could hear in the street it could be London, Cardiff, Manchester or Glasgow. Anywhere there was a council estate built to house the forgotten people. The same smells assailed her nostrils, urine, sweat and fried food, and underlying the smell of poverty was the smell of drugs and drink. She recognised the familiar musky smell of heroin addicts; she had passed two in the hallway, their glazed eyes following her up the flight of stairs. The female was emaciated and vocal, telling Joanie in no uncertain terms what she thought at having to move aside to let her pass. The male was younger, unshaven and straggly-haired. He wouldn't have noticed if a brass band had tramped through the dank lobby. He was gone from the planet and when he came back he would crash down harder than the space shuttle. But for the moment he was away, and he was happy.

She knocked tentatively on the door of the flat she was looking for. It was answered by a woman with dyed red hair and a cheerful smile.

'Joanie?'

She nodded.

'Away in, love. Did you find us all right?'

She nodded once more, not sure what she was doing now. Frightened of it all.

Inside the flat it was dramatically different. There were brightly coloured walls, everything was immaculately clean and very well lit, lamps and candles burning everywhere. The smell was fantastic: ylang-ylang, jasmine and lavender. The hallway was painted bright pink, and there was a framed poster of Marilyn Monroe opposite the front door.

The walls of the lounge were painted a deep green, and the furniture was all pale green Habitat and tubular glass tables. Joanie felt better about being here. If it had been dirty or neglected she would have turned around and gone home. She actually wondered for a moment if that was what she secretly wanted, just to turn around and leave.

But she knew she had to stay. This had gone too far now, she realised with a certainty that terrified her. The woman grinned at her, displaying uneven but very white teeth, and Joanie realised that she was much older than she had first thought.

'A cuppa, a real drink or both?' she asked.

Joanie smiled shyly.

'Vodka?'

'A lass after my own heart!'

Five minutes later they were settled on the comfortable sofa with large vodkas and Cokes.

'You look nervous, pet,' the other woman said.

Joanie smiled.

'That's probably because I am.'

The woman held out her hand and said, 'Marie Drinkwater,

though I should be called Drinkvodka by rights!'

Joanie laughed loudly.

Then Marie said seriously, 'My daughter was murdered as well. She was seven when she disappeared. They found her three days later in a neighbour's flat. Nice fella and all, or so we all thought. He had raped her and stuffed her in a bin bag. She was found shoved in a cupboard in his bedroom. Turned out he'd done it before. Served a two-year sentence for molestation and eight years for murder. He even helped us search. You see, no one thought anything bad had happened to her at that point.'

Marie drained her drink swiftly in two large gulps.

'You passed the flat on your way up. His mother still lives there – a decent woman who died inside because of her son.'

Marie poured herself another large drink.

'I never touched a drink in my life until that happened. Now I wonder what I'm doing alive when she's gone, the light of my life taken. You see, Joanie, people sympathise, but it's not until it happens to them that they finally comprehend what it's like. How many times have you read about it, a kid gone missing, and thought, how terrible, and then hugged your own kids because it wasn't them? They're still there so you turn off the TV and forget about it until the next time.'

She looked out of the window as she said sadly, 'No one else knows what the nights are like, seeing their faces, wondering if they called for you. *Knowing* they did because you were their mam and mams are so important to little kids. They believe you can do anything. Except you couldn't do anything for them when they most needed it. Needed you.'

She grasped Joanie's hand.

'And then the court case when you watch the bastard who did it get fuck all, know that they'll be out within a few years. Did you know most paedophiles reoffend within six weeks? I put it down to the arrogance of the psychiatrists, believing they've cured someone who can't be cured. If a man is a leg man he'll always be a leg man, a tit man will always be a tit man, and a man who likes children will always want *children*. You kill him, lass, or I'll do it for you if you want. I know just what you're feeling, I can see it in your eyes.'

She squeezed Joanie's hand as she said quietly, 'There's no justice in this country, not for the victims anyway. Money and property, that's all the courts care about. A bank robber would get a harsher sentence than a paedophile, think on that.'

Joanie felt as if she had finally met a kindred spirit, which to all intents and purposes she had. Marie knew what she was going through better than anyone. She had been there herself.

Now it was Joanie's turn.

Chapter Twenty

Jon Jon looked at the girl in the bed. She was black, with relaxed hair and an arse you could carry a case on. She was beautiful and she was clever and she was expensive. Very expensive. For a few hours she had been his, and she was worth every penny. She had all the moves and looked good while performing them.

A true professional.

Before they had even got down to basics she had informed him that she rarely gave it away for nothing. That the whole idea of being on the game was to make money and freebies weren't really her thing.

According to Candace, she had never even given a mercy fuck, and he believed her. 'If you don't pay, you don't stay.' The words, when she'd said them, had made him laugh.

But that was last night when he had been drunk and stoned. In the cold light of day it wasn't funny any more, though looking around her flat he had to admit she had the right idea. He only wished his mother had had her acumen and then she might have had something more to show for all her years spent on the game.

Candace was shrewd, but she was also cold and calculating. He felt she would sell her own mother for money. Money was her god, she freely admitted that. Jon Jon had been chatting to her for an hour before they had left the party and he was annoyed about that now because there had been plenty of free pussy about. The girls were all over him like a rash these days.

Now Candace was stiffing him for the bill and he didn't like it.

He had wanted her at the time, thanks to drugs and alcohol, but he had just given her the bad news: she *hadn't* been worth the money. It had been a purely professional fuck and that had annoyed him. He was like Paulie in that respect, saw himself as better than the average punter. To Candace he could have been anyone. But what, he wondered, had he actually wanted from her in the first place? Was it because she was black like him that he hadn't expected her to treat him like a John?

But she had told him outright: to her everyone was a John.

His head was fucked and he wanted an argument suddenly and she was as good a person to fight with as anyone. Because Candace was quite able to hold her corner, he could see that.

'What exactly are you telling me, boy?' she said in a low voice.

She was looking at him with her big brown eyes. He could see that she was genuinely upset by what he had just said.

Jon Jon shrugged as he said in a cocky manner, 'I don't pay for it.'

She laughed as she said with bravado, one finger pointing in his face, 'You do now. I told you before we even got in the kip what my rates were. I even brought you to my *home*. You never had to weigh out for no hotel, boy. Now you keep your end of the bargain because *I* kept *mine*.'

Her voice conveyed without saying it that she had found him lacking, in bed and out of it. It also conveyed her South London accent which last night had been smoothed over and sophisticated.

'Not me, lady. Like I say, I don't pay.'

She leaned up on her elbow and stared deep into his eyes.

'You fucking wanker.'

'I've been called worse.'

He got out of bed slowly and felt her watching him all the time. Knew she wanted to attack him, and knew she wouldn't because he was basically her employer. He had a feeling, though, that she would fight on verbally if nothing else; at least, he hoped she would.

'I'll put the word round that you're a lousy fuck and mean with it,' Candace said decisively. With that she turned her back and closed her eyes as if going to sleep.

He wandered through her flat to the kitchen and made himself a cup of coffee. He was expecting her to come after him at any second like a wild cat, but she didn't move from the bedroom.

It was some flat. Everything was beautiful and carefully chosen and suited Candace down to the ground. It was all white paint and cream carpets, drifts of voile hanging strategically from brass curtain poles.

It was also sterile, as if no one really lived here. A show home for pretend people living pretend lives. Perfect lives. It was like an advert. Which was Candace, whether she realised it or not. Like all brasses she lived behind a front, and keeping up that front was the hardest thing of all. Pretending that the job didn't bother them, pretending to like the men paying them, pretending that their lives were great because they could afford good clothes and a nice home. At least at the lower end of the market the girls were past all that bullshit.

But men who paid a small fortune needed to feel that the girl in question really did *want* them and that the money was peripheral. They were paid to pretend they admired hanging bellies, scrawny legs and wrinkled-up dicks. It was like being an actress, except no one was going to give you any award except the cash you'd already negotiated with maybe a few quid extra as a bonus. He closed his eyes, contemplating the destruction of a lovely young girl's life.

For all her smart clothes and her beautiful home Candace had nothing, she was an emotional bankrupt. No wonder his mother had almost smothered them all with maternal love. It was the only real emotion she had ever felt.

He drank the coffee and stared aimlessly out of the kitchen window, looking out across London, watching the world come to life. A few black cabs were driving down the Portobello Road after taking home some late-night revellers. He lit himself a joint and toked on it deeply.

He wondered what he was doing hanging around here. After climbing out of her bed, why was he still in Candace's flat? More to the point, why were things like this happening to him more and more lately? It was as if he *wanted* to feel hurt and upset, *wanted* to feel used. Perhaps that was why he did it.

At least when he was disgusted with himself he was feeling something. Since Kira he feared he had lost any real feeling and that frightened him. As he puffed on the joint he remembered her face and smiled.

That was when he went back to the bedroom. Candace was still lying as he had left her and he put one hand gently on her shoulder to turn her round to face him. He expected her to be pouting, still upset over his refusal to pay, and he was going to pay her now, even pay her extra. He couldn't take it out on her, she was basically a good kid. And at least she had been honest, hadn't dressed it up as cab money. Mind you, at her prices it would have been some cab ride.

At the end of the day a deal was a deal after all. And she had been up front about it even if her rates were a bit stiff.

Then he realised she really *was* asleep because she pushed his hand off roughly and turned over once more snoring softly as she fell deeper into sleep.

He couldn't believe it.

Jon Jon started to laugh gently.

Candace honestly didn't give a fuck. She had accepted what he had said, and he admired her for that as well. She had swallowed her knob without a row of any kind. She knew she couldn't win this fight so she'd just put it down to experience. Candace didn't know it but she went up one hundredfold in his estimation because of her pragmatic reaction.

He sat on the edge of the bed and laughed until gradually he began to cry. He felt so lonely, so very lonely and hurt and unhappy. These were feelings he was still not used to. Doubted he would ever get used to. Kira's disappearance had left a gaping hole in his life which no one would ever be able to fill. That was the trouble with losing someone so young. You only ever remembered them as a child, never saw their faults because as yet they didn't have any. They were still unspoiled, still good inside and out.

Jon Jon put his head in his hands and sobbed, and all the while Candace slept beside him.

He had never felt so alone in all his life before.

He had done everything for his mother and his sisters, and the one time he wasn't there this tragedy had befallen them. He felt responsible. It was *his* fault. He had not looked after Kira properly, been there when she needed him. He would have to live with this guilt for the rest of his life.

If he had been there that day nothing would have happened to her. She would still be with them; he would still be ironing her school uniform and making her breakfast. He would be at home every night instead of staying with a procession of slappers and prostitutes, looking for something he was never going to find. Now his whole family was broken, smashed to pieces by someone they'd thought they could trust. But he would make them pay, Tommy and his father. He was going to Birmingham this morning, and Sheffield after that if he had to.

Suddenly he felt an arm around his shoulders.

'You OK?'

Finally Candace was awake.

'Yeah, I'm OK.'

She kissed him gently on his forehead.

'This one is free, if you want it?'

She raised one perfectly plucked eyebrow, looking very beautiful and very young.

He smiled.

'I couldn't raise a smile, love, let alone anything else.'

'Thinking about your sister, Jon Jon?'

She sounded real now. The posturing of the tom long gone, Candace was being herself.

He nodded.

'It must be terrible, not knowing what happened to her. That man who's gone missing . . . is there a price on his head?'

He nodded, watching her warily.

''Course there is.'

'And if someone knew something that might . . .' she coughed nervously '. . . and I only say *might* sort of lead to you finding them . . . could the money be paid in private? Like, no one would ever know where you got your information from?'

He was nodding again, wondering where she was going with this.

She knelt up on the bed and slipped both arms around his neck. He could feel her small breasts pressing against his back and it stirred him. Even in the state he was in she still affected him.

'You know there are people who are into kids, don't you? People who would pay for a child. Do pay for them, in fact.'

Jon Jon turned his head to look at her.

'Exactly what are you on about?'

Candace sighed. Then sitting down beside him she pulled the sheet around herself and said seriously, her lovely face earnest and worried, 'This is between me and you, right? It goes no further than this room.'

He nodded. Her fear was almost tangible, he didn't want to make her even more nervous.

'Of course. Tell me.'

He was getting impatient; the joint he had smoked was making him feel paranoid now. It felt like his head was about to explode.

'I mean it. You must promise you will never say you heard this from me, right?'

He had had enough now. It was like talking to MI6.

'For fuck's sake, Candace, I *promise.* Now tell me what you know.'

She stared at him as if still unsure whether or not she could trust him. Finally she said: 'It's Jesmond. You know him, I take it?'

He nodded once more, his face creasing into a frown.

'What about him?'

She sighed. He knew she was frightened, but she also wanted the money. Candace was one of the few brasses he had met who actually saved, looked to the future.

'I heard from one of the other girls – you know the way we talk together – that he catered for the more child-loving customer. It's normally boys although a few little girls have gone through his house apparently. Dahlia told me. One of her sisters is a crack head and she rented out her daughter, Mirabell. The kid's in care now – she was used for a party. Some party, eh? Bet it weren't jelly and ice cream they gave her. But Dahlia . . . fuck, man, she hates Jesmond. Bad mouths him at every opportunity. The little girl was nine years old and a cutie as well. Jesmond himself likes little girls, you see. Young as possible according to the rumours.'

Jon Jon was staring at her, trying to digest what she was saying.

'Jesmond? I never heard that about him before.'

She could hear the disbelief in his voice so she nodded and said quickly, 'You never heard any of this from me, right? But if it turns out Jesmond knows something, you owe me, OK? If those Thompson blokes were into kids, chances are they'd have had dealings with him, being local and into the same shit. He might know where they are now; he keeps all his punters in his head, see, writes nothing down but he videos them, does a lot of internet sites. I worked for him a few years back. Schoolgirl stuff, you know.'

He was staring at her as if he had never seen her before in his life.

'You did nonce stuff?'

Candace sighed.

'Nah, silly. It was big girls dressed as little girls, you know the kind of scam. It was good poke and no one saw your face.'

He was having trouble taking it all in but he could see her logic. If Tommy and his father were into all that then it was logical they'd have contacts who were like-minded. Jesmond would need to keep his punters' identities in his head; no one in their right mind would write anything like that down.

'If anything comes of it, do I get the reward?' Candace pressed.

He nodded.

'You'll get the reward all right.'

He left her then, and for a little while his trip North was forgotten. He had to get his head around what he had just been told.

Marie and Joanie were outside the Sunny Day nursing home. Marie had been observing the place for days and knew that the big fat patient with the terrible burns came out after lunch every day. Jeffrey Palmer they called him. She called him piece of shit. Just looking at him made her want to puke. Knowing what he had done to that child, what he was guilty of. This was not only the easiest money she had ever earned, it was also the most satisfying.

Now she was going to lead his victim's mother to him, and it was almost a religious experience for her. Sweet revenge for what had happened to her own child also. Marie saw it as her mission in life to wipe predators like this off the face of the earth.

Lorna and Pippy were in the pub together. It was just on eleven in the morning and they were both already well on the way to drunkenness. The social worker had turned up early for the baby and Lorna had been absolved of her maternal responsibilities sooner than she had expected. After that she had gussied herself up, which for Lorna meant a quick wash under the arms and a lavish spray of perfume, a comb through her hair and her least dirty jeans and T-shirt on. Now she was in the pub drinking Bulmer's cider with large brandies mixed in, and negotiating herself a fee for turning Pippy on to Jon Jon Brewer's little sister. What a touch!

'Her mum's on the bash, ain't she?' he enquired.

Lorna nodded.

'She's all right, old Joanie, in fairness. Never got a bad word to say about anyone.'

'So what brings little Jeanette into my fold? Why don't she just get her brother to pimp her?'

Lorna raised her eyes to the ceiling in annoyance.

'Oh, use your fucking loaf, Pip! She don't want to go gaming as such, just wants to earn a few quid sometimes. Not every bleeding minute of the day And she ain't a bad-looking kid.'

'How old?'

'Fourteen or thereabouts, tries to look older.'

Pippy grinned.

'A schoolie!'

She laughed with him.

'I said I'd sound you out like. See if you was interested.'

Pippy wiped a grubby hand across his unshaven chin.

'For a fee, of course?'

'Of course. Hundred quid.'

Lorna smiled again.

'Up front. I know *you.* If you hand me the poke now I can have her round yours whenever you like.'

'Fair enough. You miserable bitch.'

She screamed with laughter at his words.

'Hark who's fucking talking! You ain't exactly Justin Timberlake yourself.'

'By the time I'm finished with the little Brewer she won't give a fuck who I am, love, she'll fuck a table if I tell her to.'

Lorna knew it was true. Pippy terrified his girls, and the only reason Lorna herself had got off lightly was because she was an addict and for some reason he liked her. Pippy didn't need to scare her; she was already willing to do anything required to get a fix. She also looked awful nowadays so he only went near her when he was out of his box. His clients weren't over-keen either, especially since the kids. Stretch marks gave the game away when you were only supposed to be fifteen. But Jeanette was perfect for what he wanted, and he would fuck with her head within weeks.

By then even Jon Jon wouldn't be able to control her.

But Lorna was just shrewd enough to remind herself that Jon Jon Brewer would launch her into outer space if he ever found out about this, to say nothing of his mother. Joanie could handle herself as well. She wouldn't thank Lorna for introducing her daughter to the life.

She was in over her head, really playing with fire, but she could feel the heroin in her jeans pocket, and its allure was far stronger than her fear of Jon Jon Brewer. So long as she kept her lip buttoned it'd be OK.

She took herself off to the toilets for a livener. As the needle slipped into her vein she felt the release of all her tension, all her hurt. She sat on the grubby toilet seat and gradually lay back against the dirty pipes, all the time inhaling the fumes of someone else's faeces. Lorna closed her eyes and let the good times roll.

Jesmond was meeting his accountant who was actually his debt collector, but his nickname was 'the accountant' because he kept records of all Jesmond's transactions. Unlike some of the other men who worked for him, Bernard Lee had never done any debtor out of a penny they didn't owe. Once they had paid, they had paid. But if you didn't pay, then he was far more vicious than all the other collectors put together.

Bernard's way of getting his money was to harm a family member, not the person who actually owed the money. His logic had always been, why put a man in hospital when he could be out grafting to get the poke he owed? Put his wife in hospital, however, and guilt coupled with terror got them out grafting faster than anything.

It was, as far as Bernard was concerned, sound economics.

He was well liked by his inner circle of friends, always good to the people he cared about, and lived with a nice girl and their two nice little boys and his partner really did think he was an accountant.

He *was* in fact a qualified accountant but sorting out clients' books and tax returns didn't do it for Bernard. He lived in the stockbroker belt of Surrey, to all outward appearances Mr Middle Class. But Bernard had a kink in his nature, had become aware of it as a young man. He could inflict pain and suffering on anyone, did not need any personal grudge or cause for anger against them. He had no hang ups about harming others whatsoever, especially if money was involved.

He was a big man, handsome in a blond rugged way, with a magnetic personality. He had taken a job debt-collecting to fund his way through university and accidentally discovered his true calling in life. He had finished his studies, knowing he would need some kind of legitimate front to cover what he was really going to do. Twenty years later he was rich, successful and respected. He had made a killing in property investment, among other things, and lived in luxury and tranquillity.

Jesmond respected him, and he respected Jesmond. They didn't visit each other's houses, didn't need to. They were rarely even seen together but worked well as a team, each enjoying the other's company. It made for a very profitable relationship.

Now they sipped cappuccinos at the back of a hostess club Jesmond owned and chatted.

'So what do you want me to do?'

Jesmond shrugged. He was big, heavy and running to fat as he was getting older from too many pints of Guinness and white rums, too much goat and rice and fried plantain bananas.

'It's fifteen grand now with the compound interest so I want him hurt. Or should I say, I want someone close to him hurt. He has a teenage son, nice kid by all accounts, bright as a button, could get into Oxford. How about putting the frighteners on him?'

Bernard nodded.

Kids were always a good lever for getting people to pay up. He guessed the boy's father would borrow the money from another lender and worry later about paying them back. He didn't give a toss as long as he got his cut. He took a third for himself from every mark and it was easy money. No one had *ever* not paid Bernard Lee.

He wrote the latest instruction down on his to-do list. He had a busy couple of days ahead and should pull in just under forty grand cash. A nice little earner.

Jon Jon walked into this cosy little domestic scene, all smiles and bonhomie. He knew about Bernard who also worked for Paulie at times so he wasn't too trashed to see him, but he was wary. Bernard had that effect on everyone who knew him.

'Hello, Jon Jon.'

Bernard sounded genuinely pleased to see him.

'How's everything?'

'Not too bad. Yourself?'

Bernard was aware of a slight atmosphere but didn't let it bother him. He worked for Paulie and Jesmond knew it and there was nothing he could do about it. Bernard Lee was a law unto himself. But he liked Jon Jon Brewer, saw himself in him as a young man. He liked Jon Jon's front, and Jon Jon had more front than Brighton.

Jesmond studied his visitor warily.

'What can I do you for?'

It was said in a friendly fashion and Jon Jon smiled disarmingly.

'I need a favour, some information.'

He pulled up a chair and sat down without being invited which did not go unnoticed by either of the others. Bernard stifled a laugh at the expression on Jesmond's face.

'What do you want? Did Paulie send you?'

Jon Jon shook his head. His dreads looked babyish in comparison with Jesmond's heavy head of hair.

'Well, talk then. What you waiting for?'

Jesmond was annoyed now; he felt sure he was having the piss taken out of him, just wasn't aware how.

Jon Jon looked respectfully towards Bernard Lee and raised one eyebrow slightly. Jesmond smiled now, displaying a mouthful of very expensive gold teeth. 'Anything you got to say, Jon Jon, you can say it in front of Bernard.' He was Jamaican now. It was in his voice.

Even Jesmond was reluctantly impressed by the way the boy had asked him if they should speak in private. Most people who knew Bernard wouldn't have had the guts to do it. Jesmond could also see that it had amused Bernard Lee, which was just as well.

'You know my sister is missing, Jesmond?'

The other two men were immediately contrite now; serious-faced they nodded respectfully.

'Well, I heard through the grapevine that you cater for paedophiles.'

Jesmond stared at him in shock, then his eyes flicked to Bernard. The next instant Jesmond came at Jon Jon like a demented grizzly – but there had been that momentary pause and Bernard knew that Jon Jon had hit a nerve. They jumped up together.

Before Bernard made a move Jon Jon swung back his leg and with one swift kick reduced Jesmond to a quivering wreck. He sagged to his knees, clutching his gonads and trying not to throw up on the floor.

'I got enough back up outside to start a turf war, Jesmond. Your posse's been told we're in a meeting, strictly no interruptions. You don't scare me, mate. Now all I want is some answers. So tell me: do you cater to nonces?'

'You'd better give him what he wants, Jesmond. I'm interested as well now.'

Bernard's eyes were cold as he looked at the big man sprawled on the floor before him. Jon Jon decided he would rather be in a room full of tigers than on the receiving end of that look.

Jesmond was breathing heavily; he knew that the next few sentences he uttered would make or break him with Bernard Lee. He wondered how Jon Jon had found out they were having a meet because Bernard's presence put a whole different complexion on things and they all knew it.

No one better than Bernard himself.

Then Jesmond remembered that it was Bernard who had requested this meet. Was it a set up? If so he was a dead man.

Jon Jon sat back down. Pulling out a joint, he lit it and took a deep toke before smiling at Bernard as he said, 'I'll take that as a yes then, shall I?'

Marie watched as Little Tommy was wheeled out into the fresh air. He looked gross. The fat was bad enough but the burns he had received had left his head almost bald and his skin puckered and mauve. His hands were also affected, the pudgy fingers looked webbed. None of the other patients spoke to him, but then they didn't seem to have much to say to each other either.

It was a bright day. The wind was cool, a definite chill in the air. Marie pulled her coat tighter around her but she knew it wasn't the weather that was making her cold, it was what she was about to witness.

She looked across the lawn and saw Joanie studying her prey intently. One of the nurses looked in Joanie's direction and Marie felt her heart skip a beat but Joanie had stepped back into the cover of some shrubs.

As the nurses wandered round, serving teas and giving out biscuits, Marie watched Joanie confidently skirt the shrubbery where she'd been standing. She walked towards the path leading to a public area and turned swiftly back on herself as if she had just walked out of the French doors of the visitors' room. She was carrying a large wicker shoulder bag and wearing a jaunty bright blue sun hat, a long black leather coat and gloves. The outfit was finished off with big Armani sunglasses.

Tommy saw her before anyone realised there was anything untoward going on. His cry of fear was a low moan; he was in shock at seeing her suddenly appear in front of him.

Opening her bag, Joanie took out a glass bottle. As she unscrewed its cap Tommy was staring at her, fear stark on his face.

'Please, Joanie . . .'

'Don't you dare say my name, you cunt!'

Her voice was a low hiss and Tommy realised the deadly

danger he was in. A nurse was staring at them now. So Jeffrey Palmer finally had a visitor? He didn't exactly look pleased about it. She started walking towards them.

'Excuse me, have you reported to Sister?'

She was nearly level with Joanie now and saw Mr Palmer frantically trying to move his wheelchair, but she had braked it herself. It was an unwieldy old model, the only one that could cater for his weight. He was a sitting duck.

'Hello, Tommy. Or should I say Jeffrey?'

Joanie looked at the nurse and smiled brightly, but the nurse was staring at the dirty lemonade bottle she was holding in her hand.

'I'm an old friend, love, I brought him something.'

She looked back at Tommy and even in her anger felt a stirring of pity for him. Jon Jon had done a proper job on him. But it wasn't enough, he had not paid dearly enough. There was no price too high for what he had done.

'Are you all right, Mr Palmer?'

Tommy was staring at Joanie, terrified to take his eyes off her in case she did something to him.

'Where's my baby? Come on, tell me where she is and all this can stop now.'

'Look, what exactly is going on here?'

Joanie turned to the nurse and said through gritted teeth, 'Fuck off, love, you really don't want to get involved. Believe me, you don't want anything to do with this.'

She turned to Tommy again.

'Where is she? I need to know.'

She was slowly taking the lid off the bottle and a distinctive odour was coming from it. Tommy cowered. The nurse was looking round frantically while an orderly was watching the scene, fascinated.

'Go and get some help!'

Tommy held up one arm as if to shield himself.

'I don't know where she is, I swear! Don't you think I'd tell you if I knew? I loved her as much as you did . . .'

Joanie was crying now.

'You don't know what love is. Your love is fucking sick . . .'

As she raised the bottle ready to crash it down on his head the nurse grabbed at her arm, twisting it.

The bottle slipped from her hand and the hydrochloric acid it contained splashed Tommy's legs and the nurse's shoes before the bottle smashed on the ground. Joanie punched the nurse in the face, forcing her to let go of her arm, and then she was running back the way she had come.

She turned and shouted at the writhing, sobbing man, 'I'll be back. You ain't getting away with it. Not this time.'

Marie was waiting with the engine already running in a white Sierra that had been stolen the night before.

'I fucked it up!'

Marie was laughing with nerves and adrenaline.

'He knows you can find him now, love. He'll never sleep easy in his bed after this, console yourself with that. We found the bastard once, we'll find him again.'

Chapter Twenty-One

'So what do you want then, Jeanette?'

Pippy was smiling at the girl before him. She was a cracker. Even with her face plastered in makeup the child in her was still evident. Her breasts were a bit too big for most of his clients, but there was still some good mileage in her.

He poured her out another cup of tea. As he sugared it, Jeanette looked around her. His flat was not what she'd expected at all. It was comfortable in a shabby kind of way. All the furniture was old; the Chesterfield looked worn out but wonderful to relax on. The walls were painted a pale lemon colour, and the curtains were heavy chintz. The whole place looked like something from an old black-and-white fifties film.

Pippy was different too. He still looked scruffy but he was wearing a Tag-Heuer watch and a diamond ring on his little finger. She felt he was trying to impress her and was oddly flattered.

He handed her the cup of tea and Jeanette smiled as she took it, trying her hardest to look grown-up and sophisticated.

'I just need to earn a bit of pin money, that's all.'

He grinned.

'Now let me get this right. You decided all on your own to go on the game, correct?' His voice was drenched in sarcasm. 'And you say all you want is pin money?'

She nodded.

'Then why not take a Saturday job in Tesco's stocking shelves?'

She dropped her gaze and noticed that the carpet by the fireplace was almost threadbare.

'You need a rug to go over that,' she said, pointing as she spoke.

Pippy's face was pinched with fury. It happened in the blink of an eye and suddenly she knew why they called him Mad Pippy.

'And you need your fucking head examined if you think I'm going to take *you* on.'

Jeanette stared at him, unsure what to say now. It had all been going so well, she knew he'd liked the look of her, but suddenly he looked ferocious, his brown teeth bared and looking menacing as he half smiled at her. His smile was like Jon Jon's in that it rarely reached his eyes.

Suddenly she was frightened. And to cap it all she didn't even know why she was in this room with him except that somehow it felt like she should be here. Should pay the price for all the times she had blown Kira out, told her to go away, been horrible to her. Jeanette knew she was guilty of neglect, of not loving her sister enough, and wanted to punish herself.

Every time she closed her eyes she remembered another slight she'd given her little sister, another nasty comment she had made to her, and all Kira had ever wanted was for Jeanette to like her.

And the stupid thing was she *had* liked Kira, loved her, but she hadn't known how to show it – and now it was too late and all Jeanette deserved was this – an introduction to a man as feared as he was hated. A man who could find her easy work as long as she wasn't fussy.

But perhaps she was fussier than she'd thought? Jeanette was realising new things about herself with every second that passed in this claustrophobic room.

Jealousy had been an all-consuming emotion with her since her sister had been brought home from hospital. Jon Jon had immediately fallen in love with Kira, with her blonde hair and big blue eyes. She had been like a little china doll. Everyone who saw her made a fuss of her, looked after her. Kira never had to fight to make people notice her, care about her. Not like Jeanette. There'd been a gulf between them when Kira disappeared, a gulf of Jeanette's making. She suffered because of it. She deserved to suffer some more. But like this? She wasn't so sure any more.

Pippy watched her. He could read the expressions going

across her face as if they were words. He had seen so many girls like Jeanette over the years; they were his stock in trade. Usually he used their self-hatred to foster his own ends but Jon Jon Brewer's face was superimposing itself on Jeanette's and he was unaccountably nervous.

'What did you see yourself doing? Taking on one punter a week? Two a week? Or maybe four or five a day? I mean, what exactly do you class as pin money?'

Jeanette was not ready for this kind of talk. She had assumed he would snap her up. She had not bargained on meeting any resistance to her plan. Now she had she was strangely glad but she wouldn't let him *see* that. She knew instinctively that any sign of weakness now would be a worse mistake even than coming to see him.

'You got so many girls you can pick and choose then?'

Her voice was deliberately sarcastic.

'Could be, love, or maybe I'm fussy what I and my clients touch. I mean, imagine what could happen to one of them if your brother turned up at the crucial moment, eh?'

'Very funny, Pippy.'

She stood up to go, on shaking legs.

'It's your loss.'

Pippy stayed sitting in his chair, watching her.

'Did Jon Jon send you here? Tell me the truth.'

She sighed as if he had just said the most stupid thing she had ever heard.

'Oh, yeah, he can't wait for you to pimp me out. Use your fucking loaf!'

He made no move to let her out. Jeanette forced herself to step around his chair and walk slowly down the hall to his steel-reinforced front door. She expected him to come after her at any second.

She drew back two bolts, scrabbling at one and tearing a nail in her haste to be out of this terrible place. He'd left the key in the lock. She turned it and stepped outside with a sob. Outside she started to run and didn't stop until she reached the Copeses' house, her chest and throat tight with fear and a foul taste in her mouth.

There was only Karen in and for the first time ever Jeanette was pleased to see her.

When she'd left, Pippy sat for a few minutes gnawing on his thumbnail then took out his mobile and punched in a number.

'I think we've been rumbled.'

He listened for a few seconds before turning the phone off. He'd arranged a meet for this evening and just hoped he could avoid Jon Jon Brewer till then.

Joanie was still shaking from the encounter with Tommy. One half of her wished she could have carried out her plan, the other half was glad she had been stopped.

Whatever he had done, he'd looked so bereft, so terrified, she had actually felt a flicker of pity for him. This annoyed her even as it made her feel sick to her stomach. Why should she care what happened to scum like him? If she was right, and she was convinced she was, he was the cause of her child's death.

'You OK?'

Marie's voice was low.

Joanie nodded.

'I think so.'

'You need to get back to London as quick as you can. They'll have him moved in no time at all and you're bound to be questioned. Have you covered your arse?'

Joanie had not covered her arse or any part of her anatomy for that matter.

'Nah. I didn't think . . .'

Marie sighed.

'Get on your Moby, love, and get yourself a proper alibi, OK?'

Joanie nodded once more.

'Let's get you back to London. We've plenty of time to cook a story up. You hungry?'

Joanie shook her head.

'I could do with a drink though.'

Marie laughed.

'Couldn't we all!'

Jesmond was on the spot and he knew it but fought his corner bravely. If Bernard had not been there he would not even have bothered to answer Jon Jon's charges. Would have taken him out of the ball game without a second's thought. But he was in the spotlight now and had to come out of this looking like an innocent man.

'I have never been involved in anything like that and I resent you coming steaming in here shouting the odds in front of a friend.'

'Rumours are sometimes true, Jesmond.'

It was Bernard talking now. It was almost as if he and Jon Jon had rehearsed this.

Jesmond stood up painfully to his full intimidating height and said loudly, determined to front this out, 'What is this, eh? So what if I cater now and again for the gymslip crew? They ain't really kids I use, they're girls who look young for their age, that's all. I mean, coming from you, Jon Jon, it's a bit rich considering we're in the same fucking business. You telling me you ain't got any schoolies knocking about your parlours?'

Jon Jon was aware of what he was trying to do and said as much.

'Don't try and change the subject. I am well up on you and what you are capable of. Our parlours have grown-ups in them, you know that, or are you trying to bring Paulie down to your level? And what about your little parties, eh, where the star guest is a child? I know all about them.'

Bernard Lee looked stunned. This was obviously news to him.

'What you on about, Jon Jon?'

He flicked his dreads in Jesmond's direction.

'Ask him.'

Bernard and Jesmond stared each other out. Jesmond finally shrugged as if bored.

'Don't know what he's talking about.'

He was the man again now, had regained his equilibrium.

'You can't come in here and shout your fucking mouth off without some kind of back up, and I don't mean your heavy friends. I mean without proof, and there ain't any proof because I ain't done fuck all.'

He looked out of the corner of his eye at Bernard, the man he was really trying to convince of his innocence.

'That's not what I heard,' growled Jon Jon.

'Who told you then?'

Jesmond held out his arms in supplication.

'Come on, that's the least you can do. Put your fucking money where your mouth is, boy. I am guilty of a lot of things but fucking noncing ain't one of them.'

'All I need to know is, did you ever have any dealings with Tommy Thompson or his father?'

'Did I fuck! Are you trying to wind me up or what?'

He was emphatic now, his fear of Bernard being replaced by real anger. Who the fuck did Jon Jon Brewer think he was – Big John? And more to the point, where had he got this information?

'Listen to me, you might be Paulie Martin's brown-eyed boy but that don't give you the right to come here and disrespect me. Now I am telling you, you are barking up the wrong mango tree, my son, so until you can prove my involvement in anything you had better get the fuck away from me and mine.'

The last bit was for Bernard's benefit and he knew it.

'Come on, Jes, surely you can do better than that?'

Jon Jon studied the two men covertly. There was an undercurrent here that he couldn't quite fathom. Jesmond was clearly panicking now.

'You would trounce me on the say-so of this little cunt, Bernard, after all the years we've done business together?'

He nodded.

''Course I would – if I found out you were a nonce.'

He grinned.

'I'd remove your dreadlocks myself with a pair of pliers and that would just be for starters, Sonny Jim.'

Bernard's biggest fear was of being tarred with the same brush. People would assume he was involved because he and Jesmond had worked closely together for so long, and he wasn't having that. Bernard had his standards and any fiddling about with kids deserved the death sentence in his book, whether it was inside or outside the law.

Jesmond was cornered and he knew it, but he wasn't giving up anything he didn't have to.

'Does Paulie know you're here, Jon Jon?'

'That's irrelevant, Jesmond. Stop trying to change the fucking subject.'

'I tell you what, you go and talk to him about all this, right, then come back and see me after that.'

'He's having a laugh!' Jon Jon looked at Bernard as he said incredulously, 'He is having a laugh, ain't he?'

Bernard replied seriously, 'I ain't laughing and neither are you! Now who have you got outside with you?'

'Big Earl, a couple of the others. Why?'

'Bring them in, we can have a party.'

Jesmond could not believe what he was hearing.

'You wouldn't fucking dare!'

'Well, either you tell us what we want to know or we'll force it out of you. Won't we, Jon Jon?'

Jesmond was being threatened for the first time in his life. Even as a schoolboy he had been much too big to diss. Now it seemed that like all bullies he had finally met his match. All he could do was hope to salvage something from this situation.

'You won't like what you'll hear, Jon Jon, I warn you.'

He shrugged nonchalantly even though his heart was racing inside his chest.

'I'm a big boy, I'm sure I'll cope.'

Jesmond shook his head.

'I wouldn't be too certain of that.'

Lorna smiled widely when she saw Jeanette at her front door once more. She was one of the girls now and Lorna treated her as such.

'Come on in, mate.'

Jeanette remembered to take a deep breath as she walked inside. Once you got into the lounge the smell wasn't too bad but with the toilet being in the hallway alongside the bathroom, the smell was stronger here.

'So how did you get on then?'

The place was empty of people for once, and it felt strange. Jeanette stared around her as if for the first time. In the cold light of day it looked even worse than usual.

The small kitchen had a black bin bag lying on the worktop by the sink. It was moving of its own accord, maggots breeding inside, and Jeanette felt the bile rise up in her throat.

'Pippy wouldn't have me, blew me out. Did you say anything to him?'

'He what?'

Lorna could not believe what she was hearing. Did this mean he wanted his ton back? Only the hundred quid was long gone, smack and fags had seen to that.

She was starting to panic.

'Look, Jeanette, stop worrying. I can talk him round, it's only because of fucking Jon Jon. I'll talk to him again. It'll be cool, you'll see.'

Jeanette grinned.

'I'm glad, to be honest.'

Lorna stared at her as if she was mad.

'Looking at you now, looking at this place, I realise this could have been my life. I'm bad enough as it is, all the trouble I cause, but I tell you something, girl, whatever I may be I will *never* be as bad as you are. You're fucking scum, and them babies deserve better than this. *I* deserve better than this.'

The insults finally penetrated Lorna's brain. She drew herself up to her full height as she said, 'Well, fuck off then.'

Jeanette grinned.

'I will, Lorna, don't you worry. I just felt the urge to tell you a few home truths first.'

She walked out of the maisonette and through the lobby. As she walked out of the front door she saw Jasper standing waiting for her.

'What did you have to tell Lorna?'

She shrugged.

'Just a message, that's all. Will you walk me to my mum's? I want to give the flat a good clean for her. She went off in a bit of a hurry yesterday. I thought I'd sort it out for her.'

''Course I will.'

'Shall we go out later, Jasper? See a film or something?'

'Are we cool again, Jeanette?'

She grabbed his arm and smiled at him.

'I suppose we are.'

Paulie was signing his gold away in his solicitor's office. Even though it galled him to give Sylvia anything, he knew he was doing the right thing. It was the lesser of two evils, so he took a deep breath and wrote his name.

His brief, a middle-aged Scot much taken with Versace suits and tattoos, was clever enough to specialise in clients like Paulie Martin. Danny McBane could hide money from anyone, even his clients though that was not something he advertised. If it ever went pear-shaped he could retire with the click of one button – such was his mindset and the reason he got on so well with the men he did business with. He had no morals and no scruples plus a healthy disregard for the people he dealt with. This, coupled with his aggressive personality, made him the perfect choice to represent Paulie and his porn empire.

There was nothing he didn't know about Paulie Martin, something else he had never bothered to advertise.

He made a point of finding out as much as possible about all his clients. If they were going down at any point, he was not going with them. Not if he could help it anyway. He had a family and two girlfriends to support.

'Women are cunts, Danny. When I first met Sylvia she was existing on a pittance with that mad fucking mother of hers. Fucking State hand-outs! Now she's walking away with my hard-earned cash, two houses and a grin larger than the Cheshire Cat's.' Paulie gulped his brandy before saying, 'Should have got her topped.'

It was said quietly and vehemently. He clearly meant it.

'Cheaper certainly, but by the time you'd sorted out childcare round the clock . . .'

Danny's mock-serious tone made Paulie smile.

'Cost you more in the long run. By the way, I've put in an extra clause. Once the girls are seventeen you pay for their horses, etc. at your discretion.'

'What good will that do?'

'It's a bargaining point – you may need it by then. That lot think more of their nags than they do of you. It makes no real odds, but if they kick off you have a trump card.'

Paulie was grinning now.

'Never a truer word spoken. If anyone needs a trump card now, it's me.'

'What made you marry her, Paulie? I never saw the attraction myself.'

He shrugged.

'I thought she was upmarket, and I suppose she was in comparison to me and my old woman. Sylvia had a way about her of looking down her nose at everyone. I liked that about her, though fuck knows why. She looked down her conk at me too in the end. But then, I think she had always seen me as being beneath her. Fucking hell, I hardly ever saw her beneath *me*! And when she was she never moved. I used to take her pulse while we were on the job in case she was dead.'

They laughed together.

'More sexual activity in a morgue than round my house, I can tell you.'

'You don't mean that, Paulie. Though my wife never liked her either, said she was cold.'

'She was right. Colder than a witch's tit, that's Sylvia.'

Danny smiled.

'Well, you'll be a free agent soon, back on the marriage market.'

'Never again. I will be a bachelor boy from now on.'

'You'll get caught again, we all do. Best laid plans and all that. By the way, how's Joanie these days?'

Paulie shrugged.

'Not too good to be honest. Any news?'

Danny shook his head, his thick red hair and rugged appearance making him look like a country vet rather than a solicitor.

'Nothing. But we're keeping our options open. Baxter's being a cunt but what's new there?'

'Jon Jon's on his way to Sheffield today. He got a touch before us, but he doesn't realise how much I know so bear that in mind.'

'I will. Good kid, Jon Jon, you picked well there.'

'I wonder at times, though this new club will be an earner.'
'Does he know about you?'
Paulie shook his head.
'He don't know the half of it.'
'Will you tell him?'
'I doubt it.'
Paulie stood up, annoyed with the way this conversation was going now.
'I'd best be off.'
Danny didn't get up, just smiled lazily. It never did any harm to remind people exactly how much you knew about them. It kept them on their toes.

Baxter watched Joanie as she pulled her case from the taxi. He had her bang to rights now, and found he was actually sorry about that.
As she paid the driver he saw her daughter Jeanette run out of the flats and straight into her mother's arms. He watched Joanie hug her tightly, kiss her head and hold her face between her hands as she spoke to her. He saw Jeanette pick up her mother's bag and carry it inside.
'Are we going in, sir?'
Baxter looked at the young man beside him. He was tall, painfully thin, and talked through his nose. Baxter couldn't help thinking, And this is the cream of the crop? God help the Met if so.
'Shut up, Ritter. Let her get a cuppa before we bound in and start questioning her.'
'The psychological advantage, eh, sir? Invade her home territory?'
Baxter closed his eyes in distress.
'No, Ritter, I mean she looks like she needs a cup of tea. If, and I do mean *if*, she has been to Sheffield she's probably parched by now. We have no actual proof she's been anywhere, let alone up North, and in this country you are still innocent until proven guilty. Now, is that simple enough for you to take on board?'
Ritter nodded.
'OK, sir.'

He was not sure about this bad-tempered belligerent man beside him. Sometimes it seemed like he was on the wrong side of the law himself.

Baxter took out a mobile and tried Paulie's number again.

Nothing.

He lit a cigarette and smoked it slowly.

He was timing the making of that tea; he could do with a cup himself.

Joanie and Jeanette were inside the flat. It was spotless, much cleaner than when Joanie had left it.

'Thanks, Jeanette love. It's lovely to come home to all this.'

Her gesture encompassed the whole place which had been scrubbed until it shone. There was the smell of a chicken cooking, and the washing machine was spinning. The cosy scene seemed wholly at odds with her usually troublesome daughter, and Joanie was touched to realise how hard Jeanette had worked to do just the right thing to reassure her mother. Joanie's home being clean was important to her because she was judged on that by her peers, but also because in the chaos that was her life the only thing she had ever been able to control was her environment.

As she glanced now at the daughter who had done this for her she felt a great weight lift from her shoulders. She still had two children, she still had a family of sorts, and looking at Jeanette she realised she loved this difficult child with a vengeance.

'I'm so sorry, Mum.'

Joanie held her close, enjoying the feeling. It had been so long since Jeanette had given her a hug because she really wanted to and not because Joanie needed one.

'Where did you go, Mum? I was worried about you.'

There was concern in the girl's voice.

'I went away for the night, had a bit of business. I would have told you but let's face it, Jeanette, you're never here, are you?'

There was no reprimand in her tone but it lingered in her words and Jeanette wanted to cry. She didn't, and neither did she start an argument.

'I'll make us a cuppa.'

As she busied herself there was a knock on the door. Jeanette answered it with a cheerful expression on her face. When she saw Baxter she tried to shut the door in his face. Something in his stance told her that he brought bad news.

'Go away, Mr Baxter.'

He pushed the door open and said loudly, 'I can come back with the whole force if you like, but I am coming in at some point. Get the kettle on, Joanie, will you, girl?'

He walked through to the kitchen.

'Something smells good.'

He was smiling sadly at Joanie.

'I have a know-nothing geek outside in the car so let's make this snappy. You were in Sheffield this morning, Joanie, and you need a good alibi. Which is why I am here.'

'Is this some kind of joke, Mr Baxter?'

He stared pointedly at her bag and outdoor clothes.

'Do me one favour, Joanie. Don't take me for a cunt, eh?'

She couldn't help smiling.

'As if I would do that, Mr Baxter.'

'I'm trying to help you here, you should understand that. Now make the tea and I'll tell you what we know and what you have to do.'

She made the tea slowly, her mind racing the whole time.

'My Chief Constable likes you, Joanie. It seems you have a mutual friend.'

She placed a mug of tea before him. Looking at Jeanette, she said quietly, 'Leave us alone, babe.'

For once her daughter did as she was asked without an argument.

Joanie sat opposite Baxter and said, 'Spit it out then.'

'It was you who attacked Tommy Thompson yesterday.'

He held up his hand to silence her protests.

'Will you let me talk for once! Fucking hell, Joanie, you're worse than my old woman and she takes some beating. She could interrupt Joan Rivers without breaking a sweat, her.'

He sipped at the scalding tea and then said, 'We all know it was you, but the nurse couldn't ID you properly. Little Tommy fingered you but he's retracted that thanks to a mate of mine on the force up there with a gambling problem, an ex-wife and a pregnant girlfriend. But I digress. You have been alibied by Fat Monika and a few of your cronies at the parlour who have all made statements saying you were with them last night and this morning.'

Joanie was listening to all this in amazement.

'You gave that poor nurse a good smack, Joanie, she has a black eye! Now then, I'm going to give you copies of your mates' statements so you can get your story straight, OK? Like I say, you're under the protection of my Chief and that means you walk away this time. But Joanie, listen to me, next time Paulie Martin *won't* be able to help you and neither will I. So bear that in mind for the future and get someone else to do your dirty work for you, OK?'

She nodded.

'Oh, Mr Baxter, I can't thank you enough.'

He smiled sadly.

'Just do me a favour. Keep your boat out of the frame for a while, that will be thanks enough.'

She picked up her cigarettes and he could see her hands shaking.

'Here, let me do that for you.'

He lit the cigarette and placed it in her hand. Then he lit one for himself.

'Was Monika OK about it all? We ain't exactly bosom buddies these days.'

'Monika would swear she saw Christ Himself shoplifting for a few quid, and they all got a good few quid though in fairness they were willing enough to do right by you, Joanie. Just keep your head down and your arse up for a while, though; we can't keep protecting you.'

'Any news on Tommy's father?'

'We thought we'd found him yesterday – a body turned up in Epping Forest. It wasn't him, more's the pity. He'll turn up eventually, though. Scum always rises to the surface.'

Baxter yawned.

'You gave me a fright, Joanie. I'd hate to have to arrest you for what was in effect a public service.'

She smiled.

'If it's any consolation, I'm glad in one way that I didn't finish him. Why bring meself down to his level? But when I think of my Kira . . .'

Baxter sighed heavily.

'Listen to me, Joanie, we don't actually know for sure that anything like that happened to her.'

She shook her head and said sadly, 'Yes, we do, Mr Baxter. And you know that as well as I do.'

Chapter Twenty-Two

Jesmond was smoking a joint. He had taken his time building it, and Jon Jon had kept his impatience strictly in check. He could wait. He wanted the truth, and now he was going to get it.

It was crazy to think that he was only here because he'd wanted sex with a brass and she had unloaded herself on him about Jesmond.

Unbelievable even.

But he also knew that unbelievable was the norm for people like them. Their whole lifestyle went against the grain of the average Joe on the street. And he could understand now how those people felt. He only wished he was one of them. If he had learned anything from Kira's disappearance it was that the norm was not as boring as he had once thought. In fact, now it seemed almost desirable.

His whole life was not what he had wanted it to be, what he had expected it to be, especially as he now knew that most people had no truck with his kind of life. They wouldn't want any of it, they had too much sense.

He had thought he was clever once, going against the norm, yet all he had done was trap himself in an existence that was hard, precarious, outside the accepted morality. What was clever about that?

Maybe he was growing up at last, who knew? But looking at the two men before him, he realised he didn't want to spend the rest of his days alongside heavy-duty criminals like them.

But Jon Jon was only eighteen, he still had plenty of time. At school he had been told he was naturally bright, academic even. Could be anything he wanted to be. All this from people who had never had to live under his cloud, never had to eat lunch while being taunted by older boys because their mother was on the game. It was what made him into a fighter; he had learned to protect himself, and at the same time he was protecting his mother.

He had loved her then, and he still loved her now. Whatever she was, she was worth a hundred of anyone else he had ever known. She was decent in the only way that mattered. She was honest, loyal and true, and he had to believe in her because at the end of the day she was all he had ever had. Whatever she had done, she had done for the right reasons.

He repeated it to himself like a mantra.

He was clenching his fists again, natural animosity fighting his self-imposed cool, and he forced himself to calm down.

The truth would out, he had to believe that.

At the end of the day this could all be worth shit, mere supposition. But whatever happened he would have broken a nonce so it was worth it.

It was a little bit of payback.

But today Jon Jon was seeing his life, and the business he worked in, with stunning clarity for the first time ever. In a way his mother had not had any choice. Going on the game was all she could do, all she was geared up for. It had become her life too early for her to change. But he had *chosen* this life for himself, knowing the downside because he had had to live with it all his born days.

It was how he had been described, all his life, by everyone he knew. He could still hear them: 'You know Jon Jon Brewer? His mum's on the bash/on the game/ a sort.' He had got used to it, but still it rankled, hurt him. It had led him into all this and now he wanted out, but first he wanted to see Jesmond crawl.

He was just glad Bernard had stayed around because Jesmond was far more scared of him than he was of Jon Jon.

Anyone in their right mind would be scared of Bernard, the collector who had burned a house down for a poxy seventy-five quid debt. It wasn't the money, he had said at the time, it was the principle. The debtor had fucked him off, and no one fucked off Bernard Lee. He almost roasted a whole family alive. They had only been saved by an expensive smoke alarm and the fact that the debtor's wife suffered from insomnia. That was probably due to their money problems. Debt had a habit of chasing sleep away. Your wife could leave you, your parents die, but it was debt that had the edge when it came to keeping you up at night. Debt was a great leveller because it never went away. It was there, taunting you, twenty-four seven.

But Bernard didn't care about that. He got his money and that was all that bothered him. If he would do that for seventy-five quid, what would he be capable of doing to a nonce?

Jon Jon guessed the same thoughts were going through Jesmond's head and that was why he was playing for time.

'Come on, we ain't got all fucking day.'

Bernard's voice was tight with annoyance. Jesmond tried to blank him. He needed to think and inwardly he was panicking now. As he licked the Rizla Bernard's fist landed a hefty blow on his right ear.

'Are you fucking winding me up or what? I've been served in a Harvester quicker than this! Now you were asked a question and you had better fucking start answering it.'

Bernard was sweating, his anger rising to dangerous levels. The thought that he might actually be linked to a beast was too much for him to bear.

Bernard Lee, the collector who was a by-word for cool, controlled retribution, was suddenly impatient for answers.

Jesmond was stunned, not just by the blow but by fear. If this ever got out, he was finished. And that was if he could finesse his way out of trouble with Bernard. Money could go a long way there but first he had to swallow his knob, as the saying went, and open his trap. It was the only way out now.

He was sweating, and to make matters worse he could smell himself. Never before had he felt this kind of fear.

'It started a few years ago . . .'

He took a deep toke on the joint for comfort.

The smoke hit Jon Jon and he wanted to smile. That big powerhouse Jesmond smoked scuff? Somehow this fact took the edge off what was happening. A woman's puff. A bland puff. It was a throwback from the seventies and Amsterdam. It wasn't even a nice bit of Lebanese or Acapulco Gold. Somehow this knowledge made him feel better.

'What started a few years ago?'

Bernard's voice was lower than Jesmond's and Jon Jon brought his chair nearer to take it all in. He knew he was better off letting Bernard do the talking.

Jesmond was holding on to his dreads with one hand, pulling at them nervously.

'I was approached a while back by a Rumanian geezer. Some bloke who had girls for sale.'

He was almost stuttering with nerves.

'Well, actually, that's not strictly true, I was approached *through* one of my debtors. He had paid in full and was doing well – too well, in fact. He asked me about taking some of the girls on.'

He looked at Jon Jon, trying to justify himself and his actions.

'They work all day for nix. I own their passports and make them work off the money they owe for being brought into this country. Most of them couldn't even exist without me, you know. They need me.'

Bernard laughed.

'Big-hearted Harry now, is it? You cunt! Those girls are syphed up to the eyebrows, everyone knows that, and that's not counting the ones with HIV and AIDS.'

'Not all of them . . .'

'Oh, fuck off! They're bad news, everyone knows it. The only thing they ain't fucking picked up is manners or English.'

Bernard was disgusted and it showed.

'Anyway, where are they?'

Jesmond took a deep breath. The dope had made him paranoid. He could hear his own heartbeat.

'In and around London mostly, in houses I own.' He sighed now as if he was bored. 'It's easy money, easiest I've ever earned. A fucking fortune.'

Against his better judgement Bernard was intrigued and a little bit impressed as well. He loved easy money.

'What do you mean, a fortune?'

Jesmond smiled, his gold teeth glinting in the fluorescent light. Glad to change the subject.

'Sixty grand a week.'

He was bragging now, it was his nature. He was a natural show off.

'And you kept it all to yourself, did you?'

Bernard's animosity was evident to the other two.

'Come on, man, I didn't have much choice . . .'

'You never even offered me a drink out of it! How fucking disrespectful is that?' Bernard was shaking his head reprovingly. 'Well, we both know where we stand now, don't we? You greedy black cunt!'

Jon Jon stood up. He had heard enough.

'I hate to piss on your fireworks but where *exactly* do kids come into all this?'

They both looked at Jon Jon as he spoke. He was trying to set them back on track. Jesmond felt like he had a lump of concrete lodged in his chest, so great was his fear. He also knew that once he opened up about this terrible thing, it would change all their worlds completely.

Guilt had not exactly been weighing on him so far but he knew he had to convince them otherwise. If he had had any inkling that he was in for a capture he would have had it away on his toes long before these two collared him. Now all he could do was save his own arse and tell them what they wanted to hear, making himself out to be merely an innocent bystander.

'The kids were part of the deal, see . . .'

'What are you talking about – kids? You telling me you got kids locked away somewhere?' Bernard exploded. There was disgust in his voice, in his stance even. He was itching for a fight.

'The kids ain't here! They used to be but now they end up abroad . . .'

Jesmond sighed.

'It's a long story. First I need a drink.'

Bernard nodded at Jon Jon.

'We *all* want a drink. Get a bottle down here, son, I think we're going to need it.'

Jon Jon nodded and left the room. Jesmond's minders were

outside and they looked nervous. He smiled at them.

'A bottle of Scotch and a bottle of brandy. Now.'

Jesmond's number one, a large ginger-headed man with enormous biceps and a twisted foot, forced a grin.

'All right in there? What's the score?'

Jon Jon opened his arms wide.

'What are you then? The Martin Bashir of fucking South London? You want to ask questions, change your name to Chris fucking Tarrant. You wanna go and get the drink then move your fucking white arse out of it, if you know what's good for you.'

Jon Jon wanted a row and this man would do to vent his anger on. He looked at his cronies, sensing the pent-up fury in the young blood before him. Something was going down here, and he had a feeling it was going to cut them all deeply when it came on top. He decided to be friendly but firm. Who knew what the next few weeks could bring? He could be working for Paulie's man before the month was out. He knew the score better than anyone. In their game people came and went. He had a feeling that Jesmond was about to go.

'Keep your fucking hair on!'

Jon Jon grinned sarcastically.

'Don't you worry, I will. Now get a move on, we ain't got all night.'

He wanted to laugh. Whatever came out of this it was going to benefit him, he knew that as well as he knew his own name. He could take Jesmond's girls over if he wanted. Relocate them and bank the profits.

Then he brought himself up short.

This was supposed to be about his little sister and yet he was seeing an angle in it for himself? He had actually forgotten about Kira for a few minutes. How could he have done that?

He was Paulie's brown-eyed boy all right and this knowledge was starting to scare him.

He had seen an angle for himself when he should have seen nothing but a beast.

Monika opened the door to Joanie and smiled to see her. She had missed her friend so much, and the fact that no one else had given her the time of day since they had fallen out had not helped. She had been blanked well and truly, by friends and neighbours alike.

Joanie was liked, always had been. Without her Monika couldn't keep anyone in her corner. With her she had friends, she had kudos, and she had somewhere to go anytime, day or night. She had missed her daily meander to her friend's flat, missed all Joanie's little kindnesses, missed her friendship. Especially now she had spent all the money from the newspaper.

'Come in, Joanie love.'

Joanie hugged her.

'You're a star, Monika. You came across for me, what can I say?'

She felt like crying.

Monika shrugged.

'You're me mate, me *only* mate in fact. I'm sorry for all the shit, Joanie.'

She smiled.

'Look, Mon, you came through for me and that's all that matters.'

'And what about Lazy Caroline! Can you believe that? The last favour she ever done anyone was when she stopped wearing mini-skirts! Her fucking legs! Like tree trunks . . .'

Joanie was laughing now, really laughing for the first time in ages. It felt good being here again. Monika was a comic, she made Joanie forget her troubles and that meant the world to her at the moment.

Whatever else Monika was, she was funny.

They went into the lounge and Monika poured them both a drink.

'How's Bethany?' Joanie enquired.

Monika smiled tightly.

'Let's not start rowing already!'

She grinned then, giving her friend the benefit of the doubt. They had always argued over the kids. Monika was determined to make a joke of it.

'She's OK, Joanie. Still a pain in the arse.'

'No change there then?'

They were back on their old footing. Neither of them knew how long it would last so they were enjoying it while they could. They would be arguing again before the week was out but for the moment they were sound.

'Where is she anyway?'

Joanie was genuinely interested in the answer. Her kids were always expected to tell her where they were. Monika, on the other hand, never even asked.

'Who knows, Joanie? Since little Kira went missing she hasn't been the same.'

For once Monika sounded perturbed, interested in her daughter's thoughts and feelings.

'They were close, Mon. I loved seeing them together. Kira loved her and she loved Kira.'

It was the first time Joanie had talked about her daughter without crying. Without picturing her face and seeing her terror as she had died. That was the worst, the not knowing what she had experienced before her death, because she *was* dead, Joanie knew that as well as she knew her own name. If Kira was alive still she would have known. Would have felt it.

Monika felt the tension and said loudly, 'Who'd have thought Baxter would have come up trumps, eh? Miserable old cunt he is normally!'

Joanie laughed with her.

'He didn't have much choice, did he? Paulie saw to that.'

Monika sat on the dirty sofa beside her friend and grabbed her in a warm bear hug. 'I'm glad it's all getting back to normal, Joanie. I was really worried about you, girl.'

Joanie could smell her friend's stale sweat, and the peculiar odour of fast food that always emanated from Monika. But today she was glad of it; it was familiar and anything familiar was welcome. In her own way she had missed sparring with Monika. Even though she could be the most selfish, obnoxious individual, she could also on occasion be generous and kind-hearted.

Not often admittedly, but it had been known.

Monika could also be a good listener and that was what Joanie needed at the moment: someone to pour her heart out to.

'How much did you get from the papers, Mon?'

Monika stopped smiling and her face fell back into its usual sullen lines.

'Not a lot, but enough to make life a bit easier.'

Joanie grinned.

'I should hope so and all!'

Monika grinned again, her moon face filled with relief. The subject had been broached and it was all right, she had been forgiven, though she had always known deep down that if anyone really understood her it was Joanie.

'I got a few quid left if you want it? I'll pay your cab back to Sheffield if you like.'

They both roared at that.

'Even Baxter was impressed, Joanie, you could tell.'

She poured herself another drink. 'I must be drinking more than I realise, this bottle didn't seem so empty last night!' Monika laughed again. 'It's strange but it's like you and me never fell out, ain't it? I'm glad you're back, you know that, don't you, Joanie?'

She nodded sadly.

''Course I do, mate. I feel the same.'

'I would have come with you to Sheffield if you'd asked.'

'I know, Mon.'

'I bet it felt good, didn't it?'

Joanie smiled and nodded, unwilling to say how she had really felt because she knew Monika wouldn't understand.

She didn't understand it herself.

She was saved from answering by Bethany's arrival. Joanie remembered that she had sorted through some of the Barbie stuff in Kira's bedroom and had decided to give some of it to Bethany. She didn't get a lot in the toy line and Kira would have wanted Bethany to have it, she was sure of that. Though whether Bethany would want it was a different matter.

'Just the girl I wanted to see.'

The child went white.

'What do you want to see me about, Auntie Joanie? I don't know nothing, I swear.'

She was terrified. Joanie and Monika stared at one another until Monika shrugged as if to say, What's going on here?

'Who you talking to, you little bastard!'

Here she was, finally back on track with Joanie, and then this miserable little mare had to come in and ruin it! Monika was fuming.

'Don't call her that. Come here, Bethany love.'

Joanie put her arms out as if to hug her, something Bethany had always liked because hugs were few and far between from Monika. But she stayed where she was, almost rooted to the spot.

'I don't know anything, honest!'

She was crying now.

'What are you doing round here anyway? We don't want you here!'

Joanie was stunned, Monika fit to be tied. As she stormed towards her daughter Joanie grabbed at her arm and stopped her. Bethany's eyes were wide with fear. But it wasn't fear of her mother, Joanie knew that much.

'What's the matter, Bethany? You can tell me, love.'

'I never told! They'll think I did, won't they, if you keep coming round.'

Monika was shouting now.

'What are you fucking on about, Bethany?' She looked at Joanie. 'See what I have to put up with? This child is a cunt, drives me mad.'

'Shut up, Monika.'

Joanie's voice was sharp. The little girl looked terrible and Joanie was worried about her. She went and knelt before her. There was something going down here. What, she wasn't sure, but she would find out.

'Who are you scared of, Beth? Come on, you can tell me. I'll sort them out, you know that, and if I can't, Jon Jon will. So don't you be frightened, sweetheart, just tell me what's wrong.'

She smiled at the girl, trying to calm her down and also trying to find out what she was talking about.

'You won't get into trouble, I promise, all right?'

Bethany looked stunned. Her pudgy face was still troubled and her eyes were filled with tears. She had the same wild hair as her mother, and as Monika rarely pulled it through with an Afro comb, she looked unkempt and scruffy. Joanie's heart went out to her.

'Tell me what's troubling you.'

'I can't, Joanie. Don't make me tell you, please. They'll come after me, I know they will. You don't know what they're like.'

She was crying hard now, wringing her fat little hands together. Joanie saw that the nails were bitten to the quick. She had also lost some weight though she was still solidly built. It occurred to Joanie that this child was actually a bundle of nerves, but Monika being Monika had not even noticed or asked what the matter was with her own daughter.

Joanie hugged her gently.

'Tell me and I'll sort it out for you, I promise.'

Bethany smelled of drink. It took Joanie a few seconds to register that fact. But she knew the smell. This was Monika in a kid's dress.

'Go into your bedroom, Beth, I'll be in soon.'

The girl ran off, glad of an excuse to leave them.

'She smells of drink, Mon.'

Monika laughed.

'Wouldn't surprise me, mate. You know what she's like. Remember the turn out with Kira and the Bacardi?'

Joanie shook her head, annoyed.

'I mean, Mon, she has *drinker's* breath. She is drinking seriously.'

Monika still didn't take it in. She had no real interest in what her daughter did or didn't do for that matter. Bethany was an unwanted appendage, no more and no less. To her Bethany was like a photograph, just a reminder of a vanished past. She'd be around until she was legally ready to go, and then Monika would wave goodbye. It was what most people did with their kids, she believed. Took care of them until it was time for them to leave, then breathed a sigh of relief.

But she knew what Joanie was like so she pretended to care. She plastered a concerned expression on her face and hoped it would suffice.

'Mon, that child is on the piss, love,' Joanie persisted.

'Like mother, like daughter, eh?'

Monika was bored already. Bethany had never held her interest for any length of time. Even as a baby, Monika cared about her only when she was in the mood to care. That particular mood had not been on her for a long time.

Joanie closed her eyes in distress. Here was a woman who had everything and she didn't know it. She had a daughter who loved her and yet she honestly didn't know or care about the fact. She knew nothing of the terror of having a missing child, and if she did would shrug it off like she did everything else in her life.

Joanie tried to swallow down her anger because she knew that Monika only treated her daughter the way she had been treated herself.

Monika's mother was still alive and kicking but had no interest whatsoever in her kids. Never had had, never would have. None of them found that in the least bit disturbing. It was the norm to them and they had lived all their life with that knowledge. Monika was incapable of deep feeling. It wasn't in her makeup.

'I'm going to see how Bethany is. OK, Mon?'

But Monika wasn't listening; she was pouring more drinks. Bethany was already gone from her mind.

'Tell her she's grounded for the rest of the night. Fucking cheeky mare!'

'What do you think she was talking about, Mon? Who could she be so frightened of that they made her react like that?'

Monika rolled her eyes to the ceiling.

'You know what a drama queen she is. Ignore her, she'll get over it. Probably opened her big mouth out of turn, as usual. She's always in the shit with someone.'

She took a deep swig of her drink.

'Always round that bleeding Lorna's . . . another bag of trouble, her. I wish Bethany'd fucking move in there. Might as well, she's rarely here these days.'

Joanie turned to go in search of the girl.

'Oh, leave her, Joanie. Best thing with her is to ignore her. You make a big deal out of it and we'll never hear the end of it.'

'Something is radically wrong with that child, Monika. You pour me another drink and I'll be back before you know it, OK?'

'Suit yourself.'

She was annoyed, wanting to be with Joanie herself. But Bethany as usual was getting all the attention. Monika stared at the empty bottles and shouted, 'I'll pop down the offie and get some more vodka.'

Joanie just nodded then went into the bedroom to see how Bethany was. She was lying on her bed, her pudgy body curled into a ball. Her round cheeks were stained with dirt and tears. She needed a good bath and a change of clothes. Joanie always felt the urge to clean Bethany up, had often done so over the years.

Now she sat on the edge of the bed and put a hand gently on the girl's shoulder. Bethany wouldn't look at her so she kissed the top of the child's head before saying, 'I ain't going nowhere until you tell me what's wrong with you.'

Bethany didn't answer her, but the quietness of Joanie's voice and the kindness in her tone caused her to cry harder.

Joanie was the only person who had ever shown her any kindness or care in her whole life. Who had made Christmas special. Had always let her stay over with Kira on Christmas Eve so she had something to get up for the next morning. Monika usually turned up at dinnertime, dishevelled and half drunk, but Bethany hadn't minded because she was with Kira and she was warm and fed and she had had presents. Joanie had always got her something nice to wear, pyjamas and slippers as well as a toy.

And she had repaid that kindness with betrayal.

'Please tell me what's wrong, Bethany. I just want to help you, sweetheart.'

Sobbing now, she sat up. Hugging Joanie, she whispered, 'If I tell you, do you promise not to say it was me? Promise me, Joanie?'

She pushed the girl's damp hair from her face and smiled.

'Just tell me, lovie. I can't promise anything like that until I know what's wrong.'

'Can we go to your house?'

Joanie nodded.

'Don't let me mum come, will you?'

'This is about Kira, isn't it?'

Bethany nodded, her big eyes still full of tears. She was only an eleven-year-old girl but she already knew more than most married women. It was all plain to see in those big brown eyes for anyone who could be bothered to look.

'Get your coat on, Bethany. Leave your mum to me, eh?'

Joanie walked Bethany down the road. Her hand was hurting, so strong was the child's grasp.

She didn't want to hear what her daughter's friend had to say, but she knew she must. They walked in silence, simultaneously frightened yet comforted by the other's presence.

Chapter Twenty-Three

Monika came home to an empty flat and a note from Joanie saying she would be back soon, she had to run an errand. It never occurred to Monika that Bethany might be with her friend; she was already too drunk to think straight. Didn't even bother to check on her daughter to see if she was still in her room.

Instead she poured herself another drink and put the TV on. Settling herself on the sofa, she munched her way through the goodie bag she had brought from the off-licence.

Monika was happy. She was back on her old footing with Joanie and that was all that mattered.

In fact, Joanie *owed* her big time.

She glanced at the clock and knew she should have hit the pavement by now but she couldn't be bothered. She'd had too much to drink anyway, would only end up arguing with a punter. Once Joanie was back at work she was going to try to get into a parlour. That was Monika's dream and as she had already told herself, Joanie Brewer owed her so it was the least she could do really.

She'd just sit it out until Joanie came back, then work on her. She was a mate, after all.

Jesmond was settled with a glass of brandy. He gulped it, wondering what the outcome of his revelations would be. All those years he had covered his tracks and now, just as he was ready to reap his reward, it had all blown up in his face. But he was nothing if not resilient.

He looked at Jon Jon and said, 'The Rumanian girls were followed by Czechs only they were little more than kids. Knew it all, though, before they got here. They'd been well trained. Anyway, we don't actually use them here, we sort of pass them on . . .'

'What do you mean, pass them on?'

Jesmond had the grace to look ashamed of himself.

'Sell them on.'

Jon Jon frowned at the implication.

'Who to?'

Jesmond shrugged, his heavy dreadlocks quivering.

'Pippy Light . . . he was the middleman. From what I can gather some of the girls were used here for films and the others made their way to Amsterdam. I don't know exactly what happened to them, you'd have to ask him.'

'How old were these kids?'

It was obvious from his voice that Bernard was not only shocked by what he was hearing but ready to give vent to his anger. It was in his stance, in his voice. He was clenching and unclenching his fists as if just waiting for the right moment to attack the man before him.

Which was exactly what he was doing.

Jesmond couldn't look either of them in the face.

'All different ages. I didn't exactly ask for their fucking birth certificates . . .'

Bernard kicked him hard in the knees, nearly knocking him off his chair.

'How old are we talking about here? Fifteen? Ten? Younger?'

Jesmond's mouth was so dry he could barely get the words out.

'Like I said, man, all ages.'

Jon Jon and Bernard were staring at him, both thinking that he had not disagreed with any of the ages mentioned.

'You piece of shit, you don't give a flying fuck, do you?'

Jesmond didn't dare to look up.

'It's not a matter of caring. Once the initial deal's done you take a step back from it. The kids were Pippy's department, not mine. I deal with the older girls.'

Bernard laughed sarcastically.

'*Older* girls? How old are they then? Not the big grown-up

nine year olds? Bit old for you lot, ain't they?'

Jon Jon had to hold Bernard back then and it took all his strength. Jesmond stood up from the chair and tried to move towards the door.

'Sit back down! And you, fucking calm down, will you?'

Jon Jon was trying to keep it all together now, forcing Bernard away from Jesmond with his shoulder.

'Calm down, Bernard. You can do what you want with him when I find out what I need to know, OK? Until then you fucking keep a cool head.'

He settled Bernard down with difficulty, pouring him another drink.

'I've been doing business all this time with the Gary Glitter of fucking Barking and Dagenham! Can you credit it? I'm sorry, Jon Jon, but this is fucking unbelievable.' He shook his head once more and downed the brandy in one. 'Un-fucking-believable! Of all people, you know? If it was anyone but him . . . I've worked with him, been mates with him, for so long . . .'

He poured himself another drink.

'I just can't take it on board, it's too much. Wait until I tell everyone else that they've been dealing with a nonce, a fucking beast! No one will believe it.'

'You can say that again. Now let me talk to him, OK?'

Jon Jon turned back to Jesmond who looked smaller somehow. Without his habitual hardness, his arrogance, he didn't look half so dangerous.

'What happened to me sister? Did you have anything to do with her disappearance? Did Little Tommy or his father ever come to you?'

'You'd better ask Pippy Light, Jon Jon. All that part of the business was down to him and a mate of his. I never had anything to do with it after it was set up.'

'You took the money though, didn't you?'

Jesmond looked into Bernard's eyes.

'You have got to understand. It's like I said – the money is astronomical, more than you'd ever earn with dope, coke, you name it. And it's live cargo. It can move itself if necessary.'

Jesmond wiped a hand across his face. He was trying to make

Bernard understand the hard financial reality. He knew that money was Bernard's God. Over the years they had striven jointly for it – except in this one instance.

'Come on, Jesmond. For once in your fucking life tell the truth.'

'Your sister, Jon Jon, would never have come near or by us. We never dealt in English kids, only foreign ones, and they were already broken in by the time we got them.'

Bernard and Jon Jon could not believe what they were hearing. It was chilling to listen to him talk as if what he had done meant nothing. It genuinely *didn't* mean anything to him, that was the worst of it.

'If I was a nonce and I went to Pippy, what would he offer me?'

Jesmond shook his head.

'I don't know. Like I said, you'd have to ask him. He got someone else in to help out with the specialised stuff – wouldn't tell me who. Said I didn't need to know.'

'You don't know much, do you, cocker?'

Bernard was approaching him once more and this time Jon Jon didn't attempt to stop him.

'I swear on my daughter's life I don't know anything about your little sister, Jon Jon, or the pair of cunts who hurt her.'

Jon Jon stared into his eyes and saw what he thought was the truth.

'Please, Jesmond, if you know anything . . . anything at all?'

'I don't. Maybe you should ask Paulie Martin.'

Jon Jon sighed.

'Paulie will fucking disembowel you just for mentioning his name in the same breath as Pippy.'

His voice was dismissive and this more than anything annoyed Jesmond who sneered at him and blew out air between his teeth. Bernard decided he'd been quiet long enough.

'I am going to kill you, Jes.'

He closed his eyes for a moment.

'I never would have guessed, Bernie me old mate. But go and ask Paulie about his dealings with Pippy Light, OK?'

He was resigned to his own fate now and actually trying to

help. Even Jon Jon picked up on that much. But he still dismissed what Jesmond was saying. Not Paulie, never him.

'He couldn't have known what he was dealing with . . .'

'Who are you trying to convince, Jon Jon? Me or you?'

Jesmond was past caring now, he knew he was a dead man.

'He couldn't have known. He puts money into all sorts, bankrolls loads of people. He don't always know the score . . .'

'Don't he? Ask him about the web-sites and also about the parties at a house in Clerkenwell. You fucking ask him, man, and you tell him it was me who told you to.'

'He'll kill you,' Jon Jon growled.

Bernard laughed then, rubbing his hands together as if they were cold.

'Tell him he'll have to join the queue, Jon Jon. This ponce is mine. Do me a favour, son, fill in the Rottweilers on your way out. And send in my Jimmy – he's in the car outside. Tell him I want the lighter fuel and the pliers. We're going back to the sixties for you, Jesmond, old stylie!'

He wanted revenge and Jon Jon was willing to let Bernard get it for him. He was also shrewd enough to realise Bernard wanted to know more about where Jesmond's money was stashed.

As he walked away Bernard said quietly, 'Let me know about Paulie, I've always fancied a ruck with him.'

Jon Jon laughed.

'He's talking bollocks, Bernard. Paulie is a lot of things, but a beast? Never in a million years.'

'We'll see, son. And Jon Jon . . .'

He turned round to face the collector.

'You're a good kid. If you ever fancy a change of scene, give me a call, son.'

Jon Jon nodded and left the room. As he reached Jesmond's minders the screaming started.

'What's going on, Jon Jon?'

He noticed none of them ran in to help their boss. It was the old, old story. The king was dead, long live the *new* king.

Bethany was curled up on Joanie's sofa with a glass of milk and a packet of crisps. Joanie was running her a bath. Bethany had wet herself at some point and her clothes were soaked. There was no way she could be left like she was. Joanie had given her one of her own outsize T-shirts to wear. As she picked up the discarded clothes she saw the state of Bethany's underwear. There was dried blood in her panties which had obviously been on her for days.

Joanie sighed with frustration. Poor little cow. Monika obviously hadn't bothered to tip her the wink about her periods starting. She must have been so scared. She poured some of Kira's Matey in and watched the bubbles forming through tear-filled eyes as the extent of her friend's neglect of Bethany hit home.

'Come on, love, get in here.'

Bethany walked into the little bathroom and Joanie pulled the T-shirt up over her head. She saw bruises on the girl's solid body. She didn't have proper breasts: they were just fat. Bethany was like a little Michelin girl. As she settled back in the warm water she winced.

'You sore, sweetheart?'

She nodded.

'Has someone been hurting you, Bethany?'

'I can't tell anyone, Joanie, or they'll come and get me. They told me they would.' Even though Bethany was a drama queen there was real fear in her eyes.

'Who told you that, sweetie? Tell Auntie Joanie and I promise I will take care of you.'

She could see that Bethany wanted to believe her. But fear was a stronger emotion than love at times and Joanie knew that fear was the key here. She had to go slowly or she would lose this opportunity. Bethany had to tell her the truth because she wanted to. If Joanie forced it out of her she knew she would never get the whole story.

'Can I stay here?'

It was more of a plea than a question. As Joanie stared into those big brown eyes she felt her heart jolt. This child was beautiful beneath the grime and the flab and she was unloved and needed attention. Joanie would give her all she needed. But she also knew from personal experience what usually happened to girls like Bethany. People took them and then they used and abused them.

It was what had happened to her.

''Course you can stay here, for as long as you like. But you can't drink here, you know that, don't you?'

Bethany nodded.

'I won't need to drink here, will I? I won't be on me own all the time.'

All the loneliness she'd known was in her voice, in the resigned set of her chubby shoulders. Joanie was gently washing the girl's hair. It was matted underneath and she picked up some conditioner to try and detangle it.

'Where did these bruises come from?' she asked casually.

Bethany was still lying back in the water, enjoying the feel of Joanie's hands massaging her head. Her eyes were closed and she didn't answer for a while. Joanie felt a strong urge to walk round to Monika's and launch her into outer space for her complete callous neglect of this child. Monika should never have had children; she was completely selfish, always had been and always would be. When they'd had words about this in the past, Monika had argued she was only emulating her own mother. But Joanie's own mother had not been much better, and *she* had done the best she could. She'd been determined that her own kids would not know the misery she had endured. She knew just what it was like to be Bethany but after Kira's disappearance had forgotten all about the poor kid.

Now she said, 'You have to tell me who hurt you. I mean it, Bethany, I *have* to know.'

Bethany didn't answer her, just stared at her with those big sad eyes.

'What about me mum, Joanie? Will you tell her I told you?'

'Not if you don't want me to. Now let me rinse this off your hair and then I want you to start talking, all right?'

Bethany nodded and lay back in the warm water, enjoying the comforting feel of it. She had always envied Kira her home life and felt even more guilty now as she remembered just what she had done to her.

Jealousy had at times got the better of her. Kira had always been loved and cared for, had basked in her family's attention all her life. The only time Bethany had ever felt valued was in this tiny flat when Joanie had done her best to make her feel part of the family.

Now, as she lay in the water, she felt Joanie's love enveloping her and knew she could trust her. If she had said she would take care of Bethany, that was exactly what would happen.

So she lay there and enjoyed the ministrations of her mother's best friend.

Paulie was in a meeting with Big John McClellan. John was a face from South London with his fingers in nearly every pie in the smoke. He had done twenty-three years in prison and walked out richer than when he had gone inside as he had continued to run his businesses through his sons, and being a shrewd businessman had gone from strength to strength.

John's biggest asset was the fact that he had no conscience. From the earliest days of his career he had made sure that anyone who disrespected him or tucked him up paid a high price. There was many an old lag still walking around with a scar from eyebrow to mouth, the sixties punishment for those offences.

Now he was after Paulie to come in on a deal bringing cocaine in from Amsterdam to Harwich in plastic containers of fruit. The fruit was actually filled with the white powder, and as the plastic housing had been treated with an agent to disguise the smell the dogs would overlook it.

John had already organised a couple of dummy runs and now he was ready to go into the big leagues. It would be worth a fortune to the right investors and he needed people with a decent wedge to help him secure his contacts. Hence this visit to see his old mate Paulie Martin.

He, for his part, was happy to do business with Big John because it was always a guaranteed few shillings. Big John never invested a penny without first looking at all the angles and he always made plenty of dosh.

Paulie remembered years before, the two of them sitting on a beach in Sussex waiting for a consignment of cannabis to be unloaded from small vessels. When they saw it they waded into the water to drag it on to the beach with fishing rods.

What a laugh those days had been!

It had bonded the two men and that bond had stayed close all these years. Now Jon Jon was being introduced to this face he had only ever heard about before and he was impressed. He also knew he would have to wait until they had finished their business before he could tell Paulie what was going on with Jesmond.

He listened to them talking about old times and envied them their experience even as he told himself that as soon as all this was over he was going to take stock of his own life, once and for all.

He would normally have been excited to find himself in the company of a living legend, but now too much was going on for him to really enjoy it. He glanced round Paulie's offices and took in for the first time just how expensive everything here was. It had cost plenty of money and it looked that way.

It was Paulie's nature to choose only the best, and Jon Jon knew he would be the same in his shoes. But if this was ever within his reach, he also knew he would be happy with it. Paulie, though, couldn't ever have enough. He felt that any money spent was money wasted even if it was earning him and did his best to replace it as quickly as possible.

Jon Jon was brought back to the present by hearing Paulie saying to Big John: 'Take Jon Jon with you, then. He's a good kid and he could do with the experience.'

Paulie smiled at him.

'You go with John and you listen and learn, right? Because this will be your arm of the business. You might as well learn about it from the best.'

Big John was grinning at him, and Jon Jon found himself smiling back. Big John looked like the archetypal villain: square-headed, completely bald with expensively capped teeth. Heavy-built, running to fat but still powerful enough to make most men think twice before having a row with him even if they didn't know who he was.

But it was his eyes that were his most arresting feature: pale grey and completely devoid of any feeling, except when he grinned and then he looked benevolent. Almost.

Jon Jon left with him ten minutes later to find out about the finer points of cocaine smuggling. But he was seeing Paulie at nine that night in the club in King's Cross.

He would wait. He knew he had no choice.

Joanie had dried Bethany and dressed her once more in the T-shirt, then she had made her something to eat and now they were curled up together on Kira's bed. As Bethany munched away she tried to put what she wanted to say into words but they escaped her.

She could taste the butter in the sandwiches. It was so long since she had eaten something so good. She lived on takeaways and sweets usually and it was such a novelty to be fed like this. She was also enjoying the feeling of being held by Joanie. She felt safe and warm.

But would Joanie still want her around once Bethany told her what had been happening? In the end she knew that she would just have to tell the truth and be done with it.

'Come on, Bethany. You've dithered enough for one night and your mum will be here before we know it. She must be wondering where I've got to.'

Joanie hugged the girl to her.

'No matter what you might think, love, there's nothing that can shock me or make me feel any differently towards you.'

'Are you sure about that, Joanie?'

She nodded.

Bethany put the plate on the duvet and licked her fingers slowly before replying.

'What if I was to tell you I saw Kira the day she disappeared?'

There, it was out at last, and she felt the burden of guilt start to slide from her. She could also see the stunned expression on Joanie's face and wished she could do something to make it better.

'What do you mean, you saw her, Bethany? Where?'

'We had a row up the high street. I was horrible to her, but I didn't mean it. She ran off and I followed . . .'

Joanie was trying to take in what the child was saying.

'Why didn't you tell anyone?'

Bethany lowered her eyes before she said sadly, 'I was too frightened.'

'Frightened of who, love? Tell me who you're so scared of.'

Bethany started crying again.

'Pippy . . . he took me and Kira away in his car with him when I'd caught up with her, said he was going to show us where some children played. But I knew he wasn't going to show us anything like that because . . .'

She was choking now, unable to get the words out.

Joanie's head was spinning from what she had just been told.

'Because you had already had dealings with him, is that what you're trying to say?'

Bethany nodded, unable to answer the question outright. As Joanie absorbed what she was being told she saw the distress and guilt on the child's face and felt an overpowering urge to kill Pippy.

'Where did he take Kira, sweetheart?'

'I don't know, Joanie. I was dropped off at a house in Ilford, off Mortlake Road.' Bethany was crying once more. 'The man likes me, see? He gives me things.'

'Oh, dear God, Bethany! What on earth is going on here?'

Bethany took these words as proof of her own guilt. Pulling away from Joanie, she threw herself down on the bed, burying her face in Kira's Barbie quilt where she cried her heart out.

Finally Joanie pulled her into her arms, fighting against the child who was trying to push her away.

'I'm sorry, Joanie, I never dreamed they would hurt her. It was because of her long hair and her lovely face that I told them about her. Pippy has parties, see. I've been to them. He said did I know anyone else I could bring – someone really pretty. They dress you up in makeup and let you drink and smoke. They give you tablets to make you feel funny and you can't stop laughing . . .'

She was trying to explain as best she could just what had made her do what she had.

'I like it. It's nice, see? They're nice to you most of the time, only hurt you if you try and stop them . . .'

She was crying once more. Joanie's head was spinning. She couldn't take this all in. Her overwhelming need was to find out about Kira.

'So do you have any idea where he took her, sweetheart? Where she might be now?'

Bethany shook her head.

'I never saw her again after that day. And when I asked, Pippy hit me and told me if I ever said anything to anyone they would kill me.'

'Did this have anything to do with Tommy or his father?'

Joanie had to know the answer to that question.

Bethany was crying harder than ever now. Her whole face was swollen with tears and Joanie could see that this was just the tip of the iceberg where this child was concerned. She had been carrying all this around for so long it had broken her.

'Please, Joanie, I don't want to talk about it any more.'

'You have to answer me, sweetheart. I need to know what happened to my baby.'

She was trying to keep the terror out of her voice so she didn't frighten Bethany into silence. The thought that a child had had to deal with all this was almost mind-blowing. And when the poor girl had also been abused, sexually abused, her own mother had not been interested enough to try to find out what ailed her.

Joanie remembered the blood and the fingermarks she'd seen at the top of the girl's arms and on her thighs. With her own experience of life she didn't need to think too hard to realise how they had been put there.

She hugged Bethany, smelling the difference in her after only a few hours away from her mother. She knew that Bethany would stay her responsibility now and partly take Kira's place because Joanie felt to blame for what had happened to her. She should have *seen* what was happening. She wondered at a world where a dog was removed if neglected yet a child was abandoned to her miserable life even though the school and everyone else involved could tell something was badly wrong.

'Kira told me about the photographs Jeanette took of her. I took the film into the shop and gave it to Maurice. He works there, does some of the films for Pippy. You know, the photos and that . . . I stole it with the money and the ring.'

Joanie nodded even though she had no idea what the girl was

talking about, but she knew she would find out eventually. At the moment she was just going to let her talk, get it out of her system. Only ask a question now and again. She didn't want to bombard Bethany just yet. That would come soon enough when Jon Jon was told. Only then would any of them be able to make proper sense of what had happened to her daughter.

Bethany was absolutely terrified of what she was revealing. Joanie knew she had to let her talk herself out before she would be able to put it all into some sort of order. Before she told Jon Jon anything she needed to know as much as the child did.

'Who introduced you to Pippy?'

'Lorna. It was her who said that we could earn some money, easy money, and not have to go to school.'

Joanie smiled painfully at the girl.

'Did Lorna know Tommy and his dad?'

She clammed up again.

'Can I have a drink of water, Joanie? I feel sick.'

She nodded.

'Wait here and I'll get it for you.'

In the kitchen she leaned against the worktop and felt the battering of her heart in her chest.

She was finally going to find out what had happened to her daughter, and she wasn't sure she could cope with the knowledge.

As she let the tap run she put her wrists underneath it to calm her own feeling of nausea. Her baby, her little angel, would have walked away with them like a lamb to the slaughter. That was the worst of it.

Kira would not have had the sense to see any of it for what it was, she would only have seen the smiling faces and the promise of something nice. It would never have occurred to her that anyone would want to hurt her.

Joanie filled the glass with water and went back to the bedroom with it. Bethany looked so pathetic lying there. She placed the glass on the bedside table. Sitting beside her, Joanie gently rubbed her arm and shoulder.

Bethany put up one plump hand and grasped hers.

'I am sorry, Joanie. Promise you won't blame me?'

'I would never blame you, darling, you're just a little girl. But you have to tell me all you know, OK, so I can decide what to do about it all.'

'Will you get the police?'

Joanie didn't answer that. It depended on just what she was told. She had a feeling she might like to exact revenge herself. Her hatred and loathing of Tommy were back in full now. The child wouldn't say anything about him which could mean only one thing.

As she rubbed the girl's arm and whispered words of comfort Joanie pictured Little Tommy and his father in their coffins.

Somehow that image was the only thing that made her feel better.

Chapter Twenty-Four

Big John McClellan opened the door to his flat and waved Jon Jon inside. He looked around him in utter amazement. He had never seen anything like this in his life, it was phenomenal.

The whole place was painted white and all there was in the reception room was an imposing stone fireplace and a huge cream leather sofa. On the wall hung one long painting, a fierce spattering of bright colour that Big John informed him was by Jackson Pollock.

'No guff, son, a real one. Me fucking pension!'

Big John roared with laughter at his own wit.

Jon Jon was impressed despite himself, and as he looked into the open-plan kitchen with its state-of-the-art six-foot-long wine cooler and stainless steel cupboards, he felt overwhelmed. This was the home of someone with wealth, but it was far more than that. It was an almost aggressive display of confidence and power, demanding a proper show of respect from anyone but the man who owned it.

It spoke to something deep within Jon Jon. All his life he'd appreciated the way his mother did her best to make a decent home for them. It was clean, tidy, and she had her best china and glasses and silverware all lovingly stowed away, far too 'good' for daily use.

He had never been ashamed of Joanie and the way they lived, not in any way, but he had always known that some people lived differently, in a world that was far removed from their cramped flat on a sink estate. He had always wanted somewhere he could bring anyone, no matter who they were, and see shock and delight on their face at their surroundings, at the way he lived his life, much the same as Big John was enjoying watching him take in this place now. He almost guffawed at the boy's incredulous expression.

'This is where I bring me birds, son. Me actual house, where I live with the wife, is grander but it ain't got the same sophistication, know what I mean? My old woman could blue a rollover week on the Lottery and it would still be all chintz and MFI. You'd need a pair of Ray-Bans just to walk to the downstairs toilet!'

Jon Jon knew exactly what he meant.

'But my Kathy's a good girl all the same. Been with her thirty-four years, I have, and we've seven sons. Good boys and all except for my youngest.' Big John wasn't smiling now. 'I'm afraid my boy's fell in with some bad company, including Mad Pippy Light. I've tipped him the wink more times than I care to remember. No one else has ever tried my patience to that extent and lived, but Kieron – his whole life's a bowl of shit.'

He was opening two beers as he spoke and Jon Jon knew he was in for a long night. But even with all that was happening in his quest for Kira's killer he knew he couldn't blank Big John, that would have been dangerous and futile. Big John was in confessional mode and it was his job to keep schtumm and listen.

'I know about your sister, son. Fucking scum of the earth on the streets these days. Can't trust no cunt, you remember that.' He took a long swig of his beer. 'One of me own granddaughters was nonced, by me daughter-in-law's dad of all people!'

Jon Jon looked suitably shocked.

'Fucking hell, what did you do?'

Big John laughed.

'Let's just say he ain't been seen for a long time, and won't be seen again unless Osama bin-Laden decides to blow up part of the M25.'

He finished his beer in one gulp.

'Shame that ponce wasn't in the Reader's Digest two hundred and fifty thousand pound prize draw. Now *they* would have found him!'

He laughed at his own wit.

'But those nonces . . . they're like a cancer. Kill them, that's what I say.' He flipped the top off another beer. 'It's the only way with the bastards! You have to wipe them off the face of the earth. They're a fucking cancer, and the only way to get rid of that is to cut it out once and for all. And if it still kills you, you nuke the bastard, get yourself cremated. Burn the fucker, burn away the disease!'

Jon Jon smiled at the man, wholly understanding his sentiments. Big John opened a cupboard and took out a mother-of-pearl box. It looked beautiful and very valuable.

'Skin up, son, I'm sure you're an expert. I am going to go and get this fucking suit off, OK?'

Jon Jon opened the box, resigned to the task of joint-rolling, but what he saw amazed him. It held every kind of puff imaginable and also a hefty quantity of cocaine. It even had a silver kit for cutting and snorting – no rolled-up fivers in this house! There was no denying this man knew how to live, and he was nearer sixty than twenty. That was ancient as far as Jon Jon was concerned, but John McClellan had the money to live like a king and that was all that mattered.

Jon Jon picked up a small vial of cannabis resin and opened it; he breathed in the acrid aroma and sighed. This was something he had only ever heard about, never actually experienced, but he decided on something more mellow for tonight. He was sure the coke would be out too before long so for now he chose a nice grass. He built the joint expertly, taking his time over it. For all his high opinion of himself he found he needed to impress this man.

Jon Jon was amazed to realise that he already liked and respected him. He had heard the stories about him over the years, everyone had. Big John was a legend where they lived and Paulie had been very vocal about him when he'd had a few. But those stories didn't even scratch the surface where Big John was concerned, Jon Jon was sure of that now.

As he sparked up the joint the man himself walked back into the kitchen, wearing jeans and a T-shirt and looking younger and more intimidating somehow. Jon Jon noticed that for all his size he still had some decent muscle on him, strong arms that looked like they had seen some action over the years. He had obviously kept himself in shape as best he could. But youth would out as it always had and always would. He'd told Paulie he needed some young blood in on the Amsterdam job. Were they going to get down to business soon? Only Jon Jon had things he urgently needed to discuss with Paulie.

'How's your mother?' Big John enquired.

Jon Jon sighed and shrugged helplessly.

'In bits to be honest.'

Big John looked sympathetic.

'Well, she would be, wouldn't she? That child was the light of Joanie's life according to Paulie.' He coughed and spat phlegm into the kitchen sink. 'Brasses are like that, I know.'

He saw the stiffening of Jon Jon's shoulders and laughed again heartily.

'It's all right, son, I do know what I'm on about. *My* mother was one as well. It's no secret – though no one would say it to me boatrace these days, of course, for fear of reprisals!' He sighed heavily then looked out of the kitchen window, ruminating for a few moments on his previous life. The years devoid of money or kudos.

'My old mum went on the bash when we was kids. Me dad had gone on the trot and she had eight of us to feed. Hard graft, bless her. Loved the bones of that woman, I did. She was worn out before she was fifty. Never saw me old man again until I was doing well, had made a name for meself like. Then he turned up like the poncing leech he was.' He laughed loudly, only this time it was hollow-sounding.

'What did you do?'

Big John's face set like stone.

'Same as you would if your old man turned up for a hand out: I gave him a grand and told him if I ever saw him again, I'd kill him.'

He took a deep toke on the joint.

'Never saw hide nor hair of him again, the cunt! I'd have had more respect if he'd thrown it in me face, but he slunk off just like all those times before when I was a kid. Just upped and disappeared like he always had. Left me, the eldest, to bring up me brothers and sisters, see them all right, which I did. Good riddance to bad fucking rubbish, eh?'

Jon Jon nodded sagely. Half stoned and half straight, he felt an embarrassing urge to cry.

'I never knew my old man,' he confessed.

Big John handed him the joint.

'Just as well, son, he'd only have disappointed you. Wankers always do. Now then, what were you talking to Jesmond about today?'

'What?'

Shock and surprise were evident in Jon Jon's face and voice. That was the last thing he had expected to be asked.

Big John laughed, cupping one ear to take the sting out of his words as he said matter-of-factly, 'I hear everything, son. One of the blokes who works for me, works for him. I've more grasses than Wimbledon Centre Court. It keeps the opposition in its place – bit like Tony Blair, only I don't sell them down the river when it all falls out of bed. They don't have to top themselves either, I make a point of doing that for them.'

He grinned, and Jon Jon remembered reading somewhere about tombstone teeth. He could see what that meant now.

'I've had Ginger . . . you know, his number one, otherwise known as Manky Foot? He's a raspberry ripple, but he can have a row . . . anyway, I've had him on my payroll for a couple of years. He told me that you and Bernard were after a straightener with his boss.'

He toked on the joint once more and said in his best Jeremy Paxman piss-taking voice, 'So, Sonny Jim, or Sonny Jon Jon if you prefer, I am going to cut us a couple of lines of this very expensive and might I say rather excellent Colombian marching gear while you tell me everything I need to know.'

He grinned.

'And you *will* tell me, son, understand that much.'

It was a threat and they both knew it, but a carefully judged one. It was up to Jon Jon whether or not to take umbrage. Which of course he wouldn't, he wasn't that stupid.

He was just amazed at the way his day had turned out.

'When Paulie said to come here, I thought we had a new deal

going down. I mean, that's why you went to see him, after all.'

Big John studied Jon Jon's face as he absorbed all that was being said to him. He was quick and he had savvy. Give the boy a few years and he would be a force to be reckoned with. He was also loyal, a must have in Big John's organisation.

He decided to be honest. Or at least as honest as he could be until he knew this boy was on board.

'Listen, son, I went to see Paulie today because I wanted an in to you. The Amsterdam deal may or may not occur – I've got higher priorities right now. You going after Jesmond today done my head in, took me by surprise like. Maybe a few years from now I might have expected it as the natural course of events. Someone was going to take what he had one day and it might as well be you. You've already got a good rep, I'll give you that much. But at this moment in time you're still a babe-in-arms. I deduced that you had to have a personal reason for going up against him. And, me being me, I want to know what that reason is.'

He opened the box carefully and respectfully as befitted a decent bit of gear, at the same time pointing one finger at Jon Jon.

'There's stuff you don't know yet. I'll rephrase that, *can't* know yet. But you will if I hear what I want to hear.'

Jon Jon watched as he cut two lines expertly and with the minimum of fuss. That much in itself was different. Most people talked about how good their gear was when they iced it out, bragged about the quality, how good it was. But Big John imported his own and no one in their right mind would question its quality. This was an education and Jon Jon was determined to take in every lesson he could from the evening's entertainment.

But he was still wary of saying too much, too soon. He decided to change the subject while he thought out what to do.

'How do you know my mum?'

Big John grinned.

'I remember her from years gone by. Nice woman, Joanie. No one ever had a bad word to say about her, and why would they? She's sound, done a few favours for friends over the years. Time was, when my old woman wouldn't shit till your mother had done her Tarot cards! When I was banged up they were a lifeline to Kathy. She loves your mum.'

It was good heart-warming stuff but Jon Jon wasn't fooled.

'What kind of favours did she do for friends?'

He had taken the main point and this made Big John smile. He genuinely liked this kid. For all his dreadlocks and his Kiss 100 clothes he was a shrewd little fucker, and John McClellan liked shrewd little fuckers – they made you money.

'Never you mind, you ask her yourself. But Paulie always had a soft spot for her, I know. Wouldn't admit it, of course. Him with a brass! But I tell you something, she was worth fifty of that fat whore he married. Wouldn't get an honourable mention at Cruft's, her!'

Jon Jon didn't dispute what the man was saying. He snorted a line quickly, and felt the rush almost immediately.

'This stuff will keep you up longer than an Irish marching band!' Big John was laughing again. 'So come on, what have you found out?'

Jon Jon looked at him and wondered if this was a set-up. He decided to tell it in as ambiguous a way as possible. Feel it out as he went along.

'Well, you see . . .'

'Just call me John, son.'

He'd guessed rightly that Jon Jon didn't know how to address him.

'It's complicated.'

Big John smiled and this time it didn't reach his eyes.

'Life's complicated, son. Surely your sister's disappearance proved that. By the way, I heard about Joanie trying to give that nonce an acid bath.'

'You seem to hear everything, John.'

Big John looked at him for a moment. He was obviously choosing his words carefully.

Then he said, 'Let's see if we're singing from the same hymn sheet here. I've heard a few rumours about Jesmond and Paulie and Pippy Light. Not exactly Brain of Britain is Pippy Light. When everyone else went into computers he bought his first abacus, but I digress. It's Paulie Martin I'm really interested in. I hear through the grapevine that he makes money off of little kids and I think you can enlighten me further about that.'

He paused before continuing, 'At least, I hope so. Jesmond would sell his own mother for a few beers. Pieces of shit like him can't help it, but at least he never pretended to be anything else, do you get my drift?' He sniffed loudly to make his point but also to bring the coke as far up his nose as possible.

'Now Paulie, he's a different kettle of fish altogether. You see, he acts like butter wouldn't melt. But you know Paulie's trouble, don't you?'

'No, I don't. Exactly what is his trouble?'

Jon Jon knew he was chancing his arm. Animosity was coming off Big John in waves now and when all was said and done Jon Jon worked for Paulie Martin. They were friends. But for all that Jon Jon was getting seriously antsy about the number of times he was hearing about his boss today, and from some very unexpected quarters.

'Paulie's problem, son, is he has *never* done a lump in his life, and I am very wary of anyone who's been going as long as him and never had so much as a night in the cells. Do you see where I'm coming from?'

Jon Jon could see all right, though he wasn't sure he wanted to. It was strange the way Paulie had never had his collar felt. Luck of the devil, he always said. But maybe not.

'Now I had a capture, done me time, head down, arse up. A capture and a half and all, over twenty years.'

Big John started to cut another line.

'But it's real life, ain't it? You'll do a lump one day, son, because you won't sell out your mates, see? It's all part of the learning curve for people like us.'

Jon Jon's mouth was dry from the unaccustomed cocaine. He had left it alone for months. But he also knew it was because he was getting nervous. This was clearly personal for Big John. Jon Jon had suddenly realised that he was expected to serve Paulie up to him on a plate.

'Maybe he was just lucky?'

Big John laughed again, louder this time, and then in the blink of an eye he was not smiling. Staring Jon Jon full in the face, he said, 'No one is that fucking lucky, boy. If he had that much luck going spare he'd be getting a cheque from Dale Winton. Think about it.'

Jon Jon thought about it, he didn't have much choice. It was all going pear-shaped and he didn't know what to do. He would just have to sit this out and play it by ear. There was no way he was walking out of here with the hump, he would be lucky to get as far as the lifts.

But, for all that, Big John was making a deadly kind of sense.

Jeanette walked into the flat full of smiles and good humour. Joanie wasn't in the mood for either. In fact, Jeanette was the last person she had expected to see tonight.

Time was when her daughter coming home was a cause for rejoicing, but not now. She tried to keep her temper while Jeanette poured herself a drink and informed her that she was staying the night. She said it as if she was doing her mother the favour of a lifetime.

Joanie smiled with difficulty.

'If you don't mind, love, I need the place to meself tonight.'

Jeanette grinned.

'Oh, yeah! You on a promise?'

Joanie smiled as best she could.

'You could say that.'

'Oh, come on, Mum! Tell me.'

She saw her daughter's evident pleasure and knew that whatever else had happened to this family, Jeanette had come out of it all a better person. It was what she had needed, a bit of an eye opener. But what a price Joanie had had to pay to see this other daughter of hers smile at her with real affection.

'There's nothing to tell, love.' Joanie took a vodka from her and sipped it before saying quietly, 'Just do me a favour, will you, and go back round Jasper's?'

Jeanette picked up on the nervousness in her mother's voice.

'What's going on here?'

She was suspicious now, she knew a blank when she got one.

'Nothing, love. I just need the place to meself.'

'Oh, leave it out, Mum. Do I look like a lemon?'

Jeanette was trying to make light of it all and Joanie gave her top marks for that. But she wanted her out of the house before she saw Bethany and started asking questions. She really didn't need this tonight. Jeanette would just confuse the situation.

As her daughter walked towards the bedroom she'd shared with Kira, Joanie bellowed in annoyance.

'Why can't you just for once do what the fuck I ask?'

Jeanette turned to look at her mother.

'What's going on here?'

Joanie took a deep breath before she replied, 'Please, Jeanette. Just go to Jasper's, will you?'

Her voice was tired-sounding and she looked even more battered than usual.

'Mum, please, what's going on?'

Joanie pulled herself upright and shouted as loud as she could: 'Would you just fuck off! For *once* in your life, just do what I'm asking, will you?'

Jeanette stared at her for long seconds before saying nastily, 'Well, thanks a fucking bunch, Mother.'

She was mortally offended now and Joanie wanted to make it all better but she couldn't. Not yet. Not until she had found out what she needed to know. Jeanette would just hassle the girl and that was the last thing Bethany needed now. It was taking all Joanie's own will-power not to beat the truth out of the poor kid, for all her noble thoughts. Whereas Jeanette, if she knew the score, would not think about it twice. She would punch first and think later.

She was her mother's daughter in that respect.

Jeanette stormed out of the flat and slammed the door. Joanie sank down on to the floor. She didn't know what the hell to do. For the first time in her life, she didn't know how to make it all better.

In the bedroom Bethany was shrinking into the sheets and wondering what all the shouting was about. The only thing she knew was that this trouble was over her.

Big John was flying and he looked like he was flying. He was red in the face, talking nineteen to the dozen, but his head was as clear as the water skimming a tropical beach.

But the coke had also made him aggressive and he had no intention of pussy-footing round Jon Jon any more. He said as much.

'Are Jesmond and Paulie working a flanker? It's an easy question – a yes or no will fucking suffice. I ain't in the mood now for cunting around, OK?'

Jon Jon nodded.

'I think so.'

He'd decided to burn his boats and go in with Big John, even though in his heart of hearts he knew that in reality he had no choice but to comply with what this man wanted.

That was the up side of being a legend like John McClellan. People always did what you wanted in the end. It was the law of the street, and Jon Jon had always respected that law.

Paulie was suddenly an unknown entity. Until today he had been the boy's role model, and Jon Jon had been grateful for his tutelage. But had he been messing with a beast, and the worst kind of beast imaginable at that? Was Paulie the proverbial wolf in sheep's clothing?

It looked like it. No matter how much he tried to dress things up in his head it seemed to Jon Jon like Paulie was tainted. And in their world the stench of nonce would not, could not, be tolerated.

He sighed so deeply he felt empty inside.

'According to Jesmond, he worked with Paulie and Pippy. They had girls and kids brought in from Eastern Europe then sold them on.'

He snorted another line before saying, 'I want to see Pippy about it now but according to you, your boy's in league with him so I need to know exactly where that leaves me. Do I have to go through you, John?'

He looked the man in the face, fair and square.

Big John leaned back against a granite work top, his craggy face frozen into a mask of grief. He put his head into his hands, big shoulders shaking as if he was trying not to cry. He stood like that for some minutes, the tension mounting in the room.

Then he seemed to come round and, looking up at the boy in

front of him, said seriously, 'It leaves you open to taking my boy out of the ball game, don't it?'

He held one big well-manicured hand over his mouth for a moment as if he was going to be sick, then said sadly, 'It'll kill my Kathy. He's her youngest, but I can't protect him, son. Don't want to, not if he's trafficking in kids. But you have to do it because I can't. If I did I could never look my old woman in the face again. And for all my faults, I love her, like I loved Kieron once. Weak and foolish as he was, I loved that boy.'

He was cutting lines again but Jon Jon saw his hands were shaking. When he had finished he looked at his namesake and said sadly, 'You'd better see this.'

He left the room and Jon Jon heard him walking up the wrought-iron staircase to the gallery bedroom. Jon Jon felt as if he was in some kind of dream. He wondered if this was all happening. Was this man really expecting Jon Jon to waste his youngest son for him?

When John came back into the room he handed over a paper folder, like the ones kids use at school.

'Open it, look inside.'

Jon Jon opened it with trepidation. Now it had come on top he wasn't actually sure he wanted to go any further. He felt a bit like Pandora except he knew that whatever was left in the box it would not be hope. Hope had fucked off years before and there was no chance of it ever coming back.

'Are you sure about this, John?'

The man placed a heavy hand on his shoulder.

'Your mother done a fucking blinding job with you. Everyone says so. They talk about how well you looked after her and your sisters. About what a strong person you are. I admire that, see. My eldest boys are like that. Fuckers admittedly, I ain't disputing it, but my youngest, my Kieron, he's a cunt. Only I never believed it until I saw these photos. Got them off his PC myself. There's no doubt about what he's done himself. I just needed to know if he was a client or in on the arranging like.'

He poked a finger in Jon Jon's face.

'You never tell a soul what you see in there tonight, right? My other boys will be informed but only after the event. They'll not know the half of it, just enough to shut them up. You'll understand why I want it kept quiet. I'll dispose of his body meself. But I want you to do this little job for me, and then I'll owe you, son, fucking big time.'

He cleared his throat noisily before saying: 'Now look inside that fucking folder, will you?'

'Will I see my sister?'

Jon Jon needed to know that first. Before he delved into this folder and burned his boats once and for all.

'Nah, you won't, and when you look in there you'll thank God for that fact the rest of your life. Me, I have to live with knowing my boy is a filthy pervert, and worse than that even. Someone who's made it easy for other sick fucks to ruin little children.'

Reluctantly Jon Jon opened the folder and took out the printed images. As he stared at them he felt the bile rise up inside him.

Kieron McClellan was there in glorious Technicolor with small children, girls and boys. It was enough to bring the bile from his stomach into his mouth. He threw up into the state-of-the-art kitchen sink until his ribs hurt. All he could taste was lager and cocaine. Big John rubbed his back until he was finished.

Jon Jon looked into the big man's face.

'I'm so sorry, mate.'

And he was too. To see what he had just seen and to know that the perpetrator was your own flesh and blood had to be the worst thing that could happen to anyone.

Big John opened the large American fridge and took out a bottle of Bourbon and a bowl of ice.

'I still can't get me head round it. I go over it time and time again and still I can't make any sense of it. And you know the worst of it all, don't you? Paulie Martin is financing the lot of it.'

He shook his head at the skulduggery of his one-time friend.

'Now, you in or out, son?'

Jon Jon took the bottle of Bourbon and poured them both a large drink.

'I'm in.'

Big John smiled, his first unfeigned smile of the night.

'Good lad. I knew you wouldn't bottle out. Cheers, Jon Jon. You're doing the right thing.'

Chapter Twenty-Five

Joanie smoked a cigarette and tried to calm herself down. One part of her just wanted to walk away from the flat and leave this whole sorry situation behind her. But the other half knew she had no choice. She had to sit this one out, and more importantly *sort* it out as best she could.

But even though she hated Little Tommy with a vengeance she had been hard pressed to hurt him, and in her heart of hearts wasn't sure she now wanted to know exactly what had happened to her daughter.

She had enough trouble sleeping as it was – how would she feel if she knew the full score? And as for poor Jeanette . . . Well, she would not easily forgive her mother for this night's work, especially when she found out what had really been going on. She would feel she had been pushed out, would feel she was not considered good enough to be included, which was not true but what the girl would choose to believe.

Joanie finally went into the bedroom and saw that Bethany had turned on the small portable TV and was watching *Recess* on the kids' channel.

'All right, sweetie?'

The girl turned and stared at her with dead eyes.

'Can we talk now, Joanie?'

She nodded and sat down on the bed beside her. Bethany moulded herself into Joanie's body and she instinctively hugged the child to her.

Bethany stared at the screen for a few seconds while they got comfortable then she said sadly, 'Kira was a good girl. Not like me.'

Joanie felt her heart racing once more in her chest.

'Tell me, darling. Tell Auntie Joanie how it was.'

'You see, me and Kira, we used to go round Lorna's. But Kira didn't like it there, said it was too dirty and that you would kill her if you found out about it. Then Little Tommy came on the scene and she started to spend all her time with him. I was jealous. She was always talking about him. But I knew about the Thompsons, and he knew I did.'

Joanie swallowed deeply before saying, 'What did you know, Bethany?'

She still stared at the screen, unwilling to look Joanie in the face.

'About his dad.'

'What about his dad?'

'He was always looking at her, but he was too scared of Tommy, see. I will give him that, Tommy wouldn't let his dad near Kira.'

'How do you know all this?' Joanie asked, dry-mouthed. The girl shrugged her plump shoulders.

'He used to come to one of the houses where Pippy took me.'

Joanie closed her eyes to blot out the vision those words conjured up.

'Are we talking about Tommy or his dad?'

'Not Tommy, it was his dad, Joseph. He kept away from me, though, and I always acted like I didn't know him.'

She looked at Joanie sidelong.

'But he never got near Kira, Tommy made sure of that. I know for a fact.'

So the father was the nonce. But what about Tommy? What exactly was he? Joanie led into it slowly.

'So he never touched you – Joseph Thompson, I mean?'

Bethany shook her head.

'He was too scared of me, like I said. Lorna knew him from before, see. She gets the kids for Pippy and his mate Kieron. It's Kieron who hosts the parties for men like Joseph. He loves it, and unlike Pippy he's really nice. But Tommy's dad, he liked his girls to be small – small and skinny. Blonde if possible. I was never his cup of tea. Now Kieron, he loved me . . .'

Joanie had heard enough but forced herself to carry on the interrogation.

'Where was this house you went to then?'

'The one I went to the most was in Ilford, like I said, just off Mortlake Road.' Bethany grinned then. 'I used to go to other people's houses too when I'd learned to do it properly. Pippy said I was a natural.'

It was said with a dreadful pride. The one thing she had been praised for in her life, and it had to come from a nonce. What a criminal waste of a child's innocence and trust.

Joanie felt so angry with Monika then she wondered if the friendship which had had more ups and downs than the Japanese Stock Market would survive this.

Bethany went on dreamily, 'Some of the houses were really lovely, like you see on telly. And they gave me drink and fags and laughed at me. They *liked* me, Joanie. They said so. And they gave me money. Me mum thought I got it shoplifting stuff and selling it on.'

Joanie looked down into the little girl's face. Her soft hair was drying now, springing up all over her head. It made her look so young. Her big brown eyes were sad, like the eyes of so many women Joanie had worked with over the years.

This child knew all there was to know already, and the worst of it was it would be years before the horror of that knowledge finally hit her. She wouldn't want it to, of course, and by then she would be into drugs and drink to blot out the pain of a life lived too young. All she would have left of herself was her anger, and it would be all-consuming, Joanie knew that from experience.

There was still one thing left to ask.

'What about Kira, what happened to her?'

Bethany sipped at the can of Coke beside the bed before she spoke. Joanie could see the child trying to pull herself together.

'I saw her on her way up the shops, like I said. We had a row – my fault.' She was quick to take the blame on herself. 'She ran off and I chased her. That's when Pippy Light stopped in the car and spoke to her.'

Joanie felt faint with fright.

'Go on, love.'

'He saw me, and called me over. He wanted her at a party. Said to tell Kira that he knew you, that he knew her mum like.'

She looked full at Joanie for the first time.

'You see, I couldn't *not* do it. Pippy would have hurt me, Joanie, I know he would, and even though I wanted to tell her to run, I was too scared.'

She started to cry again.

'You don't know what he's like, Joanie. One minute he's all over you, telling you how lovely you are, and then he turns. If you won't do what he tells you, he goes berserk. He hits you, spits at you. Pulls your hair out and you *have* to do what he says. It's easier that way.'

Pippy Light terrified adults. He must have laughed his head off at the naivety and easiness of these poor kids. But not her Kira. She had taught Kira well about her body and who owned it.

Bethany looked into Joanie's eyes, begging for understanding.

'You can't tell him no, Joanie. You just can't.'

She heard her doorbell then and sighed. It had to be Monika. The last person Joanie wanted to see.

'Is that me mum?'

Bethany's fear was all too plain. Monika would go mad to find her here, and the worst of it was she would go mad for all the wrong reasons.

'Stay here and keep quiet. I'll sort it out, OK?'

Joanie walked from the room with a heavy heart. She knew now beyond a doubt that her baby was dead. And she knew who was responsible.

It still didn't occur to her to call the police.

This was personal: who needed them ballsing it all up?

Pippy Light had the money for good briefs and a blinding defence based on witnesses he had bought and paid for. She couldn't let this come to court. What chance of justice was there then?

Jon Jon was rolling another joint as he listened to Big John fill him in. He knew the man needed to talk about it, needed to say it out loud to someone to get it off his chest.

Jon Jon understood that, he would have felt the same.

Of all the things that could have happened to Big John McClellan, this was the worst. He could have taken anything except the knowledge that his own son was a beast. In their world that was something you could *never* live down. It was a taint, a stain on the character of everyone related.

'When he was a kid, see, she gave him whatever he wanted. So did his brothers.'

Like many a father before him John was trying to explain his child's actions.

'He was only nine months old when I got me capture so he only ever saw me on prison visits. He was twenty-one when I finally came home. I never knew him, I realise that now. How could I, banged up all that time? In fairness to my old woman she did the best she could and the others have turned out blinding. It's a kink of nature, I reckon, don't you?'

Jon Jon nodded. He knew Big John had to believe that or he would never sleep another night in his bed in peace.

'He's twenty-four years old now and he likes having sex with little kids. What's all that about?'

He was genuinely bewildered.

Jon Jon didn't know what to say.

'They reckon it's a quirk in them, Nature playing tricks. At least you've found out in time to put a stop to it. Imagine if it had got out, John.'

Big John nodded; he was sweating at the thought of it.

'You know something else as well?' Jon Jon said.

Big John looked at him quizzically.

'They'll *all* have to go, won't they? Everyone who knew about Kieron will have to be deleted. It's fucking game over, ain't it, in more ways than one?'

Big John relaxed.

This boy knew exactly what was required of him; Big John didn't have to labour the point. And he trusted him, really trusted him. That fact amazed him more than anything else. What you saw was certainly what you got with Jon Jon Brewer. Big John would see him all right after the deed was done. This boy would be royalty in waiting, he would see to that himself. He would give Jon Jon a living that most men of their ilk only dreamed of; in fact, he was going to give him a hefty wedge of Paulie's empire.

After all, Paulie wouldn't be fucking needing it, not where he was going anyway.

He wouldn't give him *all* of it, of course, he wasn't *that* fucking grateful. But he was grateful enough to see to it that this kid never knew another poxy day in his life. He also wanted to keep him close. Keep his eye on him. Jon Jon Brewer was going to be the keeper of his biggest secret; Big John would need him close by.

Jon Jon was relaxed enough to cut the coke himself this time without asking first.

He snorted and said, 'Stop beating yourself up, John. Kieron was a one-off, mate, a fucking mutant. Just concentrate on minimising the damage, not just for yourself but for your other kids. I mean, the last thing you need is him stuck in prison on a section for being a nonce, right? So you have to make sure he's put out to grass soon as. That way everyone wins. He's gone, your old woman has a grave to visit, and you save the family name. It's simple.'

'You are one clever little bastard, boy.'

Jon Jon smiled.

'I have a score to settle as well, remember? I'll do this for me sister, the poor little cow. She wasn't all there either, you know. Not a mong or nothing like that, but she wasn't the sharpest knife in the drawer. But she was my heart. From the minute she was born and I held her, she was my heart.'

He sighed, the tears as usual never far away.

'I'll wipe the cunt who killed her off the face of the earth and enjoy every second of it. If I get banged up for twenty, thirty, forty years, it will be worth every second of the time.'

He passed the mirror with the lines piled on it evenly to Big John as he said quietly, 'So. What you going to do about those photos of him? You can guarantee they're on the computer's hard drive. They could even be winging their way around the Internet.'

He sniffed loudly before continuing, 'Those pictures were printed off his computer. Who knows who else had access to them? Who Kieron sent them to? Because that's what paedos do, you know.'

Big John, though full of cocaine and Bourbon, suddenly saw the real scale of his problem.

'The Internet's bigger than the world, mate. Filth like this lives on. It could be on someone's screen every day for the next fifty years.'

'Oh, dear God, Jon Jon. I never thought of that. We'll have to bring someone else in, I suppose. One of them computer kids. I'll have to sniff around, find someone I can get a handle on. God, this just gets worse.'

'First I'd like to see all the pictures Kieron has on his computer, and his mates' computers as well because I have a feeling I might see a member of my own family there and unlike you I won't be ashamed of that fact. Kira never went far, I'm convinced of it. I've always known in me heart it was someone close. She wouldn't have gone off with just anyone, she knew better than that. It had to be someone she knew.

'I thought it was Tommy or his dad but now, after seeing that lot and knowing what I do, I ain't so fucking sure. The fat little black girl shagging with your son is Monika the Mouth's daughter – you know, her from my estate? Works for Paulie. Me mum's best mate when they're talking, her biggest enemy when they ain't. But that's her Bethany all right, and she was my little sister's best mate. So what does that tell us, eh?'

Big John was staring into his glass; they were Waterford crystal, a hundred pounds each they had cost him. He had bought a dozen of them. The cut glass was catching the light from the spotlight above. The spectrum of colours was beautiful, warm-looking.

He threw the glass and its contents across the room full force, enjoying the sound as it smashed into hundreds of little pieces.

'I'll talk to Kieron, find out the score. You just have to finish the job, deal?'

Jon Jon nodded.

'Be an honour, mate. But I want to be there and hear it all for meself. I need to know about Paulie Martin as well as my sister. You understand that, don't you?'

Big John nodded his agreement.

'Better than you realise, son. I thought he was my mate and all. Thought he was sound. It just shows you, don't it?'

They smiled at one another, united in their grief.

Then Big John stood up and said seriously, 'Come on, we'd better get our arses in gear. I know where my boy will be this time of the night.'

Jon Jon got up quickly and waited while Big John took a couple of wraps from inside one of the kitchen cupboards.

'We'll find out what we need to know tonight, I promise you. I'll kick it out of him if necessary.'

Jon Jon didn't answer him.

He honestly didn't know what to say.

But one thing was for sure: Kieron's own father thought he was capable of killing Kira and that had sealed his death warrant.

Paulie was buzzing with energy, smiling and rubbing his hands together as he stood on the doorstep. Joanie felt the familiar pull of him as he stepped inside her flat.

'All right, girl?'

He kissed her on the mouth and she responded as she had always responded to him.

'Any chance of a quick flash and a bacon sandwich!'

It was an old Cockney term used by people who had been married for years. She laughed, but he could see her heart wasn't in it.

'You all right?'

She nodded.

'Just tired, and I'm expecting Monika round in a minute.'

'Baxter told me. That was a touch, eh, girl?'

She smiled then.

'Thanks, Paulie, I know it was you who set it up.'

He hugged her to him.

'Least I can do for me best girl, ain't it?'

It was wonderful for her to hear him talk like this. It was so rarely he let anyone see the real Paulie. The kind, good man she had loved for so long.

'Me and you go back years, Joanie. No one else has ever affected me like you.'

She was shy suddenly at his words. Normally he only spoke like that in the dark of night.

'Where's Jon Jon? I tried his mobile and I can't get him.'

She shook her head.

'Don't know. I ain't seen him and I'm surprised. I expected him to be waiting for me so he could read me the Riot Act.'

'Jeanette in?'

She shook her head.

'Only I thought I heard her telly.'

Paulie smiled as he spoke but his eyes were darting round the flat as if looking for something. For some reason Joanie decided not to tell him what she was doing, not yet. He would just lose it with Bethany and then it would all be shouting and recriminations. So she said gently, 'I was in there. I sometimes get into her bed and cuddle up. I feel closer to her that way.'

He smiled nastily.

'You're a fucking terrible liar, Joanie.'

He watched in fascination as her pupils dilated with shock at his words.

'You what!'

'Is Jon Jon in there?'

His voice brooked no lies.

'What's going on, Paulie?'

'*What's going on?* Are you having a fucking laugh, Joanie? That little bastard Jon Jon has only been round Jesmond's and slaughtered him, with fucking Loony Bernard as his bleeding sidekick! *Now* do you understand why I'm going to slap him until my arms ache when I get my hands on him? What the fuck is he up to?'

'I don't know, Paulie. I don't know what you're talking about.'

He pushed her away from him.

'Oh, don't give me that old fanny, Joanie, your kids don't shit without consulting you first. And now he's with Big John McClellan, so fuck knows what's going on because none of them are answering my fucking calls! What am I then, a Muppet all of a sudden?'

But he knew she was no wiser than he was about her son's whereabouts. It was written all over her face.

He walked into the girls' bedroom anyway and she followed him, pulling on his arm to make him turn and face her.

'What on earth is your problem? You come in here all smiles and camaraderie and then you turn on me like that! You can fuck off, Paulie Martin. I don't need all this, not tonight.'

'What exactly is going on tonight then?' he snarled.

Joanie was staring at him as if she had never seen him before, and this side of him she definitely hadn't. He looked wild-eyed, frantic with anger and impatience and something that looked like fear. But why? What had Paulie got to worry about even if Jon Jon had got himself into more trouble. He'd never turn on his boss, thought too much of him for that.

Paulie stormed into the little bedroom.

It was empty.

Then he ransacked the flat, hauling clothes out of wardrobes, ripping the curtains off the shower.

When he had finished he turned and faced her. Poking a finger into her chest, he bellowed, 'You tell that son of yours I want him. He'd better come to me as soon as he can because if I have to go on looking for him it will be much worse once I do get my hands on him. I had a meet with him at nine o'clock and he didn't show. He'd better have a fucking good reason.'

He left without saying goodbye, slamming the door behind him.

Joanie stood there in shock, staring at the front door. This was outrageous. Who the hell did he think he was? And more to the point, where was Jon Jon and what was he playing at anyway? If he wasn't with Paulie, who was he with?

She walked back into the bedroom with a heavy heart, and helped Bethany out from under the bed. The world had gone mad, there was no doubt about that.

Bethany clung to her and Joanie hugged the girl tightly.

'All right, love, he don't mean the half of it, OK? He's just upset.'

Joanie wasn't sure who she was trying to convince, Bethany or herself.

★ ★ ★

Kieron was with Pippy Light in a private member's club in Holborn. Two of his elder brothers had just come in and he was smiling as they walked over to him.

The club owner hated him and he hated Pippy. There was always trouble when they showed. Piss-taking, always too loud. When he saw the two McClellan brothers he breathed a sigh of relief. Kieron and Pippy always got their heads together when the brothers were around, acted like someone else. He automatically poured two vodka shots so they would be waiting when the boys finally reached the bar.

First there was an elaborate pecking order they had to go through. If they said hello to everyone on their way in then no one would hassle them when they finally sat down to have a drink.

He also knew that Pippy Light would be as welcome to the other McClellans as a condom in a monastery so he would shoot off as soon as he could. One thing about Pippy, he could take the hint.

Gerald, the oldest brother and a clone of his father, grinned matily.

'All right, Kieron?'

Kieron grinned back. He was higher than a 747 over the Atlantic and it showed.

'Yeah, you?'

He had the glassy-eyed look of a smack head except he was seriously buzzing. Gerald guessed it was a mixture of coke and Es. It usually was. He was annoyed by his brother's condition but didn't say anything. Pippy was studiously ignored, but he was used to it. The McClellan brothers were a force to be reckoned with and he understood that he had to take their knockbacks in his stride. He would bide his time. Pippy had an agenda, only unlike this lot he kept it to himself.

James McClellan was on his mobile, staring at Pippy as he talked. Then he was nodding his head. He turned off the phone and went over to Gerald who gave him his shot. He downed it and then said something to his brother, which seemed to make him frown as well.

The music was loud and pumping even though the place was only a quarter full. Pippy, who prided himself on having a shit detector on a par with an F14 fighter pilot's, felt maybe it was time for him to leave this company and go on the missing list. Kieron was oblivious as usual.

Pippy's worst fears were confirmed when he was included in the next round of drinks, something he had never experienced before in this company. He smiled, though, as he accepted the large Jack Daniel's and Coke. He knew how to play the same.

Kieron was swaying to the music. It was one of his favourite tracks: Tiga singing 'Hot in Here'. It was a provocative song and Kieron was mouthing the words to a young girl standing with a large black man nearby. She had blonde hair and small breasts and was obviously no more than sixteen if that.

He started singing loudly, 'It's getting hot in here . . . So take off all your clothes!' It was the ultimate insult to his woman, and his manhood.

Gerald saw the way the wind was blowing and waved the black guy down as if to say, Ignore him. That suited the man down to the ground. He didn't really want a straightener with this lot, but he also could not be seen to swallow the situation.

'Leave it out, Kieron. Anyway, drink up. We'll have one more and then the old man wants to see you both, OK?'

Kieron nodded but he wasn't happy about it, that much was evident.

'I wanted to go out, I've made arrangements.'

James laughed now, really laughed, at his little brother's words.

'Well, you'll have to unmake them then, won't you?' He waved the barman over as he said crossly, 'And stop winding people up. That's my old schoolmate Easton and he's a right decent bloke.'

He shook his head at Gerald. Kieron was normally as good as gold, he must be more out of it than usual.

'What's he want to see Pippy for?'

As out of it as he was, he knew his father wouldn't want to see Pippy Light unless it meant trouble.

James shrugged.

'You can ask him yourself in a minute. I said for him to call in or ring to let me know where to meet. Whatever suited him. So let's get another one in before he arrives, like the spectre at the feast. He'll muller you when he sees you, Kieron. You look like you've been on it, and knowing you, you have.'

He was giving him a brotherly warning. For all their father took a bit of coke or had a puff himself, he couldn't stand seeing his children do it and only Kieron and one other brother, Dennis, had ever been tempted. The other five were drinkers, pure and simple.

James included Easton and his girlfriend in the round and smiled at them, rolling his eyes at his little brother as the other man nodded his thanks. Face had been saved and the night was undisturbed as yet. But it had been a close call. The trouble with the McClellans was, you fought one, you fought them all. There weren't only the brothers and their father, they had more cousins than the Saudi Royal family. Easton wouldn't willingly take that lot on unless he had half of Railton Road with him celebrating Notting Hill Carnival, and even then he'd think twice about it. The McClellans were heavy duty.

He kept a close eye on the little brother though. If Kieron stronged it Easton would glass him, he had no choice. He nearly fainted with relief when he saw Jon Jon Brewer walk in with the father five minutes later.

Jon Jon came over to Easton and they shook hands. As young as Jon Jon was, Sippy loved him and that was good enough for Easton. Jon Jon went back to the McClellans' where both Gerald and James greeted him warmly as they had been instructed to do on the phone.

Big John observed it all.

Then he looked at Kieron and Pippy Light and felt the sickness close in once more. His Kieron had had it all handed to him on a plate. The very name McClellan gave him access to anyone and everything he wanted. Had allowed him to get away with something worse than murder.

Who ever would have dreamed that one of Big John McClellan's boys was a beast? It didn't bear thinking about, and neither did the consequences of his son's debauched lifestyle.

He had routed enough nonces in the nick, seen them beaten, burned, had joined in the fun . . . and all the time he'd had one growing up in his own family. He saw those pictures once more in his mind's eye and swallowed down the bile. He glanced at his watch. Another couple of drinks and he would be numb enough to start the ball rolling.

Jon Jon winked at him and he felt a terrible urge to cry. Was he going soft in his old age? He couldn't answer that question yet. But he trusted he would be able to before the night was out.

Pippy sat and watched it all, saw the way Jon Jon was treated. Saw the way Big John watched him as if *he* was Jon Jon's father and not some errant coon who had legged it at the first opportunity. And he knew with deadly certainty that finally it had all come on top.

He drained his drink quickly, ready to seize his opportunity to go on the trot. But he knew it wouldn't happen. He was going nowhere without the McClellans. They would all see to that.

Chapter Twenty-Six

Gerald and James were watching their father and brother, and could see that something big was going down. They were outside the club now and Jon Jon Brewer was shaking his head at them as if to warn them not to interfere.

They were both thinking the same thing.

When had an outsider ever known anything about family business that none of them knew?

Pippy was also watching the proceedings.

Then the McClellan boys saw their father grab their little brother by the throat, and instinctively went to intervene.

Big John stared at his two eldest sons. Usually his pride in his boys knew no bounds. If anyone had ever told him one of them was a beast . . .

His anger boiled over.

'Get in your car and fuck off, boys, just leave this cunt to me.'

Gerald placed one hand on his father's arm.

'Come on, Dad. Let him go home now and then we'll talk about whatever it is tomorrow, eh?'

Kieron looked at his father, saw he was coked up and said quietly, 'Come on, Dad. We don't want this being talked about all over the place, do we?'

It was a threat. Even Gerald picked up the nuance in his brother's voice and turned to stare at him.

'What have you done now, Kieron?'

It was an accusation. One he had made many times before.

Big John was grinning now.

'Go on, tell him. I *dare* you. But you ain't got the fucking guts, have you?'

Kieron didn't rise to the bait, and Big John knew that he never would. He really didn't have the nerve. He was a coward on top of everything else.

'What is all this about? What am I missing here?'

Gerald was staring from father to brother now. His powerful shoulders and arms were reminders to Kieron of just what he was dealing with here. It occurred to him then that this was one time his mother couldn't bail him out because she'd have no idea about this meeting. His father, he knew, did just what she wanted most of the time from guilt over the fact he fucked anything with a pulse at every opportunity.

James had once told him that. Dad treated their mum like that because he had been banged up for so long he had to live life to the full now. Even tried to say that she knew all about his philandering and didn't care.

But whatever the score was there, Kieron knew he was on his last life with his old man and he would have to talk his way out of this one very carefully.

Big John pointed at Gerald and said, 'Put Pippy in the car and follow us, OK? You'll know soon enough.'

It was a lightning decision but he'd decided there and then that they had to know. Once their brother vanished they'd remember tonight and wonder. Because they would want retribution for his death, it was better for all concerned if they were in on it from the off.

Also, he didn't want all the guilt heaped on him and Jon Jon. This was family business after all. He also wanted to make sure he didn't relent at the last moment. In front of his sons he always played the hard man. With his wife it was a different story. How he'd keep this from her he dare not think.

Kieron picked up on this, of course. He always had.

'Dad, does me mum know you're here?'

He stared insolently at his father as he said it.

'Get in the fucking car, you cunt!'

'Here, hold up, Dad. What the fuck has he done now? I'll sort it,' Gerald pleaded.

'No one could sort this out, son. You'll realise that before the night's out. Your so-called brother has crossed the line, and if I have my way he'll be fucking passing over it once and for all tonight.'

Gerald could not believe what he was hearing.

'Come on, Dad, you're out of your nut! Leave it till the morning. I'll take him home, Mum will be worried . . .'

'Shut the fuck up, and follow me to the breaker's yard in Romford. It's nice and private there. And whatever you do, don't let Pippy Light get away from you. I want him as well, right?'

He forced his youngest son roughly into the car. Jon Jon was already in the back seat.

Gerald walked over the road to his own car. He knew it was pointless to argue with his father when he was in this mood.

'What's going on, Ger?'

James was as worried as he was.

He shrugged.

'Fuck knows.' He looked at Pippy as he said, 'But *he* can enlighten us on the drive, if he knows what's good for him.'

Joanie and Bethany had talked until the child had fallen asleep. That was the funny thing with kids: no matter what happened to them they could still sleep. She tucked the girl in before she poured herself a large drink and sat on the sofa sipping it as she struggled to comprehend what Bethany had told her.

The two little girls had gone off with Pippy Light and some bloke called Kieron in a car. Kira had been persuaded to go with them. Bethany had been dropped off at a house in Ilford, and Joanie's baby had never been seen again.

You didn't need to be Sherlock Holmes to work out what had happened to her. Deep inside she had always known that her daughter had been murdered. It was a mother's instinct, she supposed. Now she was more worried about what Jon Jon would do when he found out. It stopped her thinking about Kira, and what had happened to her before she had died.

Joanie downed the drink in one gulp and felt the burn as it hit her stomach. She knelt on the floor and opened up her treasure cupboard. She took out all her things and looked at them once more, knowing that never again would she feel the sheer joy they had once brought her. Never again would she fantasise about having a lovely home one day, with a garden and a swing for Kira and nice plates to eat off and dinner parties full of the rich and famous.

She could never think about any of it now without remembering her youngest daughter. Never again would she know a happy day.

Little Tommy's face rose before her eyes and she pushed the image away. The guilt she felt for what he'd suffered was overwhelming and she didn't have the time or the energy to face it at the moment.

Then, going to the kitchen, she got a black bin bag and started to fill it with all her treasures, as Jon Jon used to call them.

Kira had loved looking at them with her, it had been a treat for them both. Joanie had enjoyed seeing her daughter revel in all the lovely things. Together they'd planned their dinner parties: food, course by course, and wine, everything down to the colour of the napkins and the setting of the cutlery.

Now it was all gone, every moment of innocent happiness.

Her baby was gone too and she was never coming back.

Joanie was crying as she took the bag and walked out to the rubbish shute. As she stood on the landing and looked out over the estate she wondered at a life where nothing good ever happened for long. In the rare interludes when things seemed to be going well for her, she'd always been waiting for it all to fall out of bed. Now her life had fallen apart at the seams. It was only good for tabloid fodder and neighbourhood gossip.

She looked in at the windows of the flats around her. Saw the lights, the different wallpapers, the flickering of television screens; listened to the pumping music and the screams and laughter of the teenagers hanging about the street below, and envied everyone their uncomplicated lives.

Her mother used to say that for most people life was shit; it was what everyone else in their life made it. You never had a choice really, it was other people who fucked you up. Until tonight Joanie had not understood what she had been talking about. Every person who was hurt was only hurting because they loved someone. Look at little Bethany. She loved Monika so much and it was a wasted love. The worst of it all was that, as young as she was, Bethany already knew that fact.

Joanie clasped the bin bag to her and, sinking to her knees, cried like a baby, the pain inside her chest so acute she really did think she might die from it.

'Please, Dad, listen to me for a minute, will you?'

Kieron was starting to panic now. No matter what he said to his father he was ignored or ridiculed.

Big John mimicked his voice nastily.

'*Dad, listen to me, will you?* Will I bollocks!'

Jon Jon looked at Kieron with no feeling for his distress.

'Why don't you shut up, you fucking perverted cunt?'

Kieron, some of his usual animosity to the fore now, said, 'Are you really going to let him talk to me like that, Dad? A fucking coon and you'd let him talk to *me* like that? Where's the Big John McClellan I know and loathe?'

Big John laughed.

'Oh, upset you, has he? You fucking noncing piece of shit!'

Jon Jon leaned over between the seats in front of him.

'Did you have any dealings with my sister Kira? Only I can see from the photographs your dad showed me that you know her little mate Bethany intimately.'

Big John laughed.

'That's a good one, Jon Jon, you have a way with words. Intimately. How old was she then, Kieron? Nine, ten?'

'Wouldn't you like to know?'

He started to laugh and Big John, even though he was driving, leaned backwards and attempted to punch his son in the face.

'You stroppy little bastard! I'll kill you for what you've done to me . . .'

He stopped the car in the middle of the road and jumped out. Opening the passenger door, he started to punch his son in the head and body. He was losing it. After all he had had to contend with, he was finally losing it.

It took Jon Jon all his strength and powers of persuasion to get John back into the driving seat.

People were staring at them, wondering what was going on but not willing to get involved. Looking at this big angry man, who could blame them?

'Calm down, for fuck's sake, before we all get nicked! Pull the car into the kerb, people are looking.'

Kieron was slumped in his seat, quiet at last. He was also bleeding profusely.

Jon Jon saw that Gerald and James had pulled up behind them and were watching the scene in silence. As he couldn't see Pippy he had to assume they had talked to him already.

He walked over to their car. Cupping his eyes, he looked into the back window. Pippy was lying on the seat. He was bloody and battered but still alive, and that was all Jon Jon was interested in.

Gerald opened the driver's window.

'Is it true, Jon Jon?'

He nodded.

'Jesus Christ, it can't be . . . Kieron's a fucker but he wouldn't do something like that . . .'

Jon Jon took the folder from his jacket pocket and passed it through the window. He pointed at Pippy Light.

'Don't you dare kill him. I need to talk to him about my little sister, OK?'

They nodded.

'Once I find out what I need to know he's all yours.'

As he walked back to Big John's car a police vehicle drove past them at speed, all the lights flashing and siren blaring out, looking out for the incident that had been reported.

But Jon Jon, like the others, ignored it.

As usual, they were too late.

Paulie was in his office at Angel Girls. He liked being there lately, it was the only place he could relax. Though he wasn't relaxing tonight. He was smoking a cigarette, something he only did occasionally, and in between puffs he was shredding documents. He had already destroyed all the discs he had and the computers where things might have been stored. Not that anyone else had ever been near his computers but fear and paranoia had taken over. He had felt an instant connection between Jon Jon and McClellan, knew now that the big man had somehow sussed something out. It was just too pat the way he'd showed up, trailing a moneyspinning deal, and asking if Paulie had a good man he could put on to it. But it was only when Jon Jon had blanked him by missing the meet that he had finally put two and two together.

Why had he ever let himself get involved with Jesmond and Pippy? Because it had never occurred to him that an innocent like Kira might get involved in what he had financed. Never in a million years would he have believed things could go that far. Foreign kids, they'd said. Born and brought up to it. Knew no better.

Lots of people asked him to bankroll schemes and he had financed them, for a price. He had made fortunes that way. And that was all he had done with Pippy, financed his operation. He had worked on the premise that what you don't know can't hurt you. How wrong he had been.

This was Pippy Light after all, mad as they came and into schoolies. He had known in his heart that he should never have had any dealings with Pippy or Jesmond, they were the scum of the criminal fraternity. But Jesmond had explained the economics of it all and it had seemed too good an opportunity to pass up.

It was the only reason he had given Sylvia what she had wanted. He knew he was not in a position to have his finances scrutinised too closely. So did his solicitor. Paulie had had a bad feeling about it from the off, but the potential for all that money had allayed any scruples or fears of capture he might have had.

And the worst of it all was, he was more frightened of being captured by his own peers than by Old Bill. Lily Law would have more chance of policing the Gaza Strip than the Internet, and it was this that was worrying Paulie so much. You could find almost anything there if you were out to prove something. Once his name was linked to known paedophiles he was fucked. Now Jesmond was dead, but who knew what he'd said?

Paulie had gone to Pippy's tonight and got Earl to break in for him. What he had seen on the computers there had terrified him. He had smashed up all the machinery and then torched the place, after ransacking it first of course.

But like Big John his fear was that other computers around the world now held photographic evidence of children he had helped to procure. And somewhere his name just might be there along with it, on an e-mail to Rumania or the Czech Republic. Pippy was just cunt enough to say who'd funded them.

Paulie felt hot just thinking about it.

When he'd realised Kieron was also involved it had put the fear of Christ up him, but Pippy had sworn Big John had absolutely no idea about his son and he'd believed it, knowing John as he did.

But he had not known anything about Kira. Had not asked Pippy and Jesmond for updates on their clientele or their workers for that matter. He'd had no idea they were mad enough to touch local kids, had genuinely believed her disappearance was down to some random nutter – not the international paedophile ring he'd financed in expectation of a hefty return.

It was his own overwhelming greed that had led to his downfall, Paulie knew. To that and the death of the innocent child he'd fathered. His own daughter . . . his and Joanie's. But he couldn't think about that. He had to shut it out of his head and concentrate on saving his skin.

'Kira.' He found himself talking out loud, remembering her little face. The child he had denied. 'I can't think about you. I can't bear to think . . . Oh, God, Kira, what have I done? Sweetheart, I'm sorry. I'm so sorry . . .'

Inside the breaker's yard in Romford was a large unit used for storing car parts. The two Dobermanns, Pixie and Dixie, were used to sleeping in there between their stints patrolling the yard. Tonight their owner, an old man called Arnold Jigson, had been dragged from his kip inside an abandoned Dormobile to take them home.

He had not asked any questions, merely pocketed the fifty quid without a backward glance. He was used to the skulduggery of his boss Big John and had no desire to get involved with anything that did not have a direct bearing on him or his family. If the filth asked, he had been there all night, alone. Arnold knew the score.

Gerald poured them all a drink in the unit's office space. Jon Jon rebooted the lap top and slipped in the disk he had been given by Big John.

As the screen flickered into life he watched the reactions of Pippy and Kieron. Pippy had the grace to look ashamed but Kieron's arrogance remained, as if he truly believed he had done nothing wrong.

He was prominent in all the photos, far more than the ones his father had printed off, and Jon Jon quickly realised that this must be his own personal disk, one he kept for his own private enjoyment. So where did they keep the others? The ones they sold on to like-minded perverts?

Gerald and James looked ill. They were both white and sweaty.

James dragged his eyes away from the screen and stared at his little brother. But he was lost for words, couldn't talk or even react properly so great was his shock. His father knew just what he was feeling.

'Nice thing I bred here, eh, boys? What a fucking blinding relative. Proud of him, are you? Still want him to go home to his mummy?'

Big John dragged his youngest over by the hair and shoved his face towards the computer screen.

'Go on, have a look. Be a last memory to take with you, won't it?'

He was sobbing and shaking, but Kieron was quiet and passive, allowing it all to happen. He knew he was finished. There was nothing he could say to get himself out of this.

He pulled himself away from his father and straightened up, tidying his clothes, tucking his shirt in, and smoothing down his hair. Ever the dandy.

'Where's me sister?' Jon Jon asked.

Kieron grinned.

'What you asking me for?'

'Oh, for fuck's sake, tell them what they want to know, will you? Let's get this over with.' Pippy's voice was high-pitched with tension. He just wanted it all to end as quickly and easily as possible.

Jon Jon turned to him.

'Where is she, Pippy?'

He shrugged.

'It was him.' He flicked his head towards Kieron. 'It's happened before.'

A coughing fit overtook him then. One eye was swollen and bloody and his lip was split from the beating the brothers had given him.

Kieron laughed contemptuously then looked at James as he said, 'You better get those knuckles looked at. They're all scraped and bleeding. Must have hit his teeth. Bet that hurt.'

He grinned as he continued, 'And he's HIV, did you know that?'

That was the catalyst.

Picking up a crowbar they used to lever open the crates of contraband that regularly hit the yard, James smashed it across his brother's skull. The sound was sickening. Kieron slid to the floor.

'Pick him up and sling him out in the yard. This carpet's nearly new.'

Big John sounded like an affronted housewife. Jon Jon couldn't help it, he burst out laughing. His laughter was infectious and Gerald joined in.

'Don't know what you lot are laughing at. I might have AIDS!' James said, affronted.

'Shut up, you tart!'

Kieron levered himself up on to his elbow and gasped, 'Look at you, all standing there looking so righteous. I used scum, like you lot do. They loved it once they knew what we wanted. Your little sister would still be around if she hadn't been so fucking stubborn! "Oh, no . . . Please . . . I want me mum." '

Everyone looked at him appalled as he playacted the scene. None of them could believe just what they were hearing, a dying child's last words as this man brutalised her.

He rambled on, knowing he'd caught their attention. He knew he would die tonight but he had something to tell them first. He believed that everything he had done was entirely justified.

'They were all accidents waiting to happen. That Bethany, she couldn't get enough of it, the drink and the drugs, being the centre of attention . . . Kids like being with us, we *love* them. *Really* love them.'

'Jesus fucking Christ!'

This was from Gerald, his absolute shock and disbelief evident in his expression and his voice.

'What the fuck is going down here, Dad?'

He knew that his brother really believed what he was saying, that was the hardest thing of all.

'Get him out! Get him out of my fucking sight.'

Kieron groaned as they went to lift him up. He rolled to one side and looked up at his father.

'Thanks to the Internet we ain't alone any more. There are millions of us worldwide, and one day we'll be able to be open about what we do. You ignorant bastards have all thought about it, you just ain't had the guts to *do* anything.'

'If they legalised noncing in the morning it would be too late for you, cunt,' growled Big John. 'Now shove him in the boot of one of the cars and we'll dump him in the crusher. He won't be the first to go out like that in this yard and I daresay he won't be the last.'

He turned to Pippy Light.

'You better open your trap, son, then we'll make it easy for you. But him . . .' He pointed to his son. 'He is going in conscious and fully aware of what is happening.'

Pippy knew when he was beaten. He nodded.

'Can I ask one thing before I go?'

'You can ask. Whether you get it or not is another thing entirely.'

'Don't let me mum know about any of this. Don't let anything be found, please? It would kill her.'

Jon Jon could not get over the irony of Pippy's words.

'She'd be a bit like my mum then, wouldn't she? Broken, devastated, destroyed? You've got some fucking nerve, largeing it up here and asking us to protect your family! What about *my* family? What about the families of the other kids, eh?'

Pippy swallowed.

'I'll tell you whatever you want to know.'

'Fucking right you will.'

James and Gerald dragged their brother from the office, slapping and kicking him as he tried to escape their clutches.

'Come on then, Jon Jon, let's get this show on the road, shall we?'

He nodded.

The screams and pleas of Big John's youngest son, now

retribution was on hand, affected them not one iota. But they served to make Pippy more eloquent than he otherwise might have been. Jon Jon killed him in the end. One way or another, Big John had meant to make a murderer out of him tonight and, when he finally pulled the trigger, Jon Jon found he felt nothing but relief.

Paulie finished what he was doing and lit himself another cigarette. He had sent Earl home. Now he waited patiently for his Nemesis to arrive. It was nearly dawn when Jon Jon finally came into the office above Angel Girls.

'I knew I'd find you here,' he said.

It was Paulie's newest toy, the one he'd been proudest of, and he had always valued things above people. He had aged overnight, though, looked almost ancient, and Jon Jon felt a stirring of pity for him. But he forced it deep down inside himself.

Paulie gave him a twisted smile.

'I don't suppose there's any point in saying sorry? Kira getting involved . . . that was never meant to happen.'

'Too late for that, Paulie. What does Earl know?'

'Nothing. I was going to leave that up to you. He'll swallow it. You're the business as far as he's concerned.'

Jon Jon was relieved. He'd have hated to have to take this fight to Earl as well.

'You know everything now, I take it?' Paulie continued.

He nodded again, unable to say all he wanted to say to this man. Words weren't enough to express the depth of the betrayal he felt.

'I never knew. It was all about money, see,' Paulie faltered.

'Always is, ain't it? Where you're concerned.'

Jon Jon could not keep the bitterness from creeping into his voice.

'How's Big John?'

'In bits when I left him. He wanted to come here but I said I'd sort it.'

Paulie laughed.

'I always knew I could rely on you.'

He opened the desk drawer and took out a small hand gun. He

saw Jon Jon stiffen at the sight of it and said quickly, 'It's all right, mate, this is for me. I have only one stipulation: keep my name out of any shit that comes up, will you?'

Jon Jon's face was grey with strain, his eyes shadowed.

'I can't guarantee it but I'll try, Paulie. Big John and his boys want it kept quiet, but then they would, wouldn't they?'

'What are you going to tell Joanie?'

Jon Jon shrugged.

'I really don't know and that's the truth.'

Paulie bowed his head.

'All the relevant details are in that blue folder there.'

He pointed to it then downed the last of his brandy at a gulp.

'OK. I'll sort it all out for you, Paulie.'

'Good lad. By the way, I've owned Baxter for years. His Chief Constable too. They're yours now if you need anything.'

Paulie's smile was ghastly.

'I never thought it would all end like this, son, but there you go. Life has a habit of kicking you in the teeth when you least expect it.'

Jon Jon didn't answer. He knew that far better than this wreck of a man sitting before him but forebore to point that fact out.

'I suppose there's no chance that Big John . . .'

'No chance at all. Either you do it or I do, Paulie. The choice is yours.'

Paulie sighed. It was what he'd expected. Why delay the inevitable?

'Goodbye then. Be lucky.'

Jon Jon turned away and went to the window. He stood watching the regular people below, going early to work, struggling to pay the bills and maybe have a holiday.

Normal people, living normal lives.

The gunshot was loud, but he wasn't too bothered about the noise. Paulie owned the whole building. And anyway, he had topped himself, hadn't he?

Assisted Murder might be a better description, but that was all academic now. Paulie Martin was dead, leaving Jon Jon to pick up the pieces. He felt absolutely nothing.

He wiped his fingerprints from the door handle then took the folder downstairs and sat in the deserted reception area, going through all the papers Paulie had left for him.

Half an hour later he was gone, hailing a cab and getting inside, wondering what the hell he was going to tell his mother.

Joanie sat up all night waiting for Jon Jon to come home. It was eight o'clock in the morning and Bethany was still asleep. Joanie had left a few messages on Monika's mobile but had not heard anything, nor did she expect to. Monika would emerge from her pit around lunch-time as usual, none the wiser about the whereabouts of her daughter, as was also usual.

Joanie sipped at her tea. The front door opened and she saw Jeanette coming in.

'All right, love?'

Jeanette smiled tightly.

'You're early. Want a cup of tea?' her mother said placatingly.

'Please, then I better get off to school.'

Joanie did not think she had a laugh left inside her, but hearing that statement from Jeanette proved her wrong.

'Are you having me on?'

The girl sighed and walked through to the kitchen.

'Nah, I feel like going to school today.'

Joanie was pleased. It was a start anyway.

'Bethany's asleep in your room by the way. Don't wake her, will you?'

''Course I won't. She's the last person I want nattering on at me.'

They both turned to the doorway as they heard Jon Jon come in.

'All right, girls?'

'You look fucking awful, Jon Jon. What have you been up to?'

Jeanette's voice was loud with curiosity as she took in her brother's ruined clothes and drawn face.

'Get ready for school,' he told her tersely.

Jeanette, for once, did what she was told, much to the amazement of her brother and mother.

'Sit down, Mum.'

Joanie was busy making him some tea and toast.

'Paulie was looking for you last night. Came in here like a bear with a sore arse—'

'Paulie died, Mum. He killed himself an hour ago.'

Joanie stopped what she was doing and turned to face her son.

'He what?'

'He shot himself. It's been on the cards for a while now. He had a lot of hag going on . . . his divorce, business worries.'

He was amazed at the way the lies tripped so easily off his tongue.

She looked at her son closely, saw the fine lines around his eyes and mouth.

'What's really happened, Jon Jon?'

He shrugged.

'What do you mean?'

From the moment she had first held this boy he had captured her heart. They all had, all her kids, and she knew them better than they knew themselves.

'Please tell me what's going on, Jon Jon. I'm no one's mug, I know there's more to this.'

As she said it Bethany came out of the bedroom and Jon Jon looked at her as if she was straight from his worst nightmare.

He could never again see her as a fresh-faced schoolgirl, not after what he had seen her doing – and willingly if those photos were anything to go by. Unlike his little sister who had fought all the way to the bitter end.

Joanie saw his reaction and realised that he knew.

'Go back to bed, sweetheart, and I'll bring you through a bit of breakfast.'

Bethany didn't need to be told twice. She could feel the atmosphere in the room. Jon Jon frightened her, he always had, but since Kira's going she was doubly afraid of him.

'Let Jeanette get to school and then I think we'd better talk, son.'

He nodded and carried on drinking his tea. His mother deserved the truth. Maybe, just maybe, they could put it all behind them then.

Chapter Twenty-Seven

Joanie had packed her son's suitcase and now was sipping her morning coffee liberally laced as usual with vodka.

It was as if the world had gone mad, and she was the only sane person in it. But she pushed this thought from her head as she had taught herself to do many years ago. All her life she had been pushing things from her mind, letting things go, always trying to make the best of everything. It was what you did when you had children and they still depended on you for everything, even if they didn't realise it.

Still, she liked to console herself with the fact that Paulie couldn't have known what he had been financing – even though the sensible part of her brain knew he must have had a pretty good idea.

So why couldn't she hate him?

She supposed one day she would be able to think about it all properly, and then she would put it all into perspective. Until then she would bury it away, with all the other miserable thoughts and events that had clogged her life since she could remember. She had wanted better for her kids than she had experienced, and in a small way she had achieved that. She had to comfort herself with that belief or she would never be able to live through another day. She started to make breakfast for Jeanette. A nice omelette. She was eating a lot lately and Joanie suspected that her daughter was in the club, but she wasn't going to force the issue. There had been enough fighting and arguing to last them all a lifetime; her daughter would tell her when she was ready. Plus it made Joanie feel useful and at this moment that was what she needed more than anything.

She threw some bacon under the grill and decided Jon Jon was going to have a cooked breakfast whether he liked it or not.

Once he had left the house she would get ready for Paulie's funeral. She still wasn't sure if she was going to go but she might feel the need. She had something else she needed to do as well but as yet could not pluck up the courage to see it through. Jon Jon had told her in no uncertain terms to keep well away.

He walked into the kitchen as if her thoughts had conjured him up, looking so handsome she wanted to cry. Even his dreads looked smart on him. It was his fine-boned good looks, he could carry off anything.

'Oh, Mum!'

But she could tell that the smell of bacon was working its usual magic and he would eat whatever she prepared.

'Are Rastas supposed to eat bacon?'

Jon Jon laughed gently.

'Who gives a fuck, Mum? Get it on the plate, girl.'

She loved it when they acted like everything was still normal. She could almost imagine Kira coming in and demanding the same as her big brother. See Jon Jon feeding her little bits of his breakfast to her. He had been such a good brother.

'You all ready?'

He nodded.

'Baxter's picking me up in about ten minutes.'

'You're a good boy, Jon Jon.'

He smiled and grabbed her hand.

'I had a good teacher, didn't I?'

He saw the tears come into her eyes and, standing up, hugged her. Even the smallest kindness set her off crying these days.

'Look, Mum, whatever happened it's not our fault, OK? We did the best we could and that is all anyone can do.'

'Tell me Paulie didn't know. Please, Jon Jon, promise you've told me the truth.'

'He didn't, Mum, honest to God. So stop beating yourself up about it.'

She knew when to let things rest and nodded sadly. Jon Jon couldn't keep going over things, it upset him too much.

There was a loud banging on the door and he jumped up to

answer it. Baxter's loud voice could be heard and Joanie automatically made him a cup of tea.

'That looks handsome, Joanie,' he said, with a nod at Jon Jon's unfinished breakfast.

She grinned.

'If you've got time, I can make the same for you?'

He sat down opposite Jon Jon.

'Plenty of time, mate.'

So as usual she cooked for them all. Baxter was never off the doorstep lately and Joanie was surprised to find she actually liked him.

Wonders would never cease.

Big John sat with his wife, eating a similar breakfast to Jon Jon and Baxter. Kathy was overweight but still had the pretty face that had attracted him all those years ago. She had been a good wife, had waited for him while he was inside with never a breath of scandal about her. But now she wore the haunted look of a woman bereft of her favourite child and he knew he could not make it better.

As she placed another cup of tea beside him he grabbed her ample body and hugged her.

'All right, babe?'

She tried to smile at him.

'I'll survive, John. I ain't got much choice, have I?'

Somewhere inside her she knew that there was more to her son's disappearance than met the eye. Big John and her other boys were all going through the motions of caring about what had happened to Kieron but she knew them better than they knew themselves. Kathy McClellan had learned years before never to interfere in their business and this was business, whatever they might try and spin her.

They had ransacked Kieron's room, supposedly looking for clues to his whereabouts, but she had known that they were looking for something else and whatever it was she assumed they had found it. Kieron had been her last-born, her baby. Now he was gone and no one but her seemed to care about that fact.

But she wouldn't push it. She had a strong feeling that if she was ever told the truth it would be far worse for her than not knowing.

Baxter was like a kid as they landed at Otopeni Airport in Bucharest. He was staring around him in fascination, unable to contain his excitement at being somewhere he had only ever seen on the news.

'Well, Jon Jon, we've arrived anyway. Let's hope Little Tommy was telling you the truth.'

His voice was sceptical, but Jon Jon knew the man had been honest with him. It was the least he could do in the end.

Fear had been a terrible weapon over the years. Tommy's father had terrified him, as he had terrified his mother. But he had served up his father in the end – that was the main thing, the thing he had to remember.

Tommy was sensible enough to have known that he would be tarred with the same brush, and his instinct for self-preservation had been strong. Jon Jon understood that, better than anyone.

'Get a grip, will you,' he told Baxter. 'We've got a long few days.'

But the DI was like a dog with six lamp-posts. This was all so new to him he was overwhelmed with it all. Jon Jon practically had to drag him out of the terminal and towards the waiting policeman, Michael Crasna.

Baxter shook hands with the slightly built man and then introduced Jon Jon. After they had all lit cigarettes and chatted briefly about their flight Michael led them to a waiting Mercedes. Inside was a large man called Peter who was to drive them to their destination.

'Beautiful countryside,' Baxter commented jovially.

Michael nodded, accepting the compliment.

'We are still recovering from the past. But we Rumanians, we endure.'

He shrugged and Jon Jon respected him for his quiet understatement.

'Where are we going now?'

'We are going out to a place called Rahova. It is not very nice there. I wish I could show you the mountains or maybe the parts of Bucharest that still have their historic buildings. But time is short. Maybe some other time.'

Jon Jon nodded politely but they all knew they would never come back here. He closed his eyes to stop any further conversation and tried to relax. He had noticed Peter watching him in the mirror on the dashboard and saw the sympathy in his dark eyes.

'I have arranged for you to stay in a place called Ferentari tonight. Not much better than Rahova but it will be best for you, under the circumstances.'

Jon Jon nodded once more, keeping his eyes closed.

Baxter was quiet now they were actually on their way. He realised he really had burned his boats this time and still he didn't care. He was doing the right thing accompanying Jon Jon, he knew that without a shadow of a doubt.

Joanie got out of the cab and, after asking the driver to wait, walked into East London Crematorium. She was amazed to see there was hardly anyone present.

Walking into the chapel, she saw Sylvia standing alone and a few men sitting around looking uncomfortable.

Joanie walked up to the coffin and placed her small tribute on the carpet beneath. The cheap pine coffin lay on two trestles and looked startlingly bare. Only a small cross of white chrysanthemums adorned it.

Sylvia came over to her. Joanie didn't know what she had been expecting but the sickly smile on Sylvia's face wasn't part of it.

'You can put them on the lid, if you like?'

Joanie shook her head.

'No, thanks. I only came to pay my respects.'

'Oh, aren't you staying?'

Paulie's widow was mocking her and Joanie felt the stirrings of anger.

'Not today, love. I can see you're inundated with friends, you don't need me.'

The barb hit home and Joanie stalked from the chapel. She felt better somehow, but was still sorry Paulie was going out like he was.

But, as he had always told her, you get what you pay for. And Paulie's widow had obviously decided not to waste a penny more on his sending off than she needed to.

★ ★ ★

'This is Rahova, gentlemen.'

Jon Jon opened his eyes then. He stared out of the window at the cement blocks of flats and the dirty streets.

'Low-income housing. I am sure you have the same in England?'

Michael was apologising for his country and Jon Jon felt embarrassed on his behalf.

'We do. Are we nearly there?'

Michael nodded.

'Stop the car here,' he instructed the driver.

They stepped out on a narrow side street.

'If you look around you, gentlemen, you will notice all these buildings have either blue or pink curtains.'

Baxter and Jon Jon looked around and it was true. Most of the windows did have the same style of curtains. Mainly blue, he noticed.

'These are child brothels. Depending on the colour of the curtains is whether the children are boys or girls. Very light colours mean very young boys or girls.'

Jon Jon and Baxter were staring around incredulously, the horror of what they had been told slowly sinking in.

'You're having a fucking laugh surely?'

DI Baxter, who thought he could not be shocked any more after all he had seen over the years, was absolutely in bits.

'I wish I were joking, my friend. These buildings are all owned by the Russians, and we have very little jurisdiction over them. If we close one down we run the risk of getting into trouble with our superiors who make plenty of money from turning a blind eye, I think you say. But once you do your job, we will protect you, OK? We have informed the owners what you intend and they're agreeable to it. In return we will give them a few months' grace.'

As they stood there a woman walked along with a little boy. He was crying, she was chastising him loudly. Pulling him along by his jumper, she slapped him across the face before they disappeared into the doorway of one of the buildings.

Michael sighed sadly.

'If we closed them all down this minute they would be open again within hours in different locations. But enough of our problems.'

He pointed to a drab building on the opposite side of the road.

'The flat you want is in there.'

'What number?'

'You'll see a sign outside saying *Kindergarten*. It's meant as a joke but also shows the contempt they hold us in. Most of their customers are either German or English. The man you want is in there. He is the one who takes the orders over the Internet and sees they are carried out to the specification of the customer. But you are lucky in that the Rumanian he works for wants him gone as much as you do. He is interfering with the monetary transactions.'

He sighed.

'Honour among thieves, eh?'

The shame of defeat was in his voice and Jon Jon knew that this man had run a grave risk even giving them this address in the first place. He had obviously put himself out for them and even though he would get some money, Jon Jon had a feeling it was done for more personal reasons than that.

He also knew Michael would take their money, though. And why not? He had done them a true favour.

Michael for his part was only too glad to help. As they were English this would be swept under the carpet. They needed tourism desperately here, but unfortunately this child abuse was part of the tourist trade.

Baxter ground out his cigarette.

'Come on then, let's get this show on the road.'

The heavily overweight patient was eating a banana, and in between bites chewing on a bar of Bourneville plain chocolate. The combination of the two flavours was his favourite at the moment.

He looked out of the window of his private room and over the gardens. It was lovely here in Essex. He liked the way everyone was cheerful and had a joke with you. His cup of tea was due soon and he knew the girl would let him have as many biscuits as he liked. He was living from meal to meal once more. With the absence of anyone or anything else in his life, he was reverting to his old ways.

A shadow fell across him then and he turned in the chair, expecting to see the orderly who brought in the tea. His face was wiped of all colour as he saw the woman he loved and feared standing before him.

'Hello,' she said.

He didn't answer her. He felt that his throat had closed up and his heart was going to explode.

Joanie could see his terror. He thought she was here to finish the job she had started and she felt real sorrow for him.

'Don't worry. I know you've seen Jon Jon, he told me what you had done for him, steering him towards Rumania, and we're grateful. Really grateful.'

She tried not to stare at the scars on his face. She knew he was still having treatment to eradicate the burns and also knew that skin grafts were extremely painful. The skin on his right cheek looked red and puckered, more so than on the other side of his face. His hair had grown back somewhat and he was more recognisable as the man he'd been before. It was only his eyes that had changed.

They were haunted-looking, full of fear. She understood why he felt like that and tried again to allay those fears.

'I've come to say sorry.'

He nodded then, his moon face visibly relaxing.

'Jon Jon has told you everything then?'

'Yes.'

'And you don't hold it against me?'

She sat on the bed and smiled.

'I tried to, Tommy, but I can't. How could I? I know how frightened you were of your father. I'm just sorry we didn't know more at the time. Why didn't you tell us?'

'I couldn't, Joanie. Surely you can understand that?'

She could see the sheer humiliation in his face, almost feel his embarrassment at what had happened to him at the hands of his father. Understood his need to keep it private, knew that like he had told Jon Jon, mud stuck, especially where they lived. If he had exposed his father it would only have come back on him. Joseph would have seen to that.

'When he had started the lorry driving, see, it had given me and me mum a break. But it was then that he had made all his contacts. But I did the best I could, Joanie.'

She nodded once more.

Poor Little Tommy was innocent of anything except his lifelong terror of Joseph Thompson, the man who had first raped him as a child of seven and carried on doing so until, as a cruelly obese and withdrawn teenager, he was at least spared that.

But still the cruelty continued. Tommy and his mother were beaten for the least little thing they did to annoy Joseph. With her spirit crushed and her body weakened, his wife took refuge in prescription drugs, trying to blot out the evidence of her own eyes. She knew what he'd done to their son and the knowledge was unbearable. There was worse to come.

Tommy failed to develop like normal teenagers. It seemed in some respects he'd always be a child and retained a natural affinity with them. Joseph traded on it mercilessly, using his son's continued interest in toys and children's games to lure in his unsuspecting prey. But when an outraged parent eventually called in the police and Social Services it was his son who got the blame. After all, he looked and behaved like a freak – a hulking teenager playing with dolls and speaking in a childish treble. And when they interviewed his mother, glassy-eyed on Valium and gin, she lied as her husband told her to do. Yes, he was a bit like that, her poor boy. Didn't mean any harm, though. It wasn't as if he could actually *do* anything.

Not like the monster she'd married, the big manly *normal* member of the family, who'd threatened to beat her to a pulp unless she backed him up. She did as he said, had no choice.

And since then there'd been six changes of address, five changes of name. They hadn't bothered after leaving Bermondsey. Pippy and Kieron baled them out with cash, needing Joseph's foreign contacts, and Leigh Rowe knew better than to let the story get out.

To cap it all Little Tommy wasn't really called Tommy at all. His real name was Darren Weeks. That's what they called him in hospital now, the new one that Jon Jon was paying for. The nurses there looked after him well, no reason not to. Everyone liked Darren Weeks who always had a smile and a kind word.

'I assume Jon Jon's going to sort my dad out?' he said now.

Joanie nodded without actually answering him. Instead she said, 'It looks nice here, the gardens are beautiful.'

She saw relief replace the guarded expression. They would not need to labour their explanations, he was kind that way. Joanie had apologised and that was enough for him. He needed her so much, loved her so much, because she had been the only adult ever to give him the time of day. But she had given him more than that and they both knew it.

He had betrayed that trust, they both knew that as well, but it had been because he had never dreamed his father or any of his cronies would dare touch a Brewer.

How wrong he had been.

'I wish I'd told you everything from the off, Joanie.'

'So do I, but you didn't so let's forget about it, shall we? You came through for us in the end.'

He nodded and wiped his eyes.

The tea girl came in and was amazed to see big fat Darren, as she thought of him, with a visitor.

'Cup of tea?'

He nodded and she looked at Joanie. Recognising her from the newspapers, she said gently, 'Can I get you one?'

Joanie nodded.

'Thank you, that would be lovely.'

Joanie put her hand out to Darren then and after a brief hesitation he grabbed it and held it to his chest. As he cried she comforted him as best she could.

His burned face, distorted by tears . . . she felt the shame well up until she just wanted to run away, but she didn't. Instead she stayed and spent a companionable afternoon with him. Darren Weeks had served up his own father to them and for that much she would always be grateful.

The door to the apartment building was open and they walked inside quickly.

Jon Jon was wearing a long coat. He was opening the buttons as they looked around the hallway. There were four doors leading off it and one stood open. Inside were two young girls who looked to be about nine and a boy a little older. They were all hollow-eyed and none of them smiled back at Jon Jon or Baxter but dropped their gaze to the floor. There were toys everywhere but none of the children was playing with them. They sat still on a dilapidated sofa and none of them said a word.

Jon Jon felt the bile rise in his throat.

If this was how to make a huge return on your investment he wanted none of it. Paulie would have known all about this. Jon Jon knew he would have carefully researched where his money was going, and that knowledge hurt him.

He had thought Paulie a bigger person than that, a better person.

One of the little girls rested her head on the arm of the chair and started to suck her thumb. She wanted to sleep, that much was evident. They all looked so tired.

Baxter was walking to one of the closed doors now and Jon Jon followed. As he opened it they saw a woman in her twenties undressing a young girl. The woman was wearing only a thong and a dirty white bra. She turned in surprise and then smiled at them both.

It was only on closer inspection of her scrawny body that Jon Jon realised she was still only an adolescent. The life she led had aged her face so much.

Baxter smiled encouragingly.

'Joseph?'

She sighed.

'Josef?'

He nodded matily, desperately embarrassed by the way she was dressed, the bruises on her skinny underdeveloped body. It all felt so wrong; this whole place stank of unwashed children and degradation. She pointed to another door leading off this room and they walked past her. She cuddled the little girl to her and Jon Jon realised they had to be related, the resemblance was so strong.

The next room was a bathroom. The man they knew as Joseph Thompson lay in a filthy iron bath with an adolescent girl. He turned as the door opened and the look of stunned surprise on his face was worth every hour of Jon Jon's long search for him.

'Take her out of here,' he ordered.

Baxter pulled the girl from the water. Wrapping a dirty towel around her, he led her from the room. Jon Jon kicked the door shut.

Opening his coat, he took out a piece of lead piping handed to him by Michael Crasna as they drove towards Rahova.

He tapped it across his palm as he said gently, 'Well, well, bet you never thought you'd see me again?'

Joseph tried to stand up but the lead piping smashing down across the legs soon disabused him of that notion. He was sweating with fear, knew he was never going to leave this room alive. All he could do was cower in the warm water and wait for the inevitable.

'How did you find me?'

Jon Jon spat at him then answered, 'Your son grassed you. We know everything now. About you, Jesmond, Pippy, and all the other pieces of shit you called your friends.'

'What are you going to do to me?'

Jon Jon looked into this man's eyes and knew he had wanted Kira from the first time he laid eyes on her. Knew he had planned to get her, one way or another. He was also the British contact for this hellhole, the man Jesmond and Pippy had been given as a go-between because he had been coming over for years. Joseph had made a fortune from his knowledge of this country and had fled over here, secure in the knowledge that no one would ever find him.

Now he knew different.

'You must have thought all your Christmases and birthdays had come at once when Kieron brought her to that house in Deptford. Your dream girl had arrived, and you and him laughed about it. Well, his father's seen him off so back to your question – what am I going to do to you?'

Jon Jon pretended to think about it for a few moments. Then, walking up to the trembling naked man, he swung at his knees with the pipe once more, this time splitting the bone and destroying the whole kneecap.

Joseph was screaming in agony as Jon Jon whispered, 'I'm sure I'll think of something even more fitting, aren't you?'

Joanie got into the flat and as usual the first thing she did was put the kettle on. As it boiled she lit herself a cigarette and stared out of the kitchen window. Monika would be here any minute with little Bethany. She more or less lived here now. It had been the catalyst for Jon Jon's leaving home to stay at Sippy's for a while.

But it had been time for him to go. He was moving into his new place at the end of the week and, in fairness, he understood his mother's need to take care of the girl no one seemed to want but her.

She knew why he couldn't look at Bethany. After hearing what he had seen on those photographs it had been hard for her to look at the child herself. But unlike him, she saw Bethany as a victim. Knowing she had delivered Kira to them was the real bug-bear, and Joanie had to struggle with herself every day to stop that being an issue.

Kira had fought to leave that house in Deptford, and even after they'd given her drink and tranquillisers, had still fought them. Pippy had told Jon Jon everything before he died.

Joanie was proud of the fact that her child had stood her corner even though she must have been terrified. But that was Kira all over, stubborn. With her being who she was, there was no way they would have let her out of that place alive and she must have known that. Joanie closed her eyes a moment and drew deeper on her cigarette.

Kira's body had been located where Pippy had said it would be, and that was a relief. At least Joanie could bury her child now.

Poor Kira had been in the wrong place at the wrong time. If she had not been with Bethany that afternoon it wouldn't have happened.

But Joanie would not blame Bethany. That child was a victim, just as her daughter had been. Bethany had been too frightened to say anything about the abuse she'd suffered. Now she had to live with what had happened to her, and with what she had inadvertently brought on her friend, all her life.

That had to be punishment enough for anyone.

Monika, still none the wiser as to the truth, was glad to pass her troublesome daughter over to her best friend. For a price, of course.

But even that didn't affect Joanie at the moment.

It was still so raw, still too unbelievably shocking to put into any kind of perspective. But that would come; time would heal much of it. Or at least she hoped so.

She made her tea and splashed in the vodka. She had made her peace with Little Tommy, as she still thought of him, and was on her way to some kind of peace of mind. If she could get through the next few months she knew that eventually she would climb out of this pit of despair where she was trapped.

Jeanette came in from school at twenty-past four and walked straight through to her bedroom, as was now the norm.

Joanie followed her through and said gaily, 'Good day?'

Jeanette grinned ruefully. 'I was actually at school, Mother! How could it have been a good day?'

Joanie laughed.

'I know you were at school. They still ring me in surprise every time you turn up!'

Six months before, Jeanette would have taken umbrage at her mother's words, seen them as some kind of criticism. Now she smiled.

'I like it there really, but don't tell them that!'

'I won't. Fancy a cuppa?'

Jeanette grinned.

'Er . . . no, thanks.'

Joanie said gently, 'I was the same when I was having you.'

Jeanette, who had been emptying her school bag on to her bed, stopped what she was doing and stood stock-still.

'Oh, Mum . . .'

She started to cry; she had been wondering how to break the news to her mum. Her lovely mum whom she had never really appreciated until the last few months.

'I'm sorry . . .'

Joanie hugged her errant daughter, glad of the chance to make her feel better, glad to put the girl's mind at rest.

'We'll cope, love. On a scale of one to ten, after everything else we've had to cope with, this ain't exactly a disaster, is it?'

She held her daughter close as she cried tears of relief.

God was good. Joanie had heard that expression so many times in her life. And sometimes, just sometimes, He really was.

Jon Jon was in a bar in Ferentari. It was a shit hole, full of local bullyboys and women with shifty eyes and bad boob jobs.

Baxter was chatting up a woman with bleached hair and blue eye shadow and Jon Jon wondered when he should tell him it was a man in drag. But Baxter was so far gone now he probably wouldn't notice the difference anyway.

Michael and Peter were keeping close. He smiled at them as he got another round in. They had been given five thousand pounds to spread a little joy round their police station. It was money well spent. They would make sure Joseph Thompson's death was recorded as 'Beaten to death, assailant unknown'.

Jon Jon wanted the scum he had dealt with in England to learn of his demise. It was justice of a sort, and he had Baxter to thank for going along with it.

They had been drinking steadily all evening but Jon Jon didn't feel in the least drunk. He was numb, but he had done what he had set out to do and that was cause for celebration.

He ordered another large Chivas Regal and downed it in one gulp. He was looking forward to going home next day. It was the first time he had actually looked forward to anything for so long it was a relief to know he could still feel like that.

He was given another drink by Peter.

'Cheers.'

Peter and Michael laughed as they held up their drinks and shouted: 'Cheers.'

For some reason they found that expression hysterical. They were in a celebratory mood, as was Baxter.

Jon Jon drank to a job well done, and counted the hours until he could finally be home. He needed his family more than he had ever needed them before, though he would never admit that out loud. But he felt the urge to be with his mother and sister, to make sure they were all right, had everything they needed.

He also needed to feel the love they had for each other. It was the only thing now that was keeping him sane.

Epilogue

Joanie and her two remaining children sat silently in the hearse as it arrived at the cemetery. It was a cold blustery day and they wrapped their coats well around them as they got out and stood with the other mourners.

Joanie's eyes were dragged repeatedly to the tiny white coffin that held her daughter's remains, retrieved by the police from a lock-up in Plaistow after an 'anonymous' tip-off. There'd been the remains of two other children too, East European from their dental work, but so far neither had been named.

Monika came up and smiled sadly at her friend. Jon Jon walked away from them. He could no longer stand to see either Monika or her daughter. Monika remained impervious. She had been so impressed by Jon Jon's new house and said so now loudly to Joanie – she never did have a proper sense of occasion. Joanie just smiled and agreed.

It was a lovely house, right enough, but she was happy in her old flat where she still felt at any minute she might see Kira run into a room.

Funny, but when she finally had the opportunity to live in the house she'd dreamed of, hold her dinner parties for real, she found she didn't want to. There was a lesson to be learned there somewhere, she knew, but today she didn't have the strength to think about it.

It had been a lovely service. All Kira's friends from school had attended, and all the neighbours. The flowers had been amazing.

Joanie slipped her arm through Jeanette's and they walked slowly towards Jon Jon, waiting by the graveside. They hung back as they saw Big John McClellan and his two eldest boys go over to offer their condolences.

Joanie's son was a man of substance now, and still only eighteen years old. Paulie had signed the parlours over to him before he'd topped himself. Jon Jon had not wanted to accept them at first, said it was blood money, but Joanie had made him see sense. Paulie owed them.

These days she preferred to remember him purely as her pimp: a man who'd flogged her arse for as long as it was profitable to him. A low life. A nothing.

It was far easier that way.

Jasper was here too, holding Jeanette's other hand now. Joanie accepted his presence. After the events of the last months she felt any kind of love was not to be sneezed at and as no one else would put up with Jeanette, she supposed she'd better get used to having him around. Especially as the girl was pregnant by him. Jon Jon didn't know yet, of course. She was saving it up till the right moment.

So much for Jeanette's new start at school, though already she was talking about home tutors and Joanie child-minding so that was something.

Out of the corner of her eye Joanie noticed Baxter in his good black suit. She'd noticed that about CID over the years – they all knew how to put on a show at a funeral. That way they could eyeball the mourners while paying their respects: not that there'd be anything to learn today and Baxter had turned up trumps for them in Rumania. His superiors were turning a blind eye. Paulie's legacy to them, she supposed.

So far as the general public was concerned, the police hunt for the killer of Kira Brewer and two unnamed children was still very much in progress – but the filth and Joanie's neighbours knew the real score. Sylvia had buried her husband in an unmarked grave. Pippy Light and Kieron McClellan didn't even have that much to mark their unlamented passing. The police knew full well who had settled accounts, but Big John had been plastering money around wholesale and there'd be no comebacks.

These days Joanie ran the parlour in Ilford, still involved herself with the girls and their lives. Still tried to get through the days without too much to drink, still tried to keep Bethany on the straight and narrow.

She was twelve now, revelling in the new figure that threatened to become as top heavy as her mother's. This, coupled with her precocious knowledge, made her one dangerous piece of jail bait but Joanie would do the best she could for her. The girl had loved Kira in her own way.

Jon Jon kept an eye on his mother. She was doing well today and he was proud of her. There'd been a long painful interval between the recovery of Kira's pathetic remains and today. The inquest had been a living nightmare. He'd forbidden his mother and Jeanette to go anywhere near and thanked God that they'd listened to him. The McClellans had kept close throughout, smoothing things over behind the scenes. Paulie's last bequest to him, Chief Constable David Smith, was on their payroll now, with no question of anyone being a grass in return like Paulie had been.

And finally the day they'd all dreaded had arrived – the day they would say goodbye to little Kira. So far it was going better than any of them would have believed.

Jon Jon looked around him. Even Jasper being here didn't annoy him the way it would have done. Big John had taught him a lot in the last few months, about not sweating the small stuff and the value of restraint. Plus the fact that, if a problem finally got too irksome, a man in Jon Jon's elevated position could always pay someone else to take care of it for him. But he'd see how things panned out, give his sister her chance of happiness. God knows, she deserved it.

He saw Sippy with Earl and some other cronies, sneaking a quick joint before the interment. Jon Jon smiled. There was no disrespect intended. For them weed was a sacrament and in no way out of place on this solemn occasion.

Jon Jon still had a few scores to settle, a few debts to repay, but slowly he was working his way through it all. Closure, the Yanks called it. He preferred to think of it as acceptance.

It started to rain, a fine cold spray that he knew would soak straight through the mourners' clothes. One of them was still a sick man, but had ignored doctor's orders and insisted on attending. Jon Jon opened his umbrella and went over to Darren Weeks, standing on his own. The people from the estate still thought of him as Little Tommy and no one wanted to be tainted by association. That was something Jon Jon had to fix.

He held the umbrella over them both. The other man's huge bulk spilled out one side, it was more of a symbolic gesture than anything; but its value to Darren was incalculable.

'Thanks, Jon Jon.'

'Any time, mate.'

Jon Jon knew they were being watched and that was the point. He wanted everyone to know that Darren Weeks had as much right to be here as anyone. More than most, in fact.

Jon Jon held his mother close as they said their last goodbyes to Kira. Jeanette's sobbing was loud and Joanie dimly remembered her own mother saying that you shouldn't cry while you're pregnant because the tears drain the water from around the baby. She nearly said it aloud but stopped herself in time.

She hoped Jen had a girl. Joanie needed someone unspoiled and untainted to channel her love into, and a grand-daughter would be perfect.

She stared down at her child's white coffin and silently said goodbye. The rain stopped suddenly and weak sunshine broke through the clouds. It was Kira's blessing on them as far as Joanie was concerned.

She looked at the girls from the parlours, all dressed in black, their painted faces looking solemn. Even Lazy Caroline had turned out today. The cemetery was packed out. Hundreds had come to pay their last respects.

It was like Jon Jon said: you never forgot something as terrible as this, but joy and happiness left lasting memories too. She was not to dwell on that terrible death, he had said, but to concentrate on Kira's life, short as it was.

Remember the laughter and the overwhelming love.

You just had to make new memories for yourself, hope that one day they'd be as precious as the ones you already had.

And that was exactly what Joanie was going to do.